THE
WIDOW'S
HOUSE

THE
WIDOW'S
HOUSE

BOOK FOUR OF THE DAGGER AND THE COIN

DANIEL
ABRAHAM

www.orbitbooks.net

ORBIT

First published in Great Britain in 2014 by Orbit

Map by Chad Roberts

The moral right of the author has been asserted.

A CIP catalogue record for this book
is available from the British Library.

ISBN 978-0-356-50469-8

Printed and bound by CPI Group (UK) Ltd, Croydon CR0 4YY

Papers used by Orbit are from well-managed forests
and other responsible sources.

MIX
Paper from
responsible sources
FSC
www.fsc.org   FSC® C104740

Orbit
An imprint of
Little, Brown Book Group
100 Victoria Embankment
London EC4Y 0DY

An Hachette UK Company
www.hachette.co.uk

www.orbitbooks.net

For Kat and Scarlet

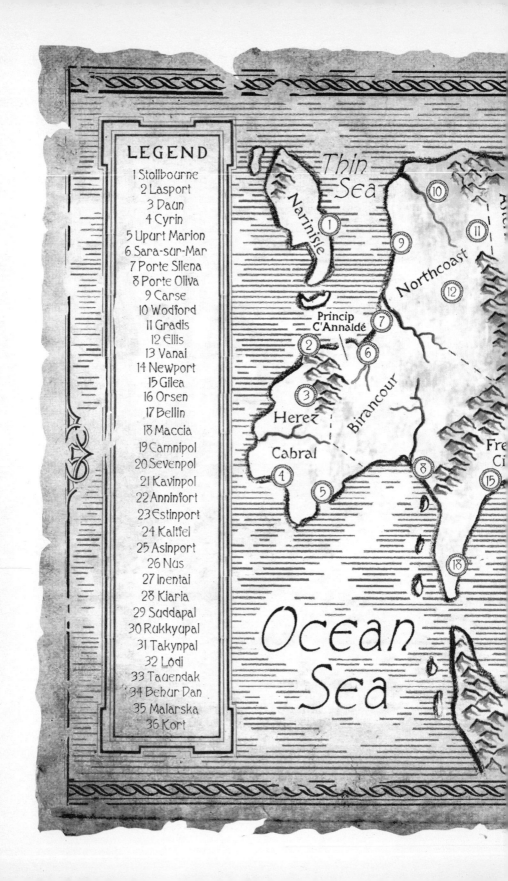

LEGEND

1 Stollbourne
2 Lasport
3 Daun
4 Cyrin
5 Upurt Marion
6 Sara-sur-Mar
7 Porte Silena
8 Porte Oliva
9 Carse
10 Wodford
11 Gradis
12 Ellis
13 Vanai
14 Newport
15 Gilea
16 Orsen
17 Bellin
18 Maccia
19 Camnipol
20 Sevenpol
21 Kavinpol
22 Anninfort
23 Estinport
24 Kaltfel
25 Asinport
26 Nus
27 Inentai
28 Kiaria
29 Suddapal
30 Rukkyupal
31 Takynpal
32 Lôdi
33 Tauendak
34 Behur Dan
35 Malarska
36 Kort

Thin Sea

Narinisle

Princip C'Annaldé

Northcoast

Birancour

Herez

Cabral

Ocean Sea

Hallskar

Antea

Sarakal

Borja

Dry
astes

Elassae

the
Keshet

Pût

nner

Sea

oneia

Prologue

Inys, the Last Dragon

The dragon rose.

With every stroke of his great wings, his sinews creaked. Before—only hours before, it seemed—he had flown this same coast, this same air, with ease. Now, rising above the ice-cracking waves taxed him. The strength he assumed was gone, and the weakness was also testimony that all his worst fears were true. He set his jaw and pressed himself up, up, up, rising to clouds that frosted his scales as he touched them. Brown earth and green water stretched below him. The snow on the ground matched the chill foam on the wave tops, and he labored.

Before—only hours, moments—the war had been at its height. The trap he had set for his mad brother, the last, desperate hope for victory, had been in its final phase. All that had remained was to convince his imperial brother that he, Inys, the last of their clutch, had died in the fall of Aastapal. And then, when mad Morade went to the island to claim his victory, to mount one last attack and drive Morade and his allies deep into the palaces and laboratories, and sink the island.

All would drown as one.

Inys had sent his friends, his lover, and the servants he trusted most to accomplish what he could not be there to complete. His scent would have distracted Morade and turned the whole business to chaos, so he had allowed himself to be buried in a secret tomb, and invoked the silence. Morade would drown, and his unclean allies with him. The madness would end, and those who remained would come and draw him back to wakefulness. Together, they would remake the world torn to ribbons by the war. Or else Morade would survive the trap, and Inys would die there, hidden in his hole, and the world would end in a delirium made of fire and false certainties.

Those had been his hopes and his fears, only hours ago, it seemed. Days at the most. Not centuries. Not millennia.

What's become of Drakkis Stormcrow? he had asked, and the slave—a Firstblood calling himself Marcus Wester—had answered. Drakkis, the most brilliant general of the slave races, had fallen long ago into legend. Her name had become only a story. The Dragon Empire that formed the world—that was the world—had fallen so long ago that a full history had grown and fallen and grown again since the last time the masters of humanity had taken to the free air. Word by word, the world was unmade before him, and Inys's great breast filled with disbelief, and then fear, and then rage. And yet this Marcus Wester who had woken him had one of the tainted at his side, and so nothing he said could be trusted. But he had also held a culling blade. By what madness could the corruption and its cure stand side by side together if not the erosion of strange ages...?

Nothing could be certain unless it was seen and smelled, touched and tasted. If Morade's weapons showed anything, it was that any report or story might be false. The ages might not have slipped away while Inys lay in the silence, dead as stone but dreaming. Morade might live. Erex might. Even Drakkis Stormcrow, short-lived though her race was, might. *Might.*

But the thin winter air was empty of dragon scent.

Inys pumped, lifting his body, and thinking against his will that his weakness was evidence that the Firstblood slave Marcus Wester had spoken truth. Inys did not know how many years a dragon had to abide in the silence to grow weak as a hatchling, and yet it had to be many. The silence had taken Sannyn for a century, and she had risen from it as from a night's rest. Her scales had been undimmed, her laughter as bright and as violent. Inys remembered her as he pushed himself—almost inch by inch, it felt—through air he should have owned. So perhaps the ages had passed. Perhaps the world was new and different and strange.

Still, even if it had been so terribly long, was he not evidence that dragonflesh could weather time itself? Might the same silence have taken others? Or perhaps there were new dragons carrying through the generations, and his incomplete death had simply dulled his senses so that he could not find them.

The land came into sight below him again, the coastline familiar only in the manner of a rough outline. The bays and heights had changed from the ones he knew. There, where the great body of the land curved to the north, had once been a thin spine of stone, just large enough for two dragons to perch upon, wings folded against each other, thick tails entwined. There, he and Erex had first pledged their love. Flying above the water now, he saw no sign of it. The waves themselves denied that it had ever been. The panic in Inys's heart shifted, but he would not let himself descend to sorrow.

Not yet.

He shifted his wings, catching the updraft from the seaside cliffs and riding the rough and unsteady air. With every turn of his gyre, more became clear. To the south, a slave town stank of weak, cold fires. Wood and coal. The thin green thread of a slave path snaked across the ground. The island, if it stood, would be north and west. The hive would be out of Inys's way, but it was so near, and the twin spurs of curiosity and fear bit his flanks.

It was a large town, and poorly designed. The slaves that traveled its streets were scattered. If there was a central task for them, it was unclear. There was a harbor with oddly made ships, a dozen or more spaces inside the town walls where work might be done but wasn't. The air had a rich stink of a thousand different things—tanners and dyers and launderers' yards, forge-hot iron and butchered meat. No purpose seemed to organize its streets, no design gave it meaning. Above the town where a true city would have had perches and feeding tables, there was nothing. If Inys had been set to create an image to capture the idea of a civilized animal that had gone feral, it would have been this.

Grief rose in his throat, and he turned away to the north. At the edge of the land, he sloped down for a moment, landing beside a rounded hut that stank of fish and slave. Birds and tiny winged lizards squeaked and fluttered and fled. Fatigue dragged him toward the bare, frost-hardened earth. His wings settled to the frozen ground and he felt no urge to lift them. He felt the despair beginning to stir in his heart and closed his eyes against it. He could not afford to feel anything, not yet. Exhaustion pulled at him, bearing him down toward a black and dreamless sleep. He let it take him.

Dreams came to him, inchoate and disturbing. He felt himself calling out in them, but could not say to whom, or to what end.

"The fuck are you doing on my land?"

Inys opened an eye. The Jasuru slave held a fisherman's axe in his broad hand, and poorly tanned furs were tied around him for warmth. His black tongue rolled behind pointed teeth, and the bronze of his scales caught the sunlight. The fear-smell was rich. Inys opened the other eye.

"Get on! I'm not afraid of you. This is my place, you get out of it!"

Inys popped the slave's belly with a foreclaw and watched the amber eyes go first wide and then dull. His grandfather's sister had made the Jasuru centuries before he'd been hatched, but not as fishers. They had been pen-keepers of the other slaves, freeing the dragons of that generation to take on other work than the dull maintenance of their servant races. They had been meant as honorable servants, halfway between the minimally altered Firstblood and the dragons themselves. As the slave died, Inys recalled the bronze of his grandfather's sister's scales, much the same color. The sharpness of her teeth. The blackness of her mouth. It was an aspect of her design that she placed a part of herself within her creation, as he had put something of himself into the black-chitined Timzinae. The weapon he had brought to the war. His answer to the chaos and madness of Morade's slave-corrupting blood spiders.

He chewed the corpse thoughtfully. The blood was hot and salty, the bones delicate and crisp. It was terrible that the three brothers and clutch-mates had turned the beauty and elegance of design against one another. To think what they might have accomplished if only Inys had not been so young. If his pranks had not struck so near his brother's heart. Or if Morade, in his rage and brilliance, had not seen how deeply the others had come to rely on the slave races they had created. When Morade's vengeance came, the blow fell where none expected it. Not in the wide, smoking air of battle, not at first. But in the lowest. With his blood spiders, he maddened the slaves until all order fell away. Only then did the full scale of his vengeance come clear.

And so perhaps there was something of his brother in the corrupted, just as there was something of his grandfather's sister in the Jasuru. Madness and the beauty of scales in sunlight. There was a poem in that somewhere, if there were any people left to speak poems to.

Inys yawned and stretched. The small meal had revived what little strength he had. He opened his wings, beating at the frigid air, testing himself. Better. Not well, but better. The shock had begun to fade, and hope was not yet dead. Not quite. There was still the island to discover. Sleep and food made the world easier to bear, if only for the moment.

Inys launched himself out over the reddened sea of sunset, skimming close to the surface until he realized that his only reason for doing so was to see his shadow on the face of the water and so feel less alone. After that, he rose. He knew the way to the island. The path to it was in his blood, as it had been in the blood of all dragons. The seat of the empire and the center of the world. The first eggs, so it was said, had risen from the womb of the earth there. The first dragons had sung their songs. It had become more than the seat of the empire; it had become the sign and symbol of all that the dragons were. The greatest workshops in the world had been there. Inys still recalled the first night he had been allowed to attend the gathering, perched beside his father's massive, fire-hot side in the vast cavern where a thousand other dragons on a thousand other perches had listened to old Sirrick declaim on the virtues of physical love. She had been ancient even then, and the beauty of her face and her form and her voice had taken Inys's breath away. She had spoken of mating—not of taking a mate or choosing a mate or living long with a mate, but the act of coupling in love— with a seriousness and maturity that would forever define for him what it meant to be wise. If he conjured up the memory, he could still feel the rush of desire and awe. Some part of his mind knew that the memory had been drawn out in part by the suspicion that he would never know the touch of his own kind again, but that thought was still small enough to ignore.

If he had won, that theater would be drowned as a sacrifice to save the world from his brother. That anyone would destroy that place was beyond even Morade's madness, and so it was the only place that a trap could be set. Inys the Ruthless, they had called him when he proposed it. True enough, but also Inys the Frightened. Inys the Ashamed.

Inys the Desperate.

He made his long way across the water as the brief winter sun doused its flame in the sea. The stars were light enough, and the moon soon rose to add its brilliance. Though he knew what he might expect, the featureless water still uneased him. The first towers should have been here. Then the Chancel of the Orbs. The oracle's spire. He could not help but wonder whether they still stood and he, in his weakness and confusion, had missed his way. It had been his scheme and intention, and still the absence of the island seemed unreal. Its destruction was a crime too vast to contemplate, even were the crime his own.

Twice he circled the wide water, his senses stretched out beyond him. The only sights were waves upon water and stars in the greater ocean above. The only scents were of fish and salt and the promise of storm weather still days away. This should have been the place, he thought, and could not be sure. Not without looking.

He took in a great breath, rose up in the air, and dove. Just before his vast flesh struck the water, he recalled Erex and the joy she had taken in night diving. He pushed the thought away. That she, whom he loved more than he did himself—she, whom he had felt and touched not more than a day before—might be dust, and ancient dust at that, could not be borne.

The cold and the pressure took him in, and Inys flew through the black water. The great, raging furnace of his flesh answered with heat and strength. For a moment, he was sure of himself as if he were young again. As if his childish folly had not ended everything.

And there in the depths, the ruins welled up, larger than dragons. The spires like mountains, encrusted with barnacles and ice coral, until it might almost have been natural. But he knew the workings of the sea too well, and the stone had slept through the long ages with him. Here was a mossy spire that had once been Keeper's Watch. There, a sunken disk of jade lay on its edge, which had once held the emperor's perch. He let the water fill his nostrils, straining for any sign of dragon scent, but there was nothing. Nowhere. The slave's words had been true. Inys closed his eyes, and the powerful, rage-filled urge to throw himself into the pits of the sea, to sink so far that he could never again rise, took him.

It took him, and then it passed. His lungs aching with protest, he turned for the surface and the stars. His tail lashed the water, punishing it, and he scented the fear of fish and eels for miles around him. When he broke the surface, his breath burst from him in a vast ball of crimson fire that turned back upon itself as it rose, unseen and meaningless, above the dark water.

The grief-fire of the last dragon lit the empty world.

On the north coast of Hallskar, Marcus Wester huddled beside the fire. To his right, the winter sea churned white ice and black water in constant and unforgiving waves. To his left, a vast wound had been gouged into the earth. Great slabs of black stone stood cracked and splintered in the frozen ground. It sank deep as a cathedral, wider than a warehouse. A dozen men with axes and shovels couldn't have dug the pit in a month. Bursting from its confinement, the dragon had made it between one breath and the next. Marcus leaned forward and threw another length of driftwood onto the fire. Green-and-blue flames danced in the stone circle of the firepit.

His daughter, Merian, would have thought the fire was beautiful, but she was long years dead now. She didn't think anything was beautiful anymore. He'd never had the chance to show her driftwood fires. Alys, his wife, would have been with the actors, sifting through the new ruins of the dragon's cave. That was unfair. She'd have been here, trying to talk him out of his gloom. Likely, she'd have managed, but she was dead too. He couldn't say that was good, but it did save him from the look of pity in her eyes. There was nothing, Marcus thought, as bleak as a success that brings no comfort.

Master Kit's footsteps on the stony beach were as familiar as his own breath. Marcus lifted a hand in greeting without bothering to look up. Kit sat beside him. With the cold, they had all taken to wearing as many of the theatrical troupe's costumes as they could, one over another. Kit was presently dressed as Orcus the Demon King, only with a thick fur hat and a frilly scarf.

"Any sign of the locals?" Marcus asked.

"A few," Kit said.

"Were they angry?"

"Yes."

"Are they coming back with torches and swords?"

"Probably," Master Kit said. "I believe they had gone to great lengths to keep the dragon's existence secret. It seemed to me they were quite … *disappointed* that we'd woken it."

"All right."

"At the very least, I think we cannot expect their help should another storm come."

"It's Hallskar in winter. Another storm is going to come."

"I think you're right."

Marcus poked at the blue fire, sending up a shower of orange embers. Nearby, Hornet called out something and Smit answered back. In the hazy white sky, gulls shrieked and wheeled. The air smelled of cold and salt. "I was hoping it would be more a situation where if we woke him, he'd explain how to defeat the spider priests. That was optimistic, wasn't it?"

"It appears to have been," Kit said.

" 'Well,' he could have said. 'It's simple. They can't stand garlic.' That would have been good."

"I rather like garlic, actually."

"You know what I mean."

"I do," Kit said. "We came and searched because they were searching and we didn't want them to find whatever it was they were looking for. They didn't. We woke the beast because we thought the enemy of our enemy might be our friend. It was a risk, and we still don't know where those choices will lead. It's possible that the things we've done will save the world."

"It's possible that Sandr will marry a Haaverkin woman, stay in Hallskar, and make a brood of little tattooed actor babies. I wouldn't bet a penny on it, though."

"I suppose I wouldn't either. But there is hope."

"Only for the hopeful."

"Are you utterly without it, then? Hope, I mean?"

Marcus laughed. "You remember who you're talking with, don't you? The sum of my hopes right now is not to die on a frozen salt coast anytime in the next three days.

That's tricky enough. Let's not borrow anything more until after."

"The dragon may still come back."

"No," Marcus said, rising to his feet. "He won't. Not anytime soon."

"You sound certain."

Marcus nodded up at the empty sky. "Can you imagine what it would be like? Waking up to find everything you loved turned to bone and ash, everything that made the world beautiful gone?"

"I take it that you can?"

"Every day the sun rises," Marcus said. "It takes some getting used to."

Clara Annalise Kalliam, Formerly Baroness of Osterling Fells

The attic of Lord Skestinin's manor in Camnipol was white. The boards of the floor and the plaster of the walls, the casement of the little dormer window, the shelves built into the wall and filled with crates and sacks. Everything was white, and it caught the winter afternoon sun and made something bright of it. Not warm to the skin, but to the eye. It made the little nest glow.

The mattress she lay on was white as well, and filled with down. The blankets pulled up to her breasts were soft wool, rich with the scent of cedar to keep away moths and now also of sex. They had been packed away for the winter season when the court was all gone from the city, and unpacked now in secrecy. Vincen Coe, the young huntsman who had once been her servant and then her lover and now both, lay spent. His long hair spread around his head like a rich auburn halo, and his breath was deep and soft. Clara Kalliam shifted, using her arm as a pillow, and considered the young man's face. The improbably long eyelashes, the soft lips, the dark scattering of whiskers just under the surface of his cheek. He was a beautiful man. Young enough to be her son. A thousand ranks below her socially. Devoted to her in a way no man in her life had ever been, except her husband.

A pigeon fluttered up against the dormer's glass, cooed in confusion, and flew away again. Clara let her body sink into the mattress, enjoying the warmth and softness and languor of her muscles.

She was not a young woman. Her hair was going white. Her skin not so taut as it had been when she was a girl. Vincen was the second man she'd lain with in her whole life, but she tried not to let her greed of him overwhelm her. A lifetime in the vicious meat-grinder of court politics had taught her that there were a thousand different reasons why people had affairs. To satisfy vanity, or for revenge, or out of sorrow. From political necessity or love of scandal. To create the story of one's self. Or to retell it differently.

She had never imagined herself as the sort of woman to conduct an illicit liaison. And even now, and despite all evidence, she didn't. Not really. Vincen was simply Vincen, and the woman she was with him, the woman who had risen from the ashes of her husband's failure and execution, who had lived in a cheap boarding house and been questioned by the regent's private inquisitors, was more real than the sugar-and-plaster woman she pretended among the court. But, of course, both were true. Her soul encompassed both of them.

"We should go," Vincen said. "We'll be missed."

"We should," she agreed.

Neither of them moved to reclaim their clothes, strewn on the white floorboards. Their intimate ritual was not done yet. The words were only the prelude to their parting. She breathed in, savoring the dust-smell of the attic and the chill of the air. Through the window, she could see the great tower of the Kingspire rising above the city. Even with the mattress on the floor, the spire's uppermost floors were too high to see. Only the red banner with its eightfold sigil, the sign and symbol of the spider goddess's temple housed in its high halls. The cloth shifted in the wind as if it were not only a religious cult's marking but the new banner of Imperial Antea. Perhaps it was.

"Are things well?" she asked.

"As well as can be," Vincen said. "I'm still a new man in an established house. It will be some time before I'm trusted. There was some resentment of Jorey."

"Of Jorey?" she said, her heart moving instantly to her son's defense. "Whatever for?"

"He married Lord Skestinin's daughter just in time to make her the daughter-in-law of a traitor."

"Oh. Well, yes. That."

"Now that he's better known as the regent's right hand than his father's son, it's turning about, though."

Clara considered the rafters. A spider's web clung in a corner, empty. In the course of three seasons, she had gone from the Baroness of Osterling Fells to the disgraced wife of a traitor to the mother of the new Lord Marshal. And in among all of those, she'd become a widow and a fallen woman, a traitor to the crown in her own right and a patriot more devout than most of the men who had the running of the empire. The court had left her in the autumn a woman barely rehabilitated, her very name tainted. When they returned, they would find themselves jockeying to be in her good graces. It left her dizzy when she thought about it, like looking up at the stars.

"Things change so quickly," she said, "and so completely."

"They don't, m'lady," Vincen said, taking her hand. He kissed the knuckle of her thumb. "Only the stories we tell about them do."

The dreaded moment came when Clara sighed and pulled the blanket aside. Knowing in the mornings that she might hope for these brief hours, she had adjusted her wardrobe to those garments she could put off and on with only minimal assistance from her servants or Vincen. She painted her face only lightly these days. When she'd lived in the boarding house, she had forgone the practice entirely. She descended from their hidden nest first, making her way by the central stair to the third-floor rooms, some of which were her own. Sabiha and Jorey's marital apartments were on the same floor, near the street. Lower down, the guest rooms and the private quarters of Lord and Lady Skestinin, who very rarely used them. He was more often away with the fleet or at his holdings in Estinport, and she was famously allergic to the politics of the court. And likely wiser and more content because of it.

But as a result, the household in Camnipol was small. Its gardens were insignificant, and it hardly commanded more land than it took to place the house. Even the kitchens and stables were small, as if added as an afterthought. The house belonged to the commander of the Imperial Navy. Jorey Kalliam resided there now as the new Lord Marshal, with his brother Vicarian and his mother, Clara. Other estates in the city might boast more wealth and more beautiful grounds, but none had the military power of the empire in so concentrated a form. Except, of course, for the Kingspire.

"It seems like we do this every day." Vicarian's voice came from Jorey's private study. The tone was on the knife edge between amused and annoyed, as it so often was with her boys. "You panic, you come to me, and I talk sense into you. We settle matters, and then as soon as I walk out of the room, you start working yourself back into a lather."

"I go back to look at the numbers again," Jorey said, his tone almost of apology. "They are frightening damned numbers, for what that's worth."

"They don't matter. We didn't win the wars on the back of numbers. Antea is chosen of the goddess. We're going to win."

"With exhausted men, a season's planting that's relying on the labor of recently captured slaves, and twice as much land to hold as we had a year ago, it seems that we've put upon the kindness of the goddess plenty long enough."

"You don't understand," Vicarian said. "She will not *let* us lose."

In the half dozen steps from the middle of the staircase to its end, Clara felt her body change as she adopted her role. Her chin rose and a polite smile took its accustomed place upon her lips. Decades she had not felt only minutes before settled on her like a shawl made from dust. She was the mother of grown men now, a widow, and—though her precise status would give etiquette masters belly knots—a woman of the court. She stepped into Jorey's study with an arched eyebrow.

"I can't help noticing that my boys are shouting at each other again," she said, teasing. "Surely we can solve the complex problems of the empire in a civil tone of voice."

Vicarian rose from his divan, smiling. Ever since he'd returned from the new temple within the Kingspire, his priestly robes included the swatch of red and the eightfold sigil, and there was a brightness in his eyes that reminded Clara of men taken by fever. It saddened her to see it, but she pretended it wasn't there. He was lost to her now, but she could pretend he would return one day.

"It's Jorey, Mother," Vicarian said. "He's seen the power of the goddess time after time, but he has a doubter's heart. Come. Help me fix him."

Vicarian took her hand and kissed her cheek. His flesh seemed warmer than the fire muttering in the grate could account for.

"I don't believe I've had authority over Jorey's heart for some time," Clara said. "Though it is sometimes pleasant to pretend otherwise. What seems to be the trouble?"

"It's the war," Jorey said, as a farmer might have said, *It's the crops*. "Ternigan's death leaves everything in a muddle."

Clara smiled. That her plot against Ternigan had borne fruit almost compensated for the fact that it had put Jorey in the old Lord Marshal's place. Before that, she'd sent anonymous letters out, reporting on the plans and ambitions of the regent to his enemies as best she could from her diminished position. So far as she could see, it had been as effective as flinging pebbles into the Division. Tempting Ternigan into treason with forged letters and false promises had deprived the army of one of its most experienced minds, she was glad to hear. That it left her still uncertain how to unseat Geder Palliako and his spider priests without unmaking the empire as a whole could only be expected. *You can't make a rug from a single knot*, as her mother used to say.

"The muddle being?" Clara asked.

"Most of the army sitting in the freezing mud outside Kiaria has been fighting for at least a year," Jorey said. "Some of them haven't seen rest since before Asterilhold. I have to go take command of the siege—"

"Which we should have done a week ago," Vicarian said.

"—but I don't know what to do with them. On one hand, putting a holding force outside Kiaria invites the Timzinae to try to break out. On the other, Father always said wars were won and lost over cookfires, and when I look at the supply reports, pushing on seems like begging the army to break."

"They won't break," Vicarian said. "The goddess won't let us lose. Look at all of the things that we shouldn't have won already. The battle at Seref Bridge? Father should have lost that. Would have, if he hadn't had the priests. And when the Timzinae turned him against the throne, he also went against the goddess, and he lost. How many people said we might—*might*—take Nus by winter. And we took Nus, Inentai, Suddapal, and we're camped outside Kiaria. We wouldn't have stopped Feldin Maas without Geder bringing Minister Basrahip from the temple. According to your numbers, we should have lost already half a dozen times over, and we didn't. And we won't. I keep telling you that."

"And after you've said it five or six times, it even starts seeming plausible," Jorey said. "But I sleep on it, and in the morning—"

"My lords," the steward said. He was a Dartinae, and the glow of his eyes made his expression difficult to read. It seemed to Clara that he was excited. Or frightened. "The Lord Regent has arrived."

Clara and her sons went silent. The man could as well have announced that the Division had closed. It would have been as plausible.

"The Lord Regent is in the south," Jorey said. "Geder wrote that he was going to Suddapal. To get here from there, he'd have had to ride almost straight through."

"I've put him in the western withdrawing room," the steward said with a bow.

A cold dread moved down Clara's spine. There were stories, of course, of Geder Palliako's uncanny abilities. That the spirits of the dead rose up to march alongside the armies of Antea. That King Simeon pushed open his tomb to consult with the regent. To listen to all the tales, Geder Palliako was more than a cunning man. Of course, there were also stories that her fallen husband, Dawson, had been the puppet of foreigners and Timzinae, so there was only so much credence such things could bear. Still, as she walked arm in arm with Jorey, her mind was plagued by a sense of dark miracles just beyond her sight. Perhaps Geder was in Suddapal and Camnipol both. Perhaps distance had ceased to have meaning for him.

Or perhaps he'd simply ridden straight through.

Clara had known half a dozen aspects of Geder Palliako, from the awkward boy lost in the complexity of court etiquette to the frenzied executioner of her own husband, slaughtered before her eyes. He had stood over her as half-demonic judge and by her side as an ally against armed foes. He was a violent and unpredictable man, and she feared and opposed him as she would a wildfire or a plague.

The thin, ill-looking being on the divan looked up at them as they stepped in the room. His hair was lank and unwashed. His eyes were puffy and red. He rose to his feet slowly, as if in pain. When he spoke, his voice was thick with tears.

"Jorey. I'm sorry. I didn't know where else to go," the Lord Regent of Imperial Antea said. "I don't have anyone I can talk to. So I came here. I'm sorry if I'm getting in the way."

"Geder?" Jorey said, stepping toward the man. "Are you ill? You look…"

"I know. I look like hell," Geder said, then nodded to Clara. "Lady Kalliam. I'm sorry."

You murdered my husband with a dull blade and apologize to me for looking unwell, she thought. "Lord Regent," she said.

"I thought you were in Suddapal. With…" Jorey glanced at her, embarrassment showing for a moment in his eyes. "With your banker…woman…friend."

"Cithrin betrayed me," Geder said, his lips shuddering with the words. Bright tears spilled down his cheeks. "I told her that I loved her, just the way you said, and that I wanted her. And I told Fallon Broot that she and her bank shouldn't be interfered with and she…" Geder sobbed, staring at Jorey like a child with a favorite toy that had broken in his hands. "She worked with the Timzinae. And when I went to her, she left. She was gone when I came. I *loved* her, Jorey. I've never loved *anybody*."

Clara nodded to Geder and then to Jorey, and stepped slowly backward out of the room, drawing the door almost closed behind her. Almost, but not quite. She stood in the corridor, her head bowed, and listened as the most powerful man in the world, hero and regent and unquestioned leader of the empire, poured out confessions of heartbreak between sobs. Clara knew the name Cithrin. There had been a part-Cinnae girl, pale as a sprout and as fragile, who'd come to Camnipol in some previous age, when Dawson still lived. Clara recalled the girl offering condolences after Dawson's execution like it had been some particularly vivid dream. Cithrin bel Sarcour, assistant or some such to Paerin Clark of the Medean bank.

The same Paerin Clark to whom she had been sending her letters. She turned away, walking down the corridor on cat-soft feet. A thousand questions buzzed in her mind. What did the bank know? What did it suspect? What was its agenda in undermining Geder's plans to enslave the Timzinae? Some answers she could glean from listening to her boys talk in the morning. Others she might have to take her best guess and be satisfied. When she regained her own rooms, she sent the servant girl away and lay on her bed, her arms spread wide, and laughed silently. It wasn't mirth that shook her, but relief and fear.

The sun fell, turning her windows to red and then grey and then black. She lit her little bedside lamp herself and called for a servant to set a fire in the grate. She had her supper brought to her—beet soup and a thin shank of chicken. Hardly the sumptuous repast she was used to seeing in the houses of the powerful, but a thousand times better than what she would have had in the boarding house. And times, after all, were hard. Afterward, she lit her pipe and waited, her mind moving in silence.

Vincen came near midnight, his soft cough outside her door as deliberate as an announcement. She let him in and closed the door behind him. The warmth of sexuality and love was gone from his expression. And from hers.

"Well," she said. "I think we have the scandal of the season, and the court not even returned from the King's Hunt."

"Does he know, then? Does the Lord Regent suspect you?"

Clara drew fresh smoke into her lungs, frowning. "I'm not in prison or dead, so I doubt it. And why should he?"

"This can't be good, m'lady."

"It may not be. Or it may be excellent. Until now Geder has stepped from success to success. Even his failures have been recast as master strategy after the fact. This is a humiliation, and what's more, a romantic one. If there's anything Geder understands less than war, it's love. It isn't a picture that can be made lovely by a different frame."

"He won't lose power over it. If anything, people will see him with greater sympathy."

"Worse than sympathy. Pity. The hero of Antea will be remade as a victim. And I will wager you anything you like that Geder will take comfort in it. He is entirely too ready to point out the ways in which he's been wronged, when what he ought to do is make light of it."

"So this...is a good thing?"

"You're the one that said it. It isn't we who change, but the stories about us. This will make him less a creature of awe. Less the great man from legend. It may remind the noble houses that Geder and his priests are capable of losing, and if it does, that will be a very fine thing indeed," Clara said. Her tobacco was spent, and she leaned forward, tapping the ashes out into the fire. "I feel sorry for the girl, though. She's done us a favor, and for payment, she's about to become the most hated woman in the world."

Cithrin bel Sarcour, Voice of the Medean Bank in Porte Oliva

The sea had never been home for Cithrin bel Sarcour. Her life had been grown around the Medean bank as a vine around a trellis, and so the great waters of the world had been one part roadway that linked all ports and one part supplier of fish and salt and oil. Vaster than the lands on her maps, the sea had been defined by where it connected and what could be taken from it. That it was also a place had never entered her mind before now.

The winter days spent on the Inner Sea were brief, bright, and cold. The nights were black. Ice coated the decks and frost formed on the rigging by moonlight, melting only reluctantly with the coming of dawn. The shore was a darkness on the northern horizon, and Cithrin looked at it from the rails wishing she might never touch land again. Behind her little ship was the wreckage of the five cities of occupied Suddapal. Before her, Porte Oliva. One, a city that had fallen to the murderous ambitions of Antea. The other, her home. And somewhere beyond the black line to the north was Geder Palliako, regent of Antea and leader of the spider priests, whom—for the best of reasons—she had embarrassed and betrayed. Every hour brought her closer to the docks of Porte Oliva and the necessity of facing the consequences of her choice. She would rather have stayed at sea.

Instead, she spent her days walking the decks and her

nights in her tiny cabin, a plank across her thighs, writing and rewriting her report to the bank. She had left Suddapal with no warning, and was traveling so quickly that no courier would outpace her. The news of her decision to abandon the city and their efforts there would arrive with her. The ledgers and books in the chest under her hammock would tell the whole tale, but her report was her chance to interpret it, to shape for the others what she had been thinking and why she had done what she'd done. Every night she tried, and every morning scraped the ink from the parchment and began again until the morning came with no more nights behind it.

Yardem Hane, the head of her guard company now that Marcus Wester was gone, stood on the deck at her side. His great ears were cocked forward, as if he were listening to the waves. She pulled her black wool cloak tight around her shoulders and let the wind bite at her face. The smoke from Porte Oliva's chimneys rose in the north, white against the winter blue.

"Well," she said, "this will be interesting."

"Yes, ma'am," Yardem said, his voice low and rolling as a landslide. "Afraid it will."

The call of seagulls grew slowly louder as the captain angled the ship in toward shore. "I did what needed to be done."

"Did."

"You'd think that would be comforting."

He turned his wide, canine head to her. "Regrets, ma'am?"

"Ask me again when I've made my report."

The seawall of Porte Oliva rose up high above the surf. As the guide boat led them in through the maze of reefs that made up the bay, Cithrin considered the stone. At the top, narrow openings showed where engines of war could be placed should the city come under siege. She had walked by them a thousand times, and only seen them as a curiosity of the architecture. The world had changed.

Once they reached the docks, she paid the captain his fees and greeted the harbormaster's assistant. The docking taxes were a simple formality, quickly assessed and quickly paid. Yardem and Enen saw to the unloading of the cargo: crates and chests, and the last few Timzinae citizens whom Cithrin had been able to bring with her. Most were children, some barely old enough to walk, sent to a city where they might know no one rather than remain in their homes and be used to force the compliance of their parents. Those who had no one to meet, Yardem rounded up, instructing them to hold each other's hands, to watch for each other, and be sure no one was lost. The sight left Cithrin on the edge of tears.

"To the counting house, Magistra?" Enen asked.

"Not yet," Cithrin said. "You go ahead of me. I think I'll spend a moment with the city first."

"Would you like me to deliver your report to Pyk?"

"Yes, if you'd be so kind," Cithrin said. "It's in the chest with the books and ledgers there. If Magistra Isadau is there..."

Enen smiled, compassion softening her grey-pelted face. Odd to think there was a time Cithrin had found the Kurtadam woman's expressions difficult to read.

"I'll tell her you're looking forward to seeing her, ma'am," the old guard said, nodding her head.

Cithrin had come to Porte Oliva as a refugee too young to own property or sign contracts. She had relied for her survival on the protection of men of violence like Yardem Hane and Marcus Wester, the counsel of professional deceivers like Master Kit and Cary and poor, dead Opal, and the training she had in matters of finance that taken the place of love in her childhood. Then, she had needed training to know how to walk as woman walked, and not a girl. Since, she had seen a slaughtered priest hung before his church, had lived in hiding while an insurrection wracked the city around her, had prepared to debase herself in the name of saving others and found that she could not. She no longer needed to remind herself to hold her weight low in her hips or to pull her shoulders back. She walked through the familiar streets of Porte Oliva as if she were older than her years because it was true now. She had become the woman she'd only pretended to be, and the weight of it was more than she'd anticipated.

Porte Oliva had always been a place where the thirteen races of humanity mixed. Otter-pelted Kurtadam with the ornamental beads worked into their fur. Thin, pale Cinnae moving through the streets like ghosts. Bronze-scaled Jasuru, thick-featured Firstblood. There were even a handful of Tralgu and Yemmu, though Cithrin had rarely seen them apart from Yardem and Pyk Usterhall. And the Drowned swam in lazy pods through the water of the bay. She had spent so much time and effort sneaking Timzinae away from Suddapal that she'd expected to see the mixture on the streets of Porte Oliva changed. It was not. There were some Timzinae as there always had been, but she could not say it was more, and after almost a year in Elassae, they seemed too few.

At the southern edge of the Grand Market, she stopped for a while, bought a cup of honeyed almonds from a street cart, and watched one of the puppet shows that made up the civic dialogue. It was a retelling of the classic story of the rise of Orcus the Demon King, with the plot and dialogue changed. The Orcus puppet was in the shape of a Firstblood man in a flowing black cloak, and when the puppeteer spoke his words, they had the accent of Imperial Antea. Geder Palliako's reputation had spread even to here, then, and Cithrin was not the only one who looked on his victories with dread. The war that the wise had said would never spread so far or last so long had swamped her. The soldiers and the priests had not come here—not yet—but the fear of them had. She wasn't sure if that left her saddened or pleased. Either way, it was good that they knew.

She left before the end of the show, dropping a silver coin in the box at the puppeteer's feet, and passed through the Grand Market. The riot of stalls and sellers shouting each other down washed around her, and she felt herself relax a degree for the first time since she'd stepped off the ship. At one stall, a man was selling expensive dresses with the weeping colors of Hallskari salt dye, and she smiled at them.

Banking and commerce were a dance of information and deception, lies and facts and all the power that gold could provide, and she knew it better than she knew herself. She had seen it in the houses of Suddapal, the courts of Camnipol, the theater cart of Master Kit's traveling company. The Grand Market of Porte Oliva was the expression of it that was most her own. If she chose, she could see it as an innocent might. Men and women jostling one another, merchants in their stalls calling or haggling or adjusting their wares. The queensmen in green and gold strolling through the chaos with bored expressions. Cithrin could see all of that, but she could also see more. The way the price of a bottle of wine in one stall rose when the competitor across the market was too busy to call out a lower one. The way that a bag of coffee was priced ridiculously high so that the bag beside it could be merely exorbitant and still seem a bargain. She could track cutpurses and unlicensed fortune tellers moving in response to the queensmen, finding the balance between turning a profit and ending in a cage outside the Governor's Palace, measuring their chances in feet from the law, in the degrees by which their faces and shoulders were turned away. Cithrin could look at the placement of the stalls, drawn by random lot at the beginning of each day, and see who had bribed the queensmen who controlled the lottery box. The state of the city was written in the chaos like an expression on a well-known face.

She stepped out the main entrance to the market and into the square beyond it feeling calmer. But only a little bit. The distraction was pleasant, but it did nothing to change the facts of her situation. That accounting would come soon enough. She nodded to the head of the guard as she passed, and he nodded back.

"Good to see you again, Magistra," he said. "Didn't know you'd come back."

"I've only just arrived," she said.

"City's not been the same without you."

"Flatterer," Cithrin said and walked on.

So far as anyone knew, she was and had always been the authorized voice of the Medean bank in Porte Oliva. That she had been underaged when she founded the bank, that the documents of foundation were forgeries, that her notary, the de-tusked Yemmu woman called Pyk Usterhall, was the true authorized power of the branch were all secrets. Another example of the banker's trade of seeming one thing and being another.

She pushed through the front doors of the café and shrugged off her cloak. The smell of the fresh coffee and cinnamon, bread and black vinegar were like coming home.

"Magistra!" the ancient Cinnae man said, his straw-thin, straw-pale fingers splayed in the air, his grin warm.

"Maestro Asanpur," she said, accepting his embrace. "I'm so glad to see you again."

"Come, sit. I will bring you your usual, eh?"

The café had been her idea. Maestro Asanpur was a Cinnae, as her own mother had been. The ancient man with the one milky eye and the touch for coffee that bordered on a cunning man's art had been happy enough to rent her the use of a back room. The café had become her unofficial office. The center of a bank that held its business in the centers of power all across the world. Or that had, when the world had been a better place. Before Vanai burned. Before Suddapal fell. Maestro Ansanpur put the bone-colored cup in front of her. The coffee was sweeter than it had been in Suddapal, more gentle. Softened with milk and left simple compared with the complex spices the Timzinae used in the country that had been their home. Sipping it was like being two different people—the woman who during her months of exile had longed for the familiar comforts, and also the traveler to whom this particular comfort was no longer familiar. Asanpur stood at her side, his hands fluttering restlessly at his hip, his face open and bright, waiting for her approval.

Cithrin closed her eyes in pleasure that was only half feigned. "It's good to be home."

The old man beamed with pleasure and went back to his kitchens. Cithrin sat quietly, waiting for her body to stop telling her that the ground beneath her was shifting with the waves. The moment only felt like peace, but the illusion was all she had, and so she cultivated it.

She had almost a full, pleasant hour before Pyk lumbered through the door. Cithrin had never asked how she had lost the great tusks that rose from most Yemmu's lower jaws, but without them, Pyk might almost have passed for a thick, brutish Firstblood. She strode up to Cithrin's side, her eye-brow hoisted.

"Magistra," Pyk said, making the word a mild insult. "Thank you so much for agreeing to meet me here."

She meant, of course, that Cithrin should have come to the counting house and delivered the report herself rather than sending it with Enen. Cithrin smiled.

"Where better?" she asked.

"Shall we?" Pyk asked, gesturing toward the door of the private room. Cithrin's belly went tight. This was the moment she had dreaded. One of them, at least. There would be others, and soon. She rose, her coffee warm in her hand. When she'd sat at the table, Pyk closed the door behind them.

"Well," the Yemmu woman said. "You've got balls. Not the sense that God gave a housefly, but balls."

Cithrin permitted herself a thin smile. It was a mistake.

"If I were you," Pyk went on, lowering herself onto the bench, "I would have changed my name, headed out to Far Syramys, and never been heard from again. A favor to the rest of us, if nothing else."

"Sorry to disappoint."

"Before I send off my recommendations, I want to make sure I've understood this. After Isadau left Suddapal, you used your old love affair with the regent of Antea as cover to build an illegal network that helped Timzinae refugees escape the city."

"No," Cithrin said. "I started before Isadau left."

"Thank you for clarifying that. And then when Palliako— who is, by the way, the most powerful man in the fucking world—started writing you love notes and offering to see you, you left him flat and came back to roost in my city."

"I'd intended to stay," Cithrin said. "I meant to carry on the masquerade as long as I could."

"So why didn't you?"

Cithrin was quiet for a moment, then nodded to herself.

"I did. I stayed as long as I could. And then, when I couldn't, I left."

"Well, at least you've got standards."

"The bank supported everything we were doing there," Cithrin said. "Isadau first and then me. Komme knew about the refugees' network. He created Callon Cane and the bounty system, or allowed it to be created. I stayed there because if I hadn't, Isadau would have stayed, and she would have been killed, and she wasn't. I saved hundreds of people from the Antean prisons, and most of them were children. Say what you like about me, we *won*."

Pyk folded her fingers together on the table. Her expression was worse than angry. It was patient.

"We're a bank. When we've won, we have less risk and more money. You've brought less money and more risk. You made the classic error. You saw something you wanted, and you bought it. For you it was Timzinae lives. For someone else it could have been fancy jewelry. It doesn't matter. It's the same mistake."

"It isn't," Cithrin said.

"It is," Pyk said, and her tone allowed no room for dissent. "Our job is to get power. Gather it up. Protect it. Not piss it away so that we can claim the moral high ground."

"We disagree about that," Cithrin said, but in truth she wasn't certain that they did. She could imagine her first teacher, Magister Imaniel, saying all the same words that Pyk did, and they held the weight of truth.

"Komme and Isadau and Paerin and I," Pyk said. "All of us were careful. We invented this Callon Cane for the bounties. We hid the payments so that no one would track them back to us. We saw to it that the contracts with the ships never listed our extra passengers. And you? You rubbed the Lord Regent's nose in shit and signed it with the company chop. You declared war on Antea in my name and in Komme's. And Paerin's and Chana's and Lauro's. If Isadau had stayed, she'd have been killed when they found her out, but we could have claimed she was acting on her own. But you? You brought it here. You brought it to me. The latest of my Cithrin bel Sarcour messes to mop up after."

She snorted with a grandiose disgust. Cithrin's jaw tightened and her heart raced like she was being attacked. She forced herself not to move, afraid any motion might end with her fleeing the room.

"The conditions are the same as before," Pyk went on. "You're the voice of the bank in name, but you've got no power. Even if you hadn't lit us all on fire, you'd still be my apprentice for a full year, so that's how it is. You agree to nothing unless I say to. You sign nothing at all, ever. Wear your fancy dresses, go to all the best dinners, be pretty for the governor, but try to take one bit of real power from me, and I'll put you in a hole. I'll forward your report and my recommendations to Carse, and we'll see what Komme wants done with you."

"What will your recommendation be?"

"That we wrap you in chains and festive paper and ship you to Camnipol with a letter of apology," Pyk said. "But that's his to decide, not mine."

She had known. Some part of her had known the moment she lost sight of Suddapal that it could be no different than this. It didn't pull the sting, or if it did, not enough.

"I'm sorry," Cithrin said softly. "I did what I had do."

"You did *not*," Pyk said. "You didn't *have* to. God didn't come up from the earth and demand it. No one held a sword to you. So don't tell me you *had* to."

Cithrin looked into the coffee, the brown swirl at the bottom. The cup had tiny pores all along the inside, and the drink clung to the texture like a man's cheek a day after he'd shaved. She thought for a moment of Marcus Wester.

"You're right," she said. "I didn't have to. This was what I chose."

"And?"

Cithrin looked up. "And I'm not sorry."

Geder Palliako, Lord Regent of Antea

I'm sorry, Cithrin said.

In Geder's imagination, she knelt before him, chains around her wrists and an iron collar at her neck. Only no, because then she'd just be saying it because she was captive. Her hands were free, then. Her neck smooth and white. Dressed in pale silks. She would have been beautiful in pale silks. She looked up at him, tears in her ice-blue eyes.

I'm sorry to have hurt you. You were only ever a good man to me, and I betrayed you. I have made terrible mistakes in my life, and this was the worst thing I have ever done.

"Why?" Geder asked the empty room. His private chambers low in the Kingspire were warm compared to the bitter spring cold, but there was still a bit of chill. The oak logs burning in the grate and the orange-white coals in the brazier filled the air with the scents of heat and smoke. They weren't quite enough to keep him from needing blankets. The private guard was stationed outside the rooms so that he could be alone with his thoughts. With his sorrow. "Why did you do that to me?"

Cithrin turned her head away. A tear streaked down her cheek. *They misled me. The Timzinae. I fought it, I told them that I knew you, that you were a good, honorable man. That I loved you, but they made me follow their schemes. I would have stayed for you if I could. I would have warned you if I could. I am so sorry, Geder.*

He shifted on his pillow, cracking his eyes for a glimpse of the real world. The light in the window was brighter now, but still had the paleness of dawn. He closed his eyes again. With his real hands stuffed unmoving in the warm pocket underneath his pillow, he imagined reaching down to her. Caressing her cheek. She looked back up at him, leaning forward. He caught a glimpse of her small, perfect breasts, and even in the privacy of his own mind, he looked away. To imagine her body was too much. Too close. The wound was too raw there, even for pretending. But his imagination had shifted toward that, and now she had her hand on his knee. His thigh.

"I've never loved anyone," Geder said through tears of his own. Real ones now. "You were the only one, ever. I've never loved anyone."

I would do anything to erase the pain I've caused you. Tell me. Tell me what you want, and I will give it to you, if only you'll forgive me.

"You don't have to do anything. Of course I'll forgive you," Geder said, as she slid up into his lap. The pale silks were gone now, and the arousal growing in his flesh brought with it a wave of humiliation so profound that his fantasy broke against it like a wave against stone. He was the Lord Regent of Imperial Antea, and he turned his face to his pillow and sobbed.

A gentle knock came from the door, followed by a young man's tentative voice. "Geder? Are you awake?"

Geder bit his lips, forcing the tears back, and wiped his eyes quickly on the edge of the blanket. "Aster?" he called, forcing pleasure into his voice. "You've finally come home. Come in, come in. I'm just...a little cold or something. Tired. Come in."

The prince and future king stepped into Geder's bed-chamber. He was thin and tall, his face darkened by days on the hunt. If he seemed not perfectly comfortable in his skin, it was as much his age as the situation of the moment.

"You're...sick?" Aster said. His voice held a tightness that didn't conceal his fear so much as show that he wished it concealed. He had seen his mother die when he was a child and his father wither and fail. All of Antea would one day be his, and it was easy to forget that he was an orphan put in Geder's care. Geder had agreed to be the steward not only of the Severed Throne, but also of a boy's passage to man-hood. He saw himself for a moment as Aster did: red-eyed, wasted by travel and despair, tangled in blankets and his night clothes. Of course he would think Geder ill. Of course the prospect would call up other ghosts. It shouldn't have happened this way. To make up for it, Geder made himself bounce up out of bed.

"I'm fine," he said. "I rode too hard from Suddapal, and I stayed up too late reading last night. Now I'm nothing but a big sleepyhead. Get me breakfast and coffee, and I'll take on the world."

Geder spread his arms wide and gave a comic roar. Aster smiled, the fear at bay again. For now at least. That was good enough. Hold away the fear and pain long enough, and perhaps Aster would grow out of it. And really, what else was there to do about it? If there was a magic for eras-ing the cruelties of the world, Geder had never found it.

"Well. Good," Aster said.

"How went the hunt? I assume it's finished and everyone's

stopping at their holdings again before the court season starts?"

"Caot's come to the city," Aster said. "And Daskellin left his holdings early for something."

"The war. Nothing to be concerned about. I'm meeting with him later."

"Minister Basrahip?" Aster asked as Geder walked to his dressing room. There had been a time that servants and guards had been on hand to strip him and wash him and dress him, treat him like a baby and laugh down their sleeves at his belly. Now he dressed himself. Power had some compensations.

"He's come with me," Geder said, pulling off his night-shirt. "He went up to the temple to...commune with the goddess, I suppose."

Geder pulled off his night clothes and stepped quickly into his undergarments. The cool air made him feel his nakedness more clearly, and he pulled on the robes he'd been wearing the night before from the pool of cloth he'd left them in before going to bed. They were wrinkled and had a bit of brown sauce on the cuff, but he could have the servants bring him something better before going out of the private rooms.

"I think I didn't do him any favors when I put the temple so high in the Kingspire," Geder called as he tied his stays. "I was thinking it would be safer and exalted, but it's a damn lot of stairs."

"He doesn't complain," Aster said. "And when the sky doors are open, the view's like being on top of a mountain."

Geder stepped back out to the bedchamber, smiling. He hadn't made himself smile in weeks. Not since the day he'd ridden into Suddapal. There was no one in the world who could have coaxed him to feign happiness except Aster, and the pretense carried perhaps a thin version of the truth with it. His gaiety was a loose scab on a festered cut, but it was in place for now. And if he wasn't whole, he was able to pretend he was. That had to be enough.

"Come! Let's get a good table, make those lazy bastards in the kitchen send us a platter of something decent, and you can tell me all the gossip I missed. Who took honors in the last hunt?"

For three hours, they lingered over the breakfast table. Aster told tales of the King's Hunt—who had taken what honors, the incident of the singer who'd celebrated the victories of Lord Ternigan only to find out the former Lord Marshal had been killed for a traitor the week before, and even a surprisingly bawdy story about a young cousin of Lord Faskellan and her handmaiden that left both of them giggling and half ashamed. The winter world of the King's Hunt was done now. The lords and ladies of the court would return to Camnipol shortly, and the work and glamour of the court season would begin. Some of the stories of the winter would persist, others would be forgotten, and the more serious blood sport of the war would once again take precedence. They didn't speak of it directly, but Geder knew that his exposure of Ternigan's duplicity and treason had been the scandal of the hunt. If it went as the destruction of his previous enemies had, his prestige in the court would only increase. And the story of what Cithrin had done to him would be common knowledge as well.

To his surprise, Geder was almost glad that they would all know how he'd been hurt. Sitting over the ruins of their eggs and oats, laughing over the image of a young noblewoman trying to disentangle herself from her servant girl,

Geder had no way to speak about the pain he'd carried since the betrayal. Aster was too young, and he had loved Cithrin too. Had missed her company. Geder wanted to shield the boy from as much of that hurt as he could, and once there were men of the court about again, there would be opportunities to commiserate.

He could already picture himself being strong and stoic. If he practiced it enough, it might even start to be true. And he remembered the relief of telling Jorey. His best friend, his oldest companion, and the only one that Geder really trusted. There wouldn't be anyone in court as good as that to speak with. It would have been too much to ask for.

And, once the day had passed its midpoint, it was to Jorey Kalliam that Geder went.

The council chamber seemed bare and austere. The formed-earth maps that showed the rise of mountains with miniature hills Geder could step over and lakes and seas with basins of blue glass beads had been passed over in favor of charts and papers. This was not a conversation about tactics, but strategy. Jorey stood at the table, his expression focused and serious as a man twice his age. Canl Daskellin sat beside him. Geder had expected only those two, but Lord Skestinin—Jorey's wife's father and commander of the fleet—sat at Daskellin's side, and Minister Basrahip smiled placidly at the table's foot, his gaze on the window grate, as if such considerations were beneath him. Lord Mecelli was still on the long, slow road back from the field, touring the captured cities and towns of Elassae and Sarakal. Geder wasn't looking forward to the man's return.

"Lord Regent," Daskellin said, rising as Geder entered. Skestinin also took his feet. Geder waved them back down.

"No need for formalities," he said. "We've all known each other long enough to dispense with that, I think."

"As you wish, Lord Regent," Skestinin said.

"Where do we stand?" Geder asked. The men were silent, each seeming to look to the others to speak first. Geder chuckled. "What is it? Is there a problem?"

"I'm worried," Jorey said. "The problem is that I'm worried."

"Don't be," Geder said. "I know this is your first large command, but—"

"Not about that, actually," Jorey said. "We have several issues we need to address, and from the reports I've had from Elassae..."

"I don't understand," Geder said, folding his arms.

"Lord Regent," Canl Daskellin, Baron of Watermarch, said. "The army is exhausted, and it is stretched thin. These are the same men who three years ago were expected to defend and expand Antea. Now they are defending Antea, Asterilhold, Sarakal, and the vast majority of Elassae. They've faced Feldin Maas's treason and Dawson Kalliam's revolt."

Geder glanced over at Jorey, but the new Lord Marshal didn't flinch at the mention of his father's name. That was good. Geder was still afraid that Jorey would blame himself for the elder Kalliam's failures.

"And now a winter siege at Kiaria and the betrayal of yet another commander," Daskellin continued. "Last summer, we thought they would get as far as Nus and perhaps a bit more. Instead, they took Nus and Inentai and Suddapal."

"And," Jorey said. The word hung in the air for a moment as he unfurled a wide parchment scroll. "Here are the dragon's roads that we control. It seems to me the greatest threat we're facing now comes from the east. The Keshet has no leaders to speak of, but they've got more nomadic princes than we have pigeons in the Division. Inentai's been the easternmost city of Sarakal for a hundred years, but before that it was the westernmost outpost of the Keshet. There will be raids, and the local forces that used to stave them off are dead or broken, because of us."

"Also the traditional families of Sarakal had ties of marriage and blood with some of the houses of Borja," Daskellin said, pointing to the map. "The siege at Kiaria isn't complete, and we have a very long, poorly defended border along the eastern edge of the empire. To the west…the Free Cities are walking on glass and hoping we don't think of them. All the kingdoms along the Outer Sea have been friendly at best and quiet at worst. Narinisle, Northcoast, Herez, Princip C'Annaldé, Cabral. They're well armed, well reinforced. They have relatively few Timzinae, and they wish us no ill."

"What makes sense," Jorey said, an apology in his tone, "is to rest any men who aren't actively in the siege in Inentai. Rotate them out to Kiaria once they have their strength back. Once Kiaria falls, we'll have broken the Timzinae plot against Antea. We'll have won."

Minister Basrahip cleared his throat and turned to Geder. His smile remained mused. "Fight where you will. The goddess will protect you."

"It's not loss that I'm worried about," Jorey said, a bit sharply. "It's the price of winning."

Geder looked at the map, scowling. There was a time when he had seen maps as something almost holy: here was the world translated into a form that could fit on a table or in a room. Now he had to struggle to see it as more than ink on parchment. Everything his advisors said could be true, and it wouldn't matter. Not really.

"What about Birancour?" he said.

"It would be very, very difficult to field an army there," Jorey said, and the words had the careful precision of practice. Jorey knew what Geder wanted. It was what he was straining against. "The south route would mean marching through the Free Cities and either the pass at Bellin or south along the coast where there aren't any dragon's roads. The north path means going through the full length of Northcoast."

"King Tracian won't pick a fight with us," Daskellin said, "but he won't let us march an army through his country any more than we'd let him through ours."

Geder put his fingertip on the map, on the southern coast of Birancour where the mountain range ended. A black smudge of ink represented Porte Oliva. His throat thickened and he had to fight to keep his voice from trembling. *I am the Lord Regent and the hero of Antea*, he thought. *I get to demand this.*

"She's there," he said. "So that's where we're going. The goddess is with us. We'll win. It'll be all right."

Jorey nodded. He had to have known. When he met Geder's gaze he looked old. Tired. It was like he'd already spent his season in the field. "We'll want to send the fleet from Nus. We can blockade Sara-sur-Mar, Porte Silena, and Porte Oliva. We can strangle their ports without having to march through anyone else's cities. The queen of Birancour's an old woman. She won't want the trouble. When she sues for peace, we can turn her into a friend and have her turn any enemy forces in her territory over to us. And this Callon Cane in Herez? Putting the fleet so close to him will likely put him to flight too."

Geder looked down at the map. Cithrin sneered. *Did you think I hadn't considered this? All of this? You can't reach me here. I'm safe from you, and there is nothing you can do about it, you sad, sick little child.* Geder's fist clenched without his willing it, crumpling the parchment in his fingers. Lord Skestinin's voice was low and reassuring.

"With the capture of Suddapal and the ships in her port, we have a modest fleet already in the Inner Sea. The round-ships are ready to go and reinforce them at your word. We can keep the trade ships from Narinisle from reaching port. That alone will make the locals ready to tie the bitch up by her thumbs."

"If we can rest the men," Jorey said, "just for a few weeks—"

"We have to go to Porte Oliva," Geder said. "There isn't anyplace else."

Jorey nodded as if he'd understood. And maybe he really had.

"I'll bring her to you," he said, then coughed out a single, mirthless chuckle. "Granted, I don't know quite how, but I'll find a way, and I will bring her to you. If that's your command."

"Do you promise?" Geder asked.

"I promise," Jorey said. "But once I do, will you let the men rest?"

"Of course," Geder said. "Lord Skestinin? As Lord Regent of Antea and on the advice of the Lord Marshal, you will prepare the fleet to blockade the ports of Birancour until such time as Cithrin bel Sarcour is handed over to us for her crimes against the empire."

"Yes, Lord Regent," Skestinin said.

"Lord Marshal," Geder said, "You will take command of the troops in Elassae and lead them to Porte Oliva by whatever path you think best."

"Yes, Lord Regent," Jorey said. And then a moment later, "I will do the best I can."

In Geder's mind, Cithrin lifted an eyebrow. Her smile was cruel and cold, and contempt flowed off of her like cold radiating from ice. She put her palm to her mouth, her shoulders trembling with merriment, and Geder felt the answering rage rising in his throat.

You don't get to laugh at me.

Clara

Clara sat perfectly still by the fire, her shoulders aching with the tension of fear held rigidly in check. On the divan, her son and daughter took a mild kind of pleasure in stripping her already fragile sense of safety to its bones.

"I had fish for dinner last night," Elisia said.

The winter months had been kind to her. The cheeks that had lost the plumpness of youth were at least not gaunt, and there was a rosiness to her cheeks that spoke of something more than rouge.

"No," Vicarian said. "You didn't."

Elisia snorted and raised her hands in an amused despair. "So what did I have, then? If your goddess sees my mind so well, tell me that."

"That's not how it works," he said, scooping another small pickle from the tray between them and popping it into his mouth. Chewing it didn't keep him from speaking. "I can't see your mind. All she can tell me is whether what you've said is truth or a lie."

Clara lifted her pipe to her lips, sucking in the smoke. Her mind raced, cataloging all that she could remember saying since Vicarian had come back from his initiation. She had known from his voice that the rites had taken her from him. Understanding now the depths and implications of that transformation felt like waking of a morning to find a viper under her pillow. What had she said, and when had Vicarian known she was not speaking truth? Had some petty act of deceit exposed her plots? Had her long court life protected her by making deflection and careful wording as natural to her as breath? She honestly didn't know, and her only evidence was that she hadn't yet been hauled before Geder's secret tribunal...

Her heart went cold. The secret tribunal, where the high priest was always in attendance. Geder would know every lie spoken. And this had been going on since...since his return from the Keshet at least. Her knees trembled and her stomach clenched until the bite of sweetbread she'd eaten when first she'd taken her place by the fire seemed as indigestible as a stone.

"Well that hardly seems useful to me," Elisia said. "What's the good of knowing that someone's lying if you can't find out what the truth is? Do you remember that cunning man we saw at court who could tell your future? Now that was something useful."

"That was a cheap fraud, sister," Vicarian said. "He had Sorran Shoat feeding him information in code all the way through the evening."

"I don't believe that," Elisia said. And then, "Was she really?"

"What about you, Mother?" Vicarian said. "Care to try?"

"Absolutely not," Clara said.

"Why not?" Vicarian smiled, but he also seemed a bit hurt. As if he were a boy who had brought some vile insect to his nurse only to be told he had to put it out and wash his hands. Despite herself, Clara felt a tug of guilt, and then more deeply of sorrow. She could still recall quite clearly what it had been like to have the newborn Vicarian placed upon her breast. It wasn't much harder to conjure who he had been as a boy, sneaking out with Barriath to ride their father's horses and play with his hunting dogs. He'd been such a beautiful, joyful child. To see him eaten by monstrosity was more than she should have to bear. "Because," she said gently, "I was raised to believe stealing secrets was rude, dear. And so were you."

The thing that had been her son laughed with his warm laugh, and clapped his palms together as he had. But any hope she'd kept that he might return to her was doubly gone now. If her crimes were exposed to him, he would not shield her. He couldn't have, even if he'd wanted to. The cruelty was monstrous.

The afternoon was a little farewell party for Lord Skestinin in whose house Clara was now permanent guest. Elisia had come now that Jorey was Lord Marshal and having once been a Kalliam weighed not so heavily upon her. Lord and Lady Skestinin's daughter—and since the marriage to Jorey, Clara's too for that—sat across the room from the three of them, her hand on the swell of her belly. Outside, a spring storm had come in from the north and was dropping tiny chips of ice from a low, grey sky. Sabiha shifted her hand and smiled. The babe was kicking, then.

"Is that all your new goddess can do?" Elisia asked.

"It's one of the best tricks," Vicarian said. "But it's not the only one."

"Because everyone says that Geder Palliako can speak to the dead. I've heard that he consults with King Simeon every night. They've been seen at the royal crypt, ever since the Timzinae tried to kill Geder."

It was your father who tried to kill Geder, Clara thought but did not say, *and I wish he'd managed.*

"Well, that isn't something I can do, but there may be more secrets than I've been brought into."

"Priests and their secrets," Elisia said, rolling her eyes.

Everyone and their secrets, Clara thought, *and God help us all*.

A servant boy announced the meal was served. Clara left her little clay pipe to burn out the remnant still in its bowl and allowed Vicarian to help her to her feet. Her flesh did not crawl when it touched his. He seemed no different than he had been before his induction into the mysteries of the spider goddess. And still she could not afford to pretend that was true.

Jorey and Lord Skestenin were already at table, Lady Skestinin at her husband's side. A warm beef soup was already being served, the steam from it rich as smoke and good, the cunning men all said, for a woman bearing a child. Sabiha eased herself into the chair beside Jorey, though strictly speaking etiquette should have placed her by her mother rather than her husband. No one commented on the lapse, Clara least of all.

The talk was light and empty. Lady Skestinin was staying in Camnipol for the season to be with Sabiha when the baby came. Once the meal was done, Lord Skestinin would begin the long carriage ride to Nus and the fleet, and from there halfway around the world to Birancour. Jorey and Vicarian would begin their journey to the south in the morning, the Lord Marshal at last taking the field after his consultations with the Lord Regent. They made the usual jokes about not getting lost on the way, and Clara laughed with them politely, the chaos of her mind hidden behind years of form and etiquette. She had to tell Vincen. As soon as she could, she had to find him and warn him to say nothing. Not even to lie. And how many, many lies had she embraced in these past months? Half of her life was fabrications. Her mind spun like a child's top as she tried in vain to recall everything she'd said and whom she had said it before.

"Clara? Are you well?" Lady Skestinin said, and Clara became aware it wasn't the first time her name had been spoken.

"I'm sorry," Clara said, and then very nearly, *I was just thinking about what the storm might do to the garden.* It was the kind of simple, social lie one told all the time. She flailed for a moment. "I was just thinking...about the war."

And then, damn them, *damn* them, tears came to her eyes. She recognized that she was on the edge of panic, but was unable to draw herself back from it. She looked down at the soup. *I have not been discovered,* she said to herself. *If they knew, I would not be here. Even if they only knew of Vincen, I wouldn't be welcome at the table. My secrets are my own.* The room was silent. Sabiha leaned forward and took her hand, and when Clara looked up, there were tears in several eyes besides her own. Lady Skestinin, Sabiha, even Jorey's.

"We will end in victory," Vicarian said. He meant it as reassurance. It was a threat, and for a moment, she could not help but believe him.

"I'm just frightened, dear," Clara said.

The thing that had been her son smiled at her, misunderstanding. It was good enough.

Once the meal was ended, Lord Skestenin said his farewells to Clara and her sons, then took a private moment with Sabiha and Lady Skestinin. Clara would dearly have loved to know what he said to them when he believed no one else could hear. This new plan to blockade Birancour couldn't have pleased him, but precisely how displeased he was would be of interest. That she was curious was the best indication that her shock was beginning to fade. It was afternoon now. As much as she wished to find Vincen, going to him now would be a danger in itself, so instead she took to her withdrawing room and sat at her writing desk, pen in hand, uncertain what if anything she should do. The storm was thicker outside. The bits of falling ice were turning to hail, the rattle of ice bending and breaking the new grass and bruising the buds of the flowers.

She had promised herself that she would not use anything she learned from her sons in the covert reports she wrote to Paerin Clark of the Medean bank. If the missives were intercepted, there could be nothing to lead back to Jorey, and so many of the things she was now positioned to discover were known only to a few. And yet because these things were little known, they were the most important to pass along.

Perhaps it was time to stop her campaign. They knew the dangers that Geder posed. They had acted against him already. And she herself had taken Ternigan from the board and sown distrust in the ranks with the unfortunate effect of putting Jorey in harm's way. *My dear friend, I fear the time has come for our correspondence to end*, she could say. There was no one to insist that she continue. And now that she felt the danger so close at her side...

But there was an attack coming, and she knew it was coming to Birancour. The priests of the spider goddess could smell out deceit, and she could warn them of that. Perhaps no one else could. But at what cost? And if some detail that she put to paper was something that only Jorey could tell, how would she live with herself, knowing that she had engineered his death?

She had her nib above the inkwell, trapped by indecision, when a soft tap came at the door. Fear set her heart racing, but there was no call. She hadn't written a stroke. She put the pen away and shifted to the divan near the window as the tapping came again.

"Hello?" she said. "Is anyone there?"

The door swung open and Jorey stepped in.

"I'm not interrupting, am I?" he asked.

"Never, dear. I was just looking at the back gardens. I'm afraid they won't escape ruin at this rate."

"What will?" he said, and it sounded only half a jest. He came to stand by her and put his hand on her shoulder. She touched his fingers with her own. For a moment, they stared together at the grey and the white and the damage that it wrought.

"It's a shame Lord Skestinin couldn't wait for better weather."

"It is. And I hope it's cleared by tomorrow, or Vicarian and I may freeze before we reach my command."

"I'm sure that won't happen, dear. The freezing, I mean. I can't speak to the weather. I've never been good about that sort of thing."

Jorey sighed, and for a moment she thought he might not speak at all. "I don't want you to be afraid, Mother. I'll see this through."

"And had it occurred to you that might be what I was afraid of?" she asked tartly, and immediately wished she could take the words back.

Jorey sank to the divan at her side. The hail tapped angrily against the glass. "After Vanai, Father told me about his own experiences in the field. About war and what it was. What it is."

"And did that help you?"

Jorey's jaw went tight. It was answer enough. In truth, she'd been cruel to ask.

"War is an evil thing that we have to do," he said. "It is what duty and honor demand. And it's terrible."

"And do you believe him?"

"Duty and honor are making demands of me," Jorey said, chuckling despite the grimness all about them, "and it's terrible, so I'd have to say I do."

"Your father was always a man of honor. What precisely that meant was sometimes surprising, but he did not waver."

"I can't either."

"Do you...Do you want to win?"

"I want the war ended," Jorey said, "and I'm not permitted to surrender, so winning's the only path I've got. And I want you and Sabiha safe. And Vicarian. Everyone, really."

"You're Lord Marshal of Antea in the teeth of a war that's already spilled over three nations. It seems odd employment for someone seeking safety for everyone."

"That's why I didn't ask for the position," he said. "I will make this all work if I can, though. I have to try."

Clara felt sorrow in her breast like a rising flood. But also pride. "We all have to, dear. In our own ways."

"I won't be here when my child's born," Jorey said. "Lady Skestinin and Sabiha...They don't have the warmest relationship. Ever since her scandal."

The scandal had happened before Jorey and Sabiha had met and fallen in love. It was now a boy old enough to be learning his letters, and being raised by a kind family in the lower quarters of Camnipol, and Sabiha loved the child. Little wonder that the girl and her mother would carry each other's scars over it.

"I understand," Clara said.

"Thank you, Mother."

Clara rose to her feet and put her arms around her youngest boy. Little Jorey who'd wept after his first hunt, but not where Dawson could see him. Who had come back from the burning of Vanai with ghosts behind his eyes. He would lead an army for a man he feared in a war he hated because it was the right thing to do. Dawson would have been proud of him too, though for very different reasons.

"I will do what I can," she whispered.

"So will I."

When he left, she took up her pen again, and began her letter.

Pregnancy sat well on Sabiha Kalliam and sorrow poorly. Between the two, they complicated her. Clara found her in the nursery with three of the house servants—two First-blood women and a Dartinae man—holding curtains to the high windows. In the grey light of the storm, Clara saw little to distinguish the different cloths. Sabiha leaned against the great carved-oak crib where before many more weeks had passed, the child would sleep and mewl and puke and coo and generally twist every heart in reach and exhaust every body in earshot. Clara found herself looking forward to it.

"Clara," Sabiha said. "Have you come to dither about window dressings? Because that's how I'm spending the day."

"It's an honorable pursuit. Painful but necessary. I've come to make sure you were well and see whether you needed anything from me in particular."

"So Jorey sent you."

"You didn't expect him to do anything else, did you? The poor thing's riding off to the service of his nation and leaving the one person he actually cares for behind. Well, two. One and a fraction."

"Two and a fraction. He loves his mother as well. Did he warn you about mine?"

"Your mother? Yes, he did."

Sabiha chuckled. "We nipped at each other once when she was tired and I was hungry. It was nothing."

Clara didn't believe that for a moment, but it was a lie she could respect. It occurred to her that Vicarian could have removed all doubt, and the thought left her feeling colder.

The servants stood still, waiting for their betters to finish their conversation, as was their place. Sabiha turned to them. "Take them all down. Yes, that one too. All of them. The light's too dim in this weather. I'll look again tomorrow when the weather's passed."

The servants nodded, thanked her, and vanished with grace and speed. They gave no sign that they were being dismissed, and everyone present knew that they were. Good help was precious. Clara hoped Sabiha was aware of the fact. When they were alone, Sabiha lowered herself to the nursing chair with a grunt.

Sabiha pulled a face, and then laughed. "The truth is, he outpaced me," she said. "I was going to come to you tonight and ask how we could conspire to care for him while he's away."

"Is he not well, then?" Clara asked, half certain she knew the answer.

"He doesn't sleep," Sabiha said. "And when he does, it isn't restful. Honestly, he's gone away some nights for fear of keeping me up. I've found him curled on a divan in the dressing room in the morning."

"Is it the war," Clara said, "or is there something more?"

"He won't say," Sabiha said, "but it's Geder. He hates Palliako, only he won't permit himself to feel it, so it's become this terrible sort of loyalty."

"Geder's been very kind to us, in his fashion. It isn't every man who would put a traitor's son in command of the army."

"I suppose not." Sabiha sighed. A vicious gust pressed at the windows and the smell of the weather seeped in around them like a perfume. "I'm afraid that even when the war ends, the man that comes back may not have much in common with the one that's leaving. Do you know what I mean?"

"I do," Clara said.

"Does it frighten you too?"

"It does. But not so much as the thought that the war might not end. Not ever. We may be chasing conspiracies and shadows for the rest of my life and yours. And his," she added, gesturing toward her belly.

"Hers."

Clara looked up into Sabiha's smile.

"The cunning man says to expect a daughter," the girl said. "Jorey won't mind, do you think?"

"He will be delighted. He's always been quite fond of girls."

"I wish I could go with him," Sabiha said. "Or if not that, I wish that you could."

"One does not take one's pregnant wife and aged mother on campaign," Clara said. "I think it would be seen as unmasculine."

"If you really want to take care of me, find a way to take care of him. There must be one."

"I wish there were. At the moment, I'm not certain what that would mean," Clara said, but a thought had begun to take form at the back of her mind. Camnipol was thick with the priests and the loose ends of her plots. It was not safe to stay. And with Sabiha asking her to look after Jorey, perhaps—*perhaps*—there was something that could be done.

Captain Marcus Wester

The great city of Rukkyupal squatted at the edge of the ice-slush sea. Massive grey walls of granite as thick as they were high marked the city's perimeter, defending the men and women of Hallskar as much from storms as war. The port itself lay outside the walls with jetties of slime-green stone and docks of pale, fresh pine. There were no old piers in Rukkyupal; the violence of the weather was such that only dragon's jade could have withstood it. Instead, there was a tradition of rebuilding what was lost, remaking what everyone knew would be destroyed and then remade again. If the motto above the city gates had been Endure and Create, it would have captured the soul of the city. Instead, the gates held worked letters in green brass that read HMANICH SON HMINA UNT, and no one Marcus had met knew what they meant.

The streets were broad and paved with brightly colored brick—yellow and green and red. Leather banners announced the businesses along the high streets and the temples and churches of a hundred different gods in the low.

The men and women of the city were almost exclusively Haaverkin. Great rolls of fat thickened their bodies and ink marked their faces. They walked through the breaking cold in light wools, brushing frost from their shoulders like it was dust. Of all the thirteen races of humanity, the only other that might have been at home in the city were the Kurtadam, and even they appeared to prefer the warmth of the south. A band of Firstblood actors coming to the city not from the south road or the port, but straggling in from the rural northern wastes, exhausted from the effort of simply not freezing to death, was as curious as finding a dozen bright-colored finches making nests at midwinter. Marcus and Kit and the players had arrived to stares of amazement and concern from the locals, and the near-universal assumption that they were all idiots.

Cary, her hair tied back, stood by the fire and looked out at the crowd, her breath coming in plumes. It wasn't the largest of the public houses near the port, but it was the warmest. The hearth was built from clay with bits of colored glass in it that let through some of the fire's light. Like the city itself, Marcus thought, it should have been ugly and wasn't. The Haaverkin sat at their tables, watching her. Hornet knelt at her side, tuning a small dulcimer. He looked up at her, nodded, and lifted the little hammers. With the first notes he struck, Cary's voice lifted, her expression cleared. Marcus, huddled beside Master Kit at the back of the room, thought she looked miserable, chilled, and unhappy. He also knew that anyone who hadn't traveled the length and breadth of the world with her wouldn't see it. The joy in her performance only seemed artificial to him because he had seen her joy unfeigned.

"Something to drink?" Kit asked. Marcus shook his head. Kit looked over at the Haaverkin boy who served the tables and lifted one finger. The boy nodded and trundled back toward the serving room, returning in a moment with a mug of steaming wine. Kit gave the boy the price of the drink and a couple of coins besides, then cradled the cup in his hands and sat forward.

"Are you actually going to drink that?" Marcus asked under his breath.

"I may not," Kit said. "I suspect thawing my fingers with it may be the best I can hope for."

The winter had been mild, and the spring early. Meaning, apparently, that the sea had only been a sheet of ice as solid as stone for three weeks and was breaking into pieces already, and the older seamen were talking about the mildness as a thing of supernatural import, leaving Marcus to reflect not for the first time that their little troupe had survived Hallskar more by luck than skill. Even so, the waves bore rough balls of ice the size of a man's torso, and the sound of the surf was like a permanent battle. This was Rukkyupal, and the ships at the port were ready to set sail through the grinding, violent waters.

The day before, Kit and Marcus had braved the docks and found a little roundship whose captain, a swarthy Haaverkin with leaf-shaped tattoos on his forehead and cheeks, was preparing his ship. Kit, with the influence of the spiders in his blood, had been the one to make the enquiries, and Marcus stayed at his side in case something unforeseen and violent happened.

"Where are your lot looking to ship to, then?" the captain shouted over the cacophony of the ice.

"We were hoping for Antea," Kit said. Years on the boards gave his voice power enough that he sounded as though he were merely speaking. It was a good trick.

The captain laughed. "It's all Antea now. Used to be I might go to Sarakal or Asterilhold. These days, it's nothing but Antea from here to Northcoast. Or Narinisle. Won't be long before it's them too, as I make it out. Here too, for that."

"Do you think so?" Kit asked. If there was dread in his

voice, Marcus only heard it because they'd been traveling together so long. "Will the war come here?"

At the ship, a young Haaverkin woman in a light leather jacket took a pole from the dock, shook it, and began scraping hunks of ice from the ship's side at the waterline. Marcus admired the strength required for the task. Give the woman a pike and an afternoon's training, and she could take down a charging horse. Taking Hallskar would be no easy thing, even with the advantage of the spiders. But the captain only laughed.

"Won't need to, will it? No, I've got a cousin works for Sannisla of Order Coopish. He says the High Council's already drafted up agreements. They're like a third-catch fisher boy with his nets on his shoulders just waiting for the girl to ask."

"What sorts of agreements?" Kit said.

The captain looked annoyed at the question, as if the answer were obvious. "Fealty. Only a question of time before the bastards at Camnipol decide they want us too, and the High Council figure we'd just as well take their taxes and temples friendly like. It's where it'd end up anyway, and fealty leaves us be otherwise. Don't care to share a slave pen with a bunch of Timzinae."

In the end, they'd paid for passage to a low port near Sevenpol, and by midday the acting troupe had brought the cart to the dock and were breaking it down. The sides slid off their hinges and folded together. The racks of costumes and musical instruments and fake swords and crowns and chalices packed into chests. Everything the company owned was compressed small enough to carry up the gangplank and stow in the roundship's hold. Hornet and Smit, Sandr and Charlit Soon, Cary and Kit and Marcus himself. As with many of the little contrivances of the theater, Marcus was impressed by the simplicity and elegance of the design. The little rack of blunt swords and trick daggers lifted from the frame and slid into the bottom of a crate without enough room for a fingernail between it and the wood. The cart's wheels came off their axles with a twist and a kick. Everything about the theater cart was made to make movement easy, to keep from being in a single place for too long. All that they kept out were a few simple props and instruments they could use to earn a few coins before the ship set out, and the poisoned sword Marcus took from among the false blades and strapped across his back. It had been weeks since he'd had to wear the thing, and the skin of his back itched a little at the venomous thing's return. Still, if something went wrong with the ship, he didn't want to take another season tracking it down or diving for the wreckage, and it wasn't as though the dragons were forging new ones to pick up in the market square.

Cary finished her song with a flourish of hands that evoked a dove's wings in flight, and the Haaverkin stamped and whistled and tossed a few grimy silver coins to her. Hornet gathered them up, radiating pleasure as if the paltry take actually deserved gratitude. Kit sighed, gave in, and drank.

"Do you think she's still in Suddapal?" Kit asked.

"Cithrin, you mean? I hope not. Even with her wits and the bank's money, going against an occupying army's bad work. And when they've got people like you on their side, and you can't even lie about it?" Marcus shook his head. "I'm hoping she's gone back to Porte Oliva or Carse. Which means about as far as you can get from here without crossing the sea, but it's an imperfect world. One way or the other, we'll find her and we'll find Yardem, and we'll tell them... Well."

"Yes," Kit said. "That we found a sleeping dragon that

might or might not be what the spider priests were looking for, that we woke it up, gave it a rough outline of human history since the fall of the empire. And then it got upset and flew away."

"Didn't say we'd covered ourselves in glory," Marcus said.

At the hearth, Hornet was tuning the dulcimer while Cary and Charlit Soon talked with each other about what the next song should be. A thick-bodied Haaverkin man opened the door, ushering in a blast of numbingly cold air, raised his tattooed eyebrows, and retreated. Marcus shifted on his bench.

"I wish that I knew what to make of it," Kit said. "Was the dragon the thing they were searching for? If it was, then why? Or was it coincidence? I don't know where it went, or what it wants, or...anything really. I did believe once that I knew the secrets of the world, and now I don't know anything."

When Marcus chuckled, Kit looked over at him with an injured expression.

"Sorry," Marcus said. "I was just thinking how much easier it was for you to speak to the virtues of doubt when you thought you understood everything."

Kit scowled, but after a moment a glimmer of amusement came into his eyes. "I suppose that is a bit funny, isn't it?"

"I didn't mean to rub ashes in the cut."

"No, no, I think you're right. I believed that I had special knowledge that no one else had, and apparently I took some comfort in it. I don't think I was aware of it at the time." Kit took another sip from his drink. "I suppose it was a bit arrogant of me, looking back at it."

"It's all right," Marcus said. "We love you anyway."

Kit's expression went still and a thin shine of tears came to his eyes.

"What?" Marcus said.

"Nothing."

"What is it?"

"It's just that when you said that just now, you meant it, and I—"

Marcus raised a palm. "Let's not talk about our feelings just now, eh? We'll have to leave after the next song or we'll miss the tide, and I'd hate to be bawling on each other's shoulders all the way out to the dock."

Charlit Soon stood up at the front of the room, her hands clasped before her. Hornet struck an interval on the dulcimer, and a huge roar came from the street. A massive, angry voice screaming the promise of violence even before the first words came. Hornet's little hammers paused in the air.

"Come *out*!" the voice shouted. "Come out, you honorless scum!"

"Someone's having a bad day," Marcus said.

"In the name of Order Murro, I call out the coward Marcus Wester. Come out, you son of a whore! Come to this street, or we will come in and haul you out by your *balls*!"

Marcus sighed and put down his cup. "And apparently it's me. Get the others together. If there's no one at the back, go out the alley and head to the ship."

"What about you?"

"If I'm there when the tide turns, we'll go to Sevenpol. If I'm not, I'll try to catch up to you farther down the road."

"And if they kill you?"

"Then I may not try very hard," Marcus said, rising to his feet.

"For the last time, come out!"

The street was wide and mottled with horse shit and filthy ice. The traffic of carts and shaggy ponies had stopped. Five huge Haaverkin men stood in a rough circle around the

door of the bar. They were naked to the waist, the order tattoos on their chest and faces bright in the afternoon light.
They had whips with bits of metal woven into the leather
in their massive fists. Marcus shrugged, loosening the poisoned sword in its sheath but not yet reaching up to draw
it. The biggest of them took a step forward and hammered
himself on the breast.

"I am Magra of Order Murro. You took the hospitality
of my order and used it to violate our sacred mysteries. We
gave you and yours shelter from the storms, and you defiled
our secrets!"

Traffic was at a stop now. The eyes of a dozen strang-
ers were on him, and more pausing every moment to see
the show. People were coming out the door behind him now
too, watching and blocking his retreat. Whipped to death
in the street of Rukkyupal wasn't what he'd had in mind.
Marcus smiled.

"Technically, that's all true," he said. "And I offer you
and your people my profound apologies. It was rude of me,
and graceless. And I'll swear to you before God and everyone that it's not going to happen again."

"You are a coward and a false net!" Magra of Order
Murro screamed, his breath equal parts fog and spittle.

"Don't know what a false net is," Marcus said. "But I
understand you're upset, and you're right to be. I'm in the
wrong on this one. Let's not compound that by making me
kill you too."

The five men growled and shook their hands. The whips
skittered against the stone and ice. Marcus drew the blade.
The steel was a nacreous green, and as soon as it cleared
the scabbard, the fumes from it stung his eyes. He took a
simple guard pose.

"I'd rather not do this," he said again. Not that he

expected the violence to stop, but he was willing to be surprised.

Magra's whip cut through the air fast as a snake. Marcus thought it had missed, but as the whip pulled back, his right ear began to sting and a trickle of blood cooled his neck. The next man moved slower and Marcus met the whip, slicing it clean. Then two more whips arced through the air. They didn't have Magra's wrist, and Marcus avoided the first of them entirely. The second raked his leg, ripping the wool and leather, but not quite biting skin. The crowd was roaring now, great fists raised and voices clamoring for violence. Marcus gritted his teeth, lunged forward, reaching out with the blade. Magra jumped back a fraction too late, and the green tip caressed the swell of the man's belly. With any other sword, it would have been little more than an insult wound. With this, it was slow death.

Maybe too slow to matter.

A whip raked Marcus's shoulder, and he spun away from it, trying to move with the motion of the lash and keep as much of his skin in place as he could. They were on all sides of him now, though the one whose whip he'd cut was staying back to avoid the attacks of his companions. No matter which way Marcus turned, at least one was behind him.

"Stop!" Kit's voice rang out. "You *cannot* win this battle. Listen to my voice! You have already *lost!*"

The man behind him pulled his whip through the air, and Marcus danced aside. Magra turned toward Kit, weapon hissing against the ground. Marcus didn't call out a warning. Kit knew what he was looking at.

"You have already lost! Everything you love is gone already. Listen to my *voice!* You can win *nothing* here," the actor roared, and the power of the spiders in his voice made what was clearly untrue plausible. If only for a moment.

A moment was enough.

Marcus bared his teeth, roaring, and charged. The Haaverkin man he'd targeted took a step back, and drew a knife with his off hand. Marcus drove the point of his sword through the man's shin, then tucked his head down and kept on running. The crowd tried to push him back toward the rough battle circle, but Marcus lifted the sword before him, feinting toward anyone who came near. His back was frigid cold now and his breath sounded too loud in his own ears. He glanced back. Kit was close behind him, head down and legs pumping wildly. Behind them, the man with the cut shin was lying flat on the street, and Magra was on his knees beside him, a confused expression on his face. The wound on the big man's belly was foaming white where it wasn't the red of blood. So perhaps the venom wasn't so slow after all. Marcus wrenched his way free of the last of the crowd and ran.

The docks were nearby and a thousand miles away. His first sprint gave way to a steady run, his breath taking up the rhythm of his feet. The streets passed by him, expressions of surprise and outrage and fear flickering before him and being left behind. He had the energy to hope the other players had gotten to the ship. If they'd escaped the attack only so that he had to go back out and retrieve them... Well, that would be disappointing.

At the gangplank leading up to the ship, the captain was arguing with Sandr and Smit. The two actors had spars in their hands, held like clubs, and as Marcus let his stride break, Cary emerged from the deck with a black hunting bow in her hands.

The captain gestured to him with a mixture of relief and alarm. "Look! They're here now! There's no call."

"Marcus!" Smit said, rushing toward him.

"Stop!" Marcus said, then carefully sheathed the sword. He wondered whether, if he'd missed the scabbard and tapped his opened back with the flat, it would have killed him. He guessed so. "All right. Safe now."

Smit and Cary helped him aboard while Sandr, Kit, and two of the Haaverkin sailors hauled up the plank. They found Hornet belowdecks, struggling into a set of boiled leather dug out of the costumes chest. Marcus sat down heavily on the deck. The ship shifted, the lines cast off. Ice pounded against its sides like monsters beating their way in.

"You're hurt," Kit said.

"I'm standing."

"You're sitting down"

"Could stand if I wanted to."

"Fair enough," Kit said. Cary clambered down with a bottle of seaman's salve and a handful of rags, and Marcus stripped off his jacket and shirt. They were ripped to rags, as was the skin beneath them. The salve stung like wasps.

"Shouldn't have stayed with me," he said.

"I couldn't see the advantage in leaving you behind," Kit said gently. "Besides which, I think it all worked out well. This once, at least."

"Kit?" Marcus said between clenched teeth.

"Yes?"

"That conversation we were having about doubt and understanding?"

"I remember it."

"Occurs to me that the secret of the world may be *don't do the same stupid thing twice*."

Cary chuckled and the old actor sighed.

"We'll work at that," Kit said.

Geder

The spring season in Camnipol opened with the usual ceremony and pomp, but without men. At the Festival of Petals, Geder sat on the dais with Aster and an empty chair. The prince, the regent, and the king. But that was not the only empty chair. Half the great men of court, it seemed, were on campaign. The sons of the great houses were with Jorey or else the occupying forces in Nus and Inentai. Or busy building up their holdings in the territories that had once been Asterilhold. Or overseeing the passage of Timzinae slaves to the farmholds. Wherever they were, it was not here, and so the hall was rich with a great overabundance of women, youths, and old men.

The ballroom was wide and tall. Paper lamps floated by the heat of their own flames, kept from scorching the ceiling only by narrow tethers. Jugglers, gymnasts, rare animals, freaks, and curious objects stood in their niches along the walls to be considered by the court. Cunning men passed through the crowd conjuring balls of flame and telling fortunes. A small orchestra played from beneath the floor, the music filling the air like a scent without the awkwardness of making room for the musicians. Wine and beer flowed freely. The meat was rich and well spiced. After two years of war, the farms of Antea might be drawing sparse crops, but for the evening at least, the ballroom was well fed to the point of decadence.

The ladies of the court had a table of their own, with all the great names present. Daskellin, Caot, Broot, Tilliaken, Skestinin. And now Kalliam again, twice. Sabiha could take her place there on the strength of her being the daughter of Lord Skestinin, but the servants whose job it was to place the seats according to custom had gnawed themselves raw over the problems that Clara presented. Geder hadn't restored Jorey to his father's barony yet, and so Clara was both mother of the Lord Marshal and wife of a traitor, honored and tainted. In the end, she'd been placed at the foot of the high table, both present and set apart. Geder would have felt awkward about it, but she was smiling and gracious, so apparently that was all working out well enough.

The dresses of the young women at court this season tended toward the bright and the revealing. Green silk-sheath gowns as bright and rich as a beetle's shell. Wire-stiffened lacework skirts of pure white that hinted at the legs within them like a thin fog that might part at any moment. Rouged lips and painted eyes. Breasts constrained by white leather corsets. All about him, Geder found invitations toward lust, and he resented each of them individually and the class of them as a whole.

"I saw Basrahip," Aster said. "Is he coming to the ball?"

Geder turned to the boy and smiled. "No, I didn't mention it to him. I didn't think he'd want to."

Three small lines drew themselves on Aster's brow, and Geder felt the urge to reach out a thumb and smooth them away again. He didn't want the boy distressed, but more and more over the course of his regency, he'd found he was unable to prevent it.

"Are you avoiding him because of Cithrin?" Aster asked,

and Geder felt it in his sternum like a punch. He answered
with a false lightness.

"Oh, probably. The goddess is the power of truth, after
all. I may not be quite prepared for that."

"It'll be all right," Aster said. "The goddess chose you,
and she knows everything. Basrahip will help."

How could he? Geder thought, but didn't say. It would
have been too hard to keep the venom out of the words.
Instead, he patted Aster's knee and nodded. The empty
chair stood behind them.

The music changed, and the ballroom floor cleared. Geder
shifted in his seat, looking behind him. His personal guard
stood at attention against the wall, ready for violence should
violence come as it had before. He might have welcomed it
over dancing.

The first girl who approached the dais was Paesha
Annerin, cousin of Lord Annerin and so related by marriage to Jorey Kalliam's sister. She was a tall girl with dark
hair and golden skin. She wore a gown of yellow silk that
clung to her thighs. She bowed before them in a pose that
let Geder see down the top of her dress to the sheer undergarments and the curve of her breasts. The tightness in his
throat might have been embarrassment or desire or rage.
When she spoke, it was to Aster.

"My prince," she said. "If you would honor me?"

"Of course," Aster said. She smiled, bowed again. Geder
had to look away. As the girl made her way back to the floor,
Aster motioned for a servant to take his cloak. The prelude
to the dance floated up through the floor and would until all
the dancers had taken their positions. There was no hurry.

"I hate it the way they all dress," Geder said.

Aster, handing away his cloak, made his expression a
query. Geder waved a hand at the ballroom.

"Look at them," he said. "They're all showing their bodies like they were fruit on a streetcart. I'm not closed-minded about these things, but there are limits, Aster. There ought to be limits."

"It looks the same as always to me," the prince said, rising. "It's just fashion." And with that, he moved out toward the floor. Geder watched him with a mixture of alarm and admiration. Aster was a boy. He'd been part of the court since he'd been born, and he knew the steps of the dances much as anyone would, but he strode out with a confidence and calm that no age or experience could guarantee. He would walk the dance with the Annerin girl, talk with her, be charming, and come back to his chair unflustered, unchanged, and without the slightest fear of being humiliated by her or by himself. Jorey was the same. Jorey had even asked Sabiha to marry him, and she'd said yes, and the two of them had been sharing a bed ever since. The raw courage it would take to ask that of a woman boggled Geder's mind, and yet to other men it was normal. Easy.

In his imagination, he saw Cithrin as she could have been, pale and perfect among the women of the court. Her Cinnae blood would have made her stand out among the overwhelmingly Firstblood nobility, but as the consort of the regent, she'd have been undeniable. He would have dressed her in pale cream with emeralds in her hair, and the whole court would have spent the season starving themselves to look like her. The tightness in his throat made it hard to breathe.

The prelude reached its crisis point and began again. Geder shuddered and forced his mind away from her. The dancers were still strolling to their places. The floor wasn't particularly crowded, and half the men on it were Geder's father's age or older. All the people who were forgoing the dance had crowded close to the wall, the concentration of them making for a hundred conversations and a mutter of shifting for position. He saw Canl Daskellin speaking with Jorey's mother. Lady Broot was standing alone near one of the jugglers with a sour expression. Three male cousins of House Caot pushed and prodded each other like they were in private. It was hard to believe that Aster was only a little older than they were. A tight group of young women stood not far from the dais. Geder only noticed them because one girl—the one standing in the center—was looking at him. He thought she was Curtin Issandrian's niece, and her name was something like Cheyla or Shaema. He couldn't quite recall. Her jaw was fixed, and bright red marks showed in her cheeks. Her mouth was thin and hard, her chin lifted a degree. She looked like a warrior steeled for battle, and for a heartbeat, Geder was afraid she would draw a weapon. Then a worse idea occurred to him. She was going to ask him to dance.

He rose, turning his back on the floor, and walked briskly to the captain of his private guard.

"I have to go. Now," he said, trying to keep the agitation out of his voice. "I have something I need to attend to. In the library. Alone."

The captain gave salute, and Geder walked out through the entrance that only he and Aster and the guards were permitted. As soon as the door was closed, Geder felt a rush of relief like pouring cool water on a burn. He took in a deep breath and let it out through his teeth. The first chords of the dance proper came through the wall, and he turned his steps back toward the Kingspire and home.

The sunsets were coming later every day, the twilight lasting longer. He wore a jacket against the chill, but he needed it less often. The seasons he remembered from his youth had been longer. As a boy in Rivenhalm, he would spend what seemed like lifetimes in among his father's books or watching the summer sun shimmer through the leaves of the trees near the river. The world had seemed dull then. It didn't anymore, and he missed that.

The white crushed gravel of the path ground beneath his feet. His guard followed at a discreet enough distance he could almost pretend he was alone. The stars glimmered in the blue-grey sky as it fell toward black. The crescent moon hung over the rooftops of Camnipol, looking so heavy and close, it seemed like a long enough ladder would reach it. High on the Kingspire, the banner of the spider goddess shifted in the breeze, the red dimmed and the pale field with its eightfold sigil almost seeming to glow with the moonlight. All this was his to keep and care for until it was Aster's. That was years away yet. For now, and for years to come, Geder was the Severed Throne. The power should have been freeing. Instead, it weighed him down.

In theory, he could do anything. He had command of life and death over all the subjects of the empire. If he wanted to, he could order any woman in the court to his bed. He'd read a book once about King Saavin of Berenholt, Berenholt being the third-age name for western Northcoast. Legend had it that Saavin had enjoyed intercourse with every woman in the kingdom before he died. The book had had woodcuts. Geder's fantasies about sex had been fueled by the stories of the long-dead king's lusty exploits. Now that he was in something like a similar position, he had to think the whole thing was a pornographic fantasy and nothing more. He couldn't imagine ordering a woman to his bed. Ordering her to hide her disgust with him and his body. Or worse than disgust. Amusement.

Nothing about the regency was what he'd expected. If a

cunning man had come to him in those days so long ago in Vanai when he'd had the worst accommodations Sir Klin could find for him, when his days had been filled with duties and errands designed to make the citizens of the once-free city view him specifically as the worst face of Antea, and told him that these were the good times, he would have laughed. What he remembered best now was finding the scholars who would hunt down old books of specula-tive essay. He remembered the joy and excitement he'd felt, curled up against the cold with his little lantern sputtering from the cheap oil, and translating words from a dozen different languages. Uncovering ideas that would never have occurred to him otherwise. Reading anecdotes that history had almost forgotten. He hadn't known he was happy then.

For a moment, he heard the voice of the fire again, saw a woman silhouetted on the walls of the burning city. He shied away from the memory. He didn't think about it often anymore, but when he did, that nightmare was still fresh. Even years later. Would Cithrin's empty compound in Sud-dapal be the same? A bit of the past that returned to hit him in the face like a scourge for years to come? For the rest of his life?

Probably.

The climb to the temple was a long one, past the royal apartments that he shared with Aster, past the great halls and meeting rooms. When he'd given the space at the King-spire's height to Basrahip for his priests and mysteries, it had been with safety against riots in mind, and to celebrate the goddess who'd brought victory to Antea in the large and Geder in particular. The decision had implications he'd never imagined, though. Including Basrahip's increasing absence from court. The great bull-shouldered priest would still attend Geder whenever asked, but the sheer burden of climbing down the stairs and then up them again gave Basrahip reason enough to stay in his cell.

It was a humble room with a mattress laid out on the stone floor, an old iron brazier, and a low table so that Basrahip, sitting on the floor, could read and write the letters that he held in such contempt. Geder, in the doorway, cleared his throat. Basrahip looked up from the page in his hand and smiled.

"Prince Geder. It pleases me to have your company. Sit with me."

Geder lowered himself to the floor with a soft grunt, his back pressed against the wall. The pile of papers on the little desk was thick as Geder's palm and scattered enough that he could see letters written by half a dozen different hands. Basrahip followed his gaze and sighed.

"I had not thought when the goddess came again to the world it would require this of me," the priest said. "I spend my days with dead words, empty of voices."

"Being Lord Regent isn't what I'd expected either," Geder said. "And there's hardly anyone I can talk with about it, too. I mean, Aster, I suppose, but he has enough to carry already. I don't want to burden him with my problems. I suppose he knows, though."

"He is a man who listens well," Basrahip said.

"I've had reports from Jorey. The army's moving west already. He sent ahead to Newport and Maccia, and the cities were entirely willing to give permission to move freely through their lands, so it looks as though he won't have to fight his way across the Free Cities."

"I am glad you are pleased with this."

"What about you? Is this all messages from the temples?"

Basrahip nodded. "Much of it. They seek my guidance on many things, but they cannot hear my voice nor I theirs.

And so we let our words die and send their corpses across the world."

"It would be easier if you could really be there."

"It would, but then I could not attend you as I promised. You are the chosen of the goddess, and so long as you have need of me, my place is here. But where there is confusion within your realm, more of my brethren are called for. Once all humanity has heard the truth of her voice, then her purity and her peace will follow."

"Oh. Are things not peaceful, then? I thought everything was going well."

Basrahip gestured at the letters, as if by their mere existence they showed the answer. "Her enemies are many, but none will withstand her. It was known that the children of lies would resist us. We spread as the light of dawn, and their resistance is powerless."

"Still. It sounds annoying at least, eh?"

"Indeed," Basrahip said with a rueful chuckle. "Also from our friend in the east. Dar Cinlama. He makes great claims, but his pages have no voice. They are shadows. Emptinesses. I long to hear his words and know."

A Jasuru in the brown robes of the priests entered the room carrying a tray with a bowl of stewed grain and goat cheese and a cup of tea. Geder scowled, trying to place the man's face, and felt a thrill of fear when he did. The assassin who'd tried to kill him on the road in Elassae and been taken by the goddess. He knelt before Basrahip now, his black eyes empty of all malice.

"My thanks," Basrahip said, and the Jasuru priest bowed and left. Geder watched in silence until the sound of footsteps had faded.

"Is it safe? Having him here? I mean, he was planning to kill me. He did kill one of your priests, didn't he?"

"That was before the goddess's hand was upon him," Basrahip said. "He will no more act against us than your cities will rebel. The truth of the goddess cannot be denied."

"Well, that's...that's good."

Basrahip took a spoonful of the stewed grain and slurped it. For a moment, Geder could imagine him as he might have been if it had not been for the goddess. A villager and goatherd in the Sinir mountains who might live a full life and die without seeing anything like a city. And here he was instead, in the center of Firstblood power in the world, sleeping on the floor and eating the same food he would have on the far side of the Keshet. Even if the goddess had given no other powers, that the man was here at all seemed miracle enough.

"And you, Prince Geder? Are you well?"

"Yes. Yes, I'm fine," he said, knowing that Basrahip would shake his head slowly at the words even as the event occurred. "I'm not fine."

"You will be," Basrahip said. "Your wounds will heal."

Geder felt a tug of hope, of something like relief. It wasn't enough, but it was enough to make him want if more. "Are you sure of that? Because right now, it seems like they'll all go on forever."

Basrahip took another bite of his food and smiled around it. "Prince Geder, I am *certain*."

Cithrin

Spring came slowly to Porte Oliva. For weeks, the winter chill hung on, breaking for a day or two or three, and then descending again upon the city. The rains that washed the streets and pulled the grey from the clouds into the gutters had a meanness to them Cithrin didn't remember. Stray cats huddled under the eaves, glaring out at the people passing by with the hungry resentment of beggars. She went through the motions of being the woman she pretended to be. Dinners and meetings, contracts and letters of transfer. It was a sham in more ways than one. She pretended to have power when she had none, and she pretended to care, though she didn't.

Cithrin's thoughts were always and only upon the war, and so when the conversations in the taprooms and alehouses changed to some other subject—when the trade ships from Narinisle would come, whether the queen in Sara-sur-Mar was going to make her Herez-born consort official, how the governor of the city had changed the tariffs in response to pressure from the free city of Maccia—it took her by surprise and left her annoyed. A year ago, Sarakal and Elassae had been nations. Today, they were subjects of the Severed Throne. For most of the merchants and tradesmen of Porte Oliva, it was only a curiosity. Or at most one factor among many in the private calculations of their work.

The ivy that grew up the side of the bank's guard quarters was brown and dead-looking, except for pale, green-fuzzed dots that would turn to leaves and flowers in the coming weeks. The stalls of the Grand Market sold winter wheat and woolen cloaks, but also seeds and bulbs and the lighter jackets and leggings that would soon come into use. By summer, the men and women of the city would be nearly nude from the heat and the dampness of the sea and the bulbs would be tulip blossoms. Everything would change, as it always did. The thought comforted Cithrin less than it would have, once.

She had returned to her old apartment over the counting house with its thin floors and the stairway that went down the side of the building. She visited the taphouse that had been her regular haunt before Suddapal, before Camnipol, before Carse. She'd been welcomed by the same serving girl, served the same beer. It felt wrong that so little had changed in the city when so very much had been transformed for her. Yes, Magistra Isadau was in the city. No, Marcus Wester was not. Despite the changes, the city was so much itself, so confident in its permanence that she could almost believe that her travels and adventures had been only a long, complicated dream. That was how little the war had touched Porte Oliva up to now, and some days she could almost pretend it would last.

"The trade ships from Narinisle?" she said, leaning her elbows on the table. "A month, I'd guess. It depends on the blue-water trade, and that varies."

"Will it affect the branch?" Isadau said, as she accepted the plate of sausage and onion that Yardem was offering her. The three of them were at the booth at the rear of the taphouse, half hidden from the common room by a sheer curtain of blue cloth with silver bells sewn to its edges.

"Not directly," Cithrin said. "The money will come in

like a tide, and that will lift us as much as anyone. But Pyk's too frightened of risk to sponsor a ship. We might hold some insurance on cargo, but even that I imagine she'd keep to a minimum."

"You sound as though you disapprove," Isadau said.

"I do. But then she'd say I'm too reckless, so I suppose we're even. At least we annoy each other."

"Likely she was wise this year," Yardem said. "The trade ships may not come at all."

"That would be a pity," Cithrin said. "Why not?"

"Pirates," Yardem said. "Rumor at the gymnasium is they've elected some sort of king."

"I thought that would be the king of Cabral," Cithrin said bitterly. "God knows enough of the pirates have got noble blood."

Yardem shook his head. "This is someone new. Came in and began organizing. Word is the pirates are halfway to being their own fleet."

"Well-disciplined pirates?" Isadau said. "What's the world coming to? Next we'll have stones heading up in the sky like birds."

The Timzinae woman was thinner than when Cithrin had first met her. The blackness of her scales was duller than it had been, and the inner eyelid stayed closed longer and more often than it had. She smiled and she laughed, but Cithrin could see the weariness pressing her like an illness. If there had been a way to lighten her burden, Cithrin would have done it, whatever it was, however much it cost her. Of all the refugees of Suddapal, Magistra Isadau was surely among the luckiest. The Medean bank was in cities across the world, and so Isadau had a place here, and in Northcoast and Narinisle and Herez. It wasn't her own situation that dulled her eyes and sharpened her laughter. It was the war and what it had done to her race, her city, her home. It was the siege in Kiaria, still dragging on. It was Geder Palliako and the spider priests who drove him.

Cithrin felt the same.

"How did the governor's dinner go?" Isadau asked.

"I pled a sick headache," Cithrin said, then took a drink of her beer. It was stronger than the brews of Suddapal or Camnipol, and that was what she liked about it. It warmed her belly a little and loosened the knot there that kept her from sleep. In truth, she'd drunk herself to bed half the nights since she'd returned to Birancour, but it didn't matter. She was always awake just after dawn, and if it had blunted her mind a little, it wasn't as though Pyk's covert and vicious control left much demand for her wits. She wiped her mouth with her cuff. "If I'd gone, it would have been true. The governor's a terrible little man."

"There might have been news," Isadau said, her voice careful.

Cithrin hunched with guilt. "I'll attend next time."

In the common room, a boy cleared his throat and began a slightly off-key warble while an older man, clearly his father, hauled out a pair of puppets. The song was an old romantic ballad, but the words had been changed here and there to make the romantic conquests of the hero into something more martial. The puppets were a seducer and his prey, but they were also Imperial Antea and... well, and whoever got in its way, Cithrin presumed. Every now and then, she caught the singer's gaze cutting back toward the little cove where she and Isadau sat. The piece had been chosen with them in mind, then. Know your audience, Kit would have said. Know them, and know how to flatter them. The piece told Cithrin something about how the city saw her. She tried to ignore it.

Isadau did not. Her gaze fastened on the little mannequins on their strings, and her eyes filled with tears. When she spoke, her voice was calm and matter-of-fact. "If he comes, he will kill us both."

"All three," Yardem said. "I'll go first. Captain'd want it that way."

Halvill stepped through the front door and shook the rain from his shoulders, blinking into the dim as his eyes adjusted. Cithrin took the opportunity to watch the other patrons watch the young Timzinae man. The truth was that Halvill had been in Porte Oliva at least as long as Cithrin had, and likely longer, back when they had called him Roach. But he was Timzinae, his new bride and their nearly arrived child natives of Suddapal. There was distaste in the keep's expression, a distrust that had not been there before. Geder and his armies had changed what it meant simply to be a Timzinae. After all, no one liked to share cake with a leper.

It was hard to reconcile that Geder with the frightened man she'd hidden with in the days of the failed Antean coup. It was also very, very easy.

Halvill caught sight of the three of them and stepped to the booth. The little curtain jingled as he pushed it aside.

"Magistra Cithrin. Magistra Isadau. Yardem," the guard said, nodding to each of them in turn. "The man from the holding company's arrived."

Paerin Clark sat in the counting house, leaning back on his stool. The slate on the wall behind him had marked odds back when the building had been a gambler's stall. Now it listed the guard rotation. Pyk was just pouring a fresh cup of water for him when Cithrin and Isadau came in. The pale man smiled and nodded to them both.

"Paerin," Isadau said, walking to him.

"Isadau," he said, standing and taking the woman in his arms as a brother or dear friend might. "Ah, it's been too long."

"You should have come to Elassae more," Isadau said, releasing him. "You look fatter. Chana has been seeing you fed."

"She does watch after her investments. Cithrin."

For a moment, Cithrin thought he might be about to embrace her too, and her body went stiff and awkward. But Paerin only nodded and smiled and sat back down. Pyk grudgingly poured out water for Isadau and Cithrin as well and then took her own low, sturdy seat. Cithrin sipped at the water to have something to do with her hands while Isadau sat across from Paerin. Paerin was Komme Medean's son-in-law, and third in command of the holding company. Isadau was the voice of the Suddapal branch, which no longer existed. Pyk was nominally Cithrin's notary, but under instructions to run the Porte Oliva branch. Cithrin had no clear idea where she stood in the hierarchy of people in the room.

"I've just come from Sara-sur-Mar," Paerin said, "and a very short audience with her majesty the queen followed by a very long meeting with her master of coin."

"That can't have been pleasant," Isadau said.

"It wasn't," Paerin said. "The opinion of the throne appears to be that the bank has filled her cities with impoverished refugees and brought her the displeasure of Imperial Antea."

Pyk cleared her throat and spat. "Clear grasp of the obvious, that one."

"Yes," Paerin said. "It was hard to argue the facts. The more interesting issue was what remedy we intended to offer her."

Cithrin's belly went tight. "Handing me back to Geder won't stop him."

"That wasn't on the table."

"Bullshit." Pyk chuckled.

"I took it off the table," Paerin said. "It was never a serious proposal. If we started handing over our people, we wouldn't have anyone manning the branches before long."

"She wants a payoff, then?" Pyk said.

"Her master of coin was kind enough to call it a loan, but that's what it comes to, yes," Paerin said, and in Cithrin's memory, Magister Imaniel said, *We never lend to people who feel it is beneath their dignity to repay.*

When Isadau spoke, her voice was tight and passionate. "If we spent every coin we have from every branch standing against those bastards, it would be cheap."

Paerin Clark's eyes were soft. He sipped his water, leaned forward, and let his stool's legs return to the ground. "With respect, Magistra Isadau, the bank doesn't see it that way."

Isadau's face went still and her inner eyelids fluttered in distress. Cithrin stepped forward, putting herself between the Timzinae woman and Paerin Clark by instinct. "Are you going to give them the money?"

"We can't," Paerin said. "If the holding company were to offer a loan to the throne of Birancour, we'd wake up the next morning with Herez, Narinisle, and Northcoast on our doorsteps demanding the same terms. Open that pipe, and it won't close."

Pyk nodded her approval, but Cithrin tilted her head. Something in the way he had said the words, and the words he had chosen, plucked at her. He didn't meet her eyes. "When you say, *We can't*, you mean the holding company."

"I do."

Pyk's expression clouded and she sucked mightily at

the gaps where her tusks had been. "You aren't saying *my* branch ought to carry the burden."

"I told her majesty's master of coin that I was unfamiliar with the details of the branch, and would come to Porte Oliva and discuss what amounts might be available to contribute toward funding the defense of the realm."

"Well," Pyk said, "you can go right straight back up there and tell her majesty that defending the realm is her part of the bargain and paying the tax is mine. I've kept my end, now she can keep hers."

"I think I might rephrase it," Paerin said. "But I think first I will stall for as much time as we can manage. We're in a bad position here."

"Some foreign king has his cock in a twist," Pyk said, waving her massive hand. "We haven't even got a branch in his puffed-up empire. Let him stew. He won't come here."

"He will," Cithrin said.

"The letters we've had from our nameless friend in Camnipol say the army is already on its way. It will be here before the middle of spring."

"Army of stick men too damned tired to lift their own swords," Pyk muttered. Isadau rose, stepped over to the Yemmu woman, and put a hand on her shoulder. Pyk sobbed once, and clamped her jaw. Cithrin had never seen the Yemmu woman frightened before. It shook her more than she'd imagined. She felt a sudden and unpleasant sense of protectivness toward her notary.

"We'll stop them, then," Cithrin said.

"That would be lovely," Paerin said. "How do you propose to manage it?"

Cithrin took a deep breath and let it out through her nose. Geder was coming with swords, arrows, fire, and the spider priests. She had an accounting book and a strongbox of coins and jewelry. Perhaps she could hire a mercenary company. Or increase the bounties offered by the imaginary Callon Cane. Or...

"I don't know," she said. "But I will find a way."

Paerin's disappointment hissed out between his teeth. All four of them were quiet for a long moment. Carts rattled past in the street. A pigeon fluttered at the window and flew away. Cithrin folded her hands over her belly where the sick knot was tying itself tight in her gut.

"Work up a proposal," Paerin said. "Send it to Carse when you have it. And we will see what we can do."

"How long do I have?" Cithrin asked.

"I don't know," Paerin said. "It isn't my deadline to set. Until Palliako's forces come. Or until the queen decides to trade you for peace. You have all the time there is between right now and whenever it's too late."

He left that night, but Cithrin barely noticed. Her world narrowed to a single, overwhelming question: how to buy herself out of a war. She spent hours talking to Yardem Hane about the fine points of hiring mercenary companies: the distinction between guarding and a field contract, the structure of payments that was least likely to have the paid swords turn aside, the delays of travel and how to overcome them. She went through the bank's books and ledgers going back as far as she could find, looking for any precedent that might apply. She reviewed the payments given out by Callon Cane, the estimates for fraud, the challenges of increasing the practice both in Herez and in other cities throughout the world.

Four days, she went without sleep. When Isadau came on the fifth day, Cithrin didn't at first notice that the woman's scales had an ashy dullness or that her movements were slow and careful. She didn't see anything of Isadau's sudden fragility until she spoke.

"I'm afraid we're too late, dear. They've blockaded the harbor."

Cithrin sat at her desk, blinking and confused. *Which harbor?* she thought. And then, *Who blockaded it? How does that change the pricing?* And then the sense of the words penetrated the armor of her focus, and she rose.

Viewed from the seawall, the Antean fleet looked like a busy day in port. Twenty ships ranging from the vast, canvas-strewn roundships to small, nimble-oared war-ships with bronze rams at their prows haunted the water just beyond the place where depth turned it a deeper blue. Fewer than half a dozen defending ships hunkered down in the bay. The harbor was too dangerous for the Antean fleet to traverse without a guide. The power and threat of the attackers was too great to permit any traffic to leave the port or enter it.

All along the seawall, men and women stood and gawked. A half dozen queensmen were shouting at one another as they assembled a ballista that hadn't seen daylight in a gen-eration. The sound of their voices in Cithrin's tired ears was like the gabble of frightened chickens. Porte Oliva was under blockade. Antea had come by water, and no one would enter or leave the city that way. She knew that she should have been worrying about an army, a full siege, but all she could think was that the trade ships from Stollbourne would not come.

The implications spread out before her as clearly as and automatically as breath. The backers of the ships would all fail. Even if the cargo did manage to come in later, any loans used to finance them would have come due. If the goods landed at some other port and came overland, there would be tariffs and shipping, and bandits alerted to the possibil-ity of wealth making its way down the dragon's roads. *All* the insurance contracts would pay out, and anyone who had taken on too many would be crippled or driven out of the market...

"I'm damned," Cithrin said. "Pyk was right about something."

Marcus

"What needs to happen," the innkeep said, his expression soft and ruminative, "is they slit the Cinnae bitch's throat and hang her on the wall as a warning to sluts."

The other people in the common room, men and women both, added their voices to his in a chorus of support. There weren't more than a dozen of them all told, but the violence of their fantasies made them seem more. Marcus leaned forward, looking into his cup. Across the table from him, Cary's smile was empty and her eyes as hard as stones.

"From what I heard, she was working with the Timzinae from the start," one of the other men said.

"All them Western Triad bastards are the same," the innkeep said. He was a gentle-faced man, his voice soft and melodious. Any words he said, however harsh, seemed to take on a kind of philosophical sorrow. "Look different on the outside, but inside, they're the same. Not saying they're all like that Cinnae piece of shit. I've known some Cinnae were fine people. Just it was in *spite* of what they was, if you see what I'm saying."

"Birancour'll give her up," a woman in the back said.

"Unless they were part of it all from the start," the innkeep said. "All those roaches that scuttled out of Elassae headed west, didn't they? There were caravans of them ready to go, and houses in Porte Oliva and Sara-sur-Mar already bought and fitted out for them."

"No, really?" the woman said, pausing in her path.

"Oh yes," the innkeep said. "Only reason Lord Geder didn't root out all the conspirators was they knew he was coming and they had their retreats in mind. They'll be running out of land soon, though. Then they can swim for blue water, and good riddance."

Marcus stood.

The keep looked over to him, eyebrows raised in polite query. "Need anything else there, friend?"

"Just going to stretch my legs and check on the others," Marcus said.

"Well, if there's anything else you need, just say it. We're all looking forward to the play tonight. Sent my boy down to Lesser Bronlet to spread the word. We should have a full yard, and no mistake."

"Kind of you," Marcus said.

They had thought to travel through Antea by avoiding the main roads and attracting as little attention as was plausible for a theater troupe. They could not have done much better. The town was hardly more than a cluster of houses at a place where dirt paths crossed. The dragon's road ran ten miles to the northwest, carrying most of the carts and carriages between Sevenpol and Camnipol. Without it, the merely human paths and roads that laced the plains and farmlands of Antea might have earned the dignity of pavement. But the eternal jade was so near and so effortless that the need never rose above the effort required. The land all around was the fresh green of springtime, the days warm, and the nights not quite cold enough to freeze. After Hallskar, it felt like the jungles of Lyoneia all over again.

Antea itself had altered. Marcus had walked its length already in his life, and while the shape of the land, the accent of the voices, and the flavors of the food remained the same, there were changes that soured all the rest of it. It wasn't only that it was near to a starving spring. Those came from time to time, and then they went. A blight might cause it, or a rogue storm. Or a war. The men who had farmed these lands were soldiers now, and some had been since the invasion of Asterilhold. The labor to manage the lands had been spent elsewhere, until now. The planted fields that the players passed were tilled. The first sprouts of a bountiful summer were pushing through the dark soil. That hadn't changed. But the men who worked the lands weren't First-blood farmers, subjects of the Severed Throne. They were Timzinae, and they were in chains.

The first time they'd seen it had been half a day out of the port of Sevenpol. There had still been snow on the ground then, and the morning ground was covered with frost. The horse Master Kit had bought, using his unnatural magics to negotiate a price so low it was barely fair, had hauled the reconstructed and creaking cart down a long, tree-lined road, heading toward the wide jade of the dragon's road, and then south. Charlit Soon had been huddled on the driver's bench, Marcus and Smit walking beside the wide, slow, turning front wheel. To their right, an old Firstblood man had been in the middle of a field, screaming in anger. The boy absorbing his abuse was perhaps as old as Magistra Isadau's nephew. The Timzinae was stripped to the waist and shivering. The morning light played off his dark scales. The old man brandished a whip made from thorn branches, not striking the boy—not yet—but terrorizing him.

Marcus had seen the shock in Smit's face. The actor was a man of good years who'd been walking the world for most of them. Marcus knew he'd seen ugly sights before, and that he would again. Scenes like it had played all through the countryside. A tree in the middle of a half-tilled field with five Timzinae men tied to it by the neck like dogs. A dead Timzinae woman, abandoned by the side of the road, her back split open by some violence Marcus hadn't seen. But no children. That had been the Lord Regent's great plan. Take the children of Sarakal and Elassae as insurance of their enslaved parents' good behavior. It left all of them ready to see Antea's far border, and Marcus only hoped when they crossed it things would be better. Not here, of course. Antea had declared the Timzinae inhuman—dragons fashioned in human form and thus the ancient enemy of the spider goddess. The atrocities would continue, but since Marcus didn't know how to stop them, at least he didn't want to watch.

In the yard outside the little inn, Kit and Sandr had lowered the side of the cart, making the little stage where they would put on their show. Hornet was placing small, dense candles in tin cups that would throw back the light all around its edge. Marcus nodded to him as he hauled himself up and into the cramped space behind the soft red curtains at the stage's back. Kit was in the long purple robes sewn with spangles at the edge that would transform him into Kil Hammerfrost, tragic king of the imaginary Kingdom of Clouds. Sandr was hunched down over a little mirror of polished metal, putting on eye-grease and rouge to become the sickly Prince Helsin, and applying it a little too thickly, Marcus thought. He shook his head.

Marcus Wester had been the most celebrated general in Northcoast, and its most feared regicide. He had trekked across two continents to confront a goddess who didn't exist and woken a dragon from the age of legend. And with all those marvels and terrors, that he had strong opinions about men's eye-grease still had the power to astonish him.

"What news?" Kit asked.

"Good news is we likely know where Cithrin and Yardem have gotten themselves to. The common wisdom puts them in Porte Oliva, probably under blockade but not siege. At least not yet. The bad news is all of Antea wants her killed slow for hurting the Lord Regent's feelings or some such."

Sandr raised a rouged sponge toward his cheek, paused, and set it down.

"I assume we won't be continuing to Suddapal," Kit said.

"I was thinking we could go back up the dragon's road, take it though Camnipol, then south to the Free Cities. Perhaps try the pass at Bellin in summer for a change," Marcus said. "The worst of the fighting is still the siege at Kiaria, and that could last another year or more, depending on how the water supply is in the caves."

"And then?"

Marcus shrugged. "Take our best guess and try it. Same as always."

"I'm afraid it may have gone too far to stop," Kit said.

"Then we'll get everyone on ships for Far Syramis and try to keep it confined to this side of the ocean," Marcus said. "If that doesn't work, we can try to find some mountain-top with a good stream, build a few houses, and kill anyone who shows up unexpectedly."

Kit's smile was dark. "I think that sounds uncomfortably plausible."

"That's me," Marcus said, tapping his temple with two fingertips, "always thinking ahead."

"I don't think I can go on tonight," Sandr said. His voice was wet and choked. His eye-grease was trailing down his cheeks in tiny black lines of tears. "I don't think I can play for these people."

Kit and Marcus exchanged a glance, and Marcus knelt down, putting a hand on the younger man's shoulder. "This isn't the place to make a stand. Time will come. I don't know where yet, and I don't know when, but it will come."

Master Kit's voice was warm and gentle, and it carried a power more than only the words. "You can do this, my friend. Listen to me. It is within your power."

Sandr was silent for a moment. He shook his head. "Do I have to?"

"We don't want to stand out," Marcus said. "Right now, we're a bunch of Firstblood actors wandering through a nation of Firstblood people. As long as that's what they see, we'll be fine. If they find out, for example, that Kit and I were working with Cithrin in Suddapal or that we tried to slaughter their new favorite goddess? Well, then being in the fields with our Timzinae friends will be the best thing we could hope for. Keep calm, and keep quiet, and let's all get through this bit alive."

"So just accept it?" Sandr asked.

"*Pretend* to," Kit said.

Sandr blinked up at the old actor. His half-painted, tear-smeared face was a mess, the illusions of color and light, pale powder and rouge ruined. He swallowed. "How long can you pretend to be something before you aren't pretending anymore?"

The three men stood silent for a long moment, then Marcus sighed. "Stop saying things that sound wise, Sandr. It upsets my sense of the world."

True to the innkeep's word, the yard was full that night. Men and women from all the surrounding hamlets had come. Kit,

Sandr, Cary, and Hornet had taken to the little stage and done a fair performance of The Kingdom of Clouds, and afterward Charlit Soon had made an encore of the queen maiden's speech from Leterpan's Hill that lifted the crowd's spirits and ended the evening with a little laughter for the audience at least. Through it all, Marcus and Smit had been in the crowd, leading the booing when the villainous Lord Stoop appeared and cheering for Prince Helsin. When a half-drunk young man tried to interrupt the performance with his heckling, Marcus had escorted him to the stables and explained why he might not want to be rude. The boy's frightened expression had made him feel good at the time and guilty later. Pretty soon, he'd be proving his manhood by kicking puppies that chewed the wrong sticks.

When the night was done, Marcus helped the players gather the coins that had been thrown on the stage and bounced down to the dirt of the yard. He cleaned out the candleholders with a work knife and fastened the stage when they hauled it up into place. Tomorrow, they'd be off again. It was a long road, and he didn't like to think what would be at the end of it. Nothing good.

Their agreement with the innkeep had been that the players would sleep in the stables, but as the last of the crowd left, he mentioned to Kit that three of the rooms hadn't been taken. Enough for the women to take a room to themselves, and the men to split the other two. So, once Kit had assured himself that the innkeep wasn't looking for more coin or one of the players to bed down with, the company accepted the extra hospitality. Sandr couldn't bring himself to thank the man. Marcus couldn't blame him.

The walls of the inn were flimsy. From his cot, Marcus could hear the snores of Hornet in the next room and the hushed voices of Cary and Charlit Soon in the one past that.

A soft wind set the rafters ticking and the lingering smell of onions reminded him how small the meal had been.

"I don't suppose you're sleeping," Marcus said.

"No," Kit answered.

"How long do you think it will take us to reach Camnipol?"

"At a guess? If the new axle holds, we could be there in a week."

"Court will be back by now. And Cithrin's mysterious correspondent."

Kit shifted on his cot, the legs creaking under his weight. The window was stretched hide, a light square in the darkness of the wall that illuminated nothing. Still, Marcus had been traveling with Kit long enough, he could imagine the man's quizzical expression.

"Are you wanting to resume that hunt?"

"I want to find some way to—"

The sound was sudden and profound, and Marcus didn't know what it was. The closest he could think was a massive stone thrown by siegecraft striking bare ground. He didn't recall rising to his feet. He was simply there, the poisoned sword in his hand, ready to be drawn. His heart was thudding in his chest.

"Marcus?" Kit whispered. "What was that?"

Marcus raised his hand for silence, the gesture useless in the black. Outside the inn, something heavy slid across the yard. Marcus stepped to the door and lifted its latch as quietly as he could.

"Get the others," he murmured. "Do it quickly. I'll go see—"

Once, years before when Marcus had been working contracts as a mercenary, he had been present at the siege of a great garrison keep at the rough, informal border between

Borja and the Keshet. The pale stone walls had stood thirty feet high, and the commander had hired a team of cunning men to undermine them. The sound when those walls came down—the thunder-deep rumble, the shriek of splintering wood, the screaming voices—was the same one that assaulted him now.

A chunk of wood struck his shoulder like a blow. He felt Kit behind him, backing him, and Marcus drew the venomed blade. The ceiling of the inn rose, a strip of stars and moonlight cracking where it was lifting from the wall. The roof of the inn creaked into the darkness like the lid of a chest swinging up. The vast head of the dragon stared down at him, its vast eyes silvered by the moonlight.

The roof tipped over, falling to the ground with a crash. People were screaming. Someone threw a lit lantern at the vast, dark bulk of the dragon that filled the yard, but missed badly. The smear of burning oil on the earth lit the beast from below as the cool moonlight did from above. Marcus held the blade before him. It felt like wielding a spoon against a forest fire.

"You," the dragon breathed. "I have followed your scent halfway across the land."

"Flattered," Marcus said, but Inys took no notice.

"I have seen it, and it was as you said. You did not lie. They are gone. They are all gone, but I will redeem my error. My workshop will be rebuilt. Those parts of ourselves we put into your kinds. I can retrieve them. I *will* retrieve them."

The dragon's tail whipped in agitation, crushing the wall of the stables. Horses were screaming in terror. People were weeping and calling out to God. The dragon's gaze slid off Marcus, then found him again. A claw larger than Marcus's body peeled back the wall of the room effortlessly. The door opened behind them, and Cary and Charlit Soon stepped in, blades in their hands. Marcus waved them back.

"This...all of this," the dragon hissed, the sharp stink of his breath filling the air, "is mine. All of it is my doing, and so I will undo it. The sky will be filled, *filled*, with dragons, and great perches will be raised again from the earth and the sea."

"All right," Marcus said. "If you say so."

The massive head rose, searching the sky as if all it said were already true. A bloom of flame rose from the black-fleshed mouth, and the dragon's wings spread until it seemed they would touch the horizons.

"This is the darkest hour of the noblest race. And rising from it shall be our greatest triumph. A glory that will echo through time itself, and change the nature of the stars."

"No reason to aim low," Cary said, and Kit shushed her. A great foreclaw folded, tightened, pressed the air before Marcus. The black talons looked sharper than spears, but Marcus made no move to parry them.

"And you," the dragon said. "Drakkis Stormcrow was to wake me, but it was you who did. So you shall be my Stormcrow. Murmus Stormcrow."

"Marcus."

"Marcus Stormcrow. You shall be my voice and my servant, my creature in this new, most glorious conquest. You shall be my general in the field of battle greater than any the worlds have ever known. We shall face down the armies of death, of nothingness, and we shall pull *life* from their corpses. *Life!*"

The last word echoed through the darkness like a great storm wind. The last dragon reared up on his back legs, screamed defiance at the sky, and toppled. The huge body crushed the wall of the stable, freeing two of the horses, which sped off shrieking into the night. The dragon's head lay against the ground, and its single raised wing folded down slowly, bending into itself like a moonflower folding at dawn.

Somewhere very close by, a man wailed in fear. A lick of flame rose from the ruined common room where the embers of the fire grate had been scattered in the splintered wood of the walls. The moon sailed uncaring above them through a vast and star-sown sky.

Cary spoke first. "Did we do something? Did we... *defeat* it?"

"No, we didn't. I'm not sure quite how he managed it," Marcus said, carefully sheathing the sword, "but I do believe our great scaled friend here is drunk."

Clara

Clara rode through the early evening rain, her pipe turned mouth-down to keep the droplets from drowning the tobacco. The lands of the Free Cities struck her as much like the cities themselves, varying from one valley to the next. The plains of southern Antea were only a day behind them now, and already she felt as if she'd ridden through three different worlds. This present landscape was made of low, rolling hills covered with a grey-green grass that seemed to collect the gloom from the clouds. The dragon's road, permanent as it was, had outlasted the hills that had once supported it. Now it undulated toward the horizon, rising here into the air like a bridge and there disappearing for a space beneath the ground. It reminded her of nothing so much as the image of a sea serpent arching through waves.

Orsen lay a day and a half a day ahead, perched on its lone mountain. She planned to turn aside before she reached it, leaving the dragon's road for the more changeable paths of mere humanity. The army, her sons at its head, would be marching for Bellin and the pass through the mountains. It was her hope and intention to meet it there or else between the city at the mouth of the pass and the fields of Birancour.

Her mount was a three-year-old gelding the color of wheat, and the hunting tent—a tiny affair that rose no more than two feet from the ground when employed—was folded across its back. She did not regret that she would not be spending yet another night in it, breathing air heated by her own breath and fighting to make the unkind ground do for a mattress. Vincen Coe rode beside her. In Camnipol, where she had been Lady Kalliam and he a huntsman of no particular rank, he would have ridden behind her. She preferred him where he was.

The question that remained as they trekked across the damp, grey hills toward the flickering torches of the wayhouse was who precisely he should be.

"Not husband," she said. "Son. It's simply more plausible."

"To who?"

"To everyone," Clara said. "A woman of my age simply isn't married to a man like you. Even if they accepted the tale, it would stand out. I prefer not to be memorable."

"I think you underestimate the world, my lady."

"Do you, now?"

"If you believe we're the strangest thing in it? Yes."

"You are my son, I am your mother. We are making our way to Maccia to take up residence with my sister now that your father is dead."

"Yes, my lady."

"You're laughing at me. I can hear it in your voice."

"Yes, my lady."

"And don't call me *my lady*. You'll give the game away."

"Yes, Mother," Vincen said. As if in answer, Clara's gelding sighed.

The sun, shrouded by clouds, did not set. The world only grew darker by degrees. The constant patter of rain was broken by the rumble of distant thunder. Her hands and hips ached, and when they drew into the wayhouse's yard and the grooms splashed out through the mud to take their horses, she mostly felt pleased that the day was done, and that there would be a warm room and a bowl of something to eat.

The house itself was low and dark, the thatch roof black with the damp. The smell of beer and roasted peppers washed over her as she ducked through the doorway.

"Let me do the talking," Vincen murmured. "You can't help sounding like you belong in a ballroom."

Clara nodded and clamped her lips tight around the stem of her pipe. The common room was low-ceilinged and smoky. The keeper was a broad-shouldered Jasuru woman with a scar across her cheek that complicated her bronze-green scales.

"Evening, friends," the keep said, baring her pointed teeth in a smile that managed to be warm and welcoming. "Hard weather for riding."

"Seen worse," Vincen said. "The wife and I need a room for the night, if you have any."

"Silver if you don't mind sharing. Two if you're looking for privacy."

"Two it is," Vincen said, putting an arm around Clara's shoulder. "And perhaps a bowl of something to eat? Whatever you've got back there smells wonderful."

"You're kind to say it," the keep replied, waving at the blackwood table. "Take a seat, and I'll bring your bowls and beers. At two silver, you're already paying for it."

Clara lowered herself to the bench, her back and knees creaking. Vincen sat at her side, scooped up her hand, and laced his finger with hers.

"You are a terrible man," Clara said softly.

"You are a beautiful woman," he replied. "And your accent is fine."

Jorey and Vicarian had left before the court season had the chance to begin. They'd shared a carriage drawn by a team twice as large as the carriage required. Jorey was in haste, rushing to do what needed to be done and have it over. She'd watched it clatter away down the street, turning to the south when it could and vanishing from sight. Sabiha, standing beside her, had wept quietly as much from exhaustion as sorrow. The baby was taking more and more of the girl's reserves, and Clara had taken Sabiha's hand in her own, thinking to offer her strength. As if a few fingers laced together could do that.

Over the following days, her suspicion that there was indeed a way to leave the court behind began to take root. And more than a way, a *need*. All her schemes among the lower classes of the city had rested on finding men and women loyal to her, who would lie for her. Now she saw that her armor was made of paste and paper, and the urge to flee the city before she could be found out grew with every day. And still, despite all her growing plans and unspoken analysis, the arrival of the high families was a shock.

The year before, Clara had watched from the gutters as the carriages arrived. Even those who had caught sight of her had pretended not to. The year before *that*, she had been Baroness of Osterling Fells and her husband one of the great names of the empire. This time, the powerful families of the court arrived in Camnipol already buzzing with scandal and confusion. Lord Ternigan had been exposed as a traitor. Ernst Mecelli had also been implicated, but the Lord Regent had either determined his innocence or reached some accommodation for amnesty. In any case, both men were gone: one dead, the other touring the captured cities of the previous year's campaign. And in their place, taking command of the army as his father once had, Jorey Kalliam, husband of the somewhat tainted Sabiha Skestinin, son of the traitor Dawson Kalliam, and best friend of the Lord Regent. Clara, being a woman and so apparently having no identity of her own, was neither the baroness she had been nor the fallen woman she'd become. She was both Dawson's widow and Jorey's mother, and with every renewed acquaintance, she saw the wariness echoed again.

To her surprise, the women who had most supported her in her year of social exile seemed the most unnerved by her rehabilitation. Lady Enga Tilliaken, who had invited Clara to garden tea but not into her home, who had given Clara a cast-off dress, who had by most measures been Clara's greatest supporter, went white about the lips when they met at Lady Essian's formal luncheon the day after the opening of the season. Ogene Faskellan, a distant cousin of Clara's and one of the first to share little meals with her at a discreet bakery where they were unlikely to be seen, was brittle and polite. Even young Merian Caot, fully a woman now but with enough of the adolescent in her to treasure scandal and upheaval, was cool to her. At first it had all taken Clara aback, but soon she felt that she understood.

Fallen, she been what each of these women needed. She had filled a role in the stories they told themselves about who and what they were. Enga Tilliaken wanted to believe she was a generous soul, and Clara had been the opportunity for her pride to feed itself by condescending to accept a disgraced woman's company. For Ogene Faskellan, Clara had been a safe sort of shame. A secret and a whiff of brimstone that could safely enliven an uninspiring marriage and constrained life. Merian Caot had wanted a way to argue that she was not tied by the same social bonds as the rest of them. Taking tea with Clara had been an act of rebellion for her at an age when rebellion—or in truth only the appearance of rebellion—was part of the subtle mourning that came with womanhood in the court of the Severed Throne. And so, for all of them, Clara had failed. Tilliaken could no longer take her clandestine joy in looking down on Clara, Faskellan found no drama in her company. And for the young Caot girl, the older woman who had shown some ray of hope that court life might not be entirely constrained had instead stepped back into line. None of it had been about who Clara truly was, and so neither was it now. And still, it left her sour.

And she would have taken the little slights and tight smiles a thousand times over rather than endure the women like Erryn Meer who had distanced herself from Clara and now greeted her like the previous year had never happened. Hypocrisy was the marrow of court life and always had been. In truth, very little had changed, except her. And she, more even than her peers, was aware at every turn that she no longer fit.

The image that came to her time and again in the early days of the season was a pot-bound plant removed from its bindings and placed in a wider soil where roots could spread as they had not before. Only now she was being pushed back into that old, too-small container, and she would not fit. She was not any longer the woman she had been. She missed her husband with an ache that she thought would never entirely fade, but she would also have been hard-pressed to welcome him back, should God and angels lift him restored from the depths of the Division. Like the old stories of men taken to magical lands who could never entirely return, Clara had stepped into a wider, more violent, less certain world. She had the taste of it now, and she would never again be so tamed as she had been.

And so it became an easy thing to plot her escape.

To Enga Tilliaken, she said that she had an ailing friend in Osterling Fells and was thinking of retiring from the court for the season to oversee the cunning men as they tried to heal her. To Lady Daskellin she hinted broadly that her residence in the Skestinin manor was not entirely to Lady Skestinin's liking. At the garden tea, she praised Geder for his kindness to her family. At the spring bowling competition, she confessed to missing Dawson and Barriath and her cousin Phelia who had been wife to Feldin Maas back when the conspiracy against the throne had been thought to spring from Asterilhold. She laid the ground for any number of stories to explain her retreat and a dozen false trails to suggest where she had gone and why. All except the truth. That, she told only to Sabiha, and even then, not all.

Dawson had spoken of the art of war many times, and she had listened with half an ear. She had heard him speak of the people that follow the army to war: robbers of the dead, prostitutes, workmen too old, slow, or infirm to wield a sword but able to do small service for the soldiery at a small price. He had told her more than once that the well-being of an army could be judged by the character of its hangers-on like judging the health of a dog by the quality of its coat. Often, he'd said, the followers and small people knew things about the army that the generals did not.

The army was once again on the march. She intended to follow it quietly, at distance, and in disguise. She would blend in with the followers and learn what there was to be learned. And if she could, frustrate the campaign without destroying the man who led it. When she had been trapped in the court like a fly in sap, the idea had seemed plausible. On the road with Vincen at her side, the rashness of the errand stood out, though not enough to make her turn back.

The room was small, and the thatch above them ticked with the rain and a variety of black beetles she had previously been unfamiliar with. The smell of the mud and beer and weather almost forgave the reek of the night pot. Vincen lay in the bed beside her, snoring slightly. Both of them still wore all the day's clothes as proof against the cold, but she could still feel the warmth of his body. She was weary beyond expectation. Her back ached and her legs as well. Sleep, however, eluded her. A thousand different worries assailed her: How would she find the army, and how would she avoid being recognized, and what would happen if she were? How could the wars of Geder Palliako and his spider priests be separated from those of Antea when the same men fought the same battles for each? How much longer could she keep the grief of seeing her middle boy consumed by the goddess at bay, and what was she going to do when that dam burst?

But along with all of it was a sense of lightness that confused her at first. It wasn't simply that court was oppressive and she was no longer there. The boarding house in Camnipol had been a hundred times more pleasant than traveling, and she hadn't even joined the army yet. She had been outside court for the better part of a year, and had been miserable and frightened through most of it.

The difference was that she had been cast out before, where now she had stepped away. After Dawson's death, she had been hollowed out. Now if anything she felt too large for the world she'd lived in. The campaign would be dangerous, brutal, and exhausting, but it was what she had chosen. If she died on the road—and God knew there was enough chance of that in a war—she would die on her own terms, serving her kingdom better than Enga Tilliaken or a thousand more like her would ever conceive. She would not have expected the difference to matter greatly, and yet it did.

Vincen grunted and curled his arm under his head like a pillow. She knew it more by feel than sight. The only illumination in the room was what leaked in around the poorly hung door and the occasional flash of lightning. Clara closed her eyes, willing herself to sleep, but to no avail. And so instead, she rolled to the edge of the little bed and stood. Vincen would want her to stay in the room. They were far from Camnipol, but there would be couriers running between the throne and the army. And even that aside, the fact that the keep had taken their money did not guarantee that everyone in the place was benign.

Clara slipped the door open carefully. The hinge was a length of hard leather, and it creaked when it moved. Vincen did not wake. She pulled the door to behind her and went down the short hall to the common room. A Southling boy not more than ten years old was sweeping the floor with a rude little broom. A table of men, some Firstblood and others Kurtadam, played a card game in the corner. Clara went to sit by the fire grate.

"Help you, dear?"

The Jasuru woman loomed up out of the shadows. Clara had always heard it said that the Jasuru were bred by the dragons as soldiers. Black-mouthed, pointed teeth, scales across their bodies as a permanent light armor. But no race was ever only the thing it was intended for, not any more than a woman was only what she was told to be. Clara drew herself up and smiled.

"Trouble sleeping," she said.

"Ah. Could bring you a cup of rum if you'd care for it."

"Trade down to wine, if you've got it," Clara said, trying to speak the way she imagined Abitha Coe speaking. Vincen's comment about sounding as though she belonged in a ballroom might only have been teasing, but there was some truth in it. If her aristocratic past showed in her words, the keep gave no sign.

"Something to ease you down, but not so much you can't wake come morning," the Jasuru said with a broad wink. "You're a wise woman, you."

"Wouldn't go that far," Clara said, but the keep was already stepping to the back room. The Southling boy glanced over to her, smiled shyly, and went back to his chore. The men at the table reached some critical point in their game, groaning and chortling together, and then one of them began reshuffling the cards. When the keep returned, with an earthenware cup of wine, Clara took it with a nod that she hoped was companionable. She didn't want to treat this woman as a servant, and for more reasons than one. The wine had a bite at the front, but it finished well. Dawson would have called it cheap and common, and he would have been right. He would have meant that there was no solace or pleasure to be found in it, and that would have been wrong.

The coals in the grate warmed her knuckles and the ticking of the rain seemed calming now that she was in a dry, comfortable room and not riding through it. They would find the army within the week, she hoped, and from there, she would have to improvise with her family, her country, her lover, and her life all at stake. She would find a way to save Jorey and the throne both. Or if not both, at least one of them. There was a fair chance that this would be one of the last pleasant evenings she had for a very long time.

Clara drank her wine alone, and listened to the rain.

Marcus

The birds announced the dawn before the light came, trilling and calling to one another as if unaware that one of the fallen masters of the world had returned from legend to sleep in the ruined inn's yard. Or if not unaware, unimpressed. Marcus had stayed up the full night, waiting. Prompted by Kit and his unpleasant power to convince, the innkeep and his people had fled toward the nearby hamlets and towns. Likely it had been the wiser choice.

"When should we wake it up?" Sandr asked.

The dragon lay on its side, wings folded in against its vast bulk. Its eyes—each as wide as a man's body—were closed. Its breath was the deep, regular tide of sleep. Every now and then throughout his watch, its scaled brows had furrowed and its mouth curved in distress at whatever nightmares plagued it.

"Be my guest," Marcus said.

"Maybe another hour," Sandr said.

Marcus was amazed at how easily he could read emotion in the vast, inhuman face, the angle of its wings, and the shape of its balled claws. It reminded him of stories he'd heard about shepherds whose dogs understood them so well that an untrained man would have thought they shared a mind. Really, it was only that over generations the dogs that followed a man's expressions had been let breed while the others were killed or gelded. Only in this translation, Marcus was playing the part of the dog.

And perhaps that was apt, because he knew—they all knew—that the beast was about to wake just before the great eyes opened. The dragon's gaze swam for a moment, fixed on Marcus, lost him, and came back.

"Morning," Marcus said.

The dragon said something like *ummbru*, shifted its feet under it, and half crawled down the sward to the little river. Marcus ran along beside it. At a pool, the dragon sank its head into the water, its throat working as it drank. Marcus waited. What seemed an impossibly long time later, it pulled its head back to land. Back at the inn, Kit and the other players stood in a line, watching. They were the audience for once.

"So," Marcus said. "Feeling any better?"

"I want to die."

"Well, give it time."

"For what?"

"Either you'll stop wanting it, or you'll die. One or the other."

The dragon managed a wan smile.

"The world is emptied," it said. With its head resting on the green earth, every word vibrated. "I have killed the world."

"Well, about that. I was hoping you knew what the spiders are. We'd been under the impression they were sent by a goddess as a sign of her favor, but that didn't work out. And since they seemed to be searching for you ... I'm sorry, this is a very strange morning for me."

"They are my fault. They are my brother's vengeance."

"Your brother."

"Morade."

"Ah."

"He destroyed everything because of me."

"No goddess, then."

The dragon shifted its head to watch him with both of its eyes. "I angered him. It was cruel and it was small, and... Erex. My love is dead. She is dead. All are dead."

"Spiders aren't dead."

"They are nothing."

"We aren't dead."

"*You* are nothing."

"You aren't dead."

The dragon took a great breath and let it out slowly. Marcus more than half expected it to be scalding hot, but it was no warmer than any large animal's though it smelled of something like oil and distilled wine. The dragon rose to its haunches, spread its wings, and yawned massively. It raised its nose as if searching for some scent, then sneezed. Marcus waited.

"I should have died with them," it said. "Instead I am trapped in this graveyard world. Feral slaves like maggots in the corpse of the earth. Why did you wake me?"

"Mostly, it seemed the thing to do at the time. The spider priests were looking for you, and we thought anything they wanted, it'd be best to keep from them."

"You keep company with the tainted."

"Just the one," Marcus said. "And he's very well behaved. Killing the spider goddess was his idea."

"There is none such."

"Picked up on that. So I don't mean to pry or intrude on your mourning, but...ah..."

"What?"

"A fair part of the world I live in is in the process of grinding itself into blood and bone, and these priests look to be at the heart of it. No offense meant, but if this really is your fault, the least you can do is explain yourself."

"I do not answer to slaves."

"Make an exception. Just this once."

The vast claw moved more quickly than Marcus could react. He tried to reach back for the poisoned sword, but his arm was already pinned to his side by the tree-limb-thick claws. The dragon lifted him in the air until he was higher than the inn had been, back when it had had a roof. His ribs creaked, and he fought to draw breath. One of the players screamed. The dragon tilted its head. Anger flared in its eyes, and then died. It sagged and dropped Marcus on the riverbank. He lay back, his eyes on the blue dome of the sky, hissing between his teeth. The pain in his back subsided slowly. Probably nothing broken, but *damn.*

"We were great," the dragon said, as if it had made no violent move. "We were masters of time and space. The mysteries of all creation were bare before us. Before him. Morade, my brother. We were set to make marvels. To prove ourselves, and I was...jealous? Angry? I don't know what I was. It is too long ago. I destroyed his work as a joke. I, in my folly, expected him to be...annoyed. Displeased. He was *enraged.* He swore vengeance.

"We were complacent. I see that now. We relied on the slave races we had made," the dragon said, waving its claw at Marcus. "Your kind. We created you, we set you to your tasks, and we forgot. And why remember? Does a body keep track of every drop of blood? Does a gardener count his worms? We had our eyes on greater things. To see the despised, the small, the insignificant, and to find a weakness there...ah, that was his genius. He forged a secret tool, and in doing so, he poisoned his own mind. They were his madness made flesh."

"The spiders?"

"A corruption to drive our slaves to slaughter one another. To disrupt all the patterns that we had come to rely upon. It made their minds brittle and caught them in a dream that fractured them. We didn't see. I didn't see. The corruption spread unnoticed, and then it shattered. They killed each other over nothing. Over the colors of their shirts or their eyes, whether they drank before they ate or ate before they drank. Whether they ate beef or fowl. *Anything* became a pretext for murder."

"Wait," Marcus said. "We haven't seen that. The ones we've been fighting can smell out lies and convince people of things, but this other thing you're talking about—"

"There is no other thing. Your kind has small, fragile thoughts and you live in dreams by your nature. You make beliefs the way a dog sheds in spring."

"All right," Marcus said. "Not following."

The dragon's smile was pitying. "I will show you. If the words in the question fall in threes, I will answer no. Otherwise, yes. Do you understand?"

"Not particularly."

"You will. Bring one of the others. Not the corrupted one."

"You want me to..."

"Any of them will do."

"Wait here, then."

"There is nowhere I can go."

Marcus turned and walked back up the gentle slope. The players came forward to meet him. *What's it saying?* Mikel asked at the same time Cary asked, *Are you all right?* The gabble of voices erupted. Only Kit stayed silent.

"Sandr," Marcus said. "Walk with me."

"Did I do something wrong? I'm sorry."

"No, just...come."

As they returned to the side of the creek, the dragon was staring at the sun, turning its claws in the light and watching the scales shine. It angled its head toward them, and Sandr froze.

"It's all right," Marcus said. "If our friend here wanted us dead, we'd be dead."

"It's true," the dragon said.

"Good to know," Sandr said in a small voice.

"I know something of you," the dragon said, its voice rich and deep. "I will answer you yes or else no, and nothing else."

"What's this about?" Sandr squeaked, his gaze cutting to Marcus.

"Just do it," Marcus said.

"Ah. All right. Um..." Sandr squared his shoulders. "Is this about me?"

The dragon turned to Marcus and counted its claws. One, then two, then three. The fourth it wiggled in the air at Marcus. *If the words in the question fall in threes, then no. Otherwise...* "Yes."

"Me in particular?"

One, then two, then three. "No."

"Something about the sort of person I am?"

Three and then three. And one left. "Yes."

"Actors?"

"Yes."

"Is it a prophecy?"

"Yes."

"Does it end with us dying?"

Three and then three. Nothing left over.

"No."

Marcus watched the dragon and the actor trade questions as the morning sun warmed them. Slowly, Sandr followed the arbitrary answers one after the other to a story about a band of actors that were going to defeat the forces of darkness by seducing an enemy queen on the evening before a great battle and then fathering a new dynastic line. Sandr's eyes grew wider over time, and Marcus could almost see him trying to imagine which queen it was and judge his own chances of cuckolding some great king.

The dragon held up its claws and turned his attention back to Marcus, ignoring Sandr as if he were not there. "Imagine now that it cannot be disbelieved."

"What can't be disbelieved?" Sandr said.

"None of that was true," Marcus said.

"The prophecy?"

"No prophecy," Marcus said.

"Oh," Sandr said with a shrug. "Well, that's a bit disappointing."

The dragon reared up, its nostrils flaring, its wings spreading wide. It pointed a claw at Sandr's chest. Sandr fell back with a shriek and Marcus moved to stand between them.

"And *that* is what they cannot do," the dragon said, its voice rising to a roar like a forest fire. "They *cannot* accept when they are wrong. Once told they cannot *doubt*. And that is what my brother did, and that is why we were weakened when he struck. That is why we *died*."

"Marcus?"

"He's not mad at you, Sandr."

"He seems mad at me."

"He's not mad at you," Marcus said. And then to the dragon: "So these wars we're seeing. These priests spreading through the world again. They really think there's a spider goddess."

"Truth and belief are indistinguishable to them," the dragon said. "They believe what they believe *because* they believe. There is no escape from it. And who listens to their voices becomes like them. They drifted into madness before I slept, and they are mad still."

"Except Kit. He's not like that."

"All the corrupt are part of Morade's plan. Give your friend his own followers, and they would kill the ones who disagreed with them like ants in a bottle. I made soldiers to fight them that the corruption would not infect. I forged the culling blades. I made the one you carry now. We fought to clean the stock of slaves, but the corruption outran us. And my brother killed everyone that opposed him. I planned my last, desperate trick. I would let him believe he had won, and then strike. It meant destroying the perches we held sacred. The one thing he did not think I would sacrifice..."

The dragon's attention turned inward. It looked stunned.

"Better I had died," it said.

"Don't let's get too far ahead with that," Marcus said. "Wait here. I'm just going to take him back."

The dragon's head sank down until it was staring at itself in the rippled surface of the pool. It shifted its wings with a sound like a ship's sails creaking. Marcus took its silence as permission and led Sandr back up the hill. The others had come a bit closer now. Sandr sat on the ground and folded his arms around his knees, trembling. Marcus noticed that he was shaking too, then pushed the fact aside. He'd ignored battle panic before too, and this wasn't likely to be so different. Kit put his hand on Sandr's shoulder and said something Marcus couldn't hear. Sandr nodded, and Kit ruffled the young man's hair before he came closer to Marcus. The old actor's face was grim.

"What have you found?" he asked.

"Everything we thought was wrong."

"I'm afraid I may be growing used to that."

"Is a habit for us, isn't it? If I'm following our new friend's thread, the priests aren't here to take the world over so much as reduce it to chaos and unending violence."

"To what end?"

"To win a war that's thousands of years dead."

"Ah," Kit said sourly. "Does he know how they can be defeated?"

"From what I can tell, he was asleep before your however-many-greats-grandfather took to the ass end of the world. He knows more than we do, though. I think he's our best hope of ending this, and I expect that your old friends would have put a tree through his neck if they'd found him. That hairwash he was spouting last night about remaking the dragons and promoting me to the next Stormcrow hasn't come up. He may not remember he said it."

"Do you think it meant anything? Or was he so deeply in his cups it's meaningless?"

"Can't say. Not yet, anyway. The more immediate problem is I think our chances of passing unobtrusively through Antea have gotten markedly worse."

Kit turned and Marcus followed his gaze. The low, rolling hills of eastern Antea seemed peaceful, but the illusion would only last so long.

"How long," Kit said, "would you expect them to stay away?"

Marcus shrugged. "If it was my inn, I'd be on the way back already. See if it was safe, and if there was anything to salvage."

Kit passed his hand across his forehead. Marcus could see the confusion and fear in the gesture. Or else in himself. *If that thing had decided to kill me just now, I'd be dead*, he thought. *And instead of addressing that, I'm going to talk as if this were all perfectly normal. Just another problem that needs fixing.*

"Surely they can't harm it. Him. I can't imagine a dragon could be threatened by a few farmers and townsfolk?"

"Used to be a lot of dragons," Marcus said. "Only one left. The one thing we can be sure of is they can die. Truth, though, I'm less worried about the locals rallying than the news reaching Camnipol. I'm not greatly tempted by the prospect of answering the sorts of questions that Palliako's private guard would be prone to ask. Especially as one of your old companions would likely be in the room."

"Yes, I suppose that wouldn't be likely to go well."

"We have to get word back to Cithrin and the bank. Most wars, the enemy is looking for victory. If these spiders just want war and more war and more after that . . . well, that's a very different thing, isn't it?"

"How shall we proceed?" Kit asked.

"I think we'll have to scatter. Pairs, I think."

"Cary won't like that."

Marcus pressed his lips thin. It was too easy to forget that it wasn't Kit's company now. Or his own. "I'll talk to her about it as soon as—"

The dragon rose up on its hind legs, wings spread, and stretched its immense neck toward the forest with a hiss. Marcus held up his hand to Kit, and the old actor nodded. Marcus trotted back toward the water, uncomfortably aware of acting as a servant would when his master called but unable to respond otherwise.

"Enough of your whispers and muttering," the dragon

said. "I will not be treated with disrespect. Even now. Even if I have earned it."

"Didn't mean to keep you outside the circle," Marcus said. "It's just...well, we're in the middle of the enemy's land. Getting all you've told me back to the people who are standing against the spiders is going to be a bit of a trick."

The dragon's head drooped, the vast iris contracting as it focused upon him. The power of its regard was like the cold coming off ice.

"Why is that?" the dragon asked.

Making the harnesses took the better part of the morning, but the dragon was astonishingly deft and there was enough leather and cloth and steel to salvage from the ruined inn and stables, and from the players' cart. Rope and leather and cloth made slings on each of the dragon's legs, and then at the dragon's instruction, they crawled into them. The scales Marcus pressed his body against were as wide as his palm and iridescent in the light. The warmth of the huge body was almost uncomfortable. He and Cary and Sandr had taken the left foreleg; Kit, Charlit Soon, and Mikel the right. Smit and Hornet had each strapped onto one of the rear legs.

"I wish we could take the cart," Sandr said. "All the props. All the costumes. I've grown up in that cart. It's like a part of the company."

"We'll make another," Cary said. "And there are plenty of pieces we can play from the ground."

"It won't be the same," Sandr said.

Inys shifted, swiveling his head down to consider them. Sandr went quiet, but everything he'd said had been heard. "Better men have lost more," the dragon said, and then to Marcus. "You are ready?"

"No, but waiting won't help."

He thought he saw a bleak amusement in the vast eye, and then the leg he was strapped to tensed and shifted. The wings unfurled with a sound like sailcloth in a high wind. The last dragon took to the sky, and Marcus held on to the straps, his mind reeling as the wrecked inn and the ruined cart, the brook and the trees, the world as he'd known it, receded.

They flew.

Geder

Geder leaned forward, his elbows on the table, like a magistrate at a trial. The peasant man kneeling on the floor below him looked up, then bowed his head, then looked up again. The risers on either side of the room were filled with Geder's private guard, and Basrahip lurked behind the man where Geder could see him and the prisoner could not. Only this was not a prisoner. He had to keep reminding himself of that. The urge to throw the man in chains, have him whipped, have him thrown off the Prisoner's Span churned in Geder's guts. It was an effort to remember that the man had done nothing wrong.

He could not keep the rage from his voice.

"You're sure those were their names?" Geder said. "Cary? Hornet?"

"Y-yes, Lord Regent, sir," the peasant said. "And . . . Smit? And the other girl."

"*Cithrin?*"

"No, Charlit. Charlit Soon. And there was an old one they called Kit. And the sick one. Marcus, he was. And the skinny bastard's name was Mikel."

Geder looked over, and Basrahip nodded once. All of it was true. Geder sucked his lower lip between his teeth and bit down until the pain made him stop. "Did it eat them? Did the dragon eat them? Or did they get away?"

"All their things were there still when we came. Except the one shiny sword the sick one liked. That was gone. But the remnants of their cart were there, and the horses. And they were just...gone."

Basrahip nodded. The peasant went on. "I don't know if that great bastard ate them or they ran a different direction, my lord."

Or if they were there with *it*, Geder thought.

If it hadn't been for Basrahip, he might well have missed the incident. The business of running the empire had always been more odious than he'd expected it to be. His days were filled with letters and meetings and occasions of state. He tried to fit time with Aster in among them and include the prince in as much of it as he could. There was the whole apparatus of servants and slaves, magistrates and priests, who concerned themselves with the mundane functioning of Imperial Antea. Without them, Geder wouldn't have had time to sleep, and even if he could have done without sleep, the work would have been too much. When the report came in, he had not even seen it, and might never have, except Basrahip had given orders that any message like it be treated seriously. Any message involving dragons.

Even after the news had been brought to his attention, he hadn't taken it too much to heart. It was only now, with the priest back from his investigations and the witnesses in tow, that Geder understood the gravity of the situation.

After the peasant was sent away with Geder's thanks and a wallet filled with silver to help him rebuild his lost inn, Geder had the doors closed. His guards remained at attention, swords and bows in their hands, their eyes fixed straight ahead. Basrahip sat at his side on the lowest tier of steps, his expression sober.

"I know them," Geder said. "I know all of them, except

this Marcus and Kit, but she talked about them too. Those were Cithrin's friends. The players that hid us during the uprising."

"Yes, Prince Geder. They were."

"And they had a *dragon*."

Basrahip nodded slowly; his jaw slid forward a degree, and his fingers dug into his thighs. "The enemies of the goddess are strong, Prince Geder. And they are full of deceit. They hate her for she is the enemy of all lies, and they are creatures of falsehood and evil. The dragons were her greatest enemies. The false world they created is falling around them now, and the coming pure world has no place for their kind. It is to be expected that they would rise in their fear."

It was no coincidence, he was certain of that, and it changed everything. He had to look back and wonder now. If Cithrin had been the tool of the Timzinae from the start, then everything might have been arranged and engineered. Dawson Kalliam had been his patron and his friend. The more he looked at it, the clearer it became that his rebellion had not truly been his own. He had been the tool of the Timzinae. It seemed plausible now that Cithrin and her friends had engineered it all, even Dawson's rebellion against him, in order to undermine the goddess. And now the Timzinae's master was exposed too. Not only the shadowy Callon Cane, but the emperors of the world—the *dragons*—were rising against them. Against *him*.

"What do we do?" Geder asked.

"Do not fear this," Basrahip said. "You are the chosen of the goddess. No harm will come to you so long as you keep your faith in her. There will be dark days ahead. Desperate struggles. We must not falter."

"We won't," Geder said.

Basrahip turned, his dark eyes meeting Geder's, and the

gentle smile on his lips expressed everything he needed to say. He had heard Geder's voice, and he knew that what he'd said was true. Geder felt a rush of pride, maybe even of love, for the big man. Besides Jorey and Aster, Basrahip had been the best friend Geder had ever had. He clapped the massive shoulder. It was like hitting a stone.

"We haven't lost yet," Geder said. "We won't stop until the world's been made pure. The peace we make will last forever."

"It will," Basrahip said.

A thought stirred in his mind, something like hope surprised him. "Basrahip. Do you think…If Dawson Kalliam was tricked by the Timzinae? By the dragons? Couldn't Cithrin have been as well?"

"The tricks of the dark ones are well crafted," Basrahip said. "Without the voice of the goddess as guide, anyone might go astray."

"So maybe…maybe it really *isn't* her fault?"

"We cannot know until she stands before us and speaks with her living voice," Basrahip said. "Do that, and all will be made clear."

"No, I understand now," Geder said. "I see what this is. We'll save her. And I know how to start."

If he'd allowed it, servants would have cleaned his library every day, whether he had found a few moments to visit it or not. He didn't like having people in his things, though. Not even people whose lives he could control at a whim. Dust had gathered on his books and scrolls. The codices of old philosophical sketches he'd been paging through the last time he'd been there still spilled across the table. He didn't know how long they'd been there.

Bright afternoon light spilled in through the windows

as Geder pulled book after book from the shelves, searching for something he only half recalled. It had been part, he thought, of a longer essay. One that touched on half a dozen subjects ranging from antiquity to the nature of time to techniques of agriculture. He had the sense that it was one of Saraio Mittian's translations of Bastian Preach, but he went through all eighteen of them, and none were the right one. Perhaps one of the Orrian histories.

His hands were grey with dust and so dry he was afraid his fingertips would crack when he found it. The pages were oversized vellum, thicker than paper and soft as skin. It had been a Saraio Mittian translation, but not of Preach. It was an extended third-age copy of Chariun's Considerations. Likely, he hadn't opened the book since he'd been in his father's house in Rivenhalm. He turned the pages now, admiring the handwork, the details in the dropped capitals and the comic marginalia. The Considerations had been one of his father's favorite books, he remembered, and Geder still felt a little intimidated opening its pages. And yet if he were to trace his love of speculative essay back to its roots, they were here.

He paused over the opening pages of the second section, following the lines of script with his thumb.

Speculation is the art of thinking where no evidence is available. To say that all birds are fish is not speculation but falsehood. To say that some birds swim for a time beneath the water is not speculation, but fact, as evidenced by the northern lake hen and salt heron. It is when we step outside these places of certainty that speculation opens its gossamer wings and breathes the free air. To say that some birds may nest beneath the waves and rise to the air only to hunt is speculation for we know of no such animal, and neither can we say for certain that none such exists. It is for this reason that speculation is also the natural realm of tolerance, for judgment demands evidence, and it follows that the absence of evidence which forms the core of speculation requires the absence of judgment.

Geder sighed. He didn't remember reading those words precisely, but he could still conjure up the awe he'd felt at this book once. The reverence he'd had for it. Reading it now, it seemed painfully naïve. Puerile. It was embarrassing to think that he had once come here expecting wisdom. He turned to the back, to the additional sections that Mittian had included.

The drawings were not quite as he recalled them, but the sense of them was the same. The ruins of Aastapal and the fields where ancient battles had been fought had been a fashion in the third age, and Chariun had not only cataloged the shards and remnants that humanity had pried from the ground, but designed the mechanisms that might plausibly have employed them. The same hand that had sketched the beautiful little comic images in the margins here laid out the pieces of vast winged harpoons designed to loop through the air. Half a dozen designs of vicious hooked spears with holes at the end that would carry loops of thread no heavier than a human hair until the hooks bit dragon flesh. Then the thread was drawn, hauling stout rope through it. One whole page was dedicated wholly to the image of a dragon the size of a mansion being dragged down to its death by humans of half a dozen races. Including, to Geder's confusion, a Timzinae. Well, it was speculation after all. Likely Chariun hadn't known the Timzinae for what they were.

For hours he paged through the designs. Some were clearly fanciful. The sections on the vast, bladderlike airships fitted with prows of viciously curved metal that could tear and rend a dragon's delicate wings were beautiful, but unconvincing. The bogs of adhesive tar that were meant to foul the dragon's perch and slow or stop it taking to air were an interesting thought, but there was no guidance on how to concoct them. The ballistas modified with toothed gears that would spin bladed disks into the sky, on the other hand, seemed at least worth the effort of experiment...

He placed bits of thin cloth on each of the pages that seemed most promising to him. He didn't feel as though he had been at his study long before the book looked as if it had sprouted a dozen tongues. When he reached the end, he felt the almost forgotten tug of pleasure, the temptation to stay and page through the library for a while. Not for anything specific, though if there were other volumes that touched on the weapons that the ancient dragons used in their wars, he would be interested. Maybe not even to read them, but to find the images and sketches put there by hands a thousand years dead. To find again some small thought that had never occurred to him before and let his mind take fire with it for a time. Basrahip might deride the words as being dead things, but not the pictures, certainly? A picture wasn't true or false, it just was. And the things the drawings showed could be resurrected. Remade in a new time, and by the skilled hands of smiths who had never heard the old designers speak a word. There was a book about the making of maps, for instance, that he'd gotten years ago in Vanai, and never had the opportunity to more than skip through. In his memory, it had had pages demonstrating the different cartographic styles in half a dozen different hands. He wondered where exactly it had gotten to...

But no. Or, not no, but another time. He was Lord Regent of Antea, and the Lord Regent could spend a day looking over old books whenever he wanted. Unless the business of court intruded. And the war. And Cithrin. And the players. And, God, had they really had a dragon?

He hefted the book up under his arm and made his way down the stairs. Servants and courtiers scattered and bowed before him, but he ignored them. He called for his litter, and within moments half a dozen servants and twice the number of guards were carrying him out into the streets of Camnipol. Him and his book besides.

The smiths and armorers kept a district in the southeast of the city, tucked almost against the city wall. The smoke of the forges thickened the air. When he looked out through the windows, the men and women all along the street were bent double or even kneeling in honor of his passage. Near his destination, a particularly fat old man was being helped to his knees by two younger men.

The greatest smithy in Camnipol belonged to a massive Jasuru named Honnen Pyre. He and his apprentices rushed out to the street when Geder's litter stopped there, and they were kneeling, heads bowed, by the time he stepped down. Geder walked over to the Jasuru. He was wider across the shoulders than Basrahip, his skin so stretched by the underlying muscle that his bronze scales didn't overlap anymore, but showed a lacework of pale skin between them.

"Lord Regent, you honor my small house," the smith intoned.

"Thank you. Please don't let me...please stand up. Yes. Thank you. Please don't let me interrupt your apprentices. I only need to talk with you."

Standing, the Jasuru was no taller than Geder, but easily twice as wide and all of it muscle. He nodded to his apprentices, and they scattered back into the forge. The smith crossed his arms and nodded nervously. It was always odd for Geder, seeing men who were so much stronger than him act as though he were the threatening one. It was the office, no doubt. When Aster took the throne, all that would vanish into mist. Still, he'd enjoy it while he could.

"I have a commission for you," Geder said. "A rather large one, I'm afraid."

"You're the Lord Regent, my lord. We're yours to command," the smith said.

"Good," Geder said, pulling the book out from where it rested on his elbow. "Is there a place I can put this? I don't want to get..." He gestured at the soot and smoke all around them.

"This way, Lord Geder," the smith said.

For the next hour, Geder and the smith went over the pictures, Geder waving his hands and growing more excited with each new page. The smith remained cautious and thoughtful. It was as if Geder could see the thoughts and strategies forming in the man's brain. Slowly, the Jasuru's scowl softened, and he began nodding more than he shook his head. The harpoons with needle-eyes on the ends would be the easiest, he thought. The ballista was possible, perhaps, but there was a man he knew with greater experience in siege engines. He would be pleased to consult with him and bring a full report to Lord Geder.

When a servant came pelting from the Kingspire to remind him of a council meeting, Geder waited for the smith to sketch out copies of the weapons built to destroy the dragons. Reluctantly, he took his book back and trotted to the litter. He couldn't help but grin. It was the first moment of real happiness he'd felt since the terrible day in Suddapal he'd arrived to find Cithrin—

No, there was no point thinking of that. Not now. Instead, he opened the book again, reviewing the designs of the weapons and imagining how it might feel to wield them. He traced the lines and thought of half a dozen more questions he hadn't thought to present to the smith. Later, then. He'd have to have a long talk with the man later.

His steps were light as he passed through the lowest floors of the Kingspire, and he bounced on the balls of his feet as if he might break into a delighted little caper at any moment. He could already see the hooked spears flying into the sky, the winged harpoons thrown by modified ballistas looping through the air. Ripping through dragon wings, spilling blood on the earth like rain from a cloud. He imagined himself standing on the corpse of a great dragon the size of a house, sinking a huge two-handed sword in its belly. Cithrin would be there too, drenched in the blood of her conquered masters.

She would look up at him, tears in her eyes. *Forgive me*, she'd say, her voice breaking just a little, her breasts shuddering with her sobs. *Forgive me, Geder. I didn't know.* And he would smile and hold out his hand to her, and she would rise and take it. And they would look after Aster together until he took the throne, not only of Antea but of a purified world. And then he—

"Lord Regent?"

Geder blinked and turned back. He'd walked past the door to the meeting room without noticing he'd done it. The captain of his personal guard hovered behind him, uncertain what to do. His distress was so comical, Geder couldn't help but laugh. "I'm sorry. My mind's half gone some days, isn't it?" he said.

"Ah..." the guard captain said. "If you say so, my lord."

Cithrin

Porte Oliva did not break, but neither did it remain the same. In all its history, no army had taken it by force. The puppet shows that sprang up outside every public house, in every square and corner told of ancient battles and the bravery of Birancour. But, Cithrin noticed, alongside the epics of war and defiance, there was another genre. Comedies like The Pardoner's Wife and PennyPenny's Last Vengeance. Those stories were of clever villains tricking good people into fighting battles on their behalf. When, at the end of the laughter and violence, PennyPenny realized how he had been manipulated, he beat the duplicitous Ga-Go with a stick. Only this time Ga-Go was a pale puppet, with the light hair and eyes of a Cinnae, and instead of the traditional red confetti, tiny coins spilled from her pockets after every blow.

The Grand Market was a place of woe and agony. The few merchants whose trade hadn't been gutted by the blockade were wise enough to pretend to suffer with the rest. Some days as many as half the stalls went empty. The carts that rolled in along the dragon's road carrying grain and beer and cloth weren't enough to make up for the loss of the port. The price of bread had risen, and would rise farther. The price of meat had tripled. Generations ago, the city had spilled out past its own defensive walls, until the great stone archways seemed almost in the city's center. That geography changed now. The price of buildings within the walls rose almost tenfold, the price of those outside dropped almost to nothing. Cithrin would have liked to buy up some of those, if only as a symbol of solidarity with the city and optimism for its future. The gesture would have been empty. When Geder's army came—and it would come—those buildings would be char and ash, and the people living in them fled or left for crows. She was as sure of that as her own name.

New ships arrived to join the blockade. Larger ones, including a great roundship that Yardem told her was the flagship of the Antean fleet. The ten Antean ships stood ready to board whatever vessels dared enter the harbor, the red flag with its eightfold sigil claiming ownership of the waters and all that passed upon them. Now and then the governor sent out small harassing forces from the port, and always they were driven back, held at the piers like dogs backed into a cave. The stories in the market said that Antean ships had been harassing fishing boats all along the coast and razing the salt drying yards. Even though anyone might come or go along the roads, the sense of being under siege changed the taste of the water and the scent of the air. The serving girl at Cithrin's favorite taproom became chilly and cold when she arrived. The boy Pyk had hired to keep the counting house clean came later and later in the day, doing less and less for his pay. Maestro Asanpur's café saw fewer people at its benches and tables than was usual. Porte Oliva was the home she'd made for herself, and she ached seeing it turn against her.

The question was clear: How was Cithrin to win a war against an army that had already broken the world across its knee? How could gold and silver, silk and spice, contracts and agreements stand in the field against swords? It was ridiculous on the face of it, and like so many things, less ridiculous the more she looked at it.

Cithrin spent her days considering the world through the lens of her new question. She spoke to Yardem about mercenary companies and what was needed to build a successful campaign. She visited the blacksmiths and armorers, the millers and the cunning men, the governor and the captain of the city guard. She drank coffee with Magistra Isadau, each of them prodding the other to some insight or perspective that might open a new pathway for them.

Geder's army had the advantage of being infected by the priests, which undermined her first line of attack: pay the enemy soldiers to switch sides. It was still possible, but there would need to be other factors at work. No rational fighter would move to the side being slaughtered, no matter what the pay. But there were other places in the management of an army that were like articulated joints of heavy armor—vulnerable, if she could find a way to hit them hard enough. No matter how the priests cried and cajoled, the Antean soldiers would have to eat. If the bank were to let it be known that they would pay an inflated price for tobacco and cotton, the farmers along the path of Geder's army would till under their wheat and vegetables. No amount of false certainty could pass for food. Swords broke, arrows lost their heads. The bank could buy the ore out of Hallskar and Borja and the Free Cities. She could hire people to break the smelters in the Free Cities and Northcoast, so that Geder's forces had less chance to repair their goods and resupply. A cunning man she'd found in a tavern in the salt quarter had told her about a kind of grass that rotted out a horse's stomach. If she found the seeds for that and sowed the pastures along the dragon's roads from the east, the Antean cavalry might lose half its mounts. More, if she were lucky.

Once she started looking at it, there were a hundred tools at her disposal that could harass and degrade the enemy's army. Some were better targeted than others. Given the choice, she preferred hiring on mercenaries, paying bounties on actions against the enemy, and rewarding Anteans for desertion because they did, for the most part, what she wanted them to do and nothing more. If she convinced the Free Cities to plow under their food, the starvation that came wouldn't only hurt Antean soldiers. If she filled the bays with iron ores and broke the smelters to gravel, plows would be as difficult to replace as swords.

War was about damage, though. And if she had to starve a nation to save the world, that was something she could bring herself to do. She sat in her offices, writing out estimates and working through the wording of contracts, estimating timing and schedules, seeing what could and couldn't be done if she had a week or a month or a season. Time would be as important as gold.

She was most aware of her fear when she tried to sleep. Those nights, she would take a guard or two to the seawall and watch the blockading ships on the dark water as they patrolled the mouth of the bay or, when the wind permitted, retreated to resupply at the base they'd made on a little island just over the horizon to the southwest. Wolves at the door, and not the only pack running. During the daylight, her mind was too much at work for emotion to intrude.

She had known since Paerin Clark's visit what would come next. It still knotted her gut when it came.

Lord Mastién Juoli, the queen's master of coin, was a younger man than Cithrin had expected. He was a Kurtadam, his face covered in a thick pelt that seemed as glossy and bright as a child's, and the silver and lapis beads that were woven into it made her think of young men preening themselves before girls. The youthful foolishness was an affectation, she told herself. An encouragement to under-estimate the man. Cithrin was likely younger than he was, and she knew something about being underestimated.

"Magistra bel Sarcour," Juoli said, rising and holding out his hand as if they were friends or business acquaintances. "It is a pleasure to meet you at last. I've heard many stories."

"I'm sorry to hear that," Cithrin said, taking his fingers in her own for a moment. "I hope they were all exaggerations." The governor coughed sourly. Likely he'd been look-ing forward to making introductions. The garden around them was the green of spring, and losing the brightness of new leaves. A cage of finches sufficed for music, and even the servants were absent. Unwelcome. She sat on the stone bench across the little blackwood table from Juoli and the governor himself poured their wine and watered it.

"I have a cousin in King Tracian's court," Juoli said. "You have a reputation for speaking your mind. And, I have to say, for being unswayed by sentiment."

"Well," Cithrin said with a smile she didn't mean, "at least I'll be damned for what I am."

"The magistra has always been one of the great citizens of Porte Oliva," the governor said. It was clearly untrue. There were children just walking who'd lived in the city longer than she had, but the governor was laying claim to her. It might only have been because the master of coin was here for her and the governor had been the sort of boy who would grab a toy just because someone else wanted it. Or he might have known how precarious her position was and denied it to keep her off balance. She would understand bet-ter as she learned more, but regardless it was interesting.

"What can I do for you, Lord Mastién?" she said, and sipped her wine.

"You can help me save our nation," he said. "We have reason to believe that the army of Imperial Antea is making its way to Birancour. The blockade that's already begun will become a siege as well. Not only here, but Porte Silena and Sara-sur-Mar as well. Between us, the queen has sent letters demanding assurances that Antea will not violate our borders."

"And did Geder promise to behave?" Cithrin asked with a lightness she did not feel.

"The queen hasn't had a response. Which brings us to here."

"Because she hasn't had a response from me either."

He smiled, and she imagined there was a touch of sorrow in his eyes. "I had hoped not to bring it up, but if we are to repel the forces of the enemy, Birancour will need every resource it has. Your branch of the bank is among the most powerful institutions in Porte Oliva. It is in all of our interests to see this invasion repelled."

"It is."

"Then certainly you see the need for all the great citizens of Birancour to come together. Yourself included. You were in Suddapal, I understand." He said the words carefully. What he did not say—*You have brought this upon us*—was all the louder for his silence. Cithrin considered whether to laugh or shout, weep or be sober. She put her cup on the blackwood table with a delicate click.

"We are all aware of the particular role I've played in this," she said, keeping her voice steady. "If I turn over my bank's wealth—and let us not pretend this is anything besides surrender—what assurances will the crown offer for my safety and the safety of my people?"

"You have my word, and the promise of the queen," Lord Mastién said without hesitation. The words and their phrasing had been ready on his lips. *My word, and the promise of the queen.* It was less even than a contract, and the queen was in a position to break contracts with impunity. No collateral was offered, no minor cousin put into the bank's control as hostage. No rights to collect royal taxes. Only a word and a promise.

"There can be no more meaningful bond than that," Cithrin said. After all, if the crown had chosen to offer her something more, it could as easily have reneged. What she had suspected coming in and knew now was that the crown wasn't even willing to pretend to offer hard assurances. It wasn't a good sign. "I have had my notary reviewing our position. What I can offer the crown, I will."

"We ask nothing more," the governor said with a nod. As if he were in any position to say what the master of coin did or didn't ask. Cithrin felt a wave of contempt so profound it bordered on hatred. The taste of bile crept up the back of her tongue, and she smiled at the governor.

"I will have my accounting completed immediately," she lied.

"My thanks," the master of coin said with a little bow. She didn't think for a moment that he was taken in, but there was little else to say at this point. He'd made his demands, and she had put on a show of acceding to them. The next conversation they had would, she suspected, be less pleasant. They spent almost an hour more chatting about the small business of the kingdom and the city, drinking wine, and decrying Geder Palliako. Both men were polite, and Cithrin maintained her composure though the knot in her gut was almost at the point of pain by the time she left.

Yardem was waiting in the square outside the Governor's Palace watching a cunning man conjure fire for a group of children. The prisoners of the city stood or sat on their

platforms all through the square and the upright citizens
came by to jeer at them or, if they were family, give them food
and wash them where they'd soiled themselves. If it could
have kept the army from her door, she'd have traded places
with any of them. Yardem fell into step with her, his earrings
jingling as they walked. For almost half of the way back to
the counting house, he was quiet. When he did speak, it was
in the offhanded tones of common conversation.

"Went poorly then."

"I need wine."

"Need, or want?"

"Doesn't matter."

They stopped at the taproom, but there were too many
people there, and Cithrin felt like they were all whisper-
ing about her when she wasn't looking. She paid for a jug
of wine, carried it back to her rooms, and sat on her bed,
drinking with the steady, studied pace of long acquaintance.
The wine turned her mind fuzzy, but it didn't untie the knot
in her belly the way she'd hoped it would. She might need to
send Yardem out for a second jug.

Geder's letter was in among the papers of the bank. She
took it out again, handling the paper with the care of a street
performer with a snake.

*Oh, this is so much harder to write than I thought it
would be. Jorey says I should be honest and gentle,
and I want to be. Cithrin I love you. I love you more
than anyone I've ever known.*

How many women in the Antea court would have cut off
toes to have a letter like this one from the most powerful
man in their empire? How many could have given Geder
the sex that he mistook for love and made the same mistake

themselves? And if they both thought it, maybe that made it true. She took another mouthful of wine, this time straight from the jug. If only there had been some way to transfer the affection, if that was what it was, the way responsibility for a contract or a loan could be shifted. A letter of transfer, where she could have assigned the burden of Geder's infatuation to some baron's daughter in Sevenpol or Anninfort. Only, of course, then she couldn't have used his affection to shield her work in Suddapal, and hundreds more people would have died or suffered in slavery.

I want to sit up late at night with your head resting in my lap and read you all the poems we didn't have when we were in hiding. I want to wake up beside you in the morning, and see you in daylight the way we were in darkness.

"Cithrin?" Isadau said from the top of the little stairway. Cithrin hadn't heard her come up.

"Why is it," she said instead of hello, "that the most passionate letter I've ever had and maybe ever will have makes me want to curl up under a rock and never come out?"

"Because it was written by an unstable tyrant who kills innocent people on a whim," Isadau said, walking into the room.

"Ah. That."

"Yardem said you didn't speak of the meeting."

"What's to say? They want the money. If I don't give it to them, they'll feed me to Geder in exchange for peace. If I do give it to them, they'll feed me to him just the same. I'm not in manacles right now because I haven't said yes and I haven't said no. And I can keep that going until they feel certain that I won't give them the coin. After which..."

Isadau sat beside her on the bed and scooped Cithrin's hand in hers. The pale, smooth Cinnae fingers knotted with the black Timzinae scales. They looked like art. "After which," Isadau said softly, "they feed you to him."

"Not seeing a path I like in this."

"Give them some. A little. Promise them more if they give you time."

"I can't," Cithrin said, her voice breaking. Maybe the wine had had more effect than she'd known, because there were tears in her eyes now and her shoulders were shaking. It was a stupid reaction. It didn't change anything. "I need that money if I'm going to beat him. Everything depends on our having the gold to pay for all of it. So we can beat him."

Isadau nodded, her knuckles squeezing gently, gently against Cithrin's own. Her voice was half hum and half singing. "You know, dear. You know *that* you know. Stop now."

"I can do this. I can find a way to stop him."

"You did find a way. You found a dozen ways. But?" It was an invitation to admit the truth they'd both known for days. For weeks. Since the first day of the blockade, and possibly earlier even than that. Cithrin felt the words in her throat like vomit. And then she relaxed. Surrendered. Let hope die.

"We don't have enough coin," Cithrin said.

"If we had all the money in all the branches and the holding company and more besides, we might still not," Isadau said.

"There *has* to be a way."

"No, dear. There doesn't. Some things even gold cannot solve."

Clara

From the road to the stand of trees fifty feet from it, the land was scarred and churned to mud. Even the jade of the dragon's road was dimmed, covered over by thick, sticky earth. Clods with grass still clinging to them peppered the landscape. The air stank of smoke and shit. The trilling birdsong and the high, rain-washed blue of the sky seemed incongruous, given the destruction. Clara pulled her horse to a stop gently. She had the feeling of walking into a tomb. Here something terrible had happened, and the world was marred by it. Made worse.

Vincen went a bit farther before he realized that she'd stopped. He turned in his saddle to look back at her. His eyes spoke his concern. She took her reins tight and shook her head. The braided leather between her fingers seemed more real to her because of the carnage all around. A dog was pawing at the ground just south of them, digging at something. It looked up at them with a wary curiosity as Vincen turned back and cantered to her side.

"My lady?"

"What happened here?" she asked. "Was there a battle?"

Vincen looked around, as if seeing the destruction for the first time. His laugh was short, mirthless, as much an expression of sorrow or anger as anything gentler. "No,

Clara. There'd be bodies. This is where they camped. Perhaps a night ago. Not more than two."

"They only camped? All this?"

"All this," he said, and nodded toward the road ahead. Clara started forward, and he fell into place beside her.

Dawson had told her any number of stories about his adventures in the field, but they had all been stories of battles or camp humor. The time he had faced down Uric Saon, the leader of the little slave rebellion in the south, and scared him so badly he'd offered to sell Dawson his own men. The siege at Anninfort, and how it had ended. The night he'd been on campaign with Simeon back when he'd only been the prince and they'd started a poetry contest with the men that went so long they didn't sleep before the battle. He had, she was certain, softened much of the worst of it. When he talked of the violence his voice had taken a calmness, a care, that spoke as loud as shouting that he was reluctant to tell her everything. But even with that, she'd built the image of war being like a kind of long, terrible King's Hunt, with men as the prey.

The violence of an army's mere passage, the damage to the land that soldiers, servants, horses, and carts left behind them merely by being had never entered her mind. An army, she knew, was a huge thing, but that it should leave ruin in its wake even without the violence of battle drove home the scale and depth of the errand her sons had been sent on. Follow this back, and the mud and filth would go to Kiaria, and Suddapal before that. Inentai. Nus. Along with his conquests, Geder Palliako had made a road of scars that tracked back, in the end, to Antea. To the fields in the south where the army had assembled, and to which it had never come home.

To the west, high mountains rose, blued by distance and

height. Clara knew that on the far side, there would be Birancour. She'd never been that far to the west or south. All she really knew about it was that it was a nation of grassy plains and busy ports, that it divided Princip C'Annaldé, Herez, and Cabral from the rest of the continent, that those smaller nations sometimes resented the tariffs the throne of Birancour exacted for the privilege of passing through its roads, and that Cithrin bel Sarcour was there. Those mountains and the long, treacherous pass through them were the last barriers between her son's army and the war they shouldn't be fighting in the first place.

The day passed all too quickly. The local traffic on the road was slight. A few carts, a handful of travelers, and most of them heading the other way. The springtime sun was just above the highest snowcapped peaks when they found the bodies.

Four men, all Firstbloods, swung by their necks from a rough scaffold built of sapling trees. Flies danced and swarmed around their eyes and mouths. Their strangled faces were swollen in death beyond any recognizable human emotion. They wore the colors of Antea in their cloaks. The banner of the spider goddess, red as blood with a pale spot in the center and the eightfold sigil of the goddess within it, hung from the top bar between the hanging ropes. Clara stopped her horse, sorrow rising in her breast, and with it an anger that was almost pride.

Vincen stopped beside her. His expression was apologetic, as if she shouldn't have had to see such a thing. As if atrocity were not part of the world she'd chosen.

"They weren't killed by the enemy," he said.

"I know," she said. "They were deserters."

Dawson had told her of this too. Of the custom of taking captured deserters, sending them ahead of the army to be executed on the path, so that the whole force would march past them on the following day. Sometimes officers were set to stand by the bodies and watch the faces of the sword-and-bows as they went by. Dawson had stood that duty himself once.

She looked at the dead men and wondered who they had been. Likely she knew all the officers in the army now, by reputation and family if not on sight. These were not of that class. They'd been low men. Conscripted farmers, perhaps. Or the sort of man that lived on the sides of the Division and eked out a living doing whatever work came to hand. They had been like her, skeptical of the glory of Geder Palliako, and driven to act.

"Cut them down," she said.

"Ma'am," Vincen began, and she interrupted him.

"Don't *ma'am* me. Cut them down or wait here and I'll do it myself."

"Do we have time to bury them? If we want to join the army's tail before Bellin, we need to keep moving."

"We'll make up the time. I won't leave them on display."

Vincen sighed, then passed her his reins and dropped to the ground. It took the better part of an hour to slash the ropes and pull the dead men to the side. Vincen was right. They didn't have time to dig graves or raise cairns, but at least the corpses weren't raised like a sign outside a taphouse any longer. She left them lying side by side in the green under the trees, as if they were only resting. The banner of the goddess, they dropped in the mud. Let that be a statement and a symbol. There were still some who stood against the goddess. No one might ever see it, and of those who did, few if any would care. It didn't matter.

Resisting Geder's power and the corruption he had brought to the Severed Throne was like shouting into a storm wind. She didn't know—couldn't know—if half the things she did had any effect at all. Undermining Ternigan, of course, she had accomplished. But the letters and reports she sent? The little acts of rebellion like putting deserters on the roadside to rest? They might be wastes time and of effort with no lasting effect on the world.

But that did not make them meaningless.

"Clara," Vincen said again. She realized he'd been trying to catch her attention for some few moments. "We should continue on."

Should we, she thought, *or should we turn our back to all of this and find some pretty farmhouse by the sea to live in together until we die?* Even in the privacy of her mind, she didn't mean it.

"Yes," she said. "Let's do."

They reached Bellin just before nightfall four days later. It was a strange little city. If she didn't know to look, it might only have been a few scattered buildings by the roadside, hardly more than a farming hamlet. At night, though, the mountainside glowed like a Dartinae's eyes. Dots of brightness the color of fire all up and down the face of the cliffs. The real city was carved from the stone, and the people lived in the flesh of the mountain like moles. Vincen also pointed out the great runes cut into the mountainside. They were hard to see in the morning with the sun behind them or the afternoon when the sun had passed above the mountains and cast the city and its approach into shadow. For an hour near midday, though, the shapes of the letters were written in light and darkness across the stone. She did not recognize the script, and could not guess what they meant.

The army of Antea—Jorey's army—was camped at the mountain's base where the dragon's road passed in among the peaks. Even from a distance, she could see the movement at the edge. The forces of Imperial Antea lining up like schoolchildren, waiting their turn to go on. The others, the hangers-on like herself, would go last, of course. And so she and Vincen caught up with a ragged, unsanctioned caravan squatting in a field of wildflowers and watching men in armor and swords as they marched into the gap in the mountains and disappeared. The caravan master was a Cinnae man, thin as a stick and pale as ice, with a beard like lichen.

"Can I help you, then?" he asked as Clara walked up to him. Days in the saddle had left her thighs aching and chapped, and her gait was wide and rolling, her cloak filthy, her hair pulled back in a tight, greasy bun. She couldn't imagine looking less like a baroness of the imperial court.

"You're following them?" she asked, pointing at the army with her thumb the way she imagined her lower-class acquaintances from the Prisoner's Span might have done.

"Am, so long as the officer class don't run me off. Most of my trade's with the lower ranks, and I'm not always so appreciated as I'd hope. What's it to you?"

"Going to see my sister in Carse," Clara said. "That's the way through, only it's chock full of men with blades and opinions."

"So passage, then?"

"My man's decent with a bow," Clara said, nodding back toward Vincen. "Put him in your guard. We'll buy any food we eat."

The 'van master leaned against his blackwood cart and scratched his neck. "You mind traveling with whores?"

"No."

"You a religious?"

"Not so much that it matters."

"Well. I'm Imbert. This is my 'van, and these are my rules.

You travel with us, you do your share. Meals are two coppers each, no credit. You need money, maybe I'll hire you to do something. If you didn't bring enough coin, it's your own damn fault. You steal from me, I'll kill you. No offense, it's just the way. Bring me trouble, I'll leave you in a ditch and keep your horses."

"Fair enough."

"Fair enough," he echoed. "And you are?"

"Annalise," Clara said. "That's Coe."

"Married?"

"Not to him," she said, and the old Cinnae grinned. "How long before we get moving?"

The 'van master shrugged. "They've been moving through all morning and down by maybe a third. I'd guess our turn could come in a day, maybe two."

"Why so slow?"

"Tired out, them. The way I heard it, their Lord Regent's allied with the dead. Doesn't mind a good forced march, because the men that die along the way can still fight when they get there."

"That truth?" Clara asked.

Imbert's eyes grew troubled. "I don't know. Maybe. Tell you this, there's something damned eerie about that army, and that's not joking."

"But you follow them," Clara said.

"I do," he said, and paused. "For now, anyway."

The 'van master's guess had been a good one. The carts passed through the gates of Bellin at noon the next day. The road was filthy. Between the droppings of the horses and cart oxen and the boots of the soldiers, the green of the road was covered in a churn of milky brown stink. The mountains rose up around them craggy and ragged. Little forests of pine and aspen clung to the sides, rising up so steeply Clara felt sometimes she must be losing her balance just looking at them. The road tracked upward, the jade keeping close to the curves of the land. Twice she saw great woolly sheep high above, walking along cliffsides she would have thought too steep for anything but birds and moss. Any game had been scared into hiding by the passage of the army before her, so the only food was briny sausage and beans that Imbert's cook made in the back of one of the carts. At nightfall, they made camp on the road itself. There was no land flat enough to sleep on otherwise. The jade of the road and the stone at the roadside both defied tent stakes, so Clara and Vincen set their bedrolls beside one of the carts, and lay in the night looking up at the moon and stars and the vast, black bulk of the mountains on either side. They were filthy. They stank. Clara was developing a persistent itch on the back of her leg. She felt oddly at peace.

"Have you ever been on campaign?" she asked Vincen, her voice soft enough not to carry to the next group over.

"No," he said. "My uncle went. He was part of the siege at Anninfort."

"Which side?"

"The wrong one," Vincen said. "Wasn't his choice. My father begged him to desert, but what's a man to do? His lord tells him to go, he goes. Or he winds up like those poor bastards we found. It was hard for my mother afterward. We were part of Osterling Fells. Working for your lord husband. Keeping his kennels and cooking his food, and him part of the force that killed Uncle Hom. They came over it, though. War's war. Things happen there, you ought not carry them home with you."

"Is that what your mother said?"

"Father," Vincen said.

"I think Dawson said something very much like that to Jorey once. It's hard to think of him and Vicarian. You realize that if I wrote them a note right now, we could likely pass it hand to hand all the way to their tents without anyone walking more than a dozen steps? If they knew I was here..."

"They'd send you back."

"And they'd be scandalized. That they are going to slaughter a nation because Geder Palliako was disappointed in love doesn't strike them as obscene. But my being here would."

"You're sure of that? The part where they think the war isn't obscene, I mean. Because Jorey at least seems more like Uncle Hom."

"You mean Geder called him and he had to go?"

"Yes."

"Yes," Clara said. "You're right. It is like that."

"The other now. Vicarian."

"He isn't like that. He's here because he wants to be. Because it's an honor. Because he believes."

"The priests. They did that to him. It's not his fault."

"Perhaps. I also have a daughter whose opinions I can't admire. Children are who they are. I may love them all, but I know them too. Their feet are as much clay as my own. It hardly matters what path we've walked to become what we are. Whatever it was, we've walked it. Vicarian has too. He's become what he is. And I've lost him." She put her hand out, took his in her own. His fingers laced themselves with hers. His body was so strong compared with hers, she could could almost understand his mistake. "Those men we cut down today. You didn't want me to see them. You didn't want me to feel that they had died in the same cause more or less that I've taken up."

"I didn't see the need."

"You cannot protect me from the world or choices I've made."

She was weeping now, but gently. For Vicarian as he had been. For the boy she'd known and loved. For her child, and what he had become. What he chose, and what was chosen for him. Her chest ached with it, and yet she knew it would pass and come again and pass again. Over and over, and likely would for the rest of her days. It changed nothing.

Farther down the road, someone began playing a flute. A pair of voices rose to join it, and another voice to protest and call for silence. It was cold, but not bitter, and the air of the mountains was thin. Vincen Coe sighed deeply, looking up into the moon and the stars and the darkness. She considered the shape of his face, the place where his collarbones met. The dim had robbed all color from him and left him like a sketch by an artist who had only blue and black to paint with.

"I've told very few people that I loved them," Clara said. "And with each of them, I think I meant something a little different. Sometimes very different."

He turned to look at her. "Are you telling me that you love me?"

"I think I am," she said. "I am. I love you."

"I love you," he said, and squeezed her hand. How strange that in the depth of all this horror and war, displacement and fear, it would take so little to fill her with warmth and pleasure. She lay back, letting the hard ground bear her up. Letting her eyes follow the distant ridges of the mountains far above. The moon glowed cold white. A bird appeared, a deeper darkness against the sky, its wings spread to ride some great updraft. Only...no.

"What is that?" she said. "Is that...a hawk?"

"Hmm? Where?"

She lifted her finger, and he pulled himself over to sight along it like a stick. When she spoke again, she could hear the fear in her own voice. "What is that?"

He said something obscene and sat up, staring. His jaw was slack, his eyes wide. He shook his head.

"Vincen? Is that a *dragon*?"

Marcus

Marcus had spent years of his life bent over maps, planning his battles and campaigns. He'd looked down on mountains made from ink and rivers drawn in dust. Once, he'd even walked through one of the fairly idiotic miniature rooms where the full landscape had been recreated in tiny scale so that the generals and kings could play at striding across their territories like gods. The actual world seen from above was an utterly different thing. From his place strapped to the dragon's leg, the land curved and curled in surprising and gentle ways. A hill could begin as an irregularity of the horizon, swell as if it were reaching up toward them, and fall away. Forests became a single, uniform texture of spring green. When they passed above farmland, he could tell the crooked furrows from the true. Vast herds of elk, surprised by this unfamiliar greatness in the sky, scattered before them like he'd poured blotting sand on a bare page and blown it.

Inys's flesh was warm beneath the scales almost to the point of discomfort. The leather-and-wood slings that held them all in place creaked and groaned, and Marcus couldn't help imagining one giving way. The long, slow fall and sudden stop. The wind of their passage roared around them and made all conversation impossible, but when he craned his head to look, he saw Sandr's eyes squeezed closed, Cary's open and her hair flowing back like a child's icon of defiance. The great dragon himself was reduced to the scaled archway of his forelegs, a long, sinuous neck, and the lower jaw seen from below and ending in a sharp chin. From time to time, it screamed out a bloom of fire that stank and choked them as they flew through its dying smoke.

When they had first left the ground behind, Marcus had imagined that they would streak across Antea, rise over the mountains that divided the Free Cities from Birancour and Northcoast, and arrive in Porte Oliva in a matter of hours. The power of Inys's wings seemed unlimited. In practice, they had gone faster than the swiftest courier, but it was still the better part of a week before the snow-topped mountains appeared on the horizon, growing slowly and inexorably larger.

The endurance of the passengers had proved to be the limiting factor.

When Inys landed, claws sinking into the deep snow, Mikel was the first to free himself from the sling. He staggered forward two steps in the thigh-deep powder and collapsed. "It's all right," he called weakly. "Just leave me here. I'll be fine."

The snowfield was near the crest of one of the highest of the peaks. The glacier spread out around them, white as the moon and blue as the sky. A great cliff stood to the north, its stone face barely visible under the layers of permanent frost. Marcus released himself and then Cary and Kit. The cold bit at him, and he couldn't catch his breath. The air felt too thin to breathe. At the dragon's side, Hornet was retching loudly. Marcus made a loose snowball and went back to the sick man. Hornet took the ball with a nod and sucked on it miserably until he'd regained himself a bit.

Freed of his burden, Inys paced through the snow, his

head shifting back and forth, fire gouting between his teeth. Kit stumbled forward. There had been ice forming in his hair even before they'd landed. His face was pale where it wasn't windburned and he was as breathless as Marcus.

"Captain. I'm concerned that our friend here may have..." Kit paused, bending over with his elbows resting on his knees. After half a dozen panting breaths, he went on. "...may have overestimated our reserves."

Marcus nodded. At the cliff wall, Inys had risen up on his hind legs and was clawing at the frost, knocking down sheets of it thicker than the length of Marcus's outstretched arm. A cloud of ice crystals rose halfway up the cliff glittering silver and white in the too-bright sun.

"I'll mention that," Marcus said, took a long moment, and started the trudge over to the dragon's side. His head ached badly, and for all the water trapped in the snow and ice, the air was so dry he could feel his eyes going gritty and his mouth thick and cottoned. He scooped up a bit of snow and stuffed it in his mouth. The melt tasted oddly metallic and also wonderful.

"Excuse me," he said when he reached Inys's feet. "Might need a word. With you. This landing? Don't think it'll sustain life."

The dragon looked down. Its shrugs were unlike anything human, but still instantly recognizable.

"Your blood takes too long to thicken. If I let you stay lower, you would not grow accustomed to the heights."

"As it may," Marcus said, "we're a bit thin of food. Or shelter. And I'd prefer not to die of cold."

Inys stepped away to the east, its claws moving along the newly exposed stone face of the cliff. Behind them, Sandr was crying openly. It was an exhausted sound, empty of all emotion but fatigue. "You are weak. Untrained. Slaves such as you should be able to live a day and a night together and stand ready to do battle at the journey's end."

"Fallen world that way," Marcus said, the roughness of anger warming his voice. "But since we're what you've got to work with, you might at least consider taking better care of your fucking tools."

Inys's head flickered toward him. The eyes were filled with gold and darkness. Marcus's fast-beating heart picked up its pace and he felt a sudden lightheadedness. The dragon's chuckle seemed as violent as a landslide.

"You are ill, feral, and untrained, Marcus Wester. But you are a strong line. In better days, you would have led a thousand slaves of your own."

"Not sure whether that's flattering," Marcus said, but Inys ignored the words, his attention already turned back to the cliff wall.

"So long as my tools serve me, I shall keep them clean and sharp," the dragon said. Its claws caught on some near-invisible flaw or seam in the stone, and the dragon let out a hiss that sounded like pleasure. "Here. If time has not broken the mechanisms…"

A creaking sound rose from the mountain below them, like the hinges of the world badly in need of grease. The stone cliff face slid gracefully back, one layer and then another and then another, each perfectly symmetrical. And then with a sound like a wall falling, they moved aside, and a vast hallway glowed gold and green before them. Inys shook his wings, snow and ice falling from them onto Marcus's head and shoulders, and stepped forward. Marcus followed, gaping like a dirt-farm child dropped into a king's temple.

The hall rose in seven great tiers with pillars of dragon's jade marbled with gold holding them. Light that seemed to have no source filled the space, and the smell of plum blossoms sweetened the thin air. Huge stone statues, twice the size of any living person, showed each of the thirteen races bowed down before what seemed at first a great stone log: Firstblood, Jasuru, Cinnae, Kurtadam. Even the rare races of Haunadam and Raushadam. And the Drowned. Inys's hind claws locked around it, and the dragon hauled itself up. A perch. No one in thousands of years had seen a dragon upon its perch until now, and Marcus had to fight the urge—deep as instinct—to kneel. There were no fires and no smoke, but the bitter cold seemed to stop at the hall's entrance as if it knew it was not welcome. The flakes of snow and chips of frost and ice that fell into the place or that were tracked in by the actors' boots and cloaks melted at once and were wicked away by a web of nearly invisible grooves that laced the floor. The dragon tilted its head.

"Will this be enough of a tent for you?" it asked in a low, purring voice that rattled Marcus's spine a little.

"Ah. . . . Sure."

"I am pleased for you, little slave," Inys said. "I would have been sorry to disappoint."

"What is this place?" Smit asked, his voice soft with awe.

"When the press of the court was too great, I would come here," Inys said. "I would . . . sulk. The slaves I put here would sing to me, and I would pose questions to them to pass the days. I was the only one who came here. Except for Erex."

The dragon's gaze softened and turned inward. As Marcus watched, grief twisted the great snout and it closed its eyes, shying to the side as if steeling itself for a blow. Marcus felt a sudden sympathy for the beast. It was disorienting to see the pain he recognized so clearly translated onto such an unlikely flesh. Inys's head drooped.

"We'll rest here tonight, then," Marcus said. "Leave

again in the morning. It won't take us many more days to reach Porte Oliva."

"And what will we do there that can matter?" Inys asked, but it was clear no answer was expected. The dragon unfurled its wings, and the tips touched the walls. With a shriek, Inys leaped from the perch, launching the great body into the sky. Marcus walked to the edge of the hall, looking out over the glacier to the white-and-grey peaks of the mountains. The cold radiated, chilling his skin without biting it. Whatever dragon's craft had held the weather at bay these last few thousand years still held it. The dragon flapped its wings, growing smaller. Unburdened, it flew faster. In less than a hundred breaths, Inys was no more than a spot of darkness in the vast landscape. And then distance took the dragon and left Marcus alone with the players.

The others walked through the hall and the chambers beyond it speaking in hushed voices. Charlit Soon cried out in delight, and Sandr rushed across the space to see what she'd found. Marcus stayed where he was. Before long Cary and Kit joined him. The sun hovered over the peaks to the west. No birds flew so high as they were now. No trees grew.

"How long would you imagine it's been," Marcus said, "since someone stood in this place, looking out?"

Neither of them answered. They didn't have to.

"Did it go to get food, Marcus?" Cary asked.

"I think so."

"So it'll come back, then," she said.

"Probably."

"If it doesn't," Kit said gently. "Or should our friend become distracted by grief..."

Marcus looked out over the vast, trackless glacier. "Well, that would make for an interesting problem."

"I suppose we'll hope it doesn't come to that," Kit said.

"That was my plan."

Cary called Mikel over, and together they started looking for something to gather ice and snow in, melting it for drinking water. Marcus turned back, walking to the statues bent down to make their obeisance to the empty perch. The metal from which they were cast was unlike any he had seen before. The workmanship was beautiful. Had the artists chosen to make their subject lifelike, Marcus would have thought perhaps some dragon's magic had brought real men and women low, transforming them into art, but these were stylized just slightly. The fur of the Kurtadam made soft spirals. The Jasuru's bent head snarled at the ground, baring its pointed teeth. The Tralgu, its large ears laid back against its head, held a fist against its chest as if pressing its heart, but when Marcus looked closely, the thumb and fingers were folded together in a gesture that would have gotten Yardem into a brawl in any taproom of the Keshet.

Marcus leaned against the massive statues, imagining some human sculptor more generations ago than he could count shaping the molds from which these were cast and adding in the snarl of the Jasuru. The Tralgu's rude gesture. From even his brief acquaintance with dragons, Marcus felt sure the punishment for being disrespectful to Inys and his kin would have been death, and likely an unpleasant one. Someone had thought it worth the risk.

Smit and Hornet had made their way through some back chambers to the sixth tier and were waving down to Sandr and Charlit Soon. Their laughter was giddy and bright, fueled as much by the terror of their situation as delight. Marcus shifted the poisoned sword against his back. The shoulder it had rested against ached like he'd wrenched it.

"Kit," he called, waving the old actor toward him. "Does anything strike you about our friend?"

"It seems to me that he's in great pain."

"Other than that."

"I would say he is likely to be our best ally against my former companions."

"I was thinking more along the lines of his towering contempt toward us and the way we all seemed inclined to accept it."

"Well, yes. I suppose there is that."

"There was a mercenary captain I used to know. Arren Bassilain. Ever heard of him?"

"I can't say that I have."

Marcus leaned against the massive Tralgu, hitching himself up to rest on the statue's broad shoulders. "He had a trick. Before the campaign, he'd stop at every taproom along the way and make a thing of himself. Boast, tell tales. Spill all this hairwash about the glories of battle and how it made boys into men. Talked about how the women in a fallen city would throw themselves at the conquering army. That no man in his force ever slept alone after a battle."

Kit chuckled ruefully. Above them, Hornet and Smit were waving a brush as long as a man at the end of a long, thin pole. Marcus could imagine Inys at his perch being groomed by his slaves.

"The thing is," he went on, "Arren was a hell of a talker. By the time he reached wherever we were supposed to be fighting, he'd have taken on a couple dozen boys greener than grass and convinced they were about to have all their dreams delivered to them on a plate. Whenever the first battle came, he'd send them out first to soak up some arrows and get an idea of what the enemy's position was so that when he sent his real forces, he had that little bit more information."

"It seems a cynical and cruel thing to do," Kit said.

"My trade doesn't attract the best people. The thing is, not all of them died, and the ones that lived, some of them stayed in his troop. More and more over time. He didn't think anything of it, and I didn't either. And then one day a group of his men got together and traded stories about how he'd recruited them, got angry over it, and opened his throat for him."

"I see," Kit said, his gaze shifting around the hall. "Do you think something similar may have happened to the dragons of old?"

"I think war's like fire. It goes where it wants more often than where you'd have wanted it to," Marcus said. "We know for a certainty that the dragons fell and that the spiders fled. If you count the victor as who was standing on the field at the end, that wasn't *either* of them."

"Kit! Cary!" Sandr said, pulling Charlit Soon along behind him by the sleeve. "Charlit's got the best idea ever. We've got to do this!"

Marcus and Kit exchanged a look and stepped forward. At the base of the great perch, Charlit was smiling, her eyes bright and a little glassy. Her cheeks were red with wind burn, the same as all of them. Cary crossed her arms and nodded to her.

"I was just thinking that, with the cart gone, we'd be practicing the things we can play from the ground," Charlit Soon said. "And it struck me that Inys has never seen any of them. He's probably never even heard of PennyPenny or Orcus the Demon King or any of them."

"It would be like performing for the greatest king in the history of the world!" Sandr said. "We could do The Prisoner's Gate. Or Allaren Mankiller—"

"We can't do Mankiller without the props," Cary said. "But maybe PennyPenny and the Three Wives of Stollbourne?"

"Kit could be the third wife!" Charlit Soon said, laughter bubbling out of with the words.

Kit's smile was warm and gentle. "I suppose I could at that," he said.

"What're you talking about down there?" Hornet called from the upper tier. "Are you making jokes about us?"

"No," Sandr called. "We're going to put on a performance. Get down here and help, you lazy bastard!"

Marcus stepped away from the gabble and excitement, back to the edge of the hall. The sun had set now, and the mountains seemed crafted from distance and mist and the deepening gray-blue of night. The snowfield glowed. The players' voices rose and fell behind him, giddy and pleased and happy because they were a people who traded in that. He traded in violence, and had his whole life. He didn't see that changing now.

Far off and low between two peaks, something glowed for a moment. Smaller than a spark, but red amid the blue-lit world. A brief flame, here, and then gone. Marcus squinted. His eyes hurt from the dryness and his head still ached. In the growing gloom, it was hard to be sure that the little flame had been dragonfire, but before long, there was a little knot of moving darkness in the direction the spark had been. And then, barely visible, the great wings, and then Inys rose up from the night, the corpse of a ram in his hind claw. Marcus stepped back as the dragon landed, dropping its kill onto the floor. The thin grooves that had wicked away the snowmelt were just as effective with blood.

"I can dress that for you if you'd like," Marcus said, nodding toward the dead animal.

"I have eaten all I care to," the dragon said, its voice half exhaustion and half disdain. "This is to take care of my tools."

"Inys! Inys!" Charlit Soon called from the perch. "Come see what we've made for you!"

The dragon lumbered away toward the perch, leaving bloody claw marks behind. Marcus drew a work knife from his belt and took the dead ram by its horns while the players arrayed themselves inside and Cary began declaiming. The dragon watched with an amused expression, licking the blood from its talons.

"You know, little sheep," Marcus said, as he prepared to skin and clean it. "I really don't see how this ends well."

Geder

M y God," Aster said. "They're beautiful."

The warehouse had been cleaned out to make room for the devices. Old stone rose to rafters of whole trees, and clerestory windows spilled light across the ceiling. Geder's personal guard had taken their positions at the doors and behind him, protecting him in case of attack, but even they glanced at the massive weapons of war. The metal had been burnished until it seemed to have some deep, hidden light glowing through it. They stood taller than men and promised violence.

"We made some adjustments to the design, my lord," Honnen Pyre, the Jasuru armorer, said. He was deferential, but Geder heard the pride in his voice. "The harpoon spears from your books are a fine start, but if you see here, we fit them on a ballista. More power to hit something higher up in the air, we thought."

"Yes," Geder said, stepping up on the device. It was even more amazing than the drawings had been. The ancient plans had made the machines seem spare and elegant. A marvel only of the mind. Made real, made larger, given form and weight, they were almost like looking at the carapace of a beetle or a gigantic wasp. A human invention for the defeat and destruction of dragons. Geder put his hand against the steel, almost expecting to feel the machine breathing.

"And the reel there," the Jasuru said. "Keeps some of the tension for pulling the rope up and through. Now, it's a queen's own bear to reset the device. Those that fire her will want to make a solid hit the first time."

"It's brilliant," Geder said.

Pyre swelled with pride. "I've got a cousin that worked with the whale hunters up in Hallskar. Thought of some of the things he'd said and modified them. The way the base turns to help the men aim quick is a Hallskari thing."

Geder stepped down. "Show me the rest."

The geared arbalests with their spinning blades were smaller than he'd expected. Small enough for a three-person team to carry and operate one in the field. Now that Geder saw the device in person, he felt he had a better sense of how they would work in battle. The smith sent one of the flat, round blades up into the rafters, where it stuck fast.

"Can I try?" Aster asked tentatively.

"Can he?" Geder asked the Jasuru. "Is it safe?"

"Safe enough, my lord," he said. "Come right here, Prince Aster, sir. I'll show you how to work the tension bar."

Geder stood back, watching. He was always astounded to see how much Aster had grown and changed in only a few years. Pulling back the bar and fitting a round blade into its seat, he looked old enough almost to be a soldier. Likely there were boys his age in the field. Not royal blood, of course, but of Aster's age. When he loosed the blades, they flew up spinning and sank deep into the wood ceiling. Geder clapped with delight. It was like seeing a cunning man's show. Better, even, because it wasn't magic.

"How many can we make, and how quickly?" Geder asked.

"This is as many as we've got now," the smith said. "I could get twice this with the supplies I've got and got coming. But it won't be fast."

Geder nodded. "Do that, then. Start now. And we'll need to break these down and put them on carts going south. Do you have men to go with them? I don't want Jorey's men trying to figure out how to put this all back together without a guide."

"I've got an apprentice boy I thought I'd send with them. He's smart enough for putting it all where it goes, but he busted his shoulder a year back and can't swing a hammer to save his life. Not much use to me here. Maybe good for something out there."

"Well, he's with the campaign now," Geder said with a grin. "Have these ready by morning. We have to get them to the south quickly. We don't know when the enemy might attack."

"If they don't do it soon, they'd best not do it at all," Pyre said. And then a moment later, with a sense of awe that Geder felt himself, "God damn, my lord. We're killing *dragons*."

Jorey's reports had been coming back every few days since he'd arrived in Elassae. The troops, he'd said, were in a mild kind of disarray. That was fair. Geder had executed Lord Ternigan months ago, and apart from the ongoing siege at Kiaria—which Jorey said showed no signs of breaking— they'd had no clear idea what was going to come next. Many of them had hoped that they'd be brought back to Camnipol and the disband called. The priests were invaluable in keeping the army focused and disciplined. That was a very good thing. Geder had ready any number of histories that talked about what happened when armies rebelled against their commanders. Once the Timzinae plotters were all caught, Geder would bring home the armies and throw the largest triumph the world had ever seen. He owed the men that much, and more.

Back at the Kingspire, he went to the map room and walked across the little hills and mountains between the miniature Kiaria and Porte Oliva. Ten tiny ships sat on the blue sand that was the ocean. One flag marked Cithrin's city, and another midway between Orsen and Bellin showed where the army had been camped when Jorey had sent his last report. Fit into a room in the Kingspire, it looked so close.

The weapons would have to move quickly to catch up to the army. But armies moved slowly compared to couriers and small forces. And Jorey would be even slower once he reached Bellin and entered the long pass through the mountains, and the weapons carts didn't have to track down to Orsen. They could cross the Dry Wastes and save hundreds of miles. He chuckled and hugged himself. It was all going to work. They were going to win.

He wanted to share his happiness with someone, and spent almost an hour looking for Basrahip, who was locked away with his priests in some sort of ritual, or Aster, who was out on a ride through the countryside with Lord Caot's daughter and a few other young people of the court. His own father was still at Rivenhalm, late as always to come to court, even now that his own son was Lord Regent. And then, there was almost no one. It always surprised Geder to realize how few people were really his friends. They knew him as Lord Regent and hero of the realm, but that wasn't the same as having a friend to talk with, and letters to Jorey didn't seem quite the right thing either.

But there was his wife. Sabiha. Geder called for his palanquin and ordered the slaves to carry him to Lord Skestinin's manor. Maybe a cup of tea with Sabiha as a little celebration. He liked Sabiha. He hoped that she liked him too. He'd ask her sometime when Basrahip was around...only that seemed rude, and he didn't want to make her feel awkward.

As soon as he reached the manor, he had the sense that something was wrong. The footmen at the front of the house seemed agitated, and the door slave chained by the entry looked grey about the face as if ill. When he told the slave he'd come to see Sabiha, the man almost reared back. Another servant showed him and his guards to a withdrawing room at the back of the house. Geder haunted the windows, peeking out at the gardens as if there, hidden among the boughs, might be some explanation of why the house felt so tense.

When the door opened, the woman who came in was not Sabiha.

Lady Skestinin's smile was almost a grimace. She held her body straight and stiff, and Geder had the sense that had he been anyone else, she would not have agreed to see him. He rose to his feet, tugged between embarrassment at having made a social misstep and alarm at the woman's appearance.

"Lord Regent," she said. "This is an unexpected pleasure."

"Lady Skestinin. I was…I'm sorry, I should have sent ahead. It was a casual visit. I was thinking I would call on Sabiha."

"Ah, I am afraid she is feeling a bit under the weather. The baby is at a delicate point."

Geder glanced reflexively to the back of the room, but Basrahip wasn't there. He didn't know if Lady Skestinin was telling the truth or not. He couldn't think why she would deceive him, but he couldn't shake the sense that something more was happening.

"I didn't know. I'm sorry."

"There is no need for you to apologize, Lord Regent. Perhaps I could have a courier sent when she is more herself? Or if there is something I can do to be of service?"

"No, that's fine. I was only stopping by on a whim. Casual. Between friends."

"Of course," Lady Skestinin said, her hands clasped tightly before her like a singer about to begin a performance. Geder nodded, unsure what to say. He wished Basrahip were with him.

"I'll just... I'll just see myself out," Geder said.

"Do let me walk with you," she said. From the drawing room to the door, neither said anything. Geder bowed a bit when he left her at the door, but he didn't know what words to say, and she didn't offer any. He walked down the steps to his palanquin slowly, his brow furrowed. His head felt like it had been stuffed with cotton ticking. Something was bothering him, but he didn't know what it could be. It wasn't as though Lady Skestinin had been rude to him. If anything, by arriving uninvited and unannounced, he'd been the rude one. Except it hardly seemed to be a serious offense. Friends stopped by to visit with each other all the time. And he was the Lord Regent, after all. And Sabiha could at least have sent a note instead of her mother...

He paused with one foot in the palanquin and looked back. The footmen stood with a formal stiffness. The door slave sat, his head bent and his hand on his chain. Something wasn't right. Geder motioned to the captain of his guard.

"I'm going back," he said. "I need to see Sabiha."

"My lord," the captain said and gestured for the others to follow them.

The door slave's smile was tight and anxious as Geder walked back up the steps.

"I need to see Sabiha Kalliam," Geder said.

"I will call for Lady Skestinin again, my lord, if you—"

"No. No, I need to see Sabiha," Geder said, his tone growing harder. "Why can't I just see her?"

"She is … she is with the cunning man, my lord."

"Oh," Geder said. And then a moment later, dread blooming in his chest. "*Why?*"

The solarium was filled with light. Darkness might have been better. Sabiha Kalliam lay on the cunning man's table. Her sweat-soaked nightgown clung to her, and her face was the color of clay. The swollen arch of her belly looked huge, but Geder hadn't spent enough time around women in the last days of their pregnancies to know if it was alarming or normal. Everything else about her seemed like a sign of panic, so maybe it was too large somehow. He couldn't imagine that it could be too small. The cunning man stood with his hands over her belly, his thin fingers glowing with something that was not quite light. He was an old First-blood man with scars on his face and arms and white hair that swept up and back from his temples like he was always facing into a stiff wind.

Geder must have gasped, because Sabiha turned her head toward him. Her eyes were glassy and flat. When she saw him, there was no flicker of recognition. Geder's heart thudded in his chest and he stepped forward like he was moving into a nightmare. Sabiha's eyes tracked him, but he didn't have the sense that she saw him. Not really.

The cunning man slumped, put his hands on the table, and looked up. Sweat dripped off him like he'd sprinted through the whole city. He nodded to Geder and spoke between gasps.

"Lord Regent. How can I. Help you?"

"I came to see Sabiha," Geder said, his voice small. It struck him how inane the statement was. "Is she … all right?"

"I will not lie to you. She is not well," the cunning man said. "And the baby within her is struggling."

"It's because of the first one," Lady Skestinin said from behind him. Geder turned to her. The older woman's face was a blank. All emotion was gone from it but a deep terror. "She had the first baby. The wrong one. And it's poisoned her."

"No," Geder said. "That's not right. It doesn't work that way. I mean...does it?"

"I cannot speak to what happened before," the cunning man said. "For now, I am doing everything that can be done."

"No," Geder said. "No, you aren't. We can do more. We'll do more. Captain! Get Basrahip. And my cunning man. All the physicians."

"Your personal physicians?" the captain asked.

"Yes," Geder said. "Why are you still here?"

The captain nodded once so deeply it was almost a bow, then turned and ran from the room. Geder took Sabiha's hand. It was cold and damp.

"It's fate," Lady Skestinin said, her voice breaking on the words. "It's the punishment that's come for the first one. It is the price of her sins." A tear dropped from Sabiha's eye, tracking back to her hairline.

"No," Geder said. "It isn't. It's just she's sick and needs help."

"She was unchaste," Lady Skestinin said, tears flowing down her cheeks. "My poor baby's going to die because she was unchaste."

"What are you talking about?" Geder snapped. "People are unchaste all the time. This doesn't happen to them. Guard! See Lady Skestinin to her drawing room. Get her some...I don't know. Wine. Read poetry to her."

"My lord, our duty is to guard you."

"Don't *fucking* tell me what your duty is. I tell you. I tell *you* what your duty is. You do as I say."

"Lord Regent," the cunning man said. "It might be better not to shout."

"Oh. I'm sorry. Sabiha, I'm sorry. I didn't mean to be loud."

Behind them, Lady Skestinin's cries and wails receded. Sabiha blinked slowly, her eyelids clicking audibly when they opened. Geder was still holding her hand. The cunning man's smile was exahsuted. "My thanks, Lord Regent."

"How long has she been like that?"

"Lady Kalliam or Lady Skestinin, do you mean? The young lady became ill last evening. I have been here since they called me. The older lady...well. Grief makes the best of us mad."

"No no no," Geder said, fear rising in him, clutching at his chest. "No grief. This is Jorey's baby. This is Sabiha. There can't be grief."

"As you say, my lord," the cunning man said, then spread his hands across her belly and closed his eyes. The not-light began flickering again. Geder squatted beside the table, holding her hand because it was all he could do.

It felt like hours before his physicians arrived. There were four of them, two Firstblood women who looked as if they could be mother and daughter, a Yemmu man with his tusks carved in intricate patterns, and a Kurtadam man so ancient and stooped his pelt was grey with a few strands of rust red still showing here and there. They came through the door-way behind Geder, nodded to him, and turned to Sabiha. Her eyes seemed a little less distant now, but she still hadn't spoken. The Yemmu man gently pulled the original cunning man aside, and began a rough-syllabled chant of his own. The older woman took a silver box from her waist, opened it, and began drawing white symbols on Sabiha's forehead and hands. The smell of honey and marigolds filled the room.

"It's going to be all right," Geder said softly. "You're

going to be fine." Sabiha turned to him, as if seeing him for the first time. Her eyes went wide and her mouth twisted into a mask of disgust. Who knew what she was seeing now? He smiled reassuringly. "It's all right. It's me. Geder. I've come to help."

"Jorey—"

"It'll be all right," Geder said, and the younger woman pulled up Sabiha's dress, exposing her thighs and hips and distended belly. Geder felt himself getting lightheaded. His gorge rose, and he looked away. "It'll be . . ." He swallowed. "It'll be all right."

None of the cunning men seemed disturbed. The Kurtadam shifted himself between Sabiha's knees and put his hand gently on her sex. She grunted in discomfort, and Geder had to leave or pass out. In the hallway, he pressed his forehead to the cool stone until he was sure he wasn't going to vomit. Basrahip still hadn't come. He wanted Basrahip to be there, to advise him. The priest would know what to do if anyone did.

"Lord Regent?"

The older of the two women stood before him. He hadn't heard her come out. "Yes. I'm here. I'm all right. How is she?"

The older woman's expression was serene and sorrowful. "We will do what we can, my lord."

"That's not enough."

"These things are always delicate, Lord Palliako," she went on. "We will do everything we can. But if it comes to a choice between saving the child or the mother, my lord . . ." She held out her hands, as if offering him something he might not want.

Geder felt the air leave his lungs. "You want *me* to decide that?"

"If we knew what your preferences were, my lord, it would help to guide us."

Geder took a long, deep breath. They wanted him to choose whether Sabiha or her baby mattered more? They wanted him to give them permission to let one of them die? The fear and horror twisted in him, turning to rage in less than the blink of an eye.

"Guide you?" he said. "Here's my guidance. That is my friend in there, and her baby with her. When they come out, it will be the same. Mother and child both. Both. If there is anything else, I will whip you all to death *myself*! *Do you understand?*"

The woman stepped back. The calm of her expression was like a mask. "My lord, I do," she said.

Cithrin

Maestro Asanpur pushed his broom, his gaze cast down. The shards and splinters of glass scraped against the café's floor with each pass of the bristles. His blind eye was watering, but not so much as to call it weeping. The breeze that passed through the shattered windows would have been pleasant in other circumstances. Cithrin shifted from one foot to the other and then stepped forward, careful not to tread where the old Cinnae was cleaning. She picked up the stones from where they'd landed. They were dark and rough and fit easily in her palm. They'd been chosen for throwing. The bricks of the floor bore small white scars where they'd struck.

Maestro Asanpur poured the shattered glass into a tin bucket and held it out to Cithrin. She put the stones in carefully, like she was nestling black eggs into a nest of shards. She wasn't afraid that he would drop the bucket if she'd simply dropped them, but she wanted to do something gentle as if it would bring something gentle back to her. The impulse was much like prayer.

"I'm sorry," she said, and the old man shook his head.

"No reason, Magistra. Youth will have its day. Boys have been breaking windows as long as there have been windows."

Not because of me, Cithrin thought. But so long as he was

pretending that the violence was random, it seemed rude to insist on the truth.

With every day that the blockade continued, Porte Oliva seemed to grow darker and more surly. Twice now, she'd woken in the night to the sound of voices in the street outside the counting house. Someone had smeared shit on the front door, leaving a swath of dirty brown and a wide, masculine handprint. After that, Yardem had redone the guard rotation. Now they kept someone in the street night and day, and half a dozen in the counting house itself. He'd also put sword-and-bows outside the apartments that Komme, Pyk, and Isadau kept. He'd hired on more guards to fill the gaps, and for once Pyk hadn't objected.

Maestro Asanpur stopped his cleaning to prepare her a cup of coffee. Cithrin went to her back room and opened the little strongbox she kept there. The books hadn't been touched, but next time they might be. Or the café might be burned. She sat at the little table, running her palm over the smooth-lacquered wood, and considered where she could move her work. By being here, she was putting Asanpur and his café at risk. Maybe she should move to the taproom nearest her rooms. God knew she was spending more time drinking than doing the work of the bank anyway.

The emptiness of the ledgers showed the same truths as the broken glass. To the merchants and traders, a bank was a place to go to reduce risks. When the bank itself became the locus of uncertainty, it was like pouring poison in the water. Even the payments due on the loans Pyk had approved were coming in slow. There were stories and explanations for each of them—a child with the flux, a robbery, a delivery of wheat that hadn't come in. They didn't matter. The larger picture was unmistakable. Whether they admitted it to themselves or not, they were all waiting for the queens-men's blades to arrive and shut down the bank.

And in truth, Cithrin was waiting for it too. In the mean-time, at least the coffee was good.

When she first heard the sound of voices raised, she real-ized she had been hearing it for some time. It wasn't the sound of the Grand Market. That combination of shouts and laughter and complaint was as familiar to her as breath. This was something else. A slow roar that built, voice upon voice, in a chorus like the surf against stones. Cithrin's belly went tight. She put her cup on the table with a thump that slopped coffee and milk onto the boards and stippled the ledger. She didn't stop to blot it clean. Heart in her throat, she stepped into the café's main room, ready to meet her doom if it waited for her there.

Maestro Asanpur stood in the doorway, shifting from side to side as if he were angling for a better view. Outside, people were running. The Grand Market had emptied. The queensmen who guarded it had left their posts. Cithrin came closer and put her hand on the old man's thin shoulder, torn between relief and alarm.

"What is it?" she asked.

"I can't say, Magistra," the old Cinnae said. "They're all shouting, but I can't tell what they're saying."

"They're going toward the salt quarter," she said, her mind dancing across the possibilities. The blockaders were attacking, and the citizens running to battle. Geder had sent an army after all, and they were fleeing it. There was fire, perhaps, or a plague.

Yardem appeared on the far side of the square in his heavy armor. Four other guards were at his side; two Firstblood men, a bronze-scaled Jasusu woman who was new to the company, and Halvill the Timzinae. Cithrin stepped out to meet them, her chin high. The stream of people had thinned by the time they reached her.

"Pyk sent us, ma'am," Yardem said. "I think you'll want to see this."

The crowd on the seawall was so dense, Cithrin was certain people would be crushed. Adolescent boys and girls were climbing up to stand or sit on the raised areas above the clifflike drop to the rocks below. Ancient ballistas had been installed in the gaps since the start of the blockade, though no enemy had ever come near enough to draw their fire. Merchants and carters and street puppeteers pressed themselves in the gaps between the engines of war and the pale stone, staring out to sea. Cithrin's jaw ached and her belly felt like she was going to be sick. Yardem sighed, squared his shoulders, and leaned close to her, speaking loud to be heard over the voices of the crowd.

"Put your hand in my belt, and stay close."

"Where are we going?"

"The front," he said with a wide, canine grin. He turned and Cithrin looped her fingers around the wide, dark leather of his belt, pulling herself close to his back so that no one could force their way between them. Yardem shouted for the people to make way, then waded into the crowd. Halvill and the Jasuru women took positions at Cithrin's side, their faces fixed in expressions of boredom tempered by the threat of violence. People shouted at them, jostled shoulders against them, pushed. Step by slow step, they made their way through the pack. Even under the open sky with a breeze coming off the water, the air was heavy and close with their bodies and their breath.

And they were clear of it, stepping past a line of the bank guards with drawn blades to a platform at the seawall's edge. Pyk stood by a small white table, a jug and cup forgotten at her side and a long bronze spyglass pressed to her eye. Out in the deep water beyond the harbor's edge the tall sails of the blockade stood as they had for weeks, their sails struck. But beyond them, three much smaller curves of white showed against the western water. Small sails in low ships. Cithrin squinted, trying to make out what they were by force of will.

"Pyk," she said. "What's happening?"

"The mad bastards took their island," the Yemmu said. "Look at that. *Look* at that."

"I can't see anything," she said. Pyk grunted and handed her the spyglass.

It took her a moment to find anything more than waves on the water. The first ship that came into focus was one of the roundships. Its deck was awash with men. She could see the flash of drawn swords, though there seemed to be no fighting. In the crow's nest, a pack of sailors pointed crossbows to the west. Cithrin followed the water until she found the little sails. They belonged to small galleys with single, triangular sails and no more than a dozen oars. Beside the roundships, the three ships looked like little more than rafts. The flags that flew from their masts had a crest that Cithrin didn't recognize.

"Who are they?" she said. "What are they doing?"

"You'll recall there was some mad bastard organizing the pirates into a fleet?" Pyk said. "That appears to be him."

"Does he know that he's got three tiny little ships going against ten Antean roundships?" Cithrin asked. "Because it seems someone hasn't mentioned the fact to him."

Yardem cleared his throat. "Wind's against the round-ships," the Tralgu rumbled. "The galleys are outmatched, but they'll only have to face one ship at a time. Until the wind shifts, anyway."

"And after that?" Cithrin asked.

"More then," he said.

The first of the galleys drew close to the roundship. Seeing them side by side, the folly of the attackers seemed to pass into madness. The men in the galley stood with raised shields while the Antean sailors rained arrows and cross-bow bolts and barrels down on them. Boarding the round-ship from the galley's low deck would be like climbing a cliff under attack with a force twice their size waiting at the top to slaughter them. The galley's oars shifted, and the little ship darted forward. An obscure movement in the center of the galley caught Cithrin's attention. Four men rushed toward the galley's prow with what looked like spears with strange, curving blades instead of points. The galley shifted and turned, seeming almost to dance in the water. One of the spearmen fell back, dropping his odd spear, but the other three found their way under the roundship's stern. They reached up, sawing wildly. The sailors on the round-ship's deck swarmed like ants with a kicked hill.

A roar like thunder came from the city, rising up all around her at once. And then as quickly as it had come in, the galley reversed oars and pulled away from its enemy. Pyk's laughter cut through the cacophony. Cithrin took the spyglass from her eye and was astonished to see her notary capering and making rude gestures with both of her hands. On the piers below the seawall, the makeshift fleet of Porte Oliva was putting out to sea: fishing boats and trading ships that had been trapped in port, guide boats.

"Yardem," Cithrin shouted. "What happened? I don't understand."

The Tralgu held out his wide palm, and Cithrin handed over the spyglass. Yardem stepped forward, frowning. Cithrin waited for what seemed like hours, looking from Yardem to the ships on the water. The two other galleys seemed to be advancing on the second of the roundships. The ship that the first galley had approached was turning now, shifting in the wind. The two galleys darted in toward the second roundship and Yardem chuckled.

"What?" Cithrin demanded, tugging on Yardem's arm.

"They're cutting the rigging and breaking the rudders," Yardem said, turning to look away from the ships to the coast stretching out east of the city. "They'll be adrift." A moment later, he made a low chuffing sound that it took Cithrin a moment to recognize as laughter.

"What?" she asked.

"Permission to gather the company guard, miss? Tides being what they are, I expect our Antean friends will be running aground before nightfall. Wouldn't mind being there to meet them."

The great roundship lay on the beach, its masts at an angle to land and water. Two others stood out to sea, the current turning them slowly and at random. The wind had shifted, coming in from the sea, carrying the scent of brine and smoke. On the western horizon, the setting sun painted the sky red and gold. Two dozen Antean sailors stood in the surf, waves washing up around their knees. They wore scowls and carried long knives hardly shorter than swords.

Facing them on the shore were the company guard of the Medean bank along with half a dozen queensmen. A larger troop of queensmen was riding the coast, waiting for the next ships to run aground. Yardem stood near the front of the crowd. Anyone who didn't know him better would have thought he was bored. Cithrin knew better. She sat a brown gelding she'd taken from the stables.

"Stand your ground, men," an old Firstblood called to the Antean sailors. He had a grey beard and a thick, powerful build. Yardem looked over to her, and Cithrin nodded him on. His ears flicked once and he stepped forward.

"Hoy, Antea," he shouted, his voice throbbing with a power she'd rarely heard in it before. "Name's Yardem Hane. Second to Captain Marcus Wester. We've come as escort, to take you back to the governor. We can fight first if you'd like."

"Hane?" the bearded man said. "I know your name. You're the bank girl's tool."

"Yes," the Tralgu said, drawing his sword as if it were the most natural thing in the world.

"That's her!" someone shouted, and with no other warning, the Antean sailors charged up out of the water. Yardem shouted out a signal call and the company guards shifted to meet the enemy charge with an air of calm. The bearded commander was shouting now too, trying to call his men back into order, but it was too late. The sailors and the guard came together in a clump, bodies slamming against bodies, blades clashing against blades. Cithrin watched, ready to take flight if the need arose, but fairly certain that it would not. The queensmen held the side, seeing to it that none of the sailors escaped in the chaos while Yardem and his guards—*her* guards—drove the attackers back into the water. The Anteans broke off, falling back. There were fewer of them now by a third. So far as she could see, none of hers were hurt.

"We can try that again if you'd like," Yardem called out. "We've got no other plans for the evening."

"Will you vouch for our safety?"

"No," Yardem said.

"I will," Cithrin called out. "These are my guard, and they'll take my word. Throw down your weapons and take the chain, and I'll see you safely to the governor. All of you. What comes after that is between you and him."

The bearded man spat. "I suppose I can't ask better than that," he called back. "Men! Throw down your blades."

"She'll kill us!" one of the sailors shouted.

"If she wanted to do that, we'd be dead," the bearded commander said, wading up out of the surf. He drew a short ceremonial sword from his side and took it by the blade. Cithrin turned her mount toward him and walked it forward. Yardem shadowed the Antean, his expression blank and calm.

"I offer you our surrender," the bearded man said.

"I accept," Cithrin said, taking the blade. "I am Cithrin bel Sacrour, voice of the Medean bank in Porte Oliva."

"Lord Anton Skestinin, servant to the Severed Throne."

"I'm sorry we had to meet under these circumstances, Lord Skestinin," Cithrin said.

The old man smiled up at her sourly. "You're a good liar, miss. There was a moment I almost believed you."

"In line!" Yardem shouted. "Hands in front!"

Cithrin watched while the enemy commander and his men were manacled. The queensmen took control of them once it was done. Cithrin ordered half a dozen of her guard to make the ship fast, running ropes from the roundship itself to the trees nearest the waterline to keep it in place when the tide rose again. She rode back toward Porte Oliva, her head high and her belly relaxed for the first time she could remember. Yardem rode beside her.

"All respect, but I wish you hadn't come," he said. "Safer to stay back and let us handle all this."

"I had faith you would protect me," she said, and Yardem chuckled.

It was past nightfall when the Antean prisoners were marched into the square between the Governor's Palace and the cathedral. All the other guests of the magistrate's justice had been freed in celebration, and the stocks and cages, gallows and torture boxes were all empty, ready, and waiting. The crowd around them seemed to be half the city, and it was all the combined force of Cithrin's guard and the queensmen could manage to keep them from running riot. Cithrin rode forward and formally turned the prisoners over to the governor. For a moment, the pair of them faced each other in silence. She thought she saw something like disappointment in the man's face. He had been waiting for the order to put her and her company in chains, and she had complicated things. The thought made her smile wider.

Afterward, Cithrin led the full company of guards to the taproom nearest their barracks, split a purse of silver coins open on the keeper's table, and told him to keep the beer coming until the coin ran out. She sat in the back, a bottle of good wine in her hand and the taste of victory on her tongue. A group of musicians, scenting the riot and joy, made their way in and struck up a tune.

In truth, though, Cithrin knew her celebration was only part of the city's general uproar. The blockade was broken, the city freed, the ships of Porte Oliva loosed upon the seas. If it wasn't something she had done herself, the relief of it was still as sweet. She closed her eyes and felt the rhythm of the music and the fumes of the wine carry her up until she was laughing. Madly, wildly, halfway to tears from it.

Geder's hand could not reach everywhere after all. It was like someone had taken a stone off her heart she hadn't known was there. She hadn't known she intended to dance until she was already up, her arm locked with Yardem's, spinning through the little taproom like the world itself was a child's top.

The celebration went on in a trail of emptied bottles and shrieking laughter, and Cithrin threw herself into it all. Reckless and wild and joyful, and not at all out of place. All of Porte Oliva had taken to the streets. Time shifted, drawing back from itself until the world seemed to be a symbol for itself, and her hardly more than a flourish upon the page of history. She didn't know where she was any longer, or who. And then she was being cradled in Yardem's massive arms like a child being carried by her mother. And then she was in her bed, alone, with cool air on her face.

With morning came a clearer light. She pulled herself out of bed, waiting for the throb of the headache. And it came, but not with the viciousness she'd expected. So that was something. She peeled off the clothes she'd worn the day before, powdered her body, and pulled on a fresh gown and cloak. She could hear voices in the counting room below her. Yardem and Pyk and Isadau. She smiled as she made her way down the stairs. But when she reached the street, she turned right instead of left, moving through the streets alone among the crowd. Even with the blockade lifted, there were a thousand problems and threats and fears, and she would go and face them soon. The joy of relief was still in her, and she wasn't quite ready to leave it behind. Not yet.

Maestro Asanpur's café was as busy as she'd seen it in months. The broken windows were not replaced, but the last of the glass had been pulled from them and the frames had been made neat. The smell of coffee and fresh bread mixed with the shouts from the Grand Market. Cithrin bowed to the old Cinnae, and he bowed back.

"A very good day after all, then, yesterday," Asanpur said.

"And from such inauspicious beginnings," Cithrin replied.

"Let me make you some coffee, eh?"

"I would like nothing better," Cithrin said, moving back toward her private room.

Asanpur's voice held her back. "Do you know anything about this savior of ours? Have you met with him?"

"Nothing," Cithrin said. "I'd guess whoever he is, he's locked in private conference while the governor gnaws himself raw deciding whether to jail him as a pirate or welcome him as a hero."

The voice that answered came from behind her. It was deep and masculine and carried the accents of Imperial Antea. "You'd have guessed wrong."

He had risen from one of the smaller tables in the back. He looked to be younger than Marcus and older than herself. His beard was a deep nut brown and his face darkened by the sun. He stepped forward, and the café went silent. Even Asanpur forgot his coffee. "You're Cithrin bel Sarcour, then?"

"I am," she said. "And am I to understand you claim to be the genius who saved us from our enemies?"

"Not genius," the man said. "I've been warning Lord Skestinin about those rudders for years. He thought I was being overdramatic. I only took the opportunity to prove my point. I've spent the last half year poking around Herez looking for a man named Callon Cane. It seems to me that you're him too."

"I can't imagine what you're talking about," she said, and the bearded man shook his head.

"I don't believe that, Magistra. You're the one person in this world with the balls to stand against Geder Palliako."

Cithrin felt a pang of some emotion that surprised her. Sorrow, perhaps. Or regret. Or pride. "I am."

"Well, I am the enemy of your enemy. My name is Barriath Kalliam, by right of blood Baron of Osterling Fells, and I've come to help you bleed that bastard white."

Marcus

It was as if Porte Oliva had known they were coming, and what they brought. Flying low over the city, Marcus looked down into streets already made bright with celebratory cloth, squares already filled with musicians and dancing. Upturned faces flashed by him so quickly, he remembered them more than actually saw them. All were in phases of amazement, mouths open, hands pointing, eyes as wide as Southlings'. Inys skimmed above the Grand Market, his feet so low, Marcus expected to hear the canvas tenting rip. He swooped out over the salt quarter, past the seawall, out over the bay. Marcus had never seen so much traffic on water before, and all the sailors shouted as they passed overhead, and he waved down to them. Inys's great wings chuffed like sailcloth as the dragon turned in a long, slow circle and passed back over the city. There was screaming in the streets now, though whether it was excitement or terror or some combination of the two wasn't clear. They all sounded the same from where he was.

At the land side of the city, Inys backed, slowed, and touched ground. The huge black talons cut into the grass as Marcus and the players released themselves and stripped off the harnesses. Inys shook his head.

"They have taken down the perches," he said, the restrained

thunder of his voice heavy with disgust. "This little growth has no place for me."

"In their defense," Marcus said, "they weren't exactly expecting the company. Wouldn't be surprised if they invested in some amenities now there's a reason for them."

The dragon growled and turned its head toward the city. A group of queensmen in green and gold were making their way across the meadow, pikes at the ready in a formation that could have been ceremonial or defensive, depending on the need. In the center of the formation, the governor lurked in bright steel armor.

"Well, God smiled," Marcus said. "You all wait here. I'll go tell the governor which way the wind's blowing."

"I will have food and drink," Inys said. "And they will build me a true perch."

"I'll let them know that," Marcus said.

The flying harness left his legs weak and numb, but Marcus made his way across the field toward the advancing force all the same. The pins-and-needles pain would come soon, and he'd have to stand in place until it passed. And he wasn't yet certain he wanted Inys to hear everything that was said.

"Hold!" the guard captain called as Marcus drew near. Marcus raised a hand in greeting as if they were acquaintances meeting on the road. "Who are you, and what is your business with the city?"

"Marcus Wester and I live here, or I used to. Been away for a time on, you know—" He pointed back toward the dragon. Inys, freed of the harnesses, was stretching out on the greensward, scratching his back against the earth like a puppy the size of a house. "Work."

"Captain Wester?" The governor's voice trembled. "Is that really you?"

"Governor," Marcus said.

"Are you well?"

"Bit tired. Long road. Speaking as a metaphor. Wasn't as much actual road in it as usual."

The governor came to the front of the group of soldiers. Marcus had never thought much of the man, and the time away from Porte Oliva hadn't improved him. His thinning hair was slicked back in a younger man's style, and he wore more glittering rings, if that was possible. Marcus could take some solace in the fear-wide eyes and trembling lips.

"The...the dragon," the governor said, gesturing over Marcus's shoulder. Marcus shifted, and a bright flare of pain rose up through both legs as the feeling returned.

"Him. Yes," he said. "Come to consult with the magistra."

"It's...the bel Sarcour woman? It's here for *her*?"

"I imagine there'll be some other people he might want to talk to, but Inys has been out of the world for long enough, he's still running to catch up on the history. Wouldn't want to annoy him too much."

"She's free, she's perfectly free," the governor said. "We haven't detained her at all."

Marcus frowned. "All...right."

"She has always been one of the great citizens of Porte Oliva. We celebrate and support her. We always have."

"Sure she'll be pleased to know that."

They stood for a moment in silence. Marcus watched the governor's face as he went from distress to relief to a near-childlike shyness. "Do you...might I be introduced? To the dragon?"

"Probably best for the magistra to make those introductions," Marcus said. "I'm just captain of the guard. Wouldn't want to presume."

"No. No no no. Of course. That's fine. When the magistra sees fit, then."

"But if you could send word to her?"

The governor turned on his guards, lifting a glittering finger. "You heard Captain Wester. Send a runner to Magistra bel Sacrour. Now!"

The queensmen looked at one another for a moment, then one of them turned and started trotting back toward the city.

"Also, if you have any spare cattle," Marcus said, pointing back at Inys. The dragon had settled back on its haunches like a huge cat and was watching Sandr, Smit, and Charlit Soon sing and caper before it while Master Kit and Cary stood off a way, in council. "The rest of us could use a bit to eat too. Some bread, maybe. We've been eating meat and not much else since Antea."

"I will have a feast brought to you."

"And a perch. Inys was saying he'd want someplace in the city with a perch."

The governor's eyes lit up. "Of course. Of course. Men! To me!"

Marcus watched the queensmen and the governor retreat. Porte Oliva itself seemed to be watching from across the green like an uncertain boy at a dance. The great defensive wall of the city was barely visible, choked out by the dyers' yards and breweries and houses that had spilled out beyond it. Peacetime always meant people trading safety for space, and Porte Oliva had seen a long peace up to now. When the war came to the city, the people who'd made that exchange were going to regret it. Marcus shook his leg, and it only hurt a little. He turned back to where the dragon and the players sat in the sun and waited.

The group that came out was small, and he knew them by how they walked before they were close enough to see their faces. Cithrin in a deep blue blouse and skirt cut in the style of Elassae. Yardem in sparring leathers and rings in his ears.

Magistra Isadau in a pale blouse that set off the darkness of her scales. Pyk Usterhall in a plain brown robe, arms swinging belligerently at her sides. Cinnae, Timzinae, Tralgu, and Yemmu. With him there as a Firstblood, they had almost half the races of humanity, and one of the dragons who'd made them. Marcus levered himself back to his feet. The players followed behind him. Inys watched with a detached interest, as if this were just another performance put on for his benefit.

Cithrin looked older than she had in Suddapal. Her face was fuller, and while her Cinnae blood would never let her skin fall to a Firstblood brown, she was a little darker in the cheeks and around the eyes. Marcus felt a stab of sorrow he hadn't expected. When she'd gone to Carse, some lifetime ago, she'd been a girl playing at being a woman. He'd gone to Lyoneia to find the poisoned sword and the wild mountains beyond the Keshet to kill a goddess who couldn't be killed. He'd been to the cold wastes of Hallskar and flown on a dragon's foot halfway across the world. He'd seen her for a few short weeks in Elassae. It wasn't enough. She had only grown a fraction older, and yet she seemed more changed than he was. He wished he had been there to see it happen.

"Captain," she said, holding out her hands to him. The formality of the word was hard. *Magistra* floated at the back of his mouth.

"Cithrin," he said, taking her hands. "Sorry I've been gone. I was...anyway. I think we found what Palliako's men were searching for. And...ah..."

There were tears in her eyes. And then in his as well. "I knew you'd come back."

"I wanted to," he said around the lump in his throat. "I'm glad I could."

And then she was in his arms and he was in hers. A fear he had hardly known he carried uncoiled a little. She was all right. She was safe. The world hadn't broken her while he was gone, or if it had, not badly. And then the others were around them too, Cary and Kit and Smit and Hornet and Yardem's wide strong arms around them all. Marcus stood there until he felt it was time to let go again, then extricated himself from the affectionate pile while the players peppered Cithrin with questions and demands and stories. The two other bank women watched, Isadau with an air of indulgence, Pyk with a scowl. Inys, bored, looked away toward the clouds. Marcus stepped away, nodding to Yardem.

"What's our situation?" Marcus asked.

Yardem flicked his ear thoughtfully. "Complicated, sir. The Lord Regent was infatuated with Cithrin, and when she didn't return the feeling he took it poorly. Sent his ships to block the harbors. Likely has his army on the way."

"Huh," Marcus said. "You ever get the sense that man just wasn't spanked enough as a child?"

"I see it more as being rewarded for all the wrong things, sir, but I've never raised a boy."

"And you have raised a girl?"

"Younger sister, sir."

"Yardem, you are a man of endless surprises."

"Yes, sir. Turns out one of Palliako's exiles is an experienced sailor. He took over a ship, organized a small pirate fleet, and has been trying to make contact with the magistra. Now he's managed, the blockade's broken here, and we're in conversation about how to address Porte Silena and Sara-sur-Mar. Got us the commander of the Antean fleet in custody as well. Lord Skestinin. Governor has him in a private cell under heavy guard."

"Well, that's got to be a good thing."

"I think so, sir."

Marcus looked over at Cithrin and the players. Sandr and Hornet were pulling her toward Inys as if the dragon were a personal friend they couldn't wait to introduce. Marcus started walking toward the dragon too, Yardem falling in step behind him.

"Did the people associate Cithrin with the blockade?" Marcus asked.

"Yes, sir. We were expecting the queen to take her in custody. Trade her for peace."

Marcus nodded. That's what the governor had been talking about, then. Made sense. "Well, that'll be harder today than it was yesterday."

"It's good to have allies, sir."

"The general populace?"

"Vandalism. Some action against the bank. One conspiracy to assassinate her."

"How'd that last one go?"

"Took care of it without having to bother her."

"Did you tell her?"

"Didn't see reason to. She seemed busy."

"Good man."

"And you, sir?"

"Found a dragon."

"And the day you come back and take over the company?"

"That's today."

Yardem's wide, canine smile and low chuckle were his only reply.

As they approached, the dragon reared up, spread his wings, and folded them again. The tips flowed back behind the massive body like the drape of a formal dress. Without planning it, the people stood in a rough semicircle before Inys, like petitioners before a great king. Even Pyk Usterhall's head was bowed, and Marcus hadn't been entirely sure her neck bent that way. Inys looked at each of them in turn. Even having traveled as far as he had with the beast, even keeping his unease with the dragon in mind, Marcus felt a certain awe. The sense of being in the presence of something greater than the world; it was almost love. Certainly loyalty. The feeling of the sheepdog for the shepherd. It made his neck itch.

"You then," Inys said, considering Cithrin. "You are Cithrin. The one who leads the fight against the tainted ones?"

"I am," Cithrin said.

"This is as it should be," Inys said. "I am Inys. I have let the world die, to my shame. Your battle is the first step in my redemption. I will aid you. I know what the tainted are, and how they are to be defeated. I will tell you what I know, and together we will burn my brother's madness from this unending grave."

Cithrin looked up at the dragon's head, her expression solemn.

"Good," she said.

Being back in Porte Oliva was like waking from a long, uncomfortable dream. In the barracks, there were more familiar faces than he'd expected. Even with Pyk's punishing austerity and a season in Suddapal, Yardem had managed to keep most of the company together. He hadn't forgotten the puppeteers that set up it seemed at every fourth corner, performing for charity from the crowd or support from some local with a political agenda, but he hadn't precisely remembered them either. The streets were familiar, the smells of salt and coffee. The dogs that chased each other through traffic, startling horses and dodging between cart wheels with suicidal abandon. It was all familiar, except that it also wasn't.

Some of the changes were overt. The governor pardoned all the guests of the magistrate's justice and had a dragon-sized perch constructed in the square between his palace and the cathedral before nightfall. Magistra Isadau was there now too. But more than that, he remembered Porte Oliva as a place he had gnawed himself raw to leave. Before he had left, he'd been the guard captain of one of the most important companies in the city. In the kingdom, for that. He'd had the prospect of a lifetime's easy work and a comfortable retirement. Instead he'd tracked across three corners of the world. He'd been driven half mad by the jungles of Lyoneia, snuck into a temple filled with spider priests to kill a dark goddess, come near to freezing in a Hallskari ice storm, been whipped by incensed Haaverkin, strapped a venomous sword to his back, and woken the last dragon in the world. Whatever about Porte Oliva had oppressed him before was gone now. The taproom where he'd met a beautiful woman with whom he'd humiliated himself, the little room in the salt quarter where he and Yardem and Cithrin had been attacked, the places where—with the help of Master Kit and the players—they had forged the founding documents of the branch. All of it was comforting and welcoming and peaceful. He couldn't imagine now why he'd felt so chapped by it all before.

"It's because his soul is a circle," Yardem said.

"Oh fuck's sake, this again?" Marcus said, but with laughter in his voice.

"How's that?" Barriath Kalliam asked. He was younger than Marcus by a decade and a half. Maybe more. He wore his youth well, though, and he'd spent enough time at sea to have outgrown the boyish romance of violence. Sitting in the taproom nearest the company barracks, he might almost have been one of them. Marcus could imagine liking him.

"It's his nature that when he is at his lowest, he will inevitably rise. And also when he reaches the highest ground of his life, he'll fall." The Tralgu traced a circle in the air, as if showing something real. "My work is to...um..." Yardem shook his head, setting his earrings clattering. He was stupendously drunk. They all were.

"His job is to see to it that my inevitable fall doesn't wind up with me landing on anyone," Marcus said.

"More or less," Yardem agreed.

"I don't hold much with souls," Barriath said.

"Wise man," Marcus said and lifted his mug toward the keeper. She nodded and held up a finger. She'd seen him. She'd be there. That was good enough. "This Palliako. You've actually met him, then?"

"More than met him. Watched him slaughter my father."

"Ah. Sorry. Didn't know," Marcus said, though through the haze of alcohol, he suspected he had known that. At least in the abstract. "That's the sort of thing that will drive a man. Revenge. Only, between us? It's not as sweet as you think. It doesn't fix much."

"I'm willing to try it all the same."

"Wouldn't expect less," Marcus said. "What do you make of him?"

"He's...petty. Mostly that. He's a little, mean, petty man who found a gem and thinks it means God loves him."

"The gem being your empire?" Yardem asked.

Barriath stroked his beard, scowling. "Apparently so."

"He was an idiot to put you to exile," Marcus said. "If you've hurt a man that deep, better you finish him off. Otherwise, he'll be around forever, waiting for the chance to come even."

"My brothers are leading his army," Barriath said. "The Lord Marshal? My fucking baby brother. Working for Palliako. Can you believe that?"

"No," Marcus said. "Kill a man's father and then hand him your army? I can't imagine ever doing anything like that."

"Falling on a sword would seem faster," Yardem agreed. His eyelids were at half-mast. His smile wide and loose.

"And yet they've got their blades and arrows pointing toward here and not back at Camnipol," Barriath said. "I don't know how he manages it. After all he's done, I don't know how he convinces them to keep his side."

"I do," Marcus said. "I'll have Kit show you when he gets back. Only knowing won't help us when the army comes."

The keep came by, sweeping up Marcus's mug and putting a fresh one down before him. He hadn't actually had that much to drink, and he was already feeling a little swimmy. Either he'd been on the road entirely too long or carrying the poisoned sword against his back during the long flight south had affected him more than he'd realized.

"They were going to hand Cithrin to him in exchange for peace," Marcus said.

"Were going to try to," Yardem murmured.

"Now we've captured Lord Skestinin, and got a fleet and a dragon answering to her, that's going to be harder for them to accomplish," Barriath said raising his own drink in a toast. Marcus matched him, and they drank. Marcus put his mug down hard and closed his eyes. Enough. He'd had enough. He was done now. He took a deep breath and let it seep out through his nostrils.

"Well," he said, "I hope her majesty had time to work out a fallback plan."

Clara

The path through the mountains was not straight. The dragon's jade curved through forest-choked valleys and rose to cling to the sides of grey-faced mountains. The air here was thin, and the nights grew colder than the season suggested. The body of the army took the lead, and Clara's little caravan and a dozen others like it followed respectfully at a distance. If there were any travelers coming in the opposite direction, they postponed their journeys, for no one passed by them.

For seven days, Clara rode or, more often, sat her unmoving horse. Any delay in the column before her meant a dead stop, sometimes for hours, before moving slowly forward a mile or two and stopping again. She did not know the source of these delays, nor was there any way of discovering them. It was hers merely to wait and be patient. And, because it was her chosen task, to learn.

On the eighth day, the landscape broadened. Mountains still rose before them, but fewer. The valley in which they stopped spread wider. The army took up its camp along the road where there was soft ground to pitch tents on and trees to cut for wood. Clara's 'van stopped farther up, where the land was still stone and the wood harder to come by. As night fell, the dark, sweet smoke of green wood thickened the air, and cookfires filled the valley below her like stars. Clara took her little writing kit and drew a bit away from the camp. Spring was well on its way to summer, and the evening sun was slow to fade. She found a flat-topped boulder with no obvious animal nests beneath it, sat, drew the steel-tipped pen over the tarry little ink brick, and continued the already impressively long letter.

I had been aware that certain women would follow the army, doing work of a sexual nature for the benefit of the soldiers. I had not—though perhaps you had—been aware that this is only one of many trading relationships that follow in a host's wake. The army of Antea now marching is for the greatest part made of men who would otherwise be farming or plying trades in the towns and villages of Antea. They are far from home, possessed of little education, and rich with needs and desires beyond the merely sexual. The army includes a complement of scribes and couriers for the use of the highborn, but the caravans and low camps that trail include scribes and runners as well which the foot soldiers make use of for a price. The cunning men who wear the colors of the great houses are the only ones in this present valley, and more than healing, provide the service of fortune tellers, advisors, and even priests. Charms against death and illness can cost more here than they would in Camnipol. I am led to understand that there is often a trade in liquors and tobacco nearer the beginning of a campaign, though any such supplies have long been exhausted here.

It occurs to me that this unofficial and unrecognized support of the men is both significant and vulnerable.

"Lady," Vincen said. Clara looked up, putting her hand over the letter. But he was alone. The light was fading quickly now, and she doubted she would be able to return to her report before morning. It wasn't the sort of thing one wrote about the campfire where anyone might see it.

"Vincen, my dear."

"It's time to come back to the 'van."

"Ah. Supper already."

"No, ma'am. We're breaking camp."

Clara blew across the fresh ink to cure it, frowning as she did so. The fires dotting the valley below were steady. What little movement she saw had no urgency. Vincen followed her gaze and her thought.

"The 'van master's been keeping watch. There have been twice as many scouting parties sent out and come back as usual. Last pass into the plains is half a day west of here. Thinking is that the locals will try to block us there."

"And we're pulling up stakes to go ahead?"

"Back, ma'am. The 'van master prefers we be a day's ride behind when the fighting starts. Things go poorly, there can be some scatter."

"Ah, I understand," she said. Her knees protested when she stood. There had been a time, and it seemed not long ago, when riding all day and sleeping under the stars would have made her body stronger rather than just more pained. "But no."

"I thought not," he said. "We'll be staying for the battle."

"Well, I don't see wading into it with a knife, but I've come here to see the war. This is it. I can't imagine turning back now."

"There's the question of safety."

"Safety would have been Camnipol. Or else nowhere."

She started down the slope back toward the road. The stones grated under her feet, pebbles skittering ahead. Now that she knew to look, the 'van master was hitching his team to the carts. Likely he wouldn't make much distance before it got so dark he had to stop again, and yet he'd make the effort. Fear of a night attack, then. Clara wondered how realistic that was. It seemed more likely to her that the forces of Birancour would wait for late afternoon when the sun would be in Jorey's eyes.

Jorey.

It was easy to see the fires in the valley as the long arm of Geder Palliako. Perhaps she'd trained herself to look away from the fact that her sons were there too. The scouts that the 'van master had been watching had been going to and from Jorey's tent. If the 'van master's assessment was correct, he would be riding into battle the next day. In two days at the most. The Lord Marshal would be behind the main lines, keeping an eye on the battle, issuing orders, and so would be the least likely to fall in the melee. Still she could not help feeling anxious when she thought of him.

Part of her wanted to see Geder's power reach its turning point, for his reach to go as far as it would extend and begin instead to fall back. That it meant Jorey's battle lost and his army defeated complicated the feeling. She ached with fear and hope and dread, and couldn't put a simple name to any of them. All that was left was to hope that nothing broke her heart again before tomorrow ended.

"There are others staying too," Vincen said, his voice tentative.

"Vultures?" she asked, forcing her tone to be light.

"Well, and some cunning men to help with the wounded. But mostly body-pickers, yes."

"Ah, my dear," she said, tucking her arm in his, "what unexpected company we do keep."

Clara managed to wheedle two days' rations from the caravan master before he left. Salted pork, hardtack, and a bowl of beans with a crust all along the edge. There was room enough to set up their little hunter's tent, and she was sufficiently tired that to her astonishment, she slept. Dawn had broken when she woke and crawled out from under the low tent to find Vincen sitting on a stone with a spyglass in his hands. A haze of smoke greyed the air that the valley cupped, the stale remnants of yesterday's cookfires. No new fires burned.

"What's happening?" Clara asked, dreading the answer.

"Birancour's come," he said, pointing. "You can see the banners between those two hills. The queen's colors."

"And Jorey?"

"No," he said. "Vicarian's the one that went out to meet them."

"How long ago?"

"An hour."

She sat at his side and plucked the spyglass from his lap. "I wish I knew what they were saying."

"Something along the lines of *You can't come in* and *Oh yes we can*, I'd imagine."

"I believe it's a bit more complex than that," she said, putting the bronze tube to her eyes.

A white table stood in the field beyond the army, a flag of parley flying above it. Three men sat at it, so distant that even the spyglass couldn't show their faces. One wore the brown robes of the spider priests. That was Vicarian, then. Knowing that, she could see something familiar in the way he held himself. The others were in dark cloth embroidered with silver or else some light mail. She couldn't tell. The thing that had been her son raised his hands and shook his head. For a moment, she was back in Camnipol, in the little bed she and Dawson had shared, listening to the haranguing shouts of the high priest in the street. *You cannot win. Everything you love is already lost. Everything you care about is gone. Listen to my voice, you cannot win.* The morning was warm, but she shuddered.

The forces of Antea stood in ranks. Swords and pikes and bows were in their hands. At the head of each rank the banner of one of the great houses of Antea: Broot, Faskellan, Ischian. Marshallin and Hoit were there as well, though they were the court of Asterilhold. Or had been, before their kingdom fell. But then, those who had passed through Geder Palliako's private court were among the trusted.

If they had turned, if she'd seen their faces, she could have named each of them. She'd eaten at their tables, and they at hers. She'd traded gossip with their wives and mothers and daughters. They didn't turn back. But along each rank, another figure strode, walking up and down, gesturing at the men as they stood at attention. More priests. More men like Basrahip. Like Vicarian. Their faces were turned toward her, and she saw joy in them. Wide smiles, open arms. She watched them touch the shoulders and arms of the men. *You cannot lose. The goddess is with you, and nothing can stand against her. She will protect you.* She could even make out some of the words on their lips. *Protect* and *cannot* were particularly easy to recognize.

Something happened. She saw the men start. Not move, not yet, but suddenly sharpen. She moved the glass back, and the parley table had been overturned. Vicarian was on his feet now, shouting at the emissaries of Birancour. His fist was raised, and the other men were stepping back in dismay. The thing that had been her son turned dramatically and stalked back toward the Antean ranks. Jorey, in good mail on a white charger, trotted forward. For a moment, the two brothers spoke. Clara thought she saw Jorey's shoulders sag, but it might only have been her imagination.

Jorey's head turned. The rising tones that called the attack rang through the valley. Clara's throat felt like she was choking on a plum pit. On the field, the soldiers shifted into their positions.

"No need to watch this," Vincen said, putting his hand on her shoulder.

"These are my men. As much as the deserters were, these are mine. I won't disrespect them."

"Yes, ma'am," Vincen said.

The forces of Birancour poured into the valley. She couldn't think what Vicarian might have said that convinced them to charge into the morning sun, but they came nonetheless. Jorey's men fell back, not in a rout, but with the discipline of practice and plan. Wings of archers swung to the fore, loosing their shafts and falling back. Birancouri cavalry came in answer, but now the priests stood in among the soldiers. They had speaking horns to their mouths, and even at distance, Clara could hear the muddle of voices. The attacking cavalry hesitated, and with every hesitation, a few more arrows fell among them. Clara wanted them to charge. She wanted them to fall back. She wanted the men of Antea and Birancour to join together and cut the priests down where they stood. She wanted her sons back.

With a rush, the cavalry of Birancour came. Their banners floated in the breeze of their passage. Foot soldiers followed, the sun glittering off bared blades. And now the men of Antea—exhausted from months of travel and battle— surged forward to meet them. She put down the spyglass.

She would not turn away, but neither did she wish to gawk as men she could not save died.

The banners moved amid the chaos, the colors of Birancour spreading wide and then falling together. The screams of men and horses filled the world like the roar of surf, like a windstorm. The breeze shifted, and brought a smell unlike anything she had ever imagined. She sat utterly still, as if frozen. Vincen took her hand in his, and she squeezed his fingers to assure him that she was still there.

The first of the green-and-gold banners fell. The roar changed. The banners moved forward, toward the mouth of the pass and the fields of Birancour. The rout began, and the soldiers of Antea rushed after their fleeing foes, slaughtering. All banners but one, and it carried her own colors. She lifted the spyglass.

Jorey sat his charger, reins in his hands. His face was little more than a flesh-colored smudge, but he did not ride forward with his men. He watched as she did. And saw, perhaps, what she saw. It was well after midday before it ended. The Antean soldiers didn't come back, but a trickle of servants did, come to collect tents and carts and move them forward, she assumed, into the conquered army's camp. All around the bowl of the valley, the body-pickers and vultures began to inch forward, keeping wary eyes out for patrols of soldiers from either side. She stood and began walking down, one foot resolutely in front of the next. Vincen had to trot to catch up to her.

"My lady, please."

"My people, Vincen. My people, my choices. Mine."

The first body she came to was long dead, face and throat cut in a single blow. The next wasn't so fortunate. He still lived and struggled, though there was no reason in his eyes.

She poured a bit of water in his mouth, and she thought he tried to drink it, but she couldn't be sure. When he went still, she moved on. The ground was churned to mud. Men and horses lay under the sun, dead and dying. Cunning men and vultures crossed the field, giving what they could. Taking what they could. A patrol of Jorey's men arrived and began hauling away the injured of Antea. Only of Antea. The enemy were left to die.

The patrol took no notice of her or the others, and she had little care for them. Birancouri and Antean alike, she did what she could to ease the injured or dying, to help them. She bound wounds where she could, gave ease where there was ease to be given. She took nothing from the bodies of the dead. She had from them already what she needed.

"You should eat," Vincen said.

"I will."

"You keep saying that."

"It keeps being true. I will."

The evening had come. She and Vincen had made their way back to their little camp, their little tents. Somewhere far ahead, a bonfire was blazing, dark smoke rising into the indigo sky. A victory celebration. Her kingdom's victory. Her son's.

Her boots and the hem of her skirt were heavy with drying mud. Vincen held out a bit of salt pork he'd been boiling over their little fire, and she took it, bit off an end, and chewed slowly. She was aware that it tasted much better than it should have. Either she was desperately hungry or any sensation that proved her still alive had become precious. Perhaps both.

"Are you all right?" he asked.

"I will be."

"You're sure of that?"

"I am."

He lapsed back into silence. The stars came out, scattered across the sky like a snowstorm. Clara drew her writing kit out, dropped another knot on the fire, and turned her back to it so that the light fell on the page and didn't blind her. She took the pen in her hand, paused, and put it back. If ever in her life it had been time for a good pipe, the time was now. She packed the little clay bowl with leaf, lit it with a burning twig, and took the pen out again. She drew it across the ink brick, let the nib hover for a moment over the page. There had been some other thought she'd had before, some strategy for undermining Geder's army. It was no longer foremost in her mind. She let it go.

Today I stood witness as the forces of Antea won their first battle against the defenders of Birancour. I presume, though I do not know, that we will turn south tomorrow for Porte Oliva. I hope to find a courier whom I may send north to Carse, and so to you. I will post to you what information I can in hopes that it will be of use in bringing this ongoing tragedy to an end.

It is important, as we consider our present conflict, that we understand it for what it is. The war now being fought is not with the people of Imperial Antea. Nor is it against the citizens of Birancour. These are the weapons that greater forces use against each other. Put two boys to fighting each other with sticks, and the boys may come away well or poorly, but the sticks will always be shattered. The enemy is within Antea, it has bored to the center of the empire, but it is not the farmers or the bakers or the beggars in the streets of Camnipol, nor even the court itself. This war is not fought against Birancour or the Timzinae or your colleague who has earned the Lord Regent's particular wrath.

A cult of death has taken root in my kingdom, Geder Palliako at its center. And our present struggle is not how to defeat Antea, but how we may best rip out this weed and burn it before all that was once noble there is lost.

Geder

Geder woke on a low divan, his head aching. He had a knot low in his back from sitting too long without moving, and his shirt felt oily against his skin. He rose, stretched, looked out the window. In the north, the light of the rising sun was working its way down the Kingspire. The red banner of the goddess hanging from the temple at its height glowed like a fire. The rooms Lady Skestinin's house master had given him were the best in the mansion. The bed was large, the mattress soft. Geder's servants from the Kingspire had brought him his bedclothes. He couldn't face the idea of sleep. Of rest. It had no place for him.

Neither did the rising flood of reports and letters, demands and imprecations that were the Lord Regent's problem. Today, and for the past week, he had not been the Lord Regent. He'd been Jorey's freind. And Sabiha's. There was nothing he could do here. He wasn't a midwife or a cunning man. All he could do, he'd done. All that was left was to be present. The empire wouldn't fall just because he took his eyes off it for a few days.

Sabiha and the baby had had a rough week of it. The cunning men worked in groups, each taking turn over Sabiha's distended belly. Some times were better, and Sabiha was able to sleep or eat, make little jokes through gritted teeth or hold Lady Skestinin's hand as the older woman wept. Some times were worse, and Sabiha's cries sounded like she was being beaten. The sunlight came down the great tower and flooded the city. Geder tugged at his shirt and ran his fingers through his hair. His chin needed shaving, and he was hungry. But later. That was all for later.

His guard waited outside the room, and Geder gestured that if they had to follow, they should at least follow quietly. The main stair was carved marble, and the echoes of their footsteps seemed thunderous to Geder. He heard the scuttle of servants in the passageway, fleeing before him like rats before a fire, and he strained his ears for the sound of Sabiha's cries. He heard nothing, and a weary kind of relief passed through him. Today might be a good one after all. But the nearer he drew to her rooms, the more the silence followed him. There were no voices of servants. No clanking of dishes or closings of doors. Geder plucked at his sleeve, pinching cloth between thumb and forefinger. His heart rose to his throat. The constant murmur of cunning men easing mother and child was also gone. The quiet was terrible.

At the door to her chamber, he lifted his hand, afraid to go on and afraid not to. It swung open under the lightest pressure.

Sabiha lay on the bed where she'd been since the day Geder had come to see her. No cunning man stood over her, and she was curled on her side, knees draw in. Her eyes were closed, and so dark that the lids seemed blue. Her breath was deep and slow, and her hair clung to her forehead and neck like ivy against a wall. Beyond her, at the window, Lady Skestinin sat in a straight-backed chair, looking out at the garden. One of Geder's cunning men—the Kurtadam with the greying fur—stood at her side. In her lap was a bundle of soft cloth. It was perfectly still. Geder put a hand up behind him, ordering his guards to stay back. He walked forward with the sense of being in a nightmare. His gaze was fixed on the little bundle. The baby. Her skin was wrinkled and yellow where it wasn't an angry pink. Tiny stumps of hands curled against her chest. Geder felt himself start to tremble.

"What happened?" he asked. "What went wrong?"

"Nothing," the Kurtadam said softly. "They all look like this at first."

"They...they do?"

"She only needs a bit of sunlight to clear the jaundice away," Lady Skestinin said in a gentle voice. "Her mother was just the same, wasn't she? Wasn't she, love?"

The baby's eyes opened. Colorless grey and amazed. The tiny arms flailed in and out, and the vague unfocused gaze passed by Geder. Through him. The horror in his breast cracked, gave way, and an oceanic sense of relief flowed through him. The Kurtadam put a hand on his shoulder, smiling benignly.

"Give the child a bit of time and a bit more milk. She's strong, only very new. The birth was less than an hour ago."

"I didn't know," Geder said.

"I didn't imagine you'd want to watch," Lady Skestinin said.

"You were right," Geder said. "Very right. I was only... Oh God. She's all right. And Sabiha?"

"Resting," the cunning man said. "The baby must nurse, and the mother must rest. The danger has passed, though. So much as it ever does."

Geder reached down to the baby, thinking she might perhaps reach up and grab his finger with her own. Her tiny mouth opened and closed, and she made a small mewling sound. Behind them, Sabiha stirred.

"Where is she?"

"Here, daughter," Lady Skestinin said. "She's right here."

"Bring her to me."

"My lord, perhaps..." the cunning man said.

"One moment," Geder said as Sabiha took her new daughter into her arms. The woman looked so tired and so pleased. *I did this*, Geder thought. *I brought the cunning men. I made them care that they both lived. This moment is because of me*. The tears in his eyes felt like pride. Sabiha tugged at the neck of her gown, preparing to bare her breast to the child. "Yes. All right. We should go."

In the corridor, a Tralgu servant waited, her ears folded back against her skull in distress. "Lord Regent? There's... there's a man asking for you. Baron Watermarch?"

Geder patted her arm reassuringly. "It's fine. I told Lord Daskellin he could find me here if he needed me. It's not a problem. Nothing's a problem."

The servant bobbed her head. "Then, if you'll... This way, my lord."

Canl Daskellin sat in the withdrawing room, a cup of strong coffee in his hand. He wore a black leather traveling cloak of generous cut. It was a style Geder had started back when he'd returned as a hero from Vanai, and it suited Daskellin better than it did him. The baron looked older than Geder usually thought of him. Flecks of white dotted his temples and the stubble of beard like ice on dark water, and his smile was weary.

"Lord Regent," he said, rising to his feet.

"Sit, sit, sit. No need to get up. It's only us here, after all."

Daskellin smiled, but it seemed halfhearted. "As you say, my lord."

"So you've met with your counterparts from North-coast?" Geder asked, sitting on a divan. He felt tired and relaxed. He'd known Sabiha's situation had made him anxious, but he hadn't known how much so until now. His body felt like he was being lowered into a warm and soothing bath.

"Unofficially, of course. But—"

"Are they standing back? They aren't going to interfere in Birancour, are they?"

"There are no immediate plans to," Daskellin said. "But they are paying a great deal of attention."

"You explained that we aren't upset with the crown there, only that the conspiracy has its roots in Porte Oliva?"

"At the Medean bank in Porte Oliva. And since the bank's holding company is in Carse, King Tracian is feeling it might come closer to him than he'd like. He's only the second generation on the throne there, and there are people even in Camnipol who still talk about his mother as an usurper. Threats to the stability of his kingdom strike him hard. But that isn't what brought me this morning. There's news of the war."

"Oh," Geder said, sitting up a little straighter. He was suddenly very aware of being in another man's house, unbathed, unshaved, and poorly slept. He wiped his palms against his thighs. "Then, yes. All right. We should go to the Kingspire. Find Aster and Basrahip. Whatever needs to be looked at—"

"Actually, my lord, it may be best that we're here. The news isn't only for you."

Geder's worst fears—that the army had collapsed or that Jorey had been hurt or killed—were so vivid that when it came out that the blockade had been broken by a rogue fleet and Lord Skestinin taken hostage by the governor of

Porte Oliva, it was almost a relief. Lady Skestinin received the news with less calm. Her countenance, so recently softened by the arrival of her new granddaughter, went grey and craggy as a cliff face. She gripped her hands so tightly Geder expected to hear her bones creak. When she spoke, her voice was tight and controlled. Had there been ransom demands? No, there had not. Was there reason to think his lordship still lived? There was no certain information one way or the other, but the governor of Porte Olive had a reputation as a cautious and shrewd fellow, more in love with the world's luxuries than the glory of battle. The expectation was that Lord Skestinin would be held as a bargaining point when the time came to sue for peace. How would the capture of the commander of the fleet affect the campaign on land? It was only when Daskellin lifted his brows that Geder realized this last was something only he could answer.

"Ah...yes, well," he said, twisting his index finger with his off hand. "We can't let the enemy see us as weak. I mean, can we? It wouldn't be good or prudent. And with Jorey already in enemy territory, and the dragons, and I just...I mean, I don't know. I don't see how..."

"I understand," Lady Skestinin said, to Geder's surprise. The deeper he'd been into the answer, the less he'd felt he knew what he was getting at. Her hard eyes were on him, and then perhaps he did understand. He had just told her that he would not stop the war to save her husband's life. If he had to be sacrificed, he would be. Geder wanted to take that back, to assure her that he wouldn't let anything happen to her family.

Except that wasn't true.

"I will do what I can," Geder said, aware as he did how weak and equivocal he sounded.

"Use your best judgment, Lord Regent," Lady Skestinin said. "Please excuse me."

She sailed from the room, her spine straight as a mast. Geder blew his breath out. Daskellin nodded sympathetically.

"Hard day," he said. "She's added one to her family, and lost another."

"Not yet," Geder said. "Nothing's lost yet."

"I hope that you're right, my lord," Daskellin said, but he didn't sound convinced. In truth, neither was Geder.

Stepping back from his duties as the protector of the Severed Throne, even for just the time it had taken to resolve Sabiha's illness, meant a massive wave of tasks awaited him. There were invitations to a dozen different events, some given merely for the sake of form, but others that he was expected to attend. Petitions waited for him, and arrangements that needed to be made before the general audience. Reports had come from Dar Cinlama in the back roads of Hallskar and young Sir Essian from the north coast of Lyoneia outlining the progress of their explorations. Letters asking for direction and advice had arrived from the protectors of Nus and Asinport, reminding him of what he'd known since Vanai: taking a city was often simpler than managing it after. And Jorey's reports on the army's progress. And the analysis of the assaults inspired by the shadowy enemy Callon Cane and his system of bounties and rewards for attacking Antea. And arrangements to be made for Aster's birthday celebrations—there would be several. And his own father's notes from Rivenhalm about the small doings at what the old man still called Geder's home.

Geder sat at a large table, the papers that had accrued while he was worrying over Sabiha arrayed before him like an inedible feast. Polished stones kept the breeze from the narrow windows from disarranging things. He sat with his head in his hands and wondered what would happen if he accidentally lit the whole lot of them afire. The idea of starting again with a cleaned slate was powerfully attractive. But...

"May I get you some tea, Lord Regent?"

"Yes," Geder said, picking up the first of the reports. "And some food to go with it. Something sweet, with butter."

"Yes, my lord," the servant said and bowed his way out of the room.

Fallon Broot, his protector in Suddapal, was seeing a rash of suspicious fires in the fivefold city. He had sent out patrols with a spider priest assigned to each of them, but thus far hadn't discovered the arsonists. There was at least one incident when an arrow had struck the street near enough that it seemed the attackers were aiming for the priests. Ernst Mecelli, one of Geder's closest advisors along with Canl Daskellin and Cyr Emming, had paused in his review of the previous year's conquests, stopping in Inentai. He didn't say anything directly, but Geder had the sense he was worried that the temple being built there might not have enough common soldiery to support it. It probably would have been a meaningful concern if the temple hadn't also been under the protection of the goddess. But Mecelli didn't have as much inside knowledge as Geder did.

The tea and sweet cakes arrived while Geder was paging through a lengthy report from Essian about the various household rumors among the Southlings of Lyoneia. Maps of ancient treasure were apparently something of an industry down there, but the adventurer—with the help, of course, of the spider priest who had accompanied him—had discovered the name of some sort of holy woman among the Drowned who lived off the eastern coast, and he was now trying to arrange an audience with her. Sir Ammen Cersillian, presently in charge of the siege at Kiaria, reported little change. The Timzinae forces showed no signs of capitulation, and even the greatest speaking trumpets seemed unable to carry the voices of the priesthood to them. It was a pity, because the convincing gifts of the goddess were so much more efficient than those of troops. With the body of the army in Birancour, an outright assault on the Timzinae stronghold would have to wait. Keeping the enemies of Antea contained would be enough for now, Geder thought. He paused to eat his cakes before the tea went cool.

When Basrahip lumbered in, Geder felt a profound relief. Something to distract him from the papers. And he'd only barely started with them. It was going to take days just to catch up. An hour or two of friendly conversation with the priest wouldn't cost him much.

"Basrahip! Good to see you."

"My thanks, Prince Geder," the massive priest said, bowing his head.

"Things went very well at Lord Skestinin's. With Sabiha, I mean. It was all a bit dour once the news came about his lordship's being captured. But I think he's likely going to be kept safe, don't you?"

Basrahip pulled a chair out from the table and sat in it, his fingers laced together on the table. Geder was so used to seeing calm, amusement, and certainty. Now the man's wide face could have been an allegorical painting of sorrow. "I cannot say, Prince Geder. I have heard no voices. Though if you bring them here, I shall—"

"No, no, no. It's all right. Jorey's on his way to Porte

Oliva. He'll find a way. What's...Is there something the matter?"

"I fear, my prince, that I must leave you for a time."

Geder's chest ached suddenly, and the coppery taste of fear flooded his mouth. "You're *going*? You're leaving me here, but I need you. Without you—"

Basrahip raised his hand in gesture equal parts reassurance and a command of silence. "You will not be abandoned. Neither by the goddess nor me. I will have another take my place at your side. You will be well. Listen to my voice, and know this to be true. You will be well. She will not abandon you."

Geder felt his fear grow a degree lower. It did not vanish. "What's happened? Is there something I can do to help?"

"A darkness has risen in the temple at Kaltfel. We will bring the light to it. The goddess is perfect, as you know. Most of those who fight against us do so because they are creatures of lies, and they flee from her truth because they fear what they will become within her. Once they know her, those battles can be seen as the birth pangs of her coming world. Nothing more."

"I don't know," Geder said. "I've just had my first real experience with birth pangs, and they're more violent than I'd thought." He was babbling. He made himself be quiet. If Basrahip noticed his discomfort, the priest didn't mention it.

"We who feel her within our blood are made pure. But sometimes—once, perhaps, in a generation—a man who has seen her light *chooses* darkness. Knowing what she is, and feeling her power within him, he turns away of his own will. There is no evil more dangerous than this. There can be no mercy for him. One such has arisen in the temple at Kaltfel."

"What? You mean someone with the gift of the goddess, but—"

"But is spreading lies like poison in a well. A man I have known since I was a boy, who lived with me in the first temples, has become one such. He has fled into the swamps, and I, as Basrahip, must take the sacred blades with which we will hunt this new apostate."

"Do you need soldiers? Should I be worried about this?"

"It has happened before, Prince Geder, and the goddess has survived. This has all happened before."

Cithrin

Inys perched on the body of a felled tree that had been lifted between two great stone blocks. Claw marks left bright, pale lines where the bark had been stripped away, and a wide smear of blood on the pavement marked where a young bull had died that morning to satisfy the dragon's hunger. Flies hovered and buzzed, drinking from the stain. Cithrin sat at a small writing desk, her pen in her hand, a length of parchment spread out before her already half covered with notes and comments. The clouds above them were white and rounded as cotton from the boll, and the heat of early summer thickened the air.

"When the enemy was killed," Inys said, his voice low and somber, "the soldier fell, but the instruments of its blood would carry on the attack. A single tainted soldier would die, and its death could drive half a dozen others mad. My brother's spiders could gain entry through the eyes, the mouth. Other ways. Any entry where the skin was thin enough to burrow down to blood. Even the scales of the Jasuru were no protection. They would climb under the scales themselves and dig down at their roots. The soldiers were then transformed, but their brothers and sisters who still loved them could often not bring themselves to kill the newly tainted. They seemed, after all, the men and women they had been before. They loved the same, spoke the same, thought the same. Were the same, truly, except they had been poisoned, and spread whatever false certainties they carried to all those around them. I recall one battle where Erex's slaves utterly destroyed my brother's little force, only to fall on each other in rage a month later."

"And the Timzinae?"

"I fastened the scales into their skins. I built closures within them so finely wrought that their enemy's blood could not touch theirs. I armed them with swords made to shrivel the spiders and poison the blood. Even above the Yemmu or Haunadam, they were the greatest warriors of the age. Not because they were stronger or better able to withstand violence, but because all other races were vulnerable, and they were not."

Cithrin wrote it all down like a child before her tutor, her mind folding in every detail. She paused, tapping the butt of her pen against her teeth.

"But the way they can demoralize an army," she said, "with speaking trumpets, for instance. The Timzinae are just as vulnerable to being convinced by their voices, aren't they?"

"Yes, yes," the dragon said, reaching out its foreclaw and pinching at the air as if demonstrating something. "You deafen them first. A little poke in each ear, and pack them with ashes. They heal enough to fight within a month, and the scars keep the spiders clear."

"Couldn't you just pour wax in there?" Cithrin asked.

The dragon shook its head. It was a weirdly familiar gesture seen on something so large. "Such plugs can fall out in the middle of a battle. Digging out the ears means there are no errors. It is a much better strategy."

"But after the war, they're still deafened for life."

"After the war, they have served their purpose," Inys said, unfolding his wings casually.

Cithrin wrote it down, but made a note of her own to look into reliable ways to stop up people's ears. "Once they were deafened, how could someone command them in battle? A system of banners?"

"Ah, that was the genius of the Stormcrow. Commands were given by launching flames of differing color into the enemy lines. The generals remained at the rear of the force, loading their catapults with balls of resin with impurities that let them burn green or yellow or blue. When the sky above the battle changed color, the soldiers had their orders."

"I've never heard of anything like that," she said, "but I'll see what I can find."

For the better part of the morning, Cithrin listened and recorded. Some days, Inys barely responded to her questions. Others, the dragon would go on for hours about some small point in the battle against his long-dead brother that Cithrin could see no applications for. And other times, times like today, he would outline some history that left her believing the war might be ended by winter.

She had known in general terms that she'd been ridden by anxiety and fear, but she hadn't let herself actually feel it. She saw it in how poorly she slept, how angry she became with Pyk, how deeply she wept at the puppet shows she watched in the evenings. She felt she was still coming to know herself, the way she might learn about a new friend. But the coming of Marcus Wester and Inys with Master Kit and Cary and the players coupled with the unexpected lifting of the blockade left her drunk with relief. That more than anything else told her how frightened she had been before.

Near midday, Inys sighed once, spread his wings, and leaped into the sky without so much as a polite farewell. Cithrin watched until she was sure the dragon wasn't coming back right away, then stood. The bowl of fish and rice she'd eaten at dawn had long since left her belly, and she was pleased that the dragon had taken flight. She made it a point not to be the one who ended their interviews. Too much depended on Inys remaining her ally to risk offending him.

A Firstblood man from her guards—Corisen Mout—came from under the shade of the cathedral's eaves and lifted the little desk onto his back. Cithrin rolled the parchment into her fist and headed back first for the café and then the counting house and her room. All along the way, the street traffic slowed around her. Kurtadam, Timzinae, Firstblood, and Cinnae all nodded to her or glanced nervously away. Even those who pretended to ignore her were so pointed in their efforts that they might as well have stared. Between Barriath Kalliam's small pirate fleet and the arrival of Inys, the city had gone almost overnight from seeing her as the goat that led home the wolves to the savior of the city. Even the governor, whose dictates carried the force of law, was second to Cithrin bel Sarcour, voice of the Medean bank. No more stones came through Maestro Asanpur's window. No one scowled at her in the taprooms. She was fairly certain that no one had been spitting in her beer. Her mornings, she spent with the dragon. Her afternoons, with the bank.

In the café, Marcus Wester and Barriath Kalliam were sitting at a table in the back. Marcus was still thinned by his travels, his cheeks sunken and the skin of his forehead tight across the bone. He looked even older now than he had in Suddapal. Some of that was the burden of carrying the poisoned sword, but some was also time. And what he'd lost from picking up the sword, he might not get back when he put it down. The unease she felt with the thought was how she imagined it would be to have a father and realize he was growing old.

The day's heat meant that even with the windows open, the air inside felt close. Most of Maestro Asanpur's customers were sitting outside at the little tables with awnings above them for shade. By putting up with the warmth, Wester and Kalliam had the main room essentially to themselves. Only Asanpur also braved the heat.

"Coffee, Magistra?"

"And if you have any food," Cithrin said.

The old Cinnae blinked his blind eye, grinned, and walked to the back as Cithrin sat at the head of the table. Wester nodded to her, but didn't break the thread of his conversation.

"Even if we did, what would it show? He's as likely to turn against us as them, isn't he?"

"I don't know," Barriath said. "Now that you put it that way."

"Put what which way?" Cithrin asked.

"We're discussing whether to introduce Lord Skestinin to Kit," Marcus said. "Pull back the gambler's mat and show him how the pea finds its way to the shell."

"I served under Lord Skestinin for years," Barriath said. "He's a good man. Competent. Smart. He has no more reason to love the priests or Palliako than I do."

"My point being that if we show him how Camnipol's under the thumb of magic that bends minds and controls people by trotting out that we've got the same thing here, it's not a guarantee that he'll see us as precisely trustworthy and free. If he decides we're all Master Kit's puppets, we won't be ahead of where we are now."

"But your one can convince him," Barriath said.

"And Geder's can convince him right back," Marcus said.

"There's no reason to keep the truth from him," Cithrin said. "But we can't let him go."

Barriath leaned forward, his fingertips pressing into the surface of the table. "If we could bring him to our side of this. Put him back on his ships, get him his sailors, aim him back toward Antea, it would undermine Palliako like nothing else."

Maestro Asanpur stepped back into the room with a cup of coffee in one hand and a plate of cheese and dried apples in the other. He put them in front of Cithrin with a smile. The salt and cream of the cheese and the sweetness of the apples was better than a feast.

"Or he might be on our side from here to Northcoast and then change his mind and come sink every ship you've got," Marcus said. The younger man scowled, but Marcus pressed on. "Unless we're willing to send Kit to go on murmuring in the man's ear every morning, we can't be sure what he'll do, and I don't know about the two of you, but I'm not willing to use him that way."

"If he would even agree to it," Cithrin said and sipped her coffee. "He's been reluctant to use his powers in the past."

"Well," Marcus said, "he'll have to get over that when Palliako's land forces arrive. If we get a dozen priests with speaking trumpets howling that we might as well give up, he'll be needed behind the wall convincing us it's not true."

"Are we sure they're coming here?" Barriath said. "The queen's in Sara-sur-Mar."

"This isn't about the queen," Cithrin said. "It's about me."

For a long moment, all three of them were silent. She could see that neither of them wanted to agree with her, but they couldn't bring themselves to deny what they all knew was true. She popped another bit of dried apple into her mouth.

"I suppose we can ask Kit to do his cunning man's show in the prison," Marcus said. "Assuming the governor's willing."

"He will be if I ask him," Cithrin said.

"Do you think he has a command from the queen to take you into custody yet?"

"I imagine he had it before either of you arrived," Cithrin said. "Having and acting upon are two different things."

Before she went back to the counting house, she stopped in her rented room in the rear of the café. In the time since Barriath and Inys had arrived, the back payments due to the bank had—mysteriously or perhaps not—started to come in a flood. Coin was flowing into her coffers, but not only from that. People had begun buying letters of exchange. The sea lanes were open now, and the tradesmen and wealthy classes of Porte Oliva knew that war was coming. Spice and tobacco, gold and jewelry had begun to make their way to Pyk's table, and sealed and ciphered letters handed back across. They would be redeemed at some other branch of the bank—most likely Stollbourne or Carse—at a percentage of their original worth. It was a pattern Cithrin had seen before, a sign of fear and of the coming war. This time, it carried no anxiety for her. The knot in her belly was as lax as it had ever been. Not gone. Never gone. But at its ebb.

When she stepped into the counting house, Pyk and Magistra Isadau were laughing with each other. If the café had been warm, the counting house sweltered. Wide, dark parches of sweat marked Pyk's armpits and the space under her breasts, but she didn't seem put out. Isadau sat by the little window and waved her greeting to Cithrin as Yardem closed the door behind her.

"Back from your little squat at the Lizard Emperor's feet?" Pyk asked, but her words didn't have even their usual bite. "What wisdom for the ages did the great bastard lay out before you today?"

"He suggested we poke out all our soldiers' ears before

they go on the field," Cithrin said. "Keep them from losing their fighting spirit."

"That seems a bit extreme," Isadau said. Her voice was light, but Cithrin could still hear the strain in it. She wished she could share her relief and calm with Isadau. But perhaps with time it would come.

"Any price is cheap when you don't value the coin," Pyk said. "That dragon's impressive, and no doubt. But the way I see it, he'd trade us all for another of his own kind. But give him this. He's good for business."

Cithrin leaned against the wall and lifted her brows. Isadau's grin brought out one of her own. "More people, then?"

Pyk waved her hands at the table. "Suddenly half the city's falling all over itself to place deposits with us. Everyone that's leaving wants letters of exchange. Everyone who's staying wants to buy their way into our good graces."

"Are we too heavy with coin?"

"Hell yes," Pyk said. "And we'll stay that way until this gets resolved. I'm not making any loans to people outside the city wall, and that's half the businesses there are. Once Palliako's army's shown up and been driven off, we can see who needs help rebuilding. Buys us goodwill from the locals, and opens up the chance to get into some solid partnerships."

"And the queen?"

Pyk shrugged. "Noble blood's always disappointed when we tell them to screw off. Can't see this will be any different. Since it's you and your pet lizard driving Antea back to its huts, I can't see that she'll have much room to complain, though. And if there's a way to stay on Inys's good side once the war's done, well, even better."

Once the war's done. There was a phrase. So much of her

life had been tied to Antea and to violence even before the cult of the spider goddess had come that the thought of *after* seemed like a thing from a children's rhyme. Once, a terrible war ripped the land. Once, children were thrown into prisons to be killed if their parents tried to throw off the slavers' yoke. Once, innocent people burned with their cities because men with power decided that they should. Once, but not now.

She could barely imagine what that world would be like. She wanted to believe that all the refugees of Suddapal would go back to their homes. All the enslaved Timzinae would leave the Antean farms that had become their prisons. All the children would find their mothers and fathers again, and everything would be made right and whole. But, of course, it wouldn't. *Once the war's done* could only ever be about what came next. Hoping to go back to what the world had been was trying to build wood from ashes.

"Look at her, Isadau," Pyk said and spat between her teeth. "I ask her to do one damned thing for the bank, and she starts pouting."

"I wasn't pouting," Cithrin snapped. "I was thinking. Of course I'll cultivate Inys if I can. When this is all over."

"Pyk didn't mean it, dear," Isadau said. "Barking is her way of showing love."

"The fuck it is," Pyk said with a laugh.

"And we all love you too," Isadau said, and Pyk laughed louder.

Cithrin stepped over to Pyk's table, looking at the numbers her notary was working. They were good. The branch was healthy. Less risk, and more money. Everything Pyk had called success. She found herself thinking about what of her plans the influx of gold could have supported. With what she had now, she could have hired a solid mercenary company. Or built a new bounty exchange in Borja. Or bought out the iron ore from the mines in Hallskar to see that it never reached the forges of Antea. Anything. But not all of it. She wondered, if she'd tried, if she could have won it all on her own. Her bank against Geder's empire. Would she have been enough? Or would that have been a very different *once the war's done?*

When she looked up, Isadau caught her gaze. The older Timzinae woman smiled, but there was a hardness to it, and always would be. Cithrin felt a little tug of shame. She was not going to let herself be sorry that she'd won the battle one way and not another. None of this was about whether she was clever enough. It wasn't about her. Or Geder. This was the war of the dragons resurrected, and nothing more. Or if not nothing, only a little.

"Rumor is the queen's forces had their fingers handed back to them at the pass from Bellin," Pyk said.

"I'd heard that too," Cithrin said. "I expect the Antean army is marching south as we speak."

"Will we be ready when they come?" Isadau asked.

"We're ready now," Cithrin said. "We have a dragon."

Clara

She had heard songs, of course, about the grasses of Birancour. It was a cliché of the poets and composers, like the dust storms of the Dry Wastes or the ice coasts of Hallskar. The grasslands were an image meant to evoke a sense of unending summer and sensual languor, the high blades shifting in the sun. Her experience of them was less impressive, but that owed something to the hooves, wheels, and boots that reduced the famous grasses to a mud-caked mat that stank of shit and rotting vegetation before she passed over it. Perhaps in some other context, Birancour might have been as beautiful as its reputation.

After the battle, the armies of the queen had pulled back, not quite in retreat. They lurked in the west, blocking the paths to Sara-sur-Mar and Porte Silena like Southlings making a wall around their queen. The army turned south, toward Porte Oliva, as the queen must have known it would. Riding on her horse, her spine stiff and aching, her mind lulled by the monotony of the day's passage, Clara half dreamed it. An attacker kicking in the door of a home and bloodying the mouth of the father, the defeated man standing between the intruder and the two children he hadn't come for, and clearing the way to a third. It was an ugly dream, and surely not true. The small, domestic ways of thinking didn't apply to the grand vision of nations at war. Violence between village thugs was base and bestial. War was the field of glory, where the nobility of men was tested. Dawson had always said so, and she had thought at the time she understood. Men fought, and the victors were celebrated. She could still recall the triumph when Dawson had returned from reclaiming Asterilhold.

Only now that she had seen some of it firsthand, she did wonder. Perhaps the nobility of war came not from victory, but from accepting an enemy's surrender. Not from taking the day, but from stopping short of absolute and unending slaughter. If so, she still thought less of it than she once had. She expected better of the world.

At midday, they passed a farmhouse with flames still licking at its eaves. The walls had fallen to ash and embers, and a Cinnae man and woman hung by ropes from a wide-branched cottonwood. A plow horse lay dead on its side by a little stone well. The caravan master sent a couple of his people into the ruins to search out anything the army had overlooked. The air stank of smoke that stung Clara's nose and roughened her throat. She looked at the bodies, fighting to make the thickness in her throat be only with the dead.

They'd fought, she told herself. They'd tried to stand against the armies of Antea. They were dead because they were stupid, because they'd tried to do something foolish and doomed. It was their fault that they hung there, their bodies shifting slightly in the breeze, the motion impossible to mistake for life. Jorey's men had killed these farmers because it was war, and this was what war was built from. Not only screaming, frightened boys bleeding into a mud-churn of a meadow. Also burning farmhouses and besieged cities poisoned with plague. It was made of a thousand species of the dead, and all of them—*all* of them—ought to have known better. Even her.

"They should have run," Clara said as they passed.

"This was their home," Vincen said.

"They still should have run."

"Yes, they should."

The horse under her stumbled a bit, surprised by a little ditch that the fallen grass had covered, and the unexpected motion sent pain through her hips and back like a shower of sparks rising from a bonfire. She cried out, and Vincen was at her side in an instant. She waved him back sharply.

"I'm fine," she said.

"You're in pain."

"I'm saddle-sore," she said. "It's nothing real."

"That's real."

"You know what I mean," she said. And then a moment later, "You think we should make camp for a day and rest."

"No, I think we should ride to the front and tell your sons that you've followed them."

Clara shifted in her saddle, her eyebrows rising toward her hairline. Vincen's expression was closed, his shoulders tight, a man preparing for a blow.

"And why in the world would I do that?" she asked.

"We can't stop here. The locals won't bother us with the main force so near, but if we lag too far behind...well, those two back there likely had family. It would be hard not to take a bit of revenge if we hand it to them."

"That's a reason to stay with the 'van."

"You're getting tired, love. You're pushing yourself harder than your body can stand, and I don't want to see you beat yourself to death against this. If you send word to Jorey, he'll—"

"He'll send me back to Camnipol under guard."

"Yes, but not because you'd be a prisoner. A dozen swords to keep us safe wouldn't be all that bad a thing."

"Impossible," she said with a wave of her hand. "I've come out here to do the work. I'd be useless in Camnipol. And with Geder's priests running through the city sniffing out secrets, all this around us strikes me as *much* safer. We left there for a reason."

No place is safe, she thought. *All the world has become a battlefield.*

With two hours still to go before nightfall, the 'van master called the halt and pulled them all off to the side of the path to let some supply carts by. It had happened before, but these were not the sacks of beans and meal that she'd seen then. The ten wide carts that rolled by were piled with complex mechanisms of burnished bronze and steel, coils of braided leather rope, stacks of what looked like wheels with blades erupting from their sides, and great harpoons with loops at the back and vicious barbs at the front like something a hunter might use against an animal too large to be killed by dogs and arrows. Siege engines, she assumed, for the coming assault on Porte Oliva should they be foolish enough to refuse to hand over the banker. She imagined the great harpoons being flung into the stone walls of Porte Oliva and used to pull it down. That couldn't be right, though.

Once the supply carts had passed, the 'van master consulted with a few of his men. They debated whether to stop here or press on, and chose to stay. Clara couldn't say she was sorry for the decision.

They made camp in twilight. The days were still growing longer. Hotter. Even when the year turned its corner and the light began to wane, the heat would still rise. She wondered as she helped construct the little hunter's tent whether she would still be in the field when the heat of summer was at its worst, or when it began to cool toward winter. She could imagine Dawson, his dogs at his side, looking out over the vast muddy swath the army's passage had cut through the landscape and shaking his head. It made her sad that she could picture the dogs more easily than Dawson's face.

The familiar scattering of stars came out, and the stink of cookfires rose to meet them, her own included. There was very little wood left after the soldiers had taken what they needed, and some of the others in the 'van had resorted to trying to burn grass or else dried dung. Clara had done a thousand things in the years since Geder Palliako took the throne that she would never have expected of herself, but eating food cooked over burning shit was still beneath her standards. She lay back on her filthy blanket and listened to the songs of the cicadas calling to each other from the grass and ate dried apples and salted almonds. She would have very much liked something warm to go with them. Even just a cup of hot tea. She would do without.

She hadn't realized she was dozing until the sound of footsteps roused her. A man was tramping north through the muck, a lantern in his hand. In this fallen place, the little assemblage of glass and tin was enough to mark him as someone important. Clara sat up and arranged her hair as she might have in Osterling Fells before going to greet a guest. The habit of decades, as out of place here as a snow-flake in a fire.

As the man grew nearer, his features became clear. He wore light mail, not the boiled leather of the normal foot. His cloak was caked with dirt and dust and streaked by stains whose origins Clara could not guess, but she could make out the remnants of the black and gold of House Basen, one of the smaller houses of Asterilhold that had not participated in the conspiracy against Antea and so had been allowed to live. The scabbard that hung from his side glittered with gems. Clara wasn't sure whether she should look away, feign sleep, or get to her feet. The chances that she would be known and recognized were thin indeed, but...

"Hoy. Old woman," the man barked. She pretended she was Aly Koutunin, her friend from the mornings she'd spent at the Prisoner's Span. She bobbed her head and didn't meet the soldier's eyes. He accepted the deference as his due. "Heard there's a cunning man back here someplace. A Kurtadam named Syles."

Clara nodded again and pointed over her shoulder toward the dim bulk of the 'van master's cart. The soldier tossed something at her feet, and it took her a moment to realize it was a coin, and that to keep up appearances she should fall to her knees and scrabble for it. When Vincen reappeared with a spare handful of dry twigs, she was turning the bit of bent copper in her fingers.

"All well?" he asked as he began to prepare a little fire.

"Walk with me," she said. "There's someone I want to see."

Her thighs were chapped and angry, her muscles tight as leather bands. Her gait was more waddle than stride. The cunning man's tent was a bit better than her own, the oiled canvas standing high enough that the old Kurtadam could sit up in it. The officer was gone, and the cunning man's eyes were half closed and focused on nothing. When Clara sat at his tent's edge, his gaze flickered to her and he smiled. The teeth he still had were yellowed and blunt.

"Fortune told, then?"

"No," she said. "Not mine. What do they ask you?"

The cunning man's eyes were open wider now. In the moonlight, his dark pelt seemed tipped by silver. He tilted his head, considering her, and she held out the bent penny.

"I'll pay you if you like," she said, "but the soldiers, when they come. What sorts of things do they ask you?"

The Kurtadam smirked. "Keep your coin. I don't have anything to tell you couldn't already guess. They ask if their wives and lovers still remember them. They ask if their children are well or if a fever has carried them away in the winter. They want to know when they will find their way home. And if. And what they can do to make the world let them be who they were before they first rode to this war. They're men, they ask the questions men ask when they have been on campaign too long."

"Nothing different? They don't ask about the priests or the Lord Marshal?"

"Some do," he said warily.

"And what do you tell them?"

The Kurtadam's eyes flicked up toward Vincen and then back to her. There was a wariness in them now, and also a curiosity. "When I see something, I tell them what I see. When I see nothing, I invent. I try to comfort them. I tell them that there are difficult times ahead, but that they will weather them. Then when hard things come, I'm already halfway to right. Why are you asking me this?"

"These men are tired," Clara said. "They started this campaign going east, and then south, and now west. They come to you for comfort. For word of home and of the future. If you chose to disturb some of them instead of offering comfort..." Clara shrugged, and the cunning man laughed.

"Yes, I could place a few poisoned seeds," the cunning man said. "If the price were right. You have someone in the army that's done wrong by you? Stole your horse, maybe? Didn't pay you what he owed?"

"Perhaps," Clara said. "Let me think about it."

She was about to stand when his hand shot out, his

dark-furred fingers snapping hard around her wrist. A wave of vertigo passed through her. A blue mist seemed to crowd in at the corners of her vision, narrowing the world, and the cunning man's eyes glowed for a moment, bright as a Dartinae's. She heard Vincen call out in alarm, but it seemed to come from a great distance. The Kurtadam released her and sat back, chewing at his lips. *What did he see?* she thought. *What does he know?*

"A time will come," the Kurtadam said, "when a man you love will ask you a question you cannot answer. Your silence will shape your life."

"Is that supposed to be useful?" Clara asked, her unease making her voice sharper and more haughty than she'd intended.

He shrugged. "I see what I see. Shadows and the shadows of shadows, but for you? Truth. Remember me when it happens. It is why the soldiers come to me. Why they *trust* me. Whatever you seek vengeance for, I have the power to help you. For the right coin."

"And that is what I came to ask," Clara said, rising to her knees and then her feet. They walked back to her tent, her steps unsteady in the darkness. Vincen was at her side, present but unspeaking. She didn't know whether she wished he would take her arm or if she was pleased that he hadn't. Something about the cunning man's pronouncement had left her feeling terribly fragile. *A man you love will ask you a question you cannot answer.* She could think of far too many ways for that particular piece of prophecy to come true. Perhaps that was the point. She had little faith in oracles, but even if the Kurtadam was a fraud, he would suffice for her needs.

Back at their little camp, Vincen lit the prepared twigs. The flame smoked. She stared into it, letting the brightness blind her to what lay all around them in the night. It made the world seem smaller.

"Another vulnerability," Vincen said.

"A small one, but yes."

"Played well, you could undermine people's faith. Or start to. Set the knights fighting among themselves."

"That was my thought," she said, sick with the words. "I don't know how to do this, Vincen. I don't know how to defeat my sons and also save them. How do I undermine Geder Palliako's priests when Vicarian is one of them? How do I stop his army when Jorey commands it? I don't know if I have the strength to sacrifice my own family to this, and also don't see how I can bring myself to stop."

"I've been wondering the same," Vincen said. "Will you tell your man in Carse about the cunning man?"

"Not tonight," she said. "It's late, and I'm too tired for writing letters."

A loud pop came from the fire, followed by a low hiss of sap cooking to nothing. Green wood and trampled grass. She shuddered though she wasn't cold.

"I want him to win, Vincen. This battle against Porte Oliva and this bel Sarcour girl? I want him to win it, and I am fighting on *her* side."

"It's like that sometimes," he said.

"Oh," Clara said, and her chuckle was sharper than she'd have wished. "Have you been on this path before?"

If he heard the sarcasm in her voice, he ignored it. "Something like it, yes. Every hunter feels it sometimes. You chase the hart, you and your dogs and your lord leading the chase. And for a moment, maybe, you catch sight of it. You remember that this magnificent animal is about to die for a bit of meat we don't need and the honor of a man with nothing better to do, and you wish the hart would run. That he'd find some escape you hadn't seen, slip the pack, and vanish into the wood."

His voice had gone soft. She smiled into the little dancing flame, what she felt most was a deep and broadening sorrow. "You sound as though you were thinking of some particular incident."

"I can think of several," he said.

"Did you hate my husband?"

"No," Vincen said without even the pause of a heartbeat. "He was the baron, and he was my lord."

"If he had only been a man?"

It was Vincen's turn to chuckle, and he managed to make the sound softer and richer than she had. "Then he wouldn't have been the baron and my lord."

"What did you do those times with him when you found your loyalty tilting toward your prey? Did you never call back the dogs? Let the beast slip away?"

"No, I killed it just the same. I'm a huntsman, Clara. We both are."

Marcus

W e should be harassing their column," Marcus said.
"I don't see much point," Cithrin said lightly. "The scouts say they'll be here in a few days."

"We should have *been* harassing their column. From the first foot they put in Birancour, the queen's army should have been snapping at their heels. Wearing them down."

Cithrin shrugged in a way that made him want to shake her. Around them, the taproom was busy with its midday custom. Sausages and hot mustard, beer and wine, the twice-baked flatbread that snapped against his lips when he bit it. The preparations for the coming siege had left the outer ring of the city almost empty, and not everyone had fled to the countryside. If anything, more of them had come behind the great white wall. For the first time in generations, siege engines were being hauled back into their niches and new gates fixed in place. Porte Oliva had been a smaller city the last time an army stood outside its defenses, and the press of extra bodies in the street was the measure of it.

"The queen's throwing you to the dogs," Marcus said. "Just standing back and letting them march to us like Porte Oliva wasn't one of her own cities."

"I know," Cithrin said, taking a handful of nuts and raisins.

"That's why *we* should be doing it."

"I've talked to the governor about it," she said. "We don't have the soldiers. There are enough to man the wall and defend the port, but if we start putting together companies to put in the field, we'll be stretched too thin."

"Really?" Marcus said. "And how many battles has the governor been through?"

"None."

"Well I've seen a couple, one time and another. We're not ready for this."

Cithrin frowned. She'd grown older since the day she'd left for Carse it seemed like years before. Her face was wider now, though her Cinnae blood meant it would always be sharp at the chin and cheeks. Her shoulders were broader now, and when she moved it was less like a girl pretending at womanhood than a woman's authentic gait. When she wasn't in the room with him, he thought of her as the girl he remembered, and was a little startled every time he saw her again.

"Inys wants to wait, and I don't see that we're in a position to issue orders to a dragon," she said. Then, changing the subject, "Herez had to close down the bounty system. I think they're afraid Antea will come after Callon Cane once they're done with me."

"You should move him to Sara-sur-Mar and let Geder chase him down the queen's throat," Marcus said bitterly, and Cithrin laughed. Marcus scowled, relented, smiled. In the street, a man started shouting and another took it up. A few people in the taproom craned their necks to look out the windows or the half-open door, but Marcus could tell the sound of a traffic brawl from something serious. It was to be expected, this near to the storm.

Since the defeat of the queen's army in the north and the arrival of Inys, Marcus had seen the city fall into the old patterns. The coming violence touched everything from the mood in the taprooms to the street-corner puppet shows to the songs the workers sang while they carried their masters' crates inside the protecting ring of the wall. He hadn't seen Porte Oliva in the months before, but Yardem had told him enough of how the blockade had shaken the city to recognize the mixture of anxiety and relief that had them all drunk. They had been in danger and now they were saved. They had a champion to lead them, and a new danger to overcome. The stones themselves had found faith in the dragon and its power to protect them. Marcus knew it was an illusion because he'd been that savior himself once in an old war in Northcoast.

He'd even had faith in himself, back then.

Cithrin sighed and shook her head. "Porte Oliva's never fallen in war. Never. The only times it's been taken, someone inside the city betrayed it and opened the gates. No one's going to do that now. We know to keep out of earshot of the priests or drown them out. They're exhausted and in the middle of enemy land. We have freedom of the sea to resupply, we have well-rested soldiers protecting their own homes, and we have a dragon. We're going to be fine."

"That exhausted army's got spider priests, and they've already conquered half the world," Marcus said. "We shouldn't underestimate them. You don't know how bad this could get."

Cithrin's face went cold and she hoisted an eyebrow. "I think I do. I've lost two cities already and lived through the fighting in Camnipol. I've seen what war can do."

"No disrespect, Cithrin. You've seen a handful of squabbling noblemen and a surrender. You haven't lived through a battle. They're worse, and once they start going bad, it's usually too late to make fresh plans. However many high cards we're holding, we should have been harassing their column, and we should have been hiring mercenaries to break the siege when it comes, and we should have burned every building north of the wall rather than leave it for the enemy to shelter in."

"The governor would never agree to that," she said.

"Shouldn't ask permission, then."

"We're going to be fine," Cithrin said, and the hardness in her voice ran on the edge of challenge. She wanted to believe it. He wished that he could too. "We're going to be fine, Marcus. They can't take the city."

"All right," he said, but when he stepped outside, he turned north. The air was thick with the smell of bodies and of the sea. The spring rains were late this year, but coming. He could feel the press of weather in the air, a stillness that made even the breeze feel sluggish. The dragon's perch in the courtyard stood empty. Inys's resting claws had stripped away the bark and carved deep gouges into the pale wood beneath. They'd have to replace that soon. Unless the siege went poorly. Then it'd be someone else's problem. He looked at the sun. He'd agreed to relieve Yardem from the guardhouse. With the increase in coin and goods in the counting house strongbox and new people coming to the relatively defended city from the countryside, they'd both decided that tripling the guard was a good thought. But if he was an hour or two late, chances were Yardem would forgive him. It wouldn't be the first time.

Passing through the defense walls was like stepping into a dream. He remembered the first time he'd passed this way, besieged by beggars. The great stone wall with its arrow slits had seemed like the artifact of another time then. It marked the edge of a city that had long since outgrown it. There were no beggars there now. He assumed they'd all moved to the port. There wouldn't be many travelers arriving with charity by land.

Beyond the fresh gates, the buildings of Porte Oliva stood almost empty. The breeze set a shutter clacking open and closed and open again. A sullen dog followed him for a few streets and then wandered away. There was no new wall, no second defense. Birancour had been at peace for generations, and even before that, their wars had been in the north, at the seat of power. It showed in the architecture and the shape of the streets and the buildings that slowly grew sparser and lower, wider yards between them and more trees and grass. And then without ever passing an archway or marker, he was outside the city. He found the dragon in a meadow that had become a favorite place for its torpid sleep. The grass all around its body was smashed and dead, the dark earth showing through. Its eyes were narrowed but not closed, and it shifted to consider him without rising.

"Marcus Stormcrow," Inys said in a voice like distant thunder.

"Back with the Stormcrow thing? Thought we'd moved past that."

"I call you that, or not. As I see fit. I think of you that way or not."

"That's very flexible of you," Marcus said. "I wanted to talk about the war."

"It was terrible. It was the triumph of rage over cowardice, and I was the coward. I should have let him kill me. I should have bared my neck to him and let him take the light from my eyes. It would have been better for both of us than this."

"Yeah. Not the war I was thinking of," Marcus said, sitting on the grass beside the great head. "There's an army coming this way. We haven't done anything to slow it down or break its supply lines. The forces that could have backed us got spanked and are off pouting outside Porte Silena and Sara-sur-Mar. Everyone and their uncle seems convinced that you're going to save us all."

The dragon didn't speak, but shifted its weight, claws digging deep into the turf like a housecat kneading a pillow. Marcus waited.

"Do you know what it is to mourn, Marcus Stormcrow?"

"I do."

"There are days I can almost forget, and then I see something and think how Erex will smile to hear of it, only she will not. Not now, and not ever. Because of me."

"That's why we call it mourning," Marcus said. "And it goes on for a hell of a long time before it gets better. But between now and then, I need to know if you're planning to follow through and protect this city. Because if you aren't, I'm going to have to."

The dragon went still. Marcus leaned forward and brushed a blade of grass from his boots.

"Even Drakkis I never permitted to speak to me in such tones."

Marcus felt a sweeping urge to apologize and bit his lips against it. "We are acting like we've already won," he said. "It makes me very uncomfortable."

"I am acting as though I have lost, and I have," the dragon said.

"When you were drunk, you had hope. Something about filling the skies with dragons again."

"When I am drunk, I have hope. When I am sober, I am too much a coward to let myself die. Even if I remake them, they will be new. Different. No one will remember the things I remember. There is no one to continue those conversations. I could bring a thousand dragonets into the world and still be alone."

A thousand dragonets, Marcus thought. *That doesn't sound like a good thing either.* He pushed the thought aside for the moment. It was a problem for another time.

"All right," he said. "So I'm hearing you say that today's one of the bad days, and you're feeling hopeless and down. Have I got that about right?"

"You do not understand."

"Like hell I don't. You went to sleep and you woke up with everyone gone. I watched my wife and daughter die in front of me because I'd gotten too cocksure and full of myself. I stood witness, and I couldn't do anything about it." Marcus stopped, growling at the thickness in his throat like it was an enemy. He was courting nightmares here, but he didn't let it stop him. "I smelled their hair burn. When you set fire to someone, they keep moving a bit after they're dead. Something about the way the sinews shorten up when they cook. They were in the flame, moving. They were dead and moving. And I spent *years* like that. Dead and moving. Some days I still do. But your family trouble is about to kill some people I know. Dead or not, you need to stop it. That's the job."

Inys rolled away, curling its back toward Marcus. The folded wings looked like furled sails on a ship.

"Perhaps you do understand," the dragon said.

Marcus sat for a time. Inys didn't speak again. Didn't move. A dove fluttered by and landed on the branch of a tree at the meadow's edge, cooing loudly. Marcus coughed.

"We should be harassing their column," he said.

Inys didn't answer.

"Was I that bad?"

Yardem flicked his ears thoughtfully, the earrings jingling against each other. "You weighed less."

"I'm amazed you put up with me."

The sky above the harbor was hazy white, the bodies of hundreds of seagulls dark against it. The tall-rigged ships that had been the heart of the blockade stood out in the deep water off the harbor, transformed from enemy to protector, and the sea shone bright and rich as mother-of-pearl. Marcus and Yardem stood on the seawall looking down into the waves.

"Do you think Inys made the Drowned too?" Marcus asked. "He said he had them undermine that island. He made the Timzinae. Maybe he made the Drowned too."

"Might have," Yardem said. "Might only have found a use for them."

"I still don't like thinking of a whole race of people as tools made for a purpose. Use them and clean them and put them in the box when you're done."

"Would they be better meaningless?"

"They should be able to make their own meaning."

Yardem grunted, his ears turning back they way they did when he was being polite.

"What?" Marcus said.

"Don't see what stops them from doing that, sir. Can stab a man to death with a cobbler's awl. Can dig up weeds with a dagger. Seems to me what something's made for matters less than what's done with it."

"But *they* made us what we are. Even the Firstbloods, to judge by the way we dance to whatever tune he calls. We're all formed by a dragon's will for a dragon's plan. All of history is a gap in a war they fought using us for weapons."

"Something had to make the dragons," Yardem said. "I believe there's a larger order, and Inys is part of it just as we are."

"Any evidence for that?"

"None, sir."

"So why think it?"

"Just seems plausible."

A new voice called out from the walkway behind them. Marcus turned back. Porte Oliva stretched out. Tile roofs and white walls and narrow, cobbled streets. Kit, Cary, and Barriath Kalliam walked toward them. The two players wore new clothes of a carefully nondescript grey. Until they could amass a new supply of costumes and props, they'd fallen back on the style of Princip C'Annaldé where the performers created the illusions of their stories through only the use of their voices and bodies. Beside them, the pirate captain looked almost gaudy, though in truth his cloak and breeches were no more than anyone might wear. Barriath nodded to Marcus and then Yardem.

"Your friends here said you wanted to speak with me?"

"Do," Marcus said. "No offense to the governor and the queensmen—or the dragon, for that matter—but I'm the sort of man who likes having five or six plans deep, and you're the man at the city's back door."

"You think the fleet's likely to attack when the army comes."

"It's what I'd do," Marcus said.

"It could happen," Barriath said. "There are a few ships in the Inner Sea, mostly at Suddapal, but they're spoils of war, and the sailors for them were up in Nus until they started sailing for here. I don't see how they get those ships crewed unless they hire on mercenaries, and frankly, I've already bought the best of those."

"You'll have to tell me more about how you managed that at some point," Marcus said. "What about the blockades on Porte Silena and Sara-sur-Mar?"

"They will come south, block any supplies coming in

or escape going out. But the water's where we're strongest now. We might not be able to stop them getting here, but I'm fairly sure we'll see them coming, and the dragon wouldn't have trouble burning them all to the waterline."

If we can talk him into caring at all, Marcus thought but didn't say.

"It seems to me," Kit said, "that you are also in a rare position to advise the city defenders on the drier end. I understand that the army is commanded by your brothers. Is there any insight you can give into how you expect that conflict to play out?"

Barriath crossed his arms. His expression was equal parts pain, anger, and the cold consideration of a man accustomed to war. Marcus waited. However carefully it was put, the question was still how best go about killing Barriath's brothers. The sailor's eyes turned toward the sea, but what he was seeing, Marcus couldn't guess. Cary put a hand on his arm, and Barriath started. Her smile was encouraging, and he nodded.

"Jorey. My youngest brother. He's smart, but not experienced. I don't know how he'll do as a commander, but Father told us stories of great battles and strategies of the hunt. And this isn't his first time in the field."

Brothers and wars. If Barriath and Jorey and this third one whose name Marcus kept forgetting had all been dragons, they'd be at the mouth of the war instead of the ass end of it. "All right. With any luck it won't come to this, but I think we need to discuss what happens if—"

"Breaking the siege isn't the problem. Or it's not the one I see," Barriath went on, ignoring him. "Maybe I'm being dim, but this isn't a normal war. If the army comes and shatters itself against the walls, then what happens? Does Palliako sue for peace? If he does, and the queen accepts it, then what? Send the army and the priests back to Antea and call it victory? Or do you few march on Camnipol with as many queensmen as Birancour's willing to grudge you?"

"That's a little farther on than I'm worried about just yet," Marcus said.

"It shouldn't be. This is precisely what you should be worrying about right now. Because everything I've heard so far are ways not to lose the war. I don't see anyone thinking about what it would take to win it."

Geder

Basrahip left Camnipol with a group of eight priests behind him. They rode the finest, fastest horses Geder could get them, and they carried strange green-black scabbards strung across their backs. Geder went with them as far as the city gate, and the black-cobbled streets emptied before them, the citizens of the empire scattering like mice before a fire. Geder felt a bright dread growing in his belly with every street they passed. In some corner of his heart, he'd hoped that something would keep this from happening. The apostate in Kaltfel might be found and killed without the need of Basrahip to oversee the hunt, and so the massive priest could stay. The danger would pass like a child's dream at sunrise, and everything would be back to the way it should be. The city wall loomed high above them, and that little wisp of hope shriveled and died.

Basrahip was leaving. He was really leaving, and Geder was staying behind. There were other priests, of course. Basrahip's duties would still be done, but by someone unfamiliar. New faces and voices would take his place, and it was that prospect that shifted in Geder's belly, the fear growing. What if the new priests didn't like him? What if they thought he was an impostor, a fake? That he didn't deserve the regency? Basrahip had known him since the beginning, it seemed. They understood each other, trusted each other. Geder didn't have many friends.

The gate rose up higher than three men. Geder pulled his own horse to a halt. He'd held this gate once, after his return from Vanai. Kept it open long enough to let his army get in and push back the showfighters and mercenaries that Asterilhold had snuck inside the city. It had been a warmer day than this, and the fighting, though fierce, had been joyous. He'd saved Jorey's life that day when a thick-tusked Yemmu had been about to drive a spear through Jorey's side. Or maybe it had been a sword. Those had been better days, Geder thought. Or if they weren't, at least he remembered them that way.

"All will be well, Prince Geder," Basrahip said.

"I want to come with you," Geder said. "This apostate? I want him caught and burned and his ashes poured into the bottoms of the pisspots of every taproom in Kaltfel."

"We will never stop hunting him," Basrahip said. "His abomination will not spread."

More reports had come from Kaltfel in the days of Basrahip's preparation. The apostate priest was a man named Ovur, one of the first priests to arrive from the temple in the mountains beyond the Keshet. Geder remembered him as an older man with white threads in his hair and beard. When they had dedicated the temple in Asterilhold—the first of the new temples Geder had sworn to raise in every city he conquered—Ovur had gone to it. With the expansion of the empire to the east, no other priests had gone to his temple for the long winter previous, and when they had, the changes they'd found were dire. Ovur had been preaching that the spider goddess was centered not just in Camnipol, but was present equally in every temple dedicated in her name. Basrahip was no more or less her voice than any of the other priests, himself included. The phrase *Though there are a thousand mouths, there is only one truth* figured into his teachings. A group of the newly initiated priests arrived to aid him in keeping the temple, and one tried to correct him. Ovur had flown into a rage and beaten the man. Since then, Kaltfel had been in an uproar. And so the nine priests and their blades set out to restore the peace and keep his lies from infecting any of the other cities and temples.

Geder wished the man had just died of the pox instead. Or the city had been hit by plague. If it were plague, Basrahip wouldn't have to go. The goddess could do anything. Surely she could manage a little plague.

Basrahip held out his great hand, and Geder clasped it. He felt like a child shaking hands with a grown man. It was easy for him to forget how really large Basrahip was.

"When you're done, come back," Geder said, trying to make the words sound like the Lord Regent of Antea commanding his loyal servant and not Lehrer Palliako's little boy whining for his nurse. "The empire needs you here."

"Your empire is in her sight," Basrahip said. "Listen to my voice, Prince Geder. You are the agent of her peace. She knows what glories you are capable of, and you shall not fail."

In truth, the season was calmer and quieter than in previous years, if only because there were fewer people present. But there were still feasts and balls and luncheons. Men still dueled over questions of honor, and their mothers and wives and sisters still patched things over afterward. It looked the same as it had before, and if it felt different, it was likely only that there was so much new that needed to be thought of. The year before, the management of Nus and Inentai and Suddapal hadn't been at issue. The year before that, Kaltfel and Asinport had been the great cities of another country. So while Camnipol alone was a quieter, calmer place, the Kingspire was not. He spent most of his days in his private study with reports and letters from the protectors of the empire's newest cities and towns. There was still the grand audience to prepare for, and he'd already postponed it once.

And so there were whole days sometimes when he didn't think of Cithrin. And then, like the sudden pain of on old wound, he would. For a moment, he would remember himself as he'd been, tripping idiotically into the streets of Suddapal expecting to find a lover's embrace waiting for him. Being *stupid* enough to think Cithrin loved him. That anyone would. He saw himself with the wide, delighted grin of an idiot, his fat buffoon's arms spread to nothing and no one. And the emptiness of the bank's compound and the pity in Fallon Broot's eyes. Fallon Broot, whom Geder had ordered specifically to give privilege to Cithrin and her people. No amount of vengeance, no triumph or victory would ever wash away the bright pain of that day. It would stain his life forever, because he had believed.

That was the worst of it. Even more than the betrayal, there was the sheer, superhuman stupidity of thinking that someone like Cithrin could have feelings for someone who looked like him. His power and position, certainly. They'd been of use to her. But he had convinced himself—*genuinely* convinced himself—that she'd taken him in love. That the touch of their bodies had been something as real to her as it had been to him. Cithrin was beautiful and intelligent, and he was the heir to a third-tier holding like Rivenhalm who'd blundered into power and then thought he belonged there. And he was fat. Worse than fat, pudgy. That one night when she'd opened herself to him—

And then the memory shifted and became a thing of

longing so deep and vast it would have filled oceans. And all of it poisoned by humiliation.

"Are you all right?" Aster asked.

Geder coughed, looking around the study as if he were seeing it for the first time. Essian's latest report from Lyoneia was still in hand. He didn't know how long he'd been staring at it without seeing the words. *The Southling locals have reported two men something over a year ago and a document known as the Silas map.* He put the papers down.

"I'm fine," he said.

"You were grunting."

"Was I? I didn't notice. Probably just too long in this damned uncomfortable chair."

"You should move, then," Aster said. "Father used to take things to his rooms at the bottom of the spire all the time. He liked it down there."

"Maybe that is a good idea," Geder said, stretching. "Very, very good idea. You're a smart boy."

"Your standards are low," Aster said with a half-smile. "Doesn't take much to say you should change things if you're uncomfortable."

"It's the simple things that carry, though." He stood up. The study was a mess. Piles of papers, reports, letters. The tax ledgers and farm reports of the south reaches. The unglamorous work of running the world. He didn't enjoy it, but it had to be done. Aster, at his own desk, was working through a poetry exercise his tutor had set him. It struck Geder again how much older the boy looked. How much older he'd become. How much work there was still to be done before Aster took the Severed Throne and ruled over Antea. More than Antea. The world. He didn't realize that he intended to speak until the words were already coming out.

"You'll be better, you know. When all this is yours? You'll be better than I am. I didn't train for any of this. I barely spent time in court when I was young. You've seen all of this. Not just what I've done, but your father, when he was alive. It won't be bad."

Aster nodded without looking up. His lips pressed thin. Geder waited, unsure whether he should just leave or be patient and let the boy answer in his own time.

"You spend all day in here," Aster said.

"There's a lot of work to be done," Geder said. "A lot of changes have come, and there're decisions to be made. I'm the only one who can make them, for now."

"Why?" Aster asked, still not looking up. "You have men who serve you. You have more men serving you than anyone else in the world, probably."

"But I'm the one the goddess chose. I don't know why she did, but she did. So this is what I have to carry. And if I do enough of it now, there won't be as much for you to shoulder. When the time comes."

Aster turned his head at last, smiling but diffident. He nodded. His jaw was stronger than Geder remembered it being.

"Do you want to come out and spar a bit?" Geder asked. "We haven't done that in a while. And it would work the kinks out of my back."

"I should finish this," Aster said.

"Yes. Of course. You should. All right, I'll just head down to that fountain for a while. Take these with me."

In the corridor, his personal guard fell in behind him as he took the great sweeping staircases down toward the ground level, the gardens, the fountain. All around him, the Kingspire buzzed with activity. Not only his own servants, but the brown-robed priests who made the tower their own home now. Men passed through the halls on errands that supported the empire and the crown and the temple. Geder felt like he was the first among servants. In truth, he was looking forward to the day when he could retire to his own estate somewhere and let it all carry on without him.

He caught sight of the only Jasuru priest. A man who had been an assassin bent on Geder's death, and was now a wide-eyed servant of the goddess. He made a point of bowing to Geder every time they met, as if his body could bend itself into a living apology. Geder couldn't help but wish Basrahip were still there. He hoped things were going well in Kaltfel. The afternoon breeze was cool when he stepped outside. The gardens spread out to his left. To his right, the dueling grounds and the vast canyon of the Division. His land, for now. Everything, as far as he could see and beyond all horizons, his responsibility.

He sat by the shadowed fountain for a time, but he couldn't focus on the papers and reports here any better than he had in his study. The dead king's chambers were all around him, and he felt Simeon's presence. Water sheeted down a bronze dragon almost lost to verdigris, and Geder listened to the splashing as if there might be voices in it. Spirits in the water that could tell him something wise. Something he needed to know. There was nothing, and after a time—long or short, he couldn't say—he made his way back out into the gardens and the sunlight. Far above, the banner of the goddess was a line of black and red against the side of the spire. He lay back in the manicured grass and looked at it, and then at the distant clouds beyond. If he'd been sitting up, Canl Daskellin and Cyr Emming—two of his three closest counselors—might have noticed him sooner and been less free with their words.

"—off for weeks at a time to apprentice as a *midwife*,"

Emming said, his voice a growl. "For God's sake. Can you imagine Simeon doing that?"

"I'm not disagreeing with your particulars," Daskellin said. "But I think you're exaggerating the problem. No one in four countries is willing to cross him. Not after Dawson Kalliam. Certainly not after Ternigan. He has his dead enemy's own children toeing his line. And the ladies of the court have nothing but kind words after his unfortunate romance."

"That. Well, it's a thin line between kindness and pity, and I for one—"

"Lord Regent!" Daskellin said, his tone bluff and hearty. "We were looking for you. Prince Aster said you were in his father's old quarters, enjoying the fountain."

"I was," Geder said, sitting up. "Then I came here." Canl Daskellin stood at the edge of the path, his smile polite and rueful. It was an acknowledgment that Geder had heard them. Emming, on the other hand, was scowling severely, nodding, and fighting not to meet Geder's gaze. The old man's face was pale. To Geder's surprise, it wasn't anger that swept through him, but a strange kind of sympathy. Emming was one of the great men of Antea, and here he was, caught misbehaving. He looked like a guilty dog. If he'd had a tail, it would have been tucked between his knees. It wasn't so long since Geder himself had felt the sting of embarrassment that he couldn't recognize its distilled form in his counselor's face.

Embarassment and also fear. That he feared Geder forgave him much.

"We've had hard news, my lord," Daskellin said. "I thought it best that we speak to you at once."

Geder levered himself up to his feet, dusting bits of grass and leaf from his knees. His mind raced to a hundred different things that might have gone badly. Had Sabiha gotten sick again? Was there bad news from Jorey? Had the enemy in Porte Oliva killed Lord Skestinin, or the apostate in Kaltfel ambushed Basrahip? Or the siege at Kiaria? Could something have gone badly there? A plague among the men? An assault from behind now that the body of the army had gone west? Geder hadn't realized he carried so many catastrophes so near the top of his mind until the chance came to for one to come true, and they all spilled out, ready to be made real.

"Mecelli's written," Emming said, his gaze fixed on Geder's collarbone. "He's still in Inentai."

"The city is suffering raids," Daskellin said. "Robbers were attacking outlying towns and farms at first, but they've grown bolder. He says they've begun coming into the city proper."

"Well, we can't let that go on," Geder said. "They have to be hunted down. Stopped."

"The force left at Inentai is not a large one," Daskellin said, nodding. "When the army was at Kiaria, there was a sense that it might return east as reinforcements. With the bulk of the men in Birancour now..."

"We're stretched thin. Very damned thin," Emming said.

"It is also possible that some members of the traditional families or their relatives in Borja are sponsoring the raids," Daskellin said.

"Can we raise more troops?" Geder asked.

Daskellin's eyes answered before his words. "Raising a second army would be difficult."

"Hired swords, my lord," Emming said. "That's the path to go. The Keshet's lousy with them, and garrison duty's what they're trained at. Get a few hundred of them for a season. Just until the problem in the west's cleared up. We've got the coin for it."

"Yes, that makes sense," Geder said.

"Mercenary companies are certainly an option," Daskellin said. "Mecelli thought we might reach for that, and he was...skeptical. There is a precedent in the east for companies to switch sides if a better offer is made. If we count on professional soldiers to die for us rather than take bribes from the enemy, it may not go as gracefully as we'd like."

"We can find out if they're loyal," Geder said. "There's a temple in Inentai. They just ask."

"Yes," Daskellin said, "and knowing that there's a force of armed men who won't answer to the throne guarding Inentai is better than not knowing, but it's still a problem."

"What then?"

"With respect," Daskellin said, "mercenaries are best used where they aren't needed. I suggest we hire companies to stand guard where there *isn't* trouble. Asinport. Nus. Even Suddapal. Then the Antean blades can go to Inentai and ride against the raiders."

"Good," Geder said. "Yes. We'll do that."

"We can do this once, my lord," Daskellin said. "If something else happens? A revolt in Nus or a slave uprising on the farms. If Herez or Cabral or Narinisle throw in with Birancour? We'll have to make choices, or we're in very real danger of all of it falling into chaos."

"No," Geder said. "It's fine. This isn't like other wars. This is the goddess reclaiming the world. The old ways don't apply. Everything is going to be just fine."

"Damned right," Emming said, nodding hard. "*Damned* right."

Daskellin's smile was thinner, the angle of his head not as deep. "I hope you are correct, Lord Geder."

Clara

The assault itself began in flame.

Over the long years of peace, the city of Porte Oliva had outgrown its own defenses. Buildings spilled past the defensive wall and out into the open land. By the time the army arrived, they were empty as a plague town. The soldiers walked through the outlying buildings and then sent forward a priest under the flag of parley. Clara saw none of it, but the reports filtered back quickly. How the parley had been refused, arrows raining from the top of the wall and driving the priest back. How the voices of Porte Oliva had jeered and sung and drowned out the priest's words. How the chance of surrender had been squandered.

After that, the army had pulled back, out into the open fields. Clara had found her own camp surrounded by soldiers' tents, and the Lord Marshal's banner not a hundred yards away. Jorey was so close she could have walked to him. The banners of the other houses took their places around the perimeter of the city—Caot and Essian and Flor and Broot. The first sign of fire came with the fall of twilight, thin pillars of white smoke rising into the air from one place and another around the exposed belly of the city. And then, with night, the flames.

"He's a careful one, this new Lord Marshal," the caravan

master said, eating his bowl of beans and salt by the fire. He sounded approving, and Clara felt a stab of pride.

"I don't understand," a young Dartinae woman said. She was a seamstress who sometimes also shared a bed with the soldiers. Her name was Mita or Meta. Something like that. "He could have used those buildings as cover. Gotten in right by the wall. Now he can't attack until the fire's burned out, and even then, he'll be marching over embers to get there."

"That was never cover," the caravan master said. "That was the first line of defense. Straight trap, and meant to seduce him. March his men in under it to keep the arrows off, just like you were thinking. Only then it'd be the queensmen who started the fire and our boys burning in it. Kalliam's boy's too smart to take the easy path. Don't know how he's getting past that wall, though."

When the time came to bed down for the night, the 'van master took her and Vincen aside. "Look, I can't help but notice you two like setting up a ways off from the rest of us. That's fine. I got no opinion on it. But tonight? Might be best if you kept close. Soldiers before a battle can be…well, rowdy, eh? Mistakes get made. Better all around if we keep close and cheer them on."

The smoke thickened the air, and the flames of the city danced and leaped and muttered. When she woke on the grey, ashen morning, her eyes stung and her throat felt raw. Where the day before there had been houses and businesses, stables and dyers' yards, there was now smoking ash, blackened timber, a few low stone walls. And beyond it, the great wall of Porte Oliva, blackened with soot. It looked like a city already fallen. Jorey's scouts made forays into the grey and black and red, reporting back, Clara assumed, how much the coals still burned, how hard or simple it would be to cross the new-made ruins and spill the same destruction on the far side of the wall.

"Are you all right?" Vincen asked.

Clara nodded at the defensive wall. "It's a high wall, and it seems they know what the priests are capable of. Do you think it might hold?"

"What I've heard, Porte Oliva's never fallen to attack," Vincen said.

"I can believe that," Clara said.

Near midday, the worst of the fire seemed to have passed. All around them, the soldiers began to prepare. Siege engines were assembled—trebuchet and catapult, ballista and the strange new spear throwers that had passed them on the road. A vast array of mechanisms all built toward violence.

And then, as they began to rise, the voices.

"The goddess is with you. You *cannot* fail." It wasn't Vicarian's voice, but neither did it carry the accents of the Keshet. When the priest passed by, one hand lifted to the sky and the other holding a speaking trumpet, his face strong and bright and severe, she didn't recognize him, but he did not have the wiry hair and long face of Basrahip or the others like him. This man had been born in the same Antea that she had known, and had been remade. "Her strength is *yours*. Her purity is *yours*. The servants of lies tremble before you now, and you cannot fail."

"Why is he saying that?" Vincen asked.

"To give them courage," Clara said. "To assure them that they will win."

"That they...Oh. I understand."

In the background, a group of nearby soldiers took up the chant *cannot fail, cannot fail, cannot fail.* Clara turned to Vincen. He looked older in the smoke-stained light. "What did you think it meant?"

"I was taking it more that they dared not fail. Must not. *You cannot fail, for if you do the consequences will be unimaginably dire.* Something like that."

"Yes," Clara said. "Words can so often mean what you take from them rather than what was intended."

They sat huddled by the 'van master's cart. The chant seemed to spread around them, the men of the army—men who had been farmers and tradesmen two years before and were practiced killers now—lifting bared steel and shouting as if their words alone could bring down the city's defenses. *Cannot fail, cannot fail, cannot fail.* She could hear both meanings in the words now. It occurred to her that if things went poorly, Jorey and Vicarian might both die today. Two of her sons might not see the sunset. She might not. It was a battle, and anything might happen.

Worse, when the priest walked by again, the speaking horn to his lips, his face a mask of religious ecstasy, Clara found herself wanting to take comfort in his words and slogans. *You are the chosen of the goddess. She will protect you.* She wanted to give herself over to the hope that it might be true, that Jorey was blessed and special and that he, at least, would live to see his wife and baby.

She didn't know she was weeping until Vincen took her hand. He didn't speak, but his gaze met her, and she found herself taking some strength from his simple presence.

A roar went up. A thousand voices lifted together. The first of the siege engines had loosed its stone. Clara watched it arc up over the newly made wasteland and strike the wall. The sound of the impact came with the stone already falling to the ground, and four more catapults swung. Four more stones battered at the vast and uncaring walls of Porte Oliva. For hours, Jorey's forces flung stones, trying to crack the battlements and the great gate. Many of the shots fell against the wall's face, but some few scraped across the top or fell past it into the city to effects Clara could not guess.

She heard the horns sound, the orders called out, but she couldn't make out the words. Men streamed forward around her and the rest of the caravan. Thin, hard-faced men in motley armor and beards. Her countrymen. The servants of the Severed Throne, as much as was she, rushing to spend their deaths to avenge Geder Palliako's sexual humiliation. And Jorey at their head. The ranks formed in the ashes. The catapults threw their last rounds before the advance. Six siege towers began the slow approach through the ruins, each following a trail the scouts had marked out for them. They were like slow giants, lumbering forward, the forces of the army advancing behind them, using them as cover. For now, the defense from the wall began in earnest. Great bolts from ballistas arcing over the ashy land. And in the siege towers, answering bolts, and also, more terribly, the voices of the priests, shouting their dreadful certainties. From where she sat, they were only muddled echoes that bounced from the wounded side of the wall. She wondered what the defenders of the city heard and if they believed. And if they did, how would they react? She closed her eyes, back again in another battle, Dawson at her side, as Basrahip shouted to a square that they had already lost, that everything they loved was gone, that there was no hope. There was no hope here. No victory was possible. Geder's priests would win or else Jorey would lose, and there was no ending that would not pour acid on her heart.

"Ah, Vincen," she said.

His gentle grip on her hand tightened and did not let go.

On the field, a covered battering ram rolled toward the gates, arrows and stones raining down onto it. Two of the siege towers had become fouled in the debris of the burned city, and men were scampering out in front, pulling away blackened beams and stones. Smoke rose where the passage of the army had exposed coals still hot from the night's long fire. The air all around her stank of ashes. The first of the siege towers came to the wall, throwing ladders up to reach the last distance to the wall's top. The queensmen of Porte Oliva swarmed toward it, their little swords no bigger than needles at this distance. The battle along the crest of the wall began. Far away to the south, a column of black smoke was rising until it found some barrier of air and grew flat along the top. She couldn't imagine what it came from, but it added to the sense of doom that covered the battlefield. The image of humanity locked in violence forever, without hope of peace.

The deep, drumlike report of the battering ram filled the air. The covered ram had reached the gate and was worrying at it like a terrier killing a rat. A shout rose, though whether from the defenders or the Antean army, she could not say. A great stone fell from the top of the wall over the gate. It struck the battering ram's protective roof a glancing blow, but perhaps something within the structure was affected. The steady boom of its attack stopped and the mechanism began, slowly, to roll back out of the way. A second tower reached the wall. More ladders rose. As she watched, a man scrambled up toward the enemy and was cast down. He fell slowly, his arms spread, his axe turning in the air beside him. Clara watched him all the way down. When he landed, he lay still. Dead, no doubt. Like that, between one breath and another, a man died before her. It wasn't the first slaughter she'd seen, and oddly, she found comfort in it. These were only men. This was merely violence. Terrible, yes. Useless and wasteful, yes. But also human. She could not say what part of the carnage that forgave.

A loud splintering came from the left, and the second siege engine to reach the wall was listing to the right. She couldn't see what had broken it, but it tipped over, not quite falling, but scattering the men who had been on its height. The ladders wheeled toward the ground, but already another tower was approaching a few dozen feet down, and a third far away to the right. The defenders would have to split their attention four ways. Maybe five. She wondered if they could.

A second battering ram made its way toward the gate, but its movement was slow, and the rain of arrows and stones seemed more concentrated now, as if with a little practice the men at the top of the wall were improving their technique. The voices of the priests still rang out, louder than the clashing of swords or the screams of the soldiers. She could not make out the syllables, but she knew the sense of them.

A horn sounded, and a company of soldiers raced across the battlefield, the banner of House Flor streaming above them. She caught sight of Jorey's banner. Banner of the Lord Marshal. It stood back from the wall, nearly as far from the violence as she was, hanging limp in the still air. She pulled her hand from Vincen's and tapped his knee. It was a moment before he took her meaning and handed her the little spyglass. It took her a moment to find him, but then there he was, sitting high in his saddle with a spyglass of his own, surveying the battle. He looked thinner than when he'd left Camnipol. His cloak was thrown back, his jaw set, and his shoulders bent in an attitude of supreme concentration. She had seen his body take that shape since he'd been a boy too small to walk. His mind was bent entirely upon the scene before him. She would have given a great deal to know what was in his mind just then.

Vicarian sat a horse just beyond him, and his expression chilled her. His smile was wide and bright, his eyes flashing in the grimy sunlight. She had also seen this—pleasure, laughter, joy—but never in this setting. To look upon this and rejoice seemed monstrous. There, in those priestly robes, was a thing that had been her son. A thing that had eaten him and now wore his skin. She had known that, but being reminded felt like being struck. She wanted to shout to Jorey to run, to get away before the corruption spread to him.

Jorey's attention shifted just as Vincen murmured, "Oh God."

A second column of smoke was rising in the south, and for a moment she thought that was what Vincen had seen. Then the flames took the crippled siege tower, lighting it like a pitch-dipped torch. The fire's soft murmur was as loud as the shrieks of the men dying within the tower. The oil that had poured down to drench it and then be set alight left a trail of flames up the soot-black side of the wall. Another of the towers stood alone, trapped, it seemed by some misfortune of the path far from the wall. The other towers had reached their places. Soldiers swarmed up the ladders, either rising to the wall through sheer will and the force of numbers or being thrown back. She couldn't guess how many men had died before her so far that day, but there were more, and with priests there to urge them on, she had no doubt that they would either win the city or die to a man. She wondered what she could write to Paerin Clark and the bank in Northcoast. *The war is a madness unto itself, and there is no ending it short of complete slaughter. The first blow has been struck, and there is no path to victory nor reconciliation nor peace.*

And yet there had to be. There must, and she—God help her—had to find it. If she did not...

"You cannot fail," she said with a sigh, "for if you do, the consequences will be unimaginably dire."

"What, m'lady?"

On the wall, a roar went up. A thousand voices lifting together in chorus that overcame mere human sound. It was like floodwaters rushing in a gully. On the top of the wall, the battle had changed, though she couldn't quite make sense of how. The motions of the men seemed more frantic, if that was possible. At the westernmost of the siege towers, a man panicked and ran off the wall, arms and legs flailing in the air as he fell to his death. Clara stepped forward, a thick dread growing in her throat. The crowd shouted again, a vast sound that seemed to echo more deeply than the space could explain. A cunning man's trick, surely. Some magic to frighten them and put the army to flight.

The dragon rose up from within the city. Its wings were spread like a monarch raising hands to claim a kingdom. The great jaw swung open, showing sword-cruel teeth and the black flesh of its tongue and mouth. It screamed again, and Clara understood. The echoing roar had not been the summed voices of the clashing armies, but this one throat opened in rage. It wheeled in the air, flame pouring from its mouth. Another of the towers close against the wall caught fire, and the screams came from all around. She felt Vincen step back, but was unable herself to move. The beast was beautiful and terrible. Its movement in the air was like a dancer's. It cried out again, and she thought there were words in the call.

Jorey's banner fell slowly, arcing down to the earth. She turned her spyglass back, fear possessing her. When she found her son, it was only his bearer who'd fled. Jorey sat where he had been, fighting to control his mount. Other men of noble blood were beside him now. Ceruc Essian,

Assin Pasillian, Myrol Caot. They wore a form of armor she had never seen before, something between scale and leather that caught the light of the burning fires. Vicarian had twisted in his saddle and was shouting at them. Jorey had eyes only for the enemy. His smile spoke less of joy than a grim and violent satisfaction.

"They knew," Clara said. "Jorey knew. He's ready for this."

"I don't think I am, Clara," Vincen said. "We should pull back. I don't think we're safe here."

Clara put up her hand, waving him to silence. By his fallen banner, Jorey lifted his fist.

The horns blew a new and unfamiliar command. The one siege tower that stood back from the rest—the one that Clara had assumed trapped by some unfortunate ground—opened, and men spilled out of it. And with them, new machines such as Clara had not seen before. Or had, but only in the carts that had made their way past her during her travels.

"What are those?" she asked.

"I don't know," Vincen said. And then, "A trap."

Cithrin

The ships that remained of the Antean Navy came as Barriath and Marcus had warned that they might, great and small, their sails catching the wind and riding into toward the port, but not so near as to be endangered by the complexities of the harbor. The guide boats remained at the docks along with the trade ships and the captured round-ships now under the command of Barriath Kalliam. Three times before, Cithrin had found herself in cities under threat of violence. In Vanai, she had escaped before the battle. In Camnipol, she had hidden until the fighting had passed. In Suddapal, she had put her tribute in the streets and prayed that the sacking army would take the wealth and spare the people.

It had never occurred to her to treat the battles as theater.

"More wine, Magistra Cithrin?"

"Thank you, Governor," she said. "I think I will."

The viewing platform had been erected by the seawall, letting them look down over the port itself and then out over the wide blue water to where the enemy waited. The sand-bars and reefs stood as the first protection of the city, the ancient ballistas and greenwood catapults along the seawall were the second, and Barriath Kalliam was the third. Three circles of defense, and only one of attack.

But the one was devastating.

The first of the enemy roundships was already burning, a plume of smoke rising up from it, black and greasy. The heat from the flames lifted it higher and higher until it seemed more like a storm cloud than the ruin of any human thing. At its top, the smoke plume flattened and began to drift. The servant poured Cithrin a fresh cup of wine as Governor Siden stared through his spyglasses and chortled. He seemed to take great pleasure in watching the enemy soldiers burn or drown or both. Cithrin preferred to see the destruction at a distance. It let her celebrate the victory with fewer pangs of conscience.

Inys, flying low along the coast, angled out again. The tip of one wing dragged along the surface of the water, leaving a spreading line of white where he turned. His back was to the city and Cithrin when he loosed his fires again, and the flame was bright as a rising sun. When Inys pulled up, working his wide wings up into the sky, a second ship was afire. The governor clapped his hands. Cithrin drank her wine and made the smile that was expected of her. It might only have been that she'd had so much trouble sleeping of late, but the victory at sea didn't fill her with joy. If anything, it seemed like a waste. All those lives. The labor that had gone to making the ships. And everything that they could have done, all of the work they might have accomplished, had they not instead been doing this.

To no one's surprise, the remaining ships began to scatter, leaving the burning hulks of their comrades behind to char and sink. A second column of smoke began to rise alongside the first. The governor stood and held his hand out to her.

"Shall we repair to the defensive wall?" he asked with a grin.

"I think we should," Cithrin replied.

The streets of the city were thick with people, but the queensmen cleared the path for them. Porte Oliva had always been a mixed city. Firstblood and Kurtadam and Cinnae. As she passed through the streets, she couldn't help picking out the dark-scaled faces of Timzinae. Refugees from Suddapal, many of them. Even with the Antean forces broken, they would shoulder much of the burden for the war. Many, many people in Porte Oliva had lost their homes and businesses already in the fire outside the wall. The Timzinae were and would be the faces that had brought the conflict to Birancour. Theirs and Cithrin's. But in the mind of the city, she had also brought the dragon, and so she would be honored, carried with the governor, plied with wine and honeybread, invited to the best viewing points to watch the slaughter. It wasn't fair, but so little was. This at least was injustice in her favor.

The viewing tower was in the highest spire of the cathedral. Walking up the tight-spiraling staircase made her legs ache and left her dizzy. The high, open air at the top did little to steady her. Yardem Hane and Pyk were there already, as was the captain of the city guard. Far below, the square that had once housed the condemned seemed terribly far away. The wall of the city stood to the north, and from her vantage, Cithrin could just see over it to the blackened ruins beyond. One siege tower stood alone and forlorn in the ashes. The others, against the defensive wall, were hidden from her sight, though a column of smoke marked where one had been set alight.

The violence was so near to her, and also separate, as if the clear air between her and the fighting were like the edge of a stage. What happened there happened there. She could imagine the press of bodies, the weight of sword and armor, the fear. She could imagine the sudden pain of an arrow in her throat, the way sound might grow distant as death came close. She could watch it all safely, from here.

"All is progressing as we'd hoped," the captain of the city guard said.

"Excellent, *excellent*," the governor said, rubbing his hands together.

"Yardem," Cithrin said. "Where's Captain Wester?"

"Had some things to see to, ma'am," Yardem said, his ears canted forward politely. She wished that the tiny stone deck were large enough to take the Tralgu aside and speak to him in something like privacy. Nothing could be said here that wouldn't be heard by everyone present, and Yardem's reply had been so diplomatic it could only mean he didn't want to say it in front of the governor. Her curiosity itched, but she turned her eyes toward the northern wall.

"What have we seen, then?" she asked.

"A little light assault by their siege engines," Yardem said. "A few small scars in the stone, I'd guess, and a few that managed to get over. One hit a stable and seems to have taken down a wall. That's the worst of it. They keep trying to scale the walls."

"Are we worried about that?"

"No," Yardem rumbled. "They're heartfelt, but the road's worn them down. Our side's rested, fresh, and guarding their own city. If it weren't for the priests, I'd call the day ours now."

"But they don't have our dragon!" Governor Siden said. "The enemy ships are already put to fire or flight."

"Yes, sir. Saw the smoke."

"And now..."

Inys flew in low over the city, wings spread wide. He passed through the square below Cithrin, the sun shining on his scales, and glided north toward the wall. Even so far above the city, she could hear the voices rise like a surge in the waves. In the square and on the wall, the citizens of

Porte Oliva raised their fists and called out. It might only have been her imagination that Inys flew where the adulation was loudest. The dragon screamed once, then again, and then cleared the wall, his shadow falling over the battlefield. This third shriek was the loudest, and the violence of it set Cithrin's heart turning a little faster in her chest. She couldn't imagine the fear it would inspire in the soldier who had to face it. Inys wheeled, wings scooping the air, and set another of the siege towers alight. The enemy's horns blared.

Something happened at the lone siege tower. It opened, and groups of men spilled out of it. From so high up, Cithrin couldn't make out the devices they were carrying. They appeared to be oversized crossbows or perhaps very small ballistas. The bolts they threw seemed no larger than needles from this distance. She could hardly believe they could do a dragon harm.

The needles caught the thin membranes of Inys's left wing, and the dragon's head turned, biting at the air below the new wounds. She glanced at Yardem, but his ears were forward in concern and confusion. Her heart began beating faster, driven by an unexpected sense of threat. Threads seemed to be rising from the ground up toward the dragon, though she couldn't imagine that was true. Inys fought to keep aloft, blasting fire toward the ground, but more needles rose to touch him. Leg, wing, neck. More threads rose. Cithrin leaned forward, her hands on the railing, clutching so hard that her knuckles ached. The dragon turned, laboring in the air that moments before he had owned. He disappeared behind the wall. A great shout rose up. The dragon had fallen. Cithrin heard herself gasp, and the sound was almost a sob. Antean horns sounded a charge.

Governor Siden's face was bloodless. "No. No no no. Our dragon," he murmured, then turned on the queensman.

"Don't just stand there! We have to help! Sound the attack! We'll free him from this trickery and end this once and for all."

"Shouldn't do that," Yardem said.

"Yes, sir," the guard captain said and bolted past the servants and down the stairs. There was little need. On the ground and at the wall's top, the soldiers of Porte Oliva were already surging forward. Cithrin willed them to go faster. To save Inys before it was too late. The dragon's voice rose in rage and agony and the governor sank to his knees. Yardem made a low grunt like he'd been punched. Cithrin turned to him. The coldness in his eyes surprised her.

"What?" she said.

"I'd thought Captain Wester was being overcautious," he said. "Owe him an apology. You need to come with me now."

"But—" She gestured at the wall that hid the battle from her.

"Ma'am," Yardem said, "they're going out after him. That means they're opening the gates. Not something that's wise to do with an experienced army on the other side."

"No, I have to see that—"

Yardem put a hand on her shoulder. His eyes were dark and hard. "Ma'am, the governor's just ordered the attack. He's *opening the gates*. The city's about to fall."

Cithrin blinked, shook her head. It was like waking up from a dream. "Oh," she said.

The stairs had been interminable when she'd gone up them. Going down was faster, easier, and seemed to take lifetimes. She expected to have nightmares running down an endless stairway, the curve of the stone walls keeping her from seeing what was only just ahead, for the rest of her life. If she lived out the day.

When they reached the square, the fighting had already spilled into the city. The streets, tightly packed before, were in chaos. Bodies surged one direction and then another, pressing together until Cithrin couldn't move her arms, couldn't breathe. Yardem raised his voice and then his bare sword. There were no Anteans near him. He was fighting their own. Refugees and workers and bakers and children. They were transformed to the enemy by the accident of being between them and where they wanted to be.

Ten horses in full barding appeared at the far side of the square, men in armor sitting astride them and hewing at the crowd. Cithrin managed to reach the far corner and thread her way through the press, following Yardem's shouts and threats. She was weeping, but she ignored it. An old Kurtadam woman with a grey-brown pelt and rheumy, confused eyes stepped into Cithrin's path, and Yardem disappeared. Cithrin shouted for him. Called his name. Screamed. She could barely hear her own voice. The crowd moved like a riptide, carrying her with it. She fought to breathe. She stumbled over something soft, and was pushed along before she could see what it was. She hoped it wasn't a body. If it was a body, she hoped it was already dead.

At the corner of the Grand Market, the churn of humanity grew thicker. Worse. Maestro Asanpur's café was shattered and overrun. The tents of the Grand Market had fallen, the space they had contained overflowing with panic and the desperate need for escape when there was no escape to be had. Cithrin screamed Yardem's name and Marcus's. She couldn't hear her own voice over the roar of the crowd.

First the roar, and then the screams.

Antean soldiers poured into the market square from two of the larger streets. People shrieked, and the pressure of flesh pushed the breath out of her. She couldn't shout.

Couldn't call for help. She thought for a moment she saw Besel a few ranks in front of her, and she tried to reach out to him until she remembered he was dead, had died before even the fall of Vanai. Words carried over the roar, inhumanly loud. *You have lost. Everything you love is already gone. There is no hope. Listen to my voice. All is lost.* The air was hot and the sounds of slaughter made it hotter. She closed her eyes. Nausea overwhelmed her. Somewhere very, very nearby, people were being cut to death with swords, and she was powerless to stop it or to avoid it.

This is war, she thought. What she'd fled in Vanai and Camnipol and Suddapal had caught her here. Her head swam, bright colors dancing before her that had nothing to do with light. The distance to her feet seemed like a day's journey. Her mind slid away, and she didn't try to hold it close.

Time changed, became meaningless. A series of moments passed with no more connection between them than images in a dream. A Timzinae man, blood pouring from his mouth. A Firstblood child huddled in a corner, her hands over her head. The cobbled street, Cithrin's cheek pressed against it as someone ground their boot against her ear.

"Are you Cithrin bel Sarcour?"

Her lip was swollen. Something had happened to her knee. Someone shook her shoulder. The words came again, in their strange accent.

"Are you Cithrin bel Sarcour?"

"No," she said.

A man's laughter. She opened her eyes. She didn't know him, but she saw the resemblance. He had the same shape of face as Master Kit. The same wiry hair. His robes were the brown of the spider priests, and he held a speaking trumpet in his hand. Soldiers stood at either side. She knew the place.

She was at the seawall, not far from where Opal had died. She hadn't thought of Opal in years. Why was her mind calling up the dead? The screams of the crowd still deafened. The air smelled like a slaughterhouse. Flies were buzzing everywhere. The slaughter was still going on. The death of her city.

"This is she," the priest said. "This is the one."

She shook her head. She was on her knees. She didn't remember being on her knees. She must have fallen in the crowd. "No," she said. "I'm not. You've made a mistake."

"Sergeant!" the man at her right called. "We've got the bitch!"

A Firstblood voice howled in triumph behind her. She shook her head, but her heart was in her belly. Better she'd died in the press. Not this. Please, anything but this.

A man stooped down beside her. He had thinning pale hair, pockmarks on his cheeks. She thought he looked sad. "All right," he said. "No one hurts her. She goes back to Camnipol, not so much as a bruise on her. Not until she gets there. Understood? You! Kippar. You're her personal guard now. Anything happens to her, you're the first to die for it."

Cithrin's gaze swam up to the new man. He stood beside the priest, fists the size of hams, shoulders as broad as a table. Yemmu blood in him, she was sure of it. When he spoke, his voice was sharp.

"Yes, sir. I'll see to it."

The priest's head snapped forward, blood splashing on Kippar's face. The massive guard stumbled back, shouting and clawing at his eyes. The two men at her shoulders dropped her and turned. The priest lay on the pale stone pavement, a crossbow bolt protruding an inch from the back of his head. Rich red blood pooled around his skull. And in the pool...

Cithrin screamed and tried to crawl away. To run. Tiny black bodies scattered from the dead priest, leaving pinprick footsteps of crimson. Someone shouted, and the Anteans, blades already drawn, closed ranks around her. The sad-faced sergeant looked around, confusion in his expression. He glanced down, dropped his blade, started screaming. Something tickled Cithrin's ankle and she slapped it hard enough to sting her fingertips. Small black legs thinner than hairs stuck to her palm, the spider's body ripped apart.

"Please, I'll go with you," she shouted. "*Let me get up!*"

She tried to stand, but someone pushed her down. Another Antean knelt beside the priest and started screaming.

"They've got a cunning man!" someone shouted. "They're using some kind of magic on us."

"Get away from the body," Cithrin shouted. "They're in his blood. *Get away from his body!*"

They ignored her. Boots tramped on stone. Voices rose in battle cries. The soldiers around her drew their blades, forgetting even her for the moment. She staggered back against the seawall itself, and her bank's guardsmen fell on the Anteans. Halvill, his dark scales marked with white lines where enemy blows had already struck him. Corisen Mout, his teeth bared. Enen, her pelt matted with and dark with blood. Yardem Hane and Marcus Wester standing side by side, their blades moving with the simple economy of men so long accustomed to violence it had become a reflex.

"There's spiders!" Cithrin screamed, and saw Marcus's head turn to her. She pointed at the fallen priest, and watched understanding bloom in the guard captain's eyes. The green sword in his hand flickered like a tongue of flame as he pushed in toward her. The Anteans, caught between the invisible threat spilling out from their dead priest and the advance of her guardsmen, retreated. Five of them were left writhing on the pavement, clawing at their own eyes and mouths and crotches. Marcus went to each in turn, sinking the poisoned sword into them, and then into the corpse of the priest. The others stood back at a respectful distance as he waved the blade slowly over the paving. A shudder of movement, almost too small to see, caught Cithrin's eye. A spider shriveled by the stinging fumes of the blade.

He reached her, sheathing the sword. He was breathing hard, laboring. His cheeks looked sunken, his eyes fever bright. When he spoke, though, it was the understated, calm tone she'd known since she'd been a lost girl with a banker's heartlessness, fleeing from a violence she barely understood. Little had changed.

"This?" he said, nodding at the city, the violence, the death that still spilled in the gutters. "It could have gone better."

Marcus

M ost days, from the seawall to the piers was the walk of minutes. A brief turn through the salt quarter with its narrow, dark streets, and then out into the broad ways built for carts and the traffic of trade. Most days, there had been puppeteers at the corners, playing out their dramas for coin. A large audience might slow things down a bit if they spilled too far into the street.

Now it was a meat grinder.

Even where there were no soldiers, there were people in the streets. Half-built barricades jutted out over the cobbles without plan or strategy. In the north, a great column of smoke might have been the Antean siege engines or the Governor's Palace or the beginning of a conflagration that would turn the city to ash. Marcus didn't know, and no answer changed what he had to do in the next hour.

Marcus and Yardem led the way, their blades clearing the way before them for the most part. The press of fear and humanity made the passage slow, and Marcus didn't want to kill anyone he didn't have to. Some of the citizens of Porte Oliva would likely survive the sack, and the ones that didn't, he preferred that the enemy killed. His arms and back ached already, and the day wasn't near done. Cithrin's arm was around Enen's shoulder. The thinness of frame that came with her Cinnae blood left her light enough that any of them but Halvill could throw her over a shoulder and run if the need came. Any of them but Halvill and himself. He tried to ignore the weakness in his arm and shoulder, the burning in his muscles that he hadn't felt wielding a blade since before his voice had cracked. He told himself it was age and indolence, but it was the venom of the blade taking its toll.

It didn't matter what it was. The job was getting Cithrin through a brief turn through the salt quarter, then the broader ways by the piers. That was all that mattered.

"She's not looking good, sir," Yardem said.

"She'll keep."

"Not sure she will."

"She'll have to."

Marcus looked over his shoulder. Blood marked Cithrin's neck and arm. He told himself it was her own, that she'd only been beaten and cut in the violence. It was a bleak thought to find comfort in, but the red hadn't been from the priest. He'd gotten there in time to keep the spiders from getting into her, at least. Still, she seemed dazed, her eyes flat and empty. She was hurt, no question. And they were a long run from safe.

A wave of bodies spewed into the intersection before them, shouting, shrieking, moving singly and together like a flock of birds. At least three of them were bleeding. Marcus and Yardem closed ranks without speaking and marched forward into the throng. A Kurtadam man, his dark, glossy pelt adorned with silver and glass beads, stopped before them, his hands out in a commanding pose.

"You! All of you! In the name of Nerris Alcion, I command you to the defense of my warehouse!"

"You should move," Marcus said, not breaking stride.

Snarling, the man put his hand against Marcus's chest. Yardem kicked the side of the Kurtadam's knee, folding it

the wrong way, and tossed him into the gutter. The mewling sounds of pain were drowned out quickly. All around
Marcus, the guards of the bank drew together, their blades
at the ready. Down the length of the street, Marcus caught
a glimpse of open space. It wasn't a good sign. The only
thing that opened a crowd like this was violence. He pushed
ahead. In the clear space, the green and gold of queensmen
dithered, caught between formation and free battle.

"Hey!" Marcus shouted. "Guardsmen! To us!"

"They can't hear you, sir."

"You try, then," Marcus said, leaning forward into the
unyielding bodies of the crowd. "People might make way
for men in uniforms."

"They can't hear anyone," Yardem said. "Wax plugs in
the ears. Against the priests."

With a roar, a dozen or so Antean soldiers as thin as
reeds rushed at the milling queensmen. Marcus spat on the
ground between his feet. "Well, God smiled," he said, then
turned again toward the port. "Make way! Move, damn it,
or we'll spit you before they can! Make a fucking *path*!"

The buildings of the salt quarter loomed, high and dark.
The smell of smoke was growing thicker. Voices all around
them were wailing, and the crowd in the street was nearly at
a standstill. In front of him, a Firstblood woman stood with
tears in her eyes. The press of humanity behind her gave
her no way to get out of Marcus's path, and her gaze was
fixed on the thin, green-patinaed blade between them. She
mouthed the words *I can't, I can't*, shaking her head, and
began to sink down to her knees.

"Stand up!" Marcus shouted. "If you fall down now,
you're dead. Stand up!"

The woman blinked, stood. He had the sense he could
have told her anything and she'd have done it. Whoever she

was, whoever she had been until now, the trauma of the day had transformed her into another kind of puppet, ready to do what she was told because the part of her that could make decisions had already surrendered. Marcus sheathed the poisoned sword and took the woman by the shoulder. He pulled her into the center of the little knot of guards, and Halvill took her from there, shoving her out behind them. One by one, Marcus ate away at the crowd in front of them, moving the guards—moving Cithrin—forward another step, and then another, and then another. It was like chipping down a mountain with a hammer, but it was all he could do, so he did it.

The crowd before them broke, the blocking bodies streaming away, diving into doorways and shifting away. Seven men in light scale armor bearing blades whipped at them, cutting the people down like grass. They might have been Antean or some group of local thugs driven mad by panic. All that Marcus cared was that they were between him and the docks and that they'd already started fighting so he didn't have to feel bad about killing them. They didn't exchange words. There was no banter. He drew his sword, Corisen Mout came to his right side, Yardem to his left. The first blow almost wrenched the blade from Marcus's hand, but then long habit flowed into him.

Yardem's longer reach drove the attackers slightly toward Corisen Mout, crowding them against the wall. Marcus's world narrowed to a few impressions, gone as soon as they arrived. The angles of the blades, the motion of shoulders. He blocked the attacks and pressed his own. The enemy weren't very good, aiming for his face instead of his body, going for the quick kill. One left his foot too far forward, and Marcus drew off the man's blade with a feint while Yardem sank his sword's point into the enemy ankle. One less. Corisen Mout fell back under a rush, and Marcus slapped the enemy's arm with the edge of his blade. The man's elbow began dripping blood at once, and the venom doubled him over screaming not five breaths later. Corisen Mout finished him, and together they slid forward. The crowd was gone now, and they were moving in another of the little clearings of violence. At least there was room.

When the enemy broke and ran, Marcus trotted after them, not so quickly as to catch up, but enough to keep that little bubble in the greater crowd open for as long as he could. They reached the broader, more open streets. Bodies lay on the cobblestones, and blood trickled in the gutters. Smoke and the smell of death thickened the air. The masts of the ships stood to the south, pointing at the sky like the leafless trunks of a winter forest. Marcus looked back. Cithrin's eyes were glazed, but still open. Her jaw set. That was as much as he had time for.

At the piers, the fighting was worse. The ships that hadn't cast off were in danger of being overrun, and their crews were locked in battle with the men and women fleeing from the city. Hours ago, they had all been allies against Antea. Now they were beating each other with bricks and fists, kicking and shrieking. Many of the boats had untied from the piers and were floating off in the water, where the brave and crazed swam toward them without any way to climb up into them. Outside the harbor, the remains of three Antean roundships burned and smoked. In the chaos, it was as if their destruction was another blow against Porte Oliva, the earlier victories turned to loss by the overwhelming collapse of the city.

At the edge of one pier, Ahariel Akkabrian, Pyk, Smit, and Hornet stood, blades drawn, before a wall of panicking citizens. One guard, one notary, and two actors against the throng. A pair of ship's boats bobbed on the water behind them, sailors ready at the oars. Magistra Isadau stood in one boat as steady as a mast, her hands clasped at her chest like a statue of abstract grief.

"Come on!" Marcus shouted, for himself as much as the others. "Just a little bit more. Push, you bastards!"

The crowd around the boats seemed dense and unyielding as stone. Marcus shoved, and they shoved back. Several of the men in the group had blades and cudgels. If it came to an open fight, the bank and her allies would win, but not without losses, and Cithrin was on the wrong side of the water for that. He sheathed his blade and nodded at Yardem. The Tralgu flicked his ears and put his own back in the scabbard, then back to back they pressed into the group, saying reassuring nonsense about there being room for everyone and the queensmen having the enemy on the run. It was like carving a groove into a wall. Creating a weak spot. When they pressed out and let Enen and Halvill and Cithrin stumble through, the crowd sensed that they'd been tricked. The roar of voices was like a storm wind, wordless and full of threat. Marcus stood on the water's edge, his heels on the last board, while Enen and Cithrin tumbled into the ship's boat with Magistra Isadau.

"Best get out now," Marcus shouted.

Smit and Pyk dropped into the second boat. Then Corisen Mout and Ahariel Akkabrian. Yardem was preparing to drop Halvill down to safety when the crowd surged, pushed from behind like a wave. A thick, solid shoulder fixed against Marcus's chest, and when he stepped back to steady himself, he was falling. Cold water forced itself up his nose, into his mouth. The padding under his armor swelled instantly, and the weight of the steel links pulled him down. His first thought was that he was drowning. The second was that his hands were empty. Above the water, people were shouting. Others had fallen in with him. Cithrin's screams were like rips in the air. Marcus filled his lungs and dove.

In the green beneath the surface, the world was quiet. Even calm. He pushed down, ears and eyes aching. There, below him, the sword turned as it fell. He kicked his legs, willing his armor to help him sink faster. Something splashed high above him. The light began to fade. He came nearer the blade. Nearer. And then he had it, his hand around the hilt. He turned. The surface of the water danced above him, the blue of the sky made green by the water and distance. The bottoms of the two boats stood solid as black clouds. A half dozen flailing bodies surrounded the nearest one. Oars dipped down toward him and then vanished as the other pulled away. Marcus aimed himself toward the second one.

His chest burned as he clawed his way up the thick water, fighting for every inch toward the dancing air. The boat nearest the shore shuddered, and a new body fell into the water, trailing an arc of bubbles and blood. It was too big to be Cithrin. He fought. The urge to breathe grew to a shriek, and he was still too far from the surface. He wasn't trying to reach the boats anymore. Not any of them. Up was all there was. His mouth opened without his willing it and a great bubble of air gouted out. *Don't breathe in*, he thought. *If you breathe the water in, that's drowning. Don't drown.*

The silver mirror of the surface shivered and teased. Five feet above him. Four. Three. The world began to grey and spin at the edges. He bared his teeth and willed his legs to kick, his arms to move. His body had been remade from clay and stone. It wouldn't move. Two feet. He lifted the sword, and its tip rose out of the water. Two feet. His sluggish body patted at the water. Two feet. Two feet.

Three feet, and sinking.

He barked out his despair, and seawater flowed into his mouth, his lungs. The pain seared him, and then there was something around him, solid and ropy. The root of a great tree. Or no. An arm. Marcus's head was in air, and he was vomiting, coughing. He was aware, distantly, of screaming voices. Anything farther than his own skin seemed to belong to some different nation. Something hard dug into his ribs like a blow. It was the edge of a boat, and he was being tipped into it. He rolled forward onto the boards. The sword was still in his hand.

"Don't...don't touch the blade," he managed.

"Clear on that, sir," Yardem said and let go his grip around Marcus's chest.

Slowly, the world expanded. The sailors working the oars were Barriath Kalliam's pirates and also Hornet working manfully alongside them with tears streaming down his cheeks. Cithrin and Magistra Isadau were huddled together at the stern, their arms around each other, their eyes wide and lost and horror-filled. Yardem, soaking and stinking of wet dog, sat beside him. Enen and Halvill were at the stern, looking back at the riot on the seafront. They were already halfway to the roundship. Marcus pulled himself to the edge of the boat and retched up another mouthful of fouled seawater.

"The other boat," he said.

"Swamped, sir. A dozen or so people fell into the water. They panicked."

"Pyk?"

"In that boat, sir."

"The guards?"

"They didn't make it out, sir."

"Go back for them, Captain," Hornet said through a sob. "*Please* go back for them. Smit's out there."

Marcus pushed himself up. The pier was fifty feet away. It could as well have been a thousand.

"He's gone, Hornet. If we go back into that, we'll be gone too. We have to get to the ship."

The heartbroken gasp came not from the actor, but from Cithrin. Carefully, Marcus put his blade back in his scabbard. *I hope you were worth it*, he thought to the sword. *The cost of having you keeps getting higher.*

At the roundship, ropes and swings were waiting to haul them up. Master Kit helped Marcus onto the swaying deck, his eyes dark. He'd seen what had happened to the other boat and been as unable to stop it as Marcus had. Mikel and Sandr and Charlit Soon grabbed Hornet as soon as the swing he rode came near, and they all collapsed together on the deck, weeping and calling Smit's name. Across the deck, Halvill and his new wife, Maha, stood, their baby between them, their foreheads touching. Only Cary stood apart, her chin lifted and her eyes dry. Marcus thought he saw hatred there, but he couldn't say for whom. Magistra Isadau and Enen came up the ropes and were lifted over the railing.

Cithrin came on board last. Her skin, always pale, was white. Even her lips were colorless.

"You knew," she said.

"I had a feeling. It was enough that I made some plans for the worst case. May have underestimated how bad it would get."

Cithrin turned to look across the deck. It was wide as a building. The boards were scrubbed, but there was still a hint of green to the old wood. The timbers creaked, and by being so near, almost matched the screams from shore. The ship's boat was being hauled back into place and the vast sails were being pulled up. When they caught the wind, they bellied out with a crack like breaking stone and the ship lurched a little.

"We've lost it all," Cithrin said.

"We have the books and ledgers," Marcus said. "The immediate wealth of the bank. The gold and jewels and spices. A couple dozen bolts of silk, I think. Hold's full of it. It's not the first time we've made this experiment. Lose a couple more cities and I'll have it down to an art. Also took the liberty of putting Lord Skestinin on the other ship over there. Figured Barriath would be in the best position to keep him."

"We've lost Porte Oliva."

"That, yes. We lost the city."

"We were supposed to win," Cithrin said. The words were almost calm.

"We didn't."

"Oh," she said, and then didn't speak again. He put a hand on her shoulder. She was trembling.

The ship's captain, a Kurtadam with a moth-eaten pelt and a missing eyetooth, strode over and nodded to Cithrin before turning to Marcus. "Himself's signaled the ready. Unless you've got more coming."

"Himself?" Cithrin asked abstractedly.

"Barriath," Marcus said, and then to the captain, "No. We're ready."

"Asked where it was you wanted to head," the captain said.

"Wherever's fastest," Marcus said. "Anyplace but here."

The Kurtadam spat over the railing and turned back, shouting orders to the sailors that Marcus didn't understand and didn't care to. His clothes were starting to dry, the salt making his skin itch. Weariness bore down on him. Cithrin looked at the city as it grew slowly more distant, the seawall becoming small enough to cover with an outstretched hand. And then a thumb. Soon the only real marks of Porte Oliva were the columns of smoke. He stood by her silently until she spoke.

"This is my fault," Cithrin said.

"It's not a matter of fault," Marcus said. "It's war. People have been doing this since—"

"Marcus!" Kit shouted.

The old actor stood at the rail. His hair was pulled back from his face, and the gauntness of age and hard living made him seem more a pirate than the pirates. Marcus stepped forward. The motion of the waves made his steps uncertain.

"I'm sorry about Smit," Marcus said.

"As am I, but I think that isn't our immediate problem."

"We have an immediate problem?"

Kit gestured out over the water, and Marcus's gaze followed the gesture. There, almost at the horizon, a black dash marked the sky. As they watched, the darkness grew larger, clearer, closer. Inys flapped twice, hauling himself above the water. His head sank low before him, like a horse on the verge of exhausted collapse. Long ropes streamed down from his body to trail behind him in the sea. His scales shone red with fresh blood.

"Well, God smiled," Marcus said sourly. "Where in hell are we supposed to put *him*."

Clara

After the defenders of the city left the safety of their walls to pour out, selling their lives cheap in the effort to free the crippled dragon, the battle moved on. It entered the city itself, and was hidden from Clara by the great, scarred walls. At one point, shortly before evening, someone in the city had tried to close the gates again, but whatever that plan was, it failed with the defenses unrestored. The falling sun spread shadows across the churned mud and ashes of the ruins outside Porte Oliva. Within the city, the sack.

She knew better than to approach the walls until her son's army had burned through its anger and its lusts, had celebrated its victory upon the bodies of the conquered. Until then, she was a creature of the fields of ash. There would be enough to learn, enough to report, when morning came and the beasts had remade themselves as men again.

Dawson had told her stories of war before. Of its glories and dangers. As she and Vincen and the other hangers-on picked through the bodies of the fallen—Antean and Birancouri alike—she could conjure up his voice. *Battle is the proving ground in which boys discover what it means to be men.* She wondered now whether he had truly believed that, or if it was only a story he'd told himself to forgive what could not be forgiven.

A Timzinae woman lay facedown in the ashes, motionless.

Dead. If she'd borne a weapon, it was lost amid the rubble. A Firstblood boy was sprawled beside her, his open eyes as empty as stones. Clara couldn't say by looking which side he'd fought on, but his frame was thin and his face gaunt, so likely one of Jorey's. A young man of Antea come to find glory in ashes and blood.

"They say the spirits of the dead ride with Geder's army," she said.

"They say a lot of things," Vincen replied. His voice was rough.

"I think it's true," Clara said, nodding at the dead boy. "He looks wasted enough he might have been dead for weeks. Months. I think perhaps we are the dead."

"I'm not," Vincen said. "And I think you aren't either."

Clara knelt by the body, checking it for any small items of value, not because she wanted them, but because it was expected of the kind of scavenger she was pretending to be. "Are you certain of that?"

"I've seen a lot of things be killed. Elk. Rabbit. Fox. Bird. Once they've died, they don't suffer. So yes. Fairly certain."

The dead boy had a little wallet folded over his belt, empty apart from a bit of oak with a mark cut into it in black. A charm against misfortune, a token from a lover or a parent, or a bit of scrap picked up and carried for no reason in particular. It didn't matter now. The only one who could have put meaning to it was past caring, and the little chip of wood was now forever and irrevocably just a little chip of wood. She tucked it in the fold of the boy's sleeve. Whatever it had been, it could rest with him. She rocked back on her haunches. Blackened timbers that had been houses and shops, launderers' yards and cobblers' stalls, stood all about, like bones made of char.

"My sons did this," she said. "My husband did much like

this in Asterilhold, and then came home to my arms. Can you imagine that? Loving someone who is capable of this?"

Vincen stood. For a long moment, they were both silent.

"Yes," he said.

"So can I," she said, "and it astounds me."

"Hey! You there!" The new voice was rough, the voice of a man hoarse from shouting.

Vincen moved between her and the approaching men, his chin high. There were five of them, all wearing armor not so different from a huntsman's leathers. One, the leader by his bearing and the adornments on his hilt, was familiar. Kestin Flor. Sir Namen Flor's first son by his second wife. Clara hunched down and tried to hide her face.

"My lord," Vincen said. "My congratulations on today's victory."

"Fuck you," Flor said, and the men with him sniggered. "You're out here desecrating our fallen, and you have the gall to congratulate me? You should be begging for mercy."

Clara's throat closed with fear. There was a madness in Flor's voice. A joy and a violence that sank her heart in black dread. Two of the soldiers moved out to the left, opening Vincen's flank.

"We've done nothing wrong," Vincen said. "We're traveling with the caravan. Supporting the soldiers."

"Feeding off us like ticks, I say," one of Flor's men growled.

"I've taken nothing from the Antean dead," Vincen said. "All I have is from the locals. You can have it, if you like. Take all of it."

"Oh, I will," Flor said, rolling the words out slowly. Tasting them. "Boys?"

They fell on him together. Four men against one. Soldiers against a man of their own nation. It was fists at first, and then when Vincen fell, feet. Clara felt as if she'd turned to stone. One of them lifted a knife.

When Clara cried out it was not the cry of animal fear that she expected. The words came out of her mouth crisply and as bright as if she'd polished them. "Kestin *Amril* Flor, you will stop this behavior at once, or by God I will have words with your mother."

The astonishment on Flor's face was instantaneous and profound. The thugs paused in their assault, turning to look first at her, and then their commander, and back again. Clara rose to her feet, not daring to look at Vincen. So long as their attention was on her, it was not on him. She had no plan apart from making them not hurt him, and didn't know what she intended next. Wise or rash, she had played her tile, and now there was nothing but to see it through. The rush of warmth and, yes, of power that surged up in her was likely an illusion, but she embraced it all the same. Flor stepped nearer, his eyes narrow and his mouth hard.

"And who the fuck are you?" he asked. She hoisted an eyebrow and watched the blood drain from his face as he found the answer to his question. "L-Lady Kalliam? What are you doing here?"

"Having my servant attacked by you and your men, it would seem," she said. The incongruity of her plain, filthy clothes, the smears of ash and mud on her face and in her hair, and her mere existence on the field of battle, she simply ignored. That which was not acknowledged did not exist. It was the simplest rule of court etiquette, and as effective as any cunning man's art.

"Give up. Who is she?" one of the soldiers asked.

The man beside him bobbed his head and smiled a tight, fearful smile. His voice was little more than a murmur. "She's the Lord Marshal's mother, you fucking ass."

The man with the knife dropped it on the ground and knelt beside Vincen. Vincen's pained grunt was sweeter than the gentlest flute. He was still alive. His rueful smile was like pouring cold water on a burn.

"I am..." Flor said, and then stumbled over any number of things that he might very well have been. Embarrassed, astounded, confused. Clara allowed herself a chilly smile. "My lady, please accept my apologies. I did not recognize you, and your man here didn't identify himself. I had no idea."

Yes, she thought, *this is all Vincen's failing*. Part of her wanted to scream at the man, accuse him. Vent her fear and anger, whatever the effect. But there were more important things to attend to. And if they were to move forward, she had to give Flor his excuse, even if it meant a bruise to Vincen's dignity.

"I see how the mistake was made, Sir Flor," she said. "I hope you can help me with its remedy?"

Flor licked his lips, uncertain what she meant. She looked down at Vincen, and up again. Flor took the hint.

"Find a litter for the lady and get her boy to the cunning men."

"He's not a soldier," the first of the men said, and the kneeling man punched the speaker's thigh.

"Do it now," Flor said, and the men scuttled away.

Clara knelt at Vincen's side. His eyes were open, but one was swelling. He held his right hand tight against his belly. Still, she had seen worse, and quite recently.

"Very sorry, my lady," he said. "I shouldn't have brought us so near the walls. I thought they'd all be in the city proper for the sack."

"You should have announced your mistress," Flor said, and Clara's mind flew to an entirely different meaning of the words. *You should have*, she thought. *You should have announced me to the world, and I should have stood by you before the court and my sons and everyone. What worse could they have done to us than this?*

"It's going to be all right, Vincen," she said, taking his left hand and holding it to her. "I'll see to it. Everything will be all right."

Vincen managed a weak laugh. "If you say so, my lady."

The mansion of Porte Oliva's newly deposed governor was as lavish as anything Camnipol had to offer barring the Kingspire itself. Its walls were covered with gold leaf, its divans upholstered in crimson silk. Scrolls with the exotic calligraphy of Far Syramys hung beside the doorway along-side portraits of the kings and queens of Birancour and a particularly gaudy and she suspected overly flattering one of the governor in a library, his eyes lifted to the mysteries of the world and his hand on a map of the city. Scented candles burned in silver holders. The fronds of potted ferns bobbed in the breeze that snaked in through the tall stone windows. A small fountain clucked to itself in the corner. The only two things that were at all out of place were a broad spill of blood slowly turning black on the golden carpet and Clara herself.

She had insisted on accompanying Vincen to the cunning men's tent the army had raised in a square not far from the defeated wall. The wounded and the dying had lain on cots of sailcloth and board or else the bare ground. The air had been thick and heavy with magic, and the weary nurse had looked over Vincen's wounds with a practiced eye even as Kestin Flor had railed at him about the importance of saving the life of Lady Kalliam's personal guard. She noticed that he made no mention of how Vincen came to be wounded, and she thought it rude to press the point. The nurse's mouth twitched into a scowl as he examined the bruises on Vincen's ribs. Still, before Clara left, she had the assurance of the old cunning man that Vincen's injuries, while uncomfortable, were far from serious, and that he would see to it that her man's care was not taken lightly. Of Clara's own clothing, he said nothing.

She wondered, sitting on the red silk cushion, what would have happened if she had not spoken. Or if she had spoken a moment later. When she closed her eyes, the knife waited for her like a dream that would not fade with the light. She packed her pipe with tobacco a servant boy had brought her. It was good leaf. Better than anything hauled along from Antea. The spoils of war, she imagined. She wondered whether whoever had bought it was still alive.

When the door opened, she rose to her feet. Jorey and Vicarian came into the room almost together. Seeing them so close rather than through a glass brought tears to her eyes. Vicarian looked bright about the eyes, merry and amused by the world and everything in it. He stood on the blood-spattered carpet, grinning and shaking his head as if he'd stepped into an unexpected party. She smiled at him, wondering whether this was another thing the goddess did to strip men of their humanity. Blind them to the horrors all around them and leave them tossing gilt balls in the slaughterhouse.

Jorey, by comparison, looked as though he had been ill. As if he still were. The pleasure and wonderment in his expression did something to allay it, but she could see the greyness of his skin, the way his cheeks were tight across the bone. From when he'd been a boy of eight, there had always been an expression he had when he was unwell. Something about his eyes or the way he held his mouth. No one else had recognized it but her and Dawson. Only her now, but there it was.

"Mother?" Jorey said. "What are you doing here?"

She shook her head. This was the moment. Whatever she said, truth or lies, would expose her. She could neither dissemble nor confess. The only alternative was to be misunderstood.

"Following you," she said. "Trying, in my own way, to help."

"Help, Mother?" Vicarian said. "How were you planning to help?"

"I know it isn't what you'd have chosen, and I suppose that's part of why I didn't send word. Or tell anyone back at home, for that matter. It isn't the sort of thing a woman of quality does, is it?"

"It really, *really* isn't," Jorey said, sitting down beside her. She scooped up his hand in her own, lacing their fingers together as if he were a child again. Vicarian brought a candle for her pipe, and she drew on the flame until the thick, fragrant smoke filled her lungs. She let tears come into her eyes. What child could press on in the face of a weeping mother? The manipulation of it disgusted her even as she embraced it. This was no time for righteousness.

"I didn't want to embarrass you," she said, and her eyes flickered toward Vicarian. *It's true. I didn't. You can't catch me out in a lie for saying that.* "And I was so frightened, there in the court with you gone." She sobbed, and it wasn't even forced. She waited for them to ask what she'd been afraid of. She could say it was Geder without, she hoped, saying why. But if they did ask that, if they *pressed*...

"Shh. It's all right," Jorey said. "I mean, it's raw madness and God help your reputation if word gets back home, but it's all right. I'm not angry."

"No?" she said.

"Of course not," Vicarian answered, as if Jorey's opinions

were identical to his own. As if the things in his blood already controlled his brother's mind. "We love you. We'll always love you. Even when you've done something a little unhinged. How long have you been following the army?"

"I... I joined it in the Free Cities. Before the pass at Bellin. We kept to the rear with the caravans. I don't think anyone suspected me of being anything out of the ordinary. Apart from Vincen. He knew, of course."

Vicarian sat, slapping his thighs. "Well, at least you had the sense to bring a guard with you. I can't imagine what you thought you could do."

"I know," she said, looking down. *You can't imagine, it's true. And if* that *changes, if you do imagine, everything is lost. Don't imagine.*

Jorey sat back in his seat, passing a hand over his chin. His sigh had laughter in it. "You don't need to go camp in the muck outside the city, do you? Tell me at least you'll accept my hospitality."

"I think my dignity would allow me to sleep in a real bed, were one on offer," Clara said, surprised to find herself blushing. Seeing herself through their eyes—sentimental, silly, unaware of the consequences of her own actions—made her feel almost as if she were the woman they thought she was. The woman she was pretending to be. The sense that Jorey was indulging her as a man might a small child or old woman left her cheeks warm.

"And if I sent you back to Camnipol with a few men to see you made it there safely," Jorey said. "Would you stay there this time?"

"I could say I would," Clara said. "If it would make you feel better."

"Tell me you would stay," Jorey said.

"I would stay," Clara lied.

Vicarian howled with laughter, slapping his thighs. "We're not getting rid of her so easily. Let her be here, brother. She won't come to harm. The goddess watches us and brings the world to our feet. She's in less danger with our army around us than from the gossips back home."

"Fine," Jorey said, lifting his palms. Dawson would have been enraged that she'd come. That she'd done something so utterly outside of her proper role. But he had been her husband, and Jorey was her son. And perhaps some part of Vicarian still was her son as well. It was a simpler thing, she thought, to tell a wife what she was allowed to be than to say the same to one's mother. She had held Jorey as a babe, had comforted him when he wept the bitter boyhood tears that no one else could ever be permitted to see. She had thought those things only love when she'd done them. She saw now they had been an investment.

She took his hand. *I am sorry*, she thought. *I love you more than I will ever say, and I am using you. I will go on using you, as long as that is what I have to do to stop Palliako and his priests. And your...the thing that was your brother. I have become a huntsman, and I am so terribly, terribly sorry.* Jorey put his hand over hers and smiled.

"Is there any news from home I might have missed during my travels?" she asked. *Further discoveries, perhaps, about who sent the false letter to Lord Ternigan?*

"You'll have left before the baby was born, then," he said. "Sabiha's named her Annalise. After you."

"Oh, no. Has she really?"

"Yes," Jorey said, "and there's a tale in it. It turns out Geder saved us again..."

Marcus

The waters off Cabral were deep blue, gentle and wide. The three roundships carved their way under the sky with a dozen smaller craft moving in among them, a fleet that answered to no king. The chuffing of the sails and the mutterings of wind were a constant, and the rolling of the ship only nauseated Marcus for the first day. The fleet moved slowly. The wounded dragon took up most of the deck of one roundship, threatening to capsize it if they hit even somewhat choppy water, and the others all cut their sails to keep pace. Marcus stood by the rail, looking across the water at Inys's unmoving head, the great bulk of his body, the torn and folded wings. It had taken a full day and night to pull the barbed spears out of the great beast's scales, and Inys had cried and wept the whole time. Marcus thought it had been less the pain of the wounds than the humiliation of having been bested by slaves and the dragon's growing despair and isolation.

Marcus kept an eye on how the others—the humans— were dealing with the loss. In his experience, military victories were all more or less alike. The rush of joy was part relief that death had been postponed for another day, part the satisfaction of overcoming a force of humanity that wished him ill. And there was a note of sorrow like a black thread in a pale cloth, that came from focusing the whole mind on a single overwhelming question and then having it melt away like ice in the sun.

Failure, on the other hand, came in varieties.

The pirate fleet seemed the least affected. They were, in essence, a group of outlaws from the first. That Barriath Kalliam had managed to forge them into a functioning alliance—for a time at least—did nothing to unmake their pasts. The rhythm of attack and retreat was old news to them, and the fall of the city laid no particular weight on their hearts. The Porte Oliva they'd lost was a destination for the prey ships they'd hunted, and the future of the city under the Antean fist was much like its past so far as they saw it. Defeat was not entirely defeat when you could sail away from it, and the novelty of the dragon lifted them all nearly to cheerfulness.

The survivors of the bank—Cithrin, Isadau, the handful of the guards—bore their injuries in silence, but Marcus suspected their cuts were deepest. In the days since their escape, Cithrin had kept to her cabin, claiming nausea. Isadau and Maha had spent their days watching Maha's baby learn to crawl on the shifting deck, but their smiles had a deadness and their clear inner eyelids were closed more than open. For the refugees of Suddapal, Porte Oliva had been the place of safety, the sanctuary from the rolling storm that was Antean hatred. And Cithrin particularly had been certain that the city could not fall, the defenders could not fail. Her mistake had been written in blood and fire, and if Marcus hadn't taken quiet but thorough measures, her life would have ended in the streets there or led her back to Camnipol in chains.

The players fell somewhere between.

"I met him in a little village outside Maccia," Kit said, leaning against the rail. "He wasn't even an actor. He was apprentice to an ironmonger. We were playing The Sand Maiden's Regret, only without the Sho-Sho part because we weren't a full company. He started answering back. Heckling. Opal was furious, but the way he delivered his barbs...he had a talent for it. Big Emmath was with us back then. You never met him. Before your time. Went after the show and beat Smit bloody for disrespect. When he came back in the morning, he must have been half bruises. He offered his apologies, and I hired him. He's been with us from that day to...well, not to this. Not any longer."

"I liked him too," Marcus said.

Kit scratched his beard. His expression was dour, but not grief-struck. "I think we became too sure of ourselves. There is a temptation, I find, after you've learned enough plays and poems, to think the world follows the same patterns. I've found precious few tales where the heroes ride the winds on dragon's wings and then die from falling off a pier."

"Comedies, maybe," Marcus said, and immediately regretted the words.

Kit chuckled and shook his head. "I don't find it so comic when it's true. I suppose that's often the case."

"He might not be dead. People survive sacks. People survive being in boats that get swamped."

Kit turned to face him. The old actor's eyes were red from the sun, and perhaps from weeping. There was more grey at his temples now than when they'd first met. "Do they survive being associates of Cithrin bel Sarcour in a city that Geder Palliako has taken, do you think?" he asked gently.

"That's less likely."

"I thought so as well. We've lost players before, Marcus. I've found that's part of the richness of the world. And its sorrow. I think the magic of my trade is that a part can be played by many people. The wise man. The lover. The curious voice in the wild. Even the enemy. Part of our work has been to step into those roles, find who we are within them, play them, and then put them aside for another to pick up and remake. In my time with it, the company has changed and changed and changed again."

"You're saying they'll be all right with this? Cary and Mikel and the rest?"

"I don't know. They may, or they may not. What Smit was to each of us was different. I'm saying that tragedy is also something we are familiar with. Sudden loss or slow, deserved or the world's caprice. We will ache and we will mourn and we will also play at the next stop with the parts rearranged. Mikel and Hornet will take Smit's lines, and people will laugh and weep just as they did before. We'll find someone new. The roles remain the same. Unless we change them."

"Suppose so," Marcus said. A cry went up among the sailors, and the ship turned a degree, creaking. Gulls wheeled in the sky, their grey bodies too many to have traveled with the ship. The shore of Cabral was too far away to see from the deck, but it was close enough for the birds to find them.

"What about you?" Kit asked. "Are you and Yardem well?"

"I've got a lot of dead friends. Sorry Smit's one, but..." He shrugged.

"And Cithrin? How is she?"

Marcus looked out into the water. He didn't answer because he didn't know.

She emerged from her cabin on the fourth day. He didn't know who'd told her about the make-do war council, but just as the midday bells rang, she rose from belowdecks,

Cary at her side. He told himself that the thinness of her face and the paleness of her skin were normal. The dark flesh under her eyes, he couldn't pretend away. She walked across the deck unsteadily, as if she hadn't become accustomed to the motion of the waves in the time since they'd fled. Maybe she hadn't. He could imagine her lying in her hammock, sleepless, for days. A thin ache bloomed in his breast. This was his fault. His and the fat lizard lying on the deck of the farthest roundship. If he'd let the dragon sleep...

"Captain," Cithrin said. Her voice was phlegmy.

"Magistra," he said, nodding his head.

"I understand we're deciding what to do from here."

"Seemed better than drifting."

"Thank you for arranging this."

"Always think it goes better when people talk," he said.

"No. All of this. Thank you for not letting me die in Porte Oliva. Or be sent back to him."

When that happens, it will be because I'm already dead, Marcus thought. All he said was "It's the job."

Cary helped Cithrin to the swing, and they lowered her into the waiting ship's boat. Yardem and Isadau were already there. Marcus went down last. They rowed to the flagship, such as it was, and went up one by one. Inys, it seemed, was not invited. Just as well.

The captain's table was a thick slab of oak with ironwork legs bolted to the deck. Stools had been set for them all. Barriath Kalliam was already at his, and two of his fleet commanders besides. One was an old Tralgu with half his left ear missing who went by Chisn Rake, the other a Timzinae woman called Shark. Lord Skestinin sat chained in a corner, his wrists and ankles in manacles of steel and leather.

After they'd gone through the formality of welcome and

taken seats, Marcus nodded at the captive. "Surprised to see the prisoner here. Not traditional to have the enemy present when you're drawing up plans."

"We do it differently in Antea," Barriath said, but his half-smile made the joke clear. "Truth is I'm not entirely certain he's an enemy. We've had the chance to talk more since we left port."

"Still in chains, though," Marcus said.

"Not entirely sure he's a friend either," Barriath said.

"Rude to speak as if I'm not present," the older man said.

Marcus scowled, then touched his forehead. "My apologies. Didn't mean to be rude." The captive nodded his acceptance. Marcus didn't like it, but if Barriath thought it was the right thing, he wasn't in a position to say otherwise. The two men had shipped together for years, and Marcus was trusting the pirate admiral with more than that already.

"So," Barriath said. "I've called this council for a reason. We've been moving slow. We're only safe because we're moving in force and we've got a dragon."

Cithrin made a painful, raw sound, part laughter, part cough. Barriath raised his hand like the master of a dueling ground awarding a point before he went on. "Two more days, and we'll be at the cape. The ships are provisioned, but the smaller ones weren't built for long journeys. We need to decide where we're going. And what happens next."

The table went quiet. Yardem flicked his ear, his earring jingling. Shark coughed discreetly into her hand.

"Seems to me," Chisn Rake said, folding his arms, "that we've got two options. We can take on the army that's already rolled through half the world, or we can stock up and head for Far Syramys. Maybe find a nice island in between where we can eat fish and fruit until we all die of sloth and indolence."

"Take it you've got a preference, father," Yardem said.

"Damned right I do," the older Tralgu growled.

"We're not running," Barriath said. "Palliako's forces are stretched past thin. He can't keep this up."

"That's what we said when they came to Porte Oliva," Magistra Isadau said. "That's why we thought we were safe."

"We *were* safe," Marcus said, "until someone opened the gates."

"Inys was being killed," Isadau said.

"And that was a shame," Marcus said. "Doesn't make opening the gates a wise choice."

Barriath raised his hand. "It's a mistake we won't make twice. What I want to know is who's at the head of this." He turned to face Cithrin. His face was as dark as hers was pale. "I came to you because you were standing against Palliako when no one else had the stones for it. Do you still?"

Cithrin blinked slowly and then laughed. Marcus wondered for the first time whether she might be drunk. "I don't...know."

Marcus felt his heart sink. *This isn't the way*, he thought. *Sit straight. Put your chin out the way Kit and Cary taught you.* The worst thing a commander could do in the face of defeat was to show weakness, to let the soldiers doubt that they were on the side fated to win. As he watched, Cithrin sank forward, resting her elbows on the table, pressing her fingers into her hair. All around the table, he saw the others looking away from her. Shark and Chisn Rake exchanged a look that seemed to carry some significance he couldn't read.

"Of course we do," Marcus said. "Won't be the first king I've killed."

"You?" Skestinin barked. "The threadbare mercenary?

You'd be better off with the bank girl, Barriath. At least she knows her limits."

"Do you have a plan, Captain?" Barriath asked.

Marcus nodded, his mind reaching in half a dozen directions at once. It wasn't that he hadn't thought about their options, but he hadn't been expected to take the role of commander. The world had a poor history of meeting his expectations.

"The dragon's still central, but more for his mind than his use in the field. Especially now that we know Antea's got weapons designed against him, we can't risk him in the battle. Barriath's right that the Antean army's fragile. They've got the priests, but those are going to be less and less an advantage the more people know what they are and find ways to get past their powers. What we need now is... well, is an army."

"Thin on the ground, those," Chisn Rake said.

"He'll find one," Yardem said.

"What? Pull one out of his asshole, will he?"

"Doubt that," Yardem said, "but he'll find one somewhere."

"Blinded by faith," the old Tralgu spat. "All you priest-caste are the same."

"I'm fallen," Yardem said pleasantly.

"Short-term," Marcus said, "is we can't stay on the water forever. Especially with Inys tipping the roundship like a raft every time he twitches in his sleep. We need to fall back, gather up allies, and make sure the Anteans aren't biting our heels the whole way."

"Does the bank still back us?" Barriath asked, turning again to Cithrin. She seemed not to have heard the question. Her pale eyes fixed on nothing. Magistra Isadau answered in her place.

"It has no choice. Cithrin and I acted against the army

directly in Suddapal and again in Porte Oliva. Callon Cane's bounty system was funded by the holding company, and if that's not known yet, it will be. Especially if they capture Pyk Usterhall alive."

"Not sure of that," Marcus said. "Pyk can't lie to them, but she's stubborn as old wood. They may get less information from her than they expect." He turned to Skestinin. "You know, now you've heard all this, we'll have to kill you rather than let you loose."

"That was true the moment you attacked my ship," Skestinin said. "And your Cinnae master guaranteed my safety."

"All fairness, sir," Yardem said, "that was only from the beach to the city. This may call for a renegotiation."

"Skestinin's under my protection," Barriath said. "He's not at issue. Callon Cane. Will Jorey come after him next?"

"Hard to do, seeing as he's a fairy tale," Marcus said.

Isadau tapped the tabletop with her fingers. "Herez disbanded the bounty board. I'd say they, at least, believe that the Anteans may track Cane down next."

"Perhaps we want them to," Barriath said, drawing the words out slowly. "If Callon Cane took shelter in some other city . . . and if there was reason for Jorey to think your mythical ally knew where Cithrin had gone to ground . . ."

"You're thinking we could wear them down by running the army up against some more enemies?" Marcus asked. "Not a bad thought."

"Serve Birancour right if you put them in Sara-sur-Mar," Isadau said, bitterness in her voice.

Barriath laughed. "All right, then. Sara-sur-Mar. If Jorey wants to fight Birancour, let's have him fight the whole damned kingdom and not just the one city they threw to the dogs."

"Not sure how we do that," Marcus said.

"You took the bank's hoard," Barriath said. "Give me enough to make a few payments. I'll play the role."

Marcus frowned. "You'd do that? Become Callon Cane?"

"Geder Palliako killed my father in front of me," Barriath said. "I'll do more than this to see him burn. Question is, where are you going while I distract my brothers? Do you have any allies left you can rally to the cause?"

"Stollbourne," Isadau said. "The bank has a branch there, and Narinisle's across the Thin Sea. So long as we have the fleet, Palliako's forces won't be able to cross to us. We can be safe there while Inys heals."

"Plus which," Chisn Rake said, "there's more ships there that know the blue-water trade."

Marcus shook his head. "It's not a place I'd pick to draw up a land army, and I'm not sure that strategies built around the dragon are the best we can make," he said, "but as safe harbors go, there's not better."

"Right, then," Barriath said. "I'll draw off the hunt in Sara-sur-Mar. The rest of the ships sail for Stollbourne. And once we've broken them and raised an army of our own, we march it down Palliako's throat, take Camnipol back, and string that bastard up by his own guts."

"Do we?" Cithrin asked. "Is that why we're doing this?"

Marcus cursed under his breath. She *was* drunk.

"What other reason would we have?" Barriath asked. His voice was sharp, and Cithrin shied away from it.

The meeting went on through the afternoon as they hashed through details. Barriath, Chisn Rake, and Shark had a long, contentious argument over who would lead the fleet in Barriath's absence and how to keep the pirates—never well known for loyalty—from turning to mutiny in the same hour that Barriath stepped off the boat. Isadau, Marcus, and Yardem composed a letter to be sent ahead by a single fast ship to apprise the Stollbourne branch of the bank of their plans, and Isadau scratched out a draft in the bank's private cipher. Through it all, two figures remained silent. Lord Skestinin listened carefully and struggled, Marcus thought, with some concern of his own. And Cithrin sat as if the conversation all around her wasn't happening and she were alone with the sound of the water lapping at the ship and the creaking of the boards.

Geder

The wind that threw itself across Camnipol the day of the grand audience didn't rise quite to the level of a storm. The cloaks of the men and women in the street flapped and fluttered, pressed tight against their bodies on one side and streamed away on the other. High, thin clouds formed and were ripped apart and formed again. Moaning and whistling and dust filled the air. Worst, through some terrible accident of angle and flow, the stink of the midden in the depths of the Division was pulled up into the high city streets. Geder couldn't take a breath without smelling rot and corruption, and even great billowing clouds of incense in the audience hall only covered it over. Sometimes the reek was so thick it seemed less a scent than a taste.

Geder sat the Severed Throne, the crown of the regent on his brows, and huddled in his cloak. His head ached. The short walk from the Kingspire to the hall had felt like a punishment. The great hall itself, wide and tall and muttering now with the voice of the wind, had impressed him as stately and grand once. Today it was a metaphor of hollowness expressed as architecture. The Severed Throne was a chair with more history than cushioning, and the mass of bodies in their cloth-of-gold and worked jewels were actually all the same people he saw at feasts and balls and council meetings, except with the ones he cared for best absent. Jorey. Basrahip.

The new priest was a thin man with one pale eye and a thin scrub of beard. He stood now in Basrahip's place, doing the same work Basrahip had done—nodding when the petitioners to the throne spoke true, shaking his head when they lied, keeping still when the words were in fact only meaningless gabble devoid of anything that could be called truth or falsehood.

"I have no wish to reopen old wounds," Curtin Issandrian said, standing before the throne with his palms out like the statue of an orator come to life. "And the question of a farmer's council has been one that's caused division and strife in years past. I have hope that in our newfound prosperity and the victories and glories of our conquests we can let go of the old arguments that divided us and consider the question with fresh eyes. And more importantly fresh hearts."

The years hadn't been kind to the man. The long, flowing hair that had been a sort of personal banner was cut between his ear and shoulder now, and ashy. His face had lost its handsomeness to an excess of jowls and a darkness at the eyes. His voice was as sweet and compelling as it had been, back when Issandrian had been the darling of the court and Geder the butt of its jokes. Everything else about him spoke of being outside the court's favor. Even his cloak was cut in last year's fashion.

"The changes we have seen over even the past year are greater," Issandrian said, "than any since the reign of King Osteban. The farm slaves we had before had entered indenture as a choice or from a magistrate's judgment. Now Timzinae work the fields under the righteous lash of Antean farmers. But the needs and skills of those farmers—good men and loyal citizens of the empire though they are—must also change. If we are to support them, they must have a voice within the court. If we are to—"

"What are you asking me for?" Geder snapped. Issandrian's speech stumbled against itself. His hands fell to his sides. Impatience bit at Geder's gut, and he leaned forward. "You want something, yes? Just say it and be done."

Issandrian glanced back at the priest. The grand audience had been more fun when no one knew that Geder's ability to tell truth from lies had rested in the grace of the spider priests. As soon as they'd inducted a wave of Anteans into the priesthood, the knowledge had entered the cycle of gossip. It was common knowledge now, and it left Geder almost feeling that the audience was with them more than him now.

"I would ask the crown to consider forming a farmer's council to advise the court," Issandrian said.

"Thank you. The answer is no. I'll hear the next petition now."

Issandrian's shoulders fell, but there was nothing for it. He bowed because he had to and was led away. The wind raked its nails across the great hall's roof and chewed at the windows. Onin Pyrellin rose next and launched into a speech about his father's service to the crown as a prelude, Geder knew, to asking that the protectorship of Nus be given to him.

It was a sign of the empire's sudden glorious expansion that so few heads of the great families were at court. Fallon Broot was ruling Suddapal. Savin Caot and Ernst Mecelli were managing the defense of Inentai from the Borjan raiders. Mikellin Faskellan was in Anninfort, consolidating the still-recent conquest of Asterilhold. Lord Skestinin was lost to the enemy. Dawson Kalliam was dead for his treason. Lord Bannien was dead for his. Mirkus Shoat, Earl of Rivencourt, dead. Estin Cersillian, Earl of Masonhalm, dead. Feldin Maas, whose barony was now Geder's, dead. Lord Ternigan, dead. King Simeon, dead. The march of victory in the field and the needed purge of corrupt elements in the court left them stretched tight as the skin of a drum. They were a court of wives, daughters, and third sons now.

He became aware that Onin Pyrellin had stopped speaking and was looking up at him expectantly. Geder pressed a hand to his cheek and looked out over the crowd. He wasn't halfway through the petitions of the nobility yet, and there was the merchant class after that, and the poor and landless after them. An endless procession of people who wanted, and he was the one they all thought could provide whatever it was. Justice or favor or status.

In the crowd, he caught sight of Sabiha Kalliam. Her mother was at her side. Little Annalise would be with the wet nurse, then, and they were here to ask him to ransom back Lord Skestinin. He would have to tell them no. And beside them, Laren Shoat, here to ask pardon for his family and a return of their titles and lands. And beside him, Namen Flor with God only knew what concerns that would be Geder's concerns too, before it was all done with.

Go home, he thought. *All of you just go home and whatever the problems were you thought you had, just forget them. Start over. Do it without bothering me.*

"I'm sorry," Geder said. "You lost my attention. Start again."

Pyrellin's mouth pressed tight, but he started in again detailing his father's glories and Geder tried to attend to it all this time.

He went on as long as he could stand it, refreshing himself

with cucumber water, apples, and cheese. The regent's crown chafed his temples, but he left it on because it was expected of him. He found that, now that everyone knew that lying before the throne was impossible, no one tried. The pale-eyed priest might almost not have been there for all the use he was, and Geder regretted the loss.

The white-gold light of afternoon pressed in through the windows and the stinking wind had died to a low, disconsolate muttering when Geder finally called the halt, thanked the court, declared once again his loyalty to the throne and to Aster who would sit it in a few years' time, and made his way out. His back ached, his head hurt, his eyes felt like someone had poured grit into them, but the grand audience was done for another year, and good riddance. The pale-eyed priest walked with him as Basrahip would have done, only Geder took no comfort in this man's presence.

"You did well today, Prince Geder," the priest said as they reached his private rooms at the Kingspire's base. "You rule with wisdom and grace."

"And you'd think the rewards would be better for that," Geder said. A servant boy accepted the regent's crown from him and scuttled away with it. "Do we have any word from Basrahip? Is he coming back soon?"

"Alas, the apostate's corruption was narrow but deep," the priest said, his hands lifted in apology as if he had some responsibility for what had happened in a different city. "The Basrahip's messengers tell me that he has rooted out much of the weed of lies and blasphemy, but one corrupted priest remains. If that man is sacrificed to her glory and her truth, he will return to us."

Geder lumbered toward the stairs, and from there to his rooms. He wondered where Aster was. He'd more than half expected the boy to attend the grand audience. It was going to be Aster's task before very long, and better that he see as many examples of it as possible before it was his ass in that damned uncomfortable chair. Geder couldn't really blame him for finding something better to do, though. He would have been elsewhere too, if he could have been.

"What do you mean, if? What else would he do with the bastard?"

"All is in accordance with her will," the priest said. "If it is her will that the apostate be sacrificed, then he will be sacrificed."

"But he's going to be killed. That's what Basrahip went out there for. He's a threat to the empire, and the empire is the chosen of the goddess. The apostate needs to die, and Basrahip'll kill him. There's no *if* in there."

"The goddess is wise beyond our knowing," the priest said, trotting a little to keep up. Geder wished he would just go away. "Her purity will cleanse the world, and all things fold to her wishes. If the Basrahip finds this apostate and ends him, it will be because she wills it."

"I don't think you understand," Geder said, reaching the stairs. "Basrahip's been very clear. The goddess has come to bring peace to the world. I'm her chosen, and so Antea is her chosen. We're spreading out and building her temples and bringing peace. That's what we do. Whatever opposes us fails. That's all."

"I have also heard the Basrahip's living voice," the priest said. He sounded a little hurt. Geder wondered if a day on the throne had left him cranky. Probably, it had. "We are not in disagreement, Prince Geder. If it is the will of the goddess, all the world will bow down before you."

Geder stopped, turned, poked the man's chest with a single stiff finger as he spoke. "What you heard Basrahip say and what I heard him say seem to be very different. I'll walk you through this one last time, and then I'm going to go eat my dinner and take my bath and sleep, I hope, until a day and a half from now. The goddess has come to bring peace to the world, and so she will. I am the chosen of the goddess, so I have her blessing and her protection. Every city I take, I raise a temple to her. Lies and deceit are purged from the world. The new age is going to dawn with the last evil of the dragons burned out of the world. Nowhere in there anywhere is an *if*."

"I fear I have given you some offense, Prince Geder," the priest said, his eyes growing wide.

"I'm not offended," Geder said, biting each word off as he spoke it. "You're not listening. When you say if—*if* the goddess wants it, *if* it's her will—it's like we don't know what's going to happen. But we do. Not all the fine, fiddly little details, maybe, but the important part is known. We're going to win. The world is going to be better and purer and right. And here's an *if* for you. *If* you aren't certain of that, you're the one who's outside of her grace."

The priest shook his head in distress. "But I am certain in my faith. I would never—"

"Stop. Just send word to Basrahip from me that I'd like him to come back as soon as he can."

"If that is your wish, Prince Geder," the priest said, bowing. Geder had to restrain himself from punching the man in the neck.

Geder dreamed that he was dead, and that Cithrin had killed him. His body was thick, his veins black with clotted blood, and he still had to rule the empire. In his dream, he was forcing himself down a long hallway, looking for the place he was meant to be. He could hear Cithrin, but every door he came to opened to the wrong rooms. If he could find her, she would be able to undo his death, but he had to find her first.

At the dream's end, he pushed open a door to find Cithrin naked in the arms of the dead King Simeon and woke up shouting. Afternoon light pressed in through the window. His shirt and hose were sticky with sweat and his body felt almost as upset and sluggish as it had before he'd laid down for his nap. He hadn't made it as far as his bath. When he rose from his bed, his back ached. It seemed unfair that sitting for the better part of a day should make him ache as much as hard work would have. He blamed the throne.

He called for fresh clothes and sent the servants away while he changed. Fresh talc soaked up the worst of the sweat, and the new robes were light. The wind had given way to cooler air, and he decided to wear a thin wool cloak along with it. He needed food and perhaps some light entertainment. Music, maybe. But when he stepped out of his rooms, Canl Daskellin was waiting for him.

"Lord Regent," he said, bowing.

"Must we?" Geder asked.

"I'm afraid there's news," Daskellin said. "If you'd prefer, I can come back in the morning, but it won't be any better then than now."

"So it's a choice of spending the evening fretting over what you've said or else fretting over what you're going to say."

"That's the shape of it, my lord." Daskellin's smile was rueful. It occured to Geder that he was the closest thing to a real friend Geder had in the city, and they barely knew one another outside the work of the court.

"All right. Come with me."

Geder tramped down to the gardens, Daskellin at his side and the royal guard trailing behind them. The gardens were thick with the scent of flowers. The perfume seemed almost too sweet after the sewer-smell of the morning. Wide red blossoms nodded in the breeze and the setting sun pulled the shadows out across the green. Servants brought chairs and chilled wine and a platter of roasted walnuts and berries glazed with honey and salt. Geder pressed a handful into his mouth.

"What's happened?" he asked. "It's Inentai, isn't it?"

"I'm afraid not," Daskellin said. "The first reports have come from Porte Oliva. The city is ours. The weapons we sent made the difference. When the dragon attacked—and the dragon did attack—we brought it down. It got away again, but injured badly. The city fell, but Cithrin bel Sarcour escaped."

Geder sat with the words, waiting to feel something. Rage, disappointment, resolve. Something. Of course she was gone. Of course it hadn't worked. Nothing went the way it should for him, not ever. He took a sip of the wine, curled his lip, and called the servant back to bring him water instead.

"What does Jorey say about finding her?"

"His first reports confirm that the dragon and the woman are in league. They left by ship, and we assume they're heading west mostly because none of our ships in the Inner Sea have seen them. They may be going to Cabral or Herez or Princip C'Annaldé. Or they may be going farther north."

"We'll have to find her," Geder said. "She's the key to it all. The Timzinae conspiracy. The dragon. Get her, and it cracks that nut. There won't be peace while she's free."

"I assumed you'd say as much, my lord," Daskellin said. "I've drawn up orders for the Lord Marshal to make chase with as much speed as is possible without exhausting the troops."

That sounded like a backhanded way to give Jorey

permission to rest in Porte Oliva, but what else was he supposed to do? And if they weren't even certain where she'd
gone...

"Fine. That's fine. Is there anything else?" Daskellin's
silence was alarming. Geder looked up. Daskellin's expression was closed and empty. Dread tugged at his belly.
"There's more?"

"The siege at Kiaria has broken," Daskellin said. "There
was a fever among the men, and the Timzinae forces inside
the fortress took advantage of it to launch a night attack.
We believe the enemy forces are small and ill-equipped, but
there is an enemy army loose in Elassae."

"No," Geder said. "That's not possible." Only maybe it
was. They hadn't taken Kiaria, hadn't built a temple in it.
Maybe the goddess wouldn't let him hold places where he
hadn't kept his bargain.

"Fallon Broot's gathered his forces in Suddapal and preparing the attack."

"Yes, of course. That's good. He has priests with him,
yes?"

"He does."

"That's going to be fine, then. He'll beat them back.
Maybe we can even get soldiers inside Kiaria this time. Put
an end to this."

"The force is smaller than it would have been," Daskellin
said. "He'd already transferred his spare blades to Inentai.
The mercenaries in Suddapal are contracted for garrison
duty, not field service."

"So renegotiate. Pay them more. We've got all of Suddapal we can sell off if we need to."

"That was my thought as well, but I wanted to consult
with you."

"Yes, of course," Geder said. "Whatever we need to do."

"And if it becomes clear that we can't hold Suddapal, my lord?"

A strange dread washed over Geder, carried by the memory of a woman's silhouette against the flames of a burning city. Vanai, boarded tight and lit to keep it from ever falling into enemy hands again. That was the question Daskellin was asking. If Broot couldn't hold back the Timzinae, would Suddapal burn? The answer should have been obvious. Geder had set precedent. This was war, after all. There was no room for sentiment. *We burn it. If we can't hold Suddapal, we burn it and everyone in it.*

"We'll decide that if we need to," Geder said. "Not something we have to worry about today. Broot's good. He'll beat them. He's very good."

"If you say so, Lord Regent."

Geder nodded to himself more than the man beside him. Perhaps it was just the unpleasant weather and the uneasing dreams, but he couldn't quite shake the feeling that it was all coming apart at the seams. The empire, the war. Even the goddess. In his mind, Cithrin smirked at him, pleased with herself. And why shouldn't she be?

She was winning.

Clara

I've taken worse beatings from my cousins back at Osterling Fells," Vincen said from behind her.

The square between the Governor's Palace and the cathedral had been emptied and the platforms razed. The icons
and trappings of half a dozen cults and mysteries, detritus of
a century of political and religious fashion, had been hauled
out of the cathedral and burned. In all, it had taken the better part of a week, and the ceremony of rededication was set
to begin at dawn, followed by demonstrations of loyalty by
the newest subjects of the Severed Throne. Clara sat on the
highest dais in a gown of sea-green silk taken from someone.
Vincen played the role of her personal guard and servant,
standing behind her. All around them, the surviving great
men and women of Porte Oliva sat on the ground in rags.
Their humiliation was, after all, part of the celebration.

"They had blades," Clara said, pretending to consider the
cathedral. In truth, given the morning mist, the glare of the
torches, and her own imperfect eyesight, the building was
little more than an indigo shadow below a dark blue sky.
When she spoke, she kept her lips as near motionless as she
could. Vincen, she presumed, would do the same.

"They didn't use them," Vincen said.

"They would have."

"Maybe, but they didn't."

"One had a knife drawn."

Vincen cleared his throat. A fanfare sounded, and the men and women of Porte Oliva knelt. Jorey emerged from the Governor's Palace, flanked by guards with bare blades. Clara watched him, but she could not help but see the fear and hatred of those he passed. For them, he was the conqueror of the city, the general who had brought them all low. Hundreds—perhaps thousands—of people in the city went to sleep at night wishing him dead or worse than dead. She wondered whether they would have had they known how little he'd wanted to come here. He was the puppet of necessity, as much as any of them. And almost against her will, it occurred to her how proud Dawson would have been of him.

She glanced up at Vincen. His face was carefully empty, but his eyes slid down toward her and a faint, complicit smile touched his lips. She breathed in deeply and returned her gaze to her approaching son.

"If we ever get back to Osterling Fells, Vincen?"

"Yes."

"Remind me to have your cousins whipped."

Clara rose as Jorey came to sit beside her on the dais. His guards arrayed themselves with Vincen. The sky had grown a shade lighter. The cathedral had begun to take on some detail. The darkness of the great doorway, the dragon's jade figures worked into the stone. Two cunning men stepped up, both Firstbloods, and apparently trained together, because when they lifted their fists to the sky, a wide white radiance filled the square. The burning torches seemed to dim, and the world all around grew darker. The cathedral's door swung open, and Vicarian stepped out. He'd traded his plain brown robes for a near-perfect white. His hair was pulled back, and his smile as he walked forward was beatific. Clara felt a knot in her throat.

She expected the thing that had been her son to come to a dais of his own, to rise up and declare the greatness of Antea from a great height. Perhaps with cunning men pouring fire and blood from the air. Instead, he looked around at the kneeling masses with a vast amusement. When he spoke, his voice carried through the space without seeming to shout.

"This is a hard day for many of you, but I've come to tell you that it is also a very, very good one. Today the goddess has come to Porte Oliva. Now, I know that isn't something that many of you can celebrate. Not yet. When the goddess came to Camnipol, I was less than delighted myself, so I know how you feel."

Vicarian stepped forward, walking among the kneeling and debased like a tutor lecturing to an overlarge collection of students. As a demonstration of personal courage, it took Clara's breath away. Any of these people might have a small blade hidden on their persons. Any of them might be desperate enough to kill the priest who had desecrated their temple, even though the punishment was death. They might all have been sheep and flowers for all the fear Vicarian showed.

"Many of you have suffered terrible losses. I understand that too. When the goddess first came to us in Antea, I lost my father. The lies of low men had taken too much of him. When the truth came to burn those lies away, it was too much for him. I loved my father. I still do. I miss him. And if I could turn away from the goddess and have him back, I would not do it. That's hard to understand now, but it will come clearer for you. For all of you. You have passed through terrible darkness and storm, and you may feel that you've lost. You haven't lost. You have been ill, and I am here as the voice of the goddess to tell you that all will be well."

Clara leaned to Jorey, putting her hand on his arm.

"This is a bit different than the way Basrahip presents himself."

"He's not here," Jorey said with a smile. "It's exactly what Vicarian's like."

For the better part of an hour, Vicarian paced among the citizens of the fallen city, explaining that the goddess was here to save the world. That all lies were clear to her, and that her voice as spoken through the mouths of her priests carried the truth with them that would shatter the false and reclaim those lost to the illusions of the world. Clara watched the people kneeling all around the square. The blankness of resentment and anger was not gone, but it was lessened. A few tried tentative, uncertain smiles. They heard his voice, but they didn't believe. Not yet.

They would.

In the end, the dawn broke, the fiery disk of sunlight burning away the last of the mist. The cathedral stood revealed, a great red banner with the pale eightfold sigil in its center announcing to the world that only one deity was welcome here and that her claim was absolute.

Afterward, Clara walked with Jorey back across the square and into the wide halls of the Governor's Palace, Vincen taking his discreet place behind Jorey's guard. They had been in the rooms so briefly, it was strange that they had become familiar. After so long following the army, sleeping in a new place every night, seeing the same rooms even twice lent a sense of permanence Clara hadn't foreseen. A breakfast of eggs and fish waited in the garden at the palace's center. Stone walls rose all around them, giving a sense of isolation and protection without going so far as to feel like a gaol. As she let a servant girl pour fresh coffee for her, Clara wondered about the people who had designed the palace, and the people who had lived in it. What they would make of her presence here.

"That went gracefully," Jorey said, lifting a poached egg into his mouth.

"Don't gulp, dear," Clara said. "And yes, I suppose it did."

"The sack was...well, those are never pleasant. I was afraid in the aftermath that holding the city would be challenging. But the spider goddess works her magic again. It shouldn't surprise me anymore."

"It always astonishes me," Clara said.

"Puts a premium on Vicarian's time, though. We lost three priests in the fighting. One burned on the ships, one at the wall, and the last took a crossbow bolt and a sword in the street-by-street work at the end. I don't know what we're going to do when the time comes to move on."

Don't ask, Clara thought. *Don't ask, and you will not be obligated to write it in a letter to anyone.* Jorey shrugged and reached for a cup of coffee for himself. A finch the blue of a noonday sky sped past them as it no doubt had passed the governor of Porte Oliva when he lived. They would believe in the goddess. They would trust in her. They would follow her.

"How long do you imagine it will be before you leave the city?" she asked, trying to keep her tone light.

"As soon as I know which direction to march, I suppose," Jorey said. "I want this done before we're pulled into a second winter campaign. And there are fewer and fewer places for her to run to. Once we have this banker, I think we'll have everything. The dragon. The Timzinae. Feldin Maas and the conspiracy in Asterilhold. It's all connected, and that woman and her bank are at the center of it."

"Why would you think that?" Clara asked.

Jorey frowned. "Everyone knows it, Mother."

"I don't," she said. "I look at it, and I see...well, people. Humanity has been struggling for power and advantage since the last time a dragon flew. Perhaps before. I don't see the need for a grand plot to explain what's normal."

"That's not how it is, Mother," Jorey said. "I've talked with Vicarian about it all the way from Camnipol, and I tried every argument. Every angle. This is the only thing that feels right."

Oh, my boy, she thought. *I should never have let you go.*

The conversation moved to safer territory, to Sabiha and Annalise, to her impressions of Birancouri food, to Jorey's continual amazement that Clara had taken it on herself to follow him. It was easier without Vicarian there. She didn't need to watch her words, or at least not so closely. It still wouldn't have done to let Vincen's name slip out in too familiar a context. She was Jorey's mother, Dawson's widow, a woman driven perhaps a bit off center by the tragedies she'd faced. Enough so, at any rate, to forgive her the occasional flight of fancy.

Too soon, Jorey squinted up into the wide square of sky and pushed his plate away.

"My talented brother's likely done with his priestly duties by now. I suppose I have to get back to work."

"Does he consult on everything, then?" Clara asked, knowing it would be a sentence in the inevitable letter if he did.

"No, it's just we're still questioning people who knew her, and he's a useful man for that kind of thing."

"I remember," Clara said. "Geder had me before a magistrate's bench that way once myself."

"And he found beyond all doubt that you were innocent," Jorey said. "It works, you see?"

We are chasing an invention of our own fancy, and so I no longer believe that Palliako's campaign can end except in an ever-broadening wave of fear and violence. Even I, who know better, find myself sometimes believing that agents of the Timzinae or the dragons or your own bank were instrumental in beginning this conflict and that Geder Palliako's actions are understandable given those which came before them. When I remind myself of the truth it feels like waking from a dream into a nation of sleepwalkers. Even talented, intelligent, kind men like the new Lord Marshal have fallen into this dream.

I began these letters in hopes of stopping the madness that has taken my kingdom and my people. I hope you will not think less of me that I now despair.

"Clara," Vincen said from the doorway, "we have to go now."

"Just a moment more," she said.

"Jorey's already waited to call the march. He'll have to start soon, and if we're following along behind again, people will start thinking you prefer it there."

"Give me a moment to finish my letter."

He left, closing the door behind him. His footsteps did not recede. She felt better, having him standing guard this way when she was writing things that were so thoroughly dangerous for them all.

*I continue my correspondence in hopes that you have
some knowledge or perspective of which I am at present unaware. My hope is that you have hope. The forces
of Antea are leaving Porte Oliva today and moving
north along the dragon's roads toward Sara-sur-Mar
and Porte Silena. It is possible that the Lord Marshal
might make the turn toward Herez and Daun, though
the news that Callon Cane and his bounties are no
longer welcome in Herez make this seem less likely to
me. The Lord Marshal has had news that, ejected from
Daun, Callon Cane has taken up his trade in Sara-sur-
Mar. If, as he believes, Cane is an adventure of your
bank, I must urge you to withdraw him to safety at
once.*

Vincen's voice came through the door as a murmur. "The
supply carts are lining up at the gate."

"You aren't anywhere near where you could see that,"
Clara said.

"You aren't anywhere near where you could be sure they
aren't."

*Jorey Kalliem has divided his force, leaving Porte Oliva
under the protectorship of his brother, a priest of the
spider goddess with all the powers and compromise
that implies. A small occupying force will also remain.
The majority of the army will proceed with the two
remaining priests. If there is any hope of victory, it is
in this: the priests are few, and their power is great.
Should they be absented from the army, it is possible
that Lord Marshal Kalliam might not push on. He is
reluctant to conduct a second winter campaign, and
should he be sufficiently slowed, the army may retreat*

to Porte Oliva to winter. I do not know what, if any-
thing, can be accomplished with that time, but

New voices came, sharp and masculine. Vincen responded
in kind. Clara grabbed a handful of blotting sand, cast it on
the paper, folded the letter, and stuffed it down the front of
her dress as the door opened and the younger son of Cyrus
Mastellin came in. He had his dead uncle's unfortunate
roundness of face, but he wore it better.

"Lady Kalliam, please forgive the intrusion, but if
you wish the escort of the Lord Marshal on your return
journey—"

"I shall be there at once," Clara said. "I was only tying up
a few last little things."

Mastellin nodded, but did not retreat. Jorey had apparently told the boy to come back with her in tow or with
permission to leave without her. In the corridor behind him,
Vincen stood quiet as a ghost, his expression too innocent
to miss his meaning. *Yes, you said as much*, she thought.
*You're very clever. And I am damned if I know how I'm to
get this letter free without drawing stares.*

"My lady," Vincen said as she passed. He was enjoying
himself entirely too much.

They left the gates behind before midday, Clara riding
with Jorey behind the advance guard. She'd said her farewells to Vicarian at his new temple the night before, speaking carefully and pleased to have the occasion behind her.
The sun was warm, and the grasslands wide and fragrant
with the ripeness that came in the falling point between mid-
summer and harvest. The story was that she would return
to Camnipol, the army acting as her escort until their paths
diverged. A small group of sword-and-bows would see her
safely back through the pass at Bellin and have her back in

the heart of empire by the close of the season. It wasn't what Clara wanted or hoped, but she'd had to resign herself to it. Otherwise her agreement would have been a lie.

The strangeness of it struck her. All the despair and fear in her letter was truth. When her mind turned to the war, and the spider goddess, the fate of her house and her kingdom, the world looked bleak and empty of redemption. But flirting with Vincen when no one was there to see or riding through the high, green grass with her son at her side and the sun in her eyes was still pleasant. Even a burning world had its moments of peace and sweetness. Perhaps even more, since they were so rare and the alternative so bitter.

The advance guard pushed on, flattening the grass as they passed so that ambush from the sides became less likely. Clara found herself imagining the track they left as the belly marks of a great dragon scratching itself on the ground. The crushed blades were prettier that way, even if it wasn't truth.

"Mother," Jorey said, intruding on her private, meaningless thoughts, "I have a favor to ask. When you turn aside, I'll be sending a courier with you. Reports for Geder."

"Will you?" she said. That was interesting. Perhaps there would be a chance to see them on the road. Copy them. Change them, even, if there were some advantage to be had.

"I also have a letter...for Sabiha. I was going to put it with the others, but if you carry it, I know it won't be delivered to the wrong place by mistake."

"Ah, one of *those* letters. I understand. I have a collection of them your father wrote to me, once upon a time."

"Mother!"

"Jorey, dear, one thing that you must be aware of by pure force of logic if nothing else? You were not the first generation to discover sex."

"I'm not having this conversation," Jorey said, but there

was laughter in his voice. Real laughter, not its bitter twin. "And thank you for agreeing to carry it. And not read it yourself."

They rode on for a time. The land was surprisingly flat, and the wind made waves in the grass like it was water and their horses were sailboats. It was lovely. That it could not last made it more so.

Cithrin

Five days after Barriath Kalliam's departure for Sara-sur-Mar in his new and unlikely role, a great pod of the Drowned appeared. They stayed with the fleet as the ships floated north, passing the rough, cruel coast that separated Herez and Princip C'Annaldé. The pale bodies floated beneath the ship where Inys lay. Sometimes they crowded so thickly there seemed more flesh than ocean. Occasionally, the dragon reached over and sank his vast head beneath the waves, and the drag set the sailors crawling over and around him, to keep the ship's course true. A few hours later, the Drowned would swarm and lift up the shining corpse of some great beast—grey-skinned squid half as long as the ship or silver-scaled tuna or ink-black flesh in a form no sailor had ever seen—from the depths like tribute being offered to a king.

Some days Marcus would take a ship's boat over and try to talk to the dragon, but more often he wouldn't. Cithrin would watch when it occurred to her that she might, but she made no point of it. Her world had changed, not to a nightmare. Nothing so bright and passionate as terror lived in her. Disappointment, yes. Despair, certainly. More than anything else, Cithrin was profoundly aware of distance. In her cabin, she would hang in her hammock, wearing the same clothes she had for a week, thick sweat making her skin sticky. Her belly was too tight for food, but she forced down bowls of salted fish as hard as leather. Her gut rebelled every time, and she kept it down through force of will. It was easy to do, because her body with its struggles and the suffering was so far away. She saw all the symptoms of her illness, but couldn't bring herself so far as alarm. If she wasted and died, she did. If not, then the world would go on taking its cuts at her until she did. Everyone died eventually. Except the dragons and the spiders and their hatred. Those, it seemed, would live forever.

Cithrin didn't sleep, though she sometimes lost consciousness. No dreams bothered her, and she was not refreshed by it. Instead, she experienced it as a stuttering of time. It was day, and then night. The sun was low in the east, playing above the coast, and then it was overhead. She felt as through her mind had developed a bad limp, one that was growing slowly worse. She drank what there was to drink, not because it helped, but because she did. She waited without knowing what she was waiting for. Her body shuddered sometimes, trembling without cause. Occasionally, late at night, she wept and put no particular importance on it. It was simply a thing that happened.

It was an oddly peaceful sort of violence. The worst of it was when someone tried to help her.

"You should come out to the light," Isadau said.

The cabin was small. There was hardly enough room to stand straight, and the walls—if the slats and beams could deserve the name—were close enough to touch both sides without stretching. Someone outside the room coughed and muttered a florid obscenity. Cithrin could hear everything around her perfectly. She assumed they could hear her too. She wished Isadau wouldn't talk, but not so much that she'd object.

"I've seen sunlight," Cithrin said. "Has it changed?"

"It's not healthy to stay too long in darkness."

The magistra of Suddapal hunched against the wall, the black scales of her skin seeming to blend in with the shadows. She was beautiful, and Cithrin wished there was something to do for her. She would have liked to be kind to her. Isadau smiled tentatively.

"There's nothing out there," Cithrin said.

"There is a great deal," Isadau said, and her hand found its way into Cithrin's. "We have lost a battle, but it is not the last. Even with his priests, Geder cannot press his campaign forever."

"He can, though," Cithrin said. "Because we can't fight him. It all keeps happening, again and again and again. Nothing will be different in Stollbourne. They'll use their fear of him to demand our gold, just the way the prince of Vanai did. And the queen of Birancour. And we'll be in the same position we had in Porte Oliva, trying to balance being too useful against not being useful enough. It hasn't worked. It's never worked. It won't."

"We can send your plans and schemes to Komme," Isadau said. "The branch in Porte Oliva didn't have the coin to make them work, but—"

"What will be cheaper for him?" Cithrin said, gently, softly. She felt she was breaking hard news to a dear friend. "Bankrupting his bank to fight a war he wants no part of, or handing me to Geder?"

"You know Captain Wester and Yardem will never let that happen," Isadau said. "You know I won't either. You are loved, Cithrin."

Her throat felt thick, and for a moment, she mistook sorrow for mere nausea. They sat in the dark, weeping quietly together while two sailors on the other side of the thin wall argued about oiled ropes and iron nails. When at length Cithrin spoke, her voice was low and rough as a child at the trailing end of a tantrum.

"I was so sure we'd win."

The books and ledgers were in the hold, and Cithrin went there sometimes. She looked through the accounts for three dead branches—Vanai, Suddapal, Porte Oliva—not because there was anything to learn there. It was like sitting with old friends and recalling sweeter times. The oldest entries were in Magister Imaniel's handwriting, the newest in Pyk Usterhall's. The dead before and the dead behind. Their voices mixed in her half-hinged memory. *It's bank policy never to lend to people who consider it beneath their dignity to repay* became *When we've won, we have less risk and more money.* She thought of Besel and of Smit. She still wore the necklace poor lovestruck little Salan had given her before going off to man the walls at Kiaria. A silver bird to care for until the war was over. Only they hadn't known then how terribly, terribly long ago the war had begun.

Her own notes were among the pages Marcus Wester had saved. Her plans and schemes from before he and the players had arrived strapped to Inys's great legs. Schedules of mercenary companies, of crop prices and iron prices and coal. A long examination written in cipher of what resources could be choked off to limit the ability of Antea—of anyone—to make the instruments of war. Alum and salt and cotton. All of it rigorous and logical and impossible as a dream. The roundships held the remaining wealth of Suddapal that Pyk had been so conservative in lending, the swollen coffers from the wise buying out letters of credit when they fled before the storm. Likely, they had more wealth on board now than all the pirates in the fleet had ever captured. It would be a miracle if they weren't all slaughtered in their sleep and their bodies thrown over the side for the sharks. Except Master Kit was there to nose out any mutiny, and Marcus would stop them, and if he didn't Inys might still take offense at what the pirates would have to do to Marcus. Fears laid against fears, making a fragile kind of stability. Not that it mattered.

In among her notes, she found another page, one not written in her hand. She knew the words without looking at them. They'd burned themselves into her eyes.

Cithrin I love you. I love you more than anyone I've ever known. All this time that I've been running Aster's kingdom and fighting to protect the empire, it's been a way to distract myself from you. From your body. Does that sound crass? I don't mean it to be. Before that night, I'd never touched a woman. Not the way I touched you.

She had had so few professions of love in her life. Sandr had muttered something along the lines, she thought, back when they were drunk and skating and stupid. Even then she'd known better than to believe it. Salan, in his boyish, fumbling way. Qahuar Em, the first lover she'd ham-handedly tried to betray. Had he ever pretended to love her? She didn't think so. He had respected her too much for that. None of them had been as heartfelt and sincere as Geder, and none of them had made her skin crawl. Even now, Geder's words felt like she'd brushed her arm against a snake.

If only there were an exchange where people could trade love for love. She could have sold Geder's devotion to some status-struck girl at the Antean court and gotten the admiration and desire of…oh, an ambassador, perhaps. Some merchant prince who'd put his heart in an awkward position and would have been much better paired with the voice of the Medean bank in Porte Oliva. Only at some point, she would have to have fallen in love with someone as well, and she was fairly certain she never had. Loving her would have been like lending to a king, a weight on her scales that would never be brought to balance. And anyway—

The profound moment appeared silently and with no fanfare. It cleared its throat, almost in apology, and between one breath and the next changed Cithrin forever. She didn't catch her breath, didn't shout. There was no feeling of exultation that demanded it. The sick chaos that she called her mind resolved like a choir lost in pandemonium suddenly finding a chord. Though she had not been asleep, she woke.

The hold all around her was as it had been: shadows and light, the acrid smell of cheap lamp oil and salt and tar, the soft paper in her hand that had once been in Geder's. She tucked the letter away, sighed, went to the ladder, and rose from the darkness into the moonlight.

She went to find the two men she needed. Marcus Wester and Kit.

"There, upon the horizon stand!" Sandr said, gesturing at the rising hills of Borja in the imagination of the sailors and the guards. Cithrin could almost imagine the red-brown earth.

Kit turned to follow Sandr's finger, his jaw tight. He was the perfect image of Sebbin Caster, the evil queen's crippled brother and, through poetic justice, the last of his house. "No rising sun e'er burned so bright! Her castle falls, and so makes right."

The applause began, Cary and Mikel leading it and the wider audience taking it up. Sandr and Kit stood motionless as the first waves of sound passed over them. Their eyes were still on fire and death, and then their false selves fell away, and they smiled and bowed. The sailors hooted and clapped their hands against their thighs. The bank guards, more accustomed to theater, showed a degree less excitement, but their pleasure was unfeigned. Across the water, Inys blew a bright plume of flame out over the waves. The silver of the moonlight and the smoky red of dragonfire seemed like a painter's contrivance. Cithrin found herself smiling and wondering if it had been only coincidence, or if the dragon had been able to follow the performance even across the wide water. She moved through the little crowd, dodging Chisn Rake when the old Tralgu and a young Dartinae sailor began to pantomime the final duel scene. Marcus and Yardem were on the port side, leaning against the railing. Yardem's eyes found her first, and his wide, canine smile was a pleasure to see.

Marcus straightened, tugged at his sleeve, and tried to look nonchalant.

"Captain," Cithrin said. "I wondered if I might have a moment?"

Marcus and Yardem exchanged a glance. Yardem flicked an ear.

"Of course," Marcus said. Cithrin nodded and walked toward the ship's bow. He took two long, fast strides to catch up and then walked beside her. The half moon hung low in the sky and stars spilled across the darkness. In the night, she couldn't make out the coast away to the east. Or maybe they'd pulled farther away from land, tracking toward the Thin Sea, Narinisle, and Stollbourne.

"You're looking... better," Marcus said. "Are you feeling well?"

"I am," Cithrin said. "But I'm afraid we're going to need to change our plans."

The moonlight made Wester a drawing of himself in black ink and watered paint. Still, she could see the skepticism in his expression. "I'm listening."

"We've made a mistake. I've made it. And I think I see the way to . . . well, not win. Nothing so straightforward as that. I think I see the way to start fighting the right battles."

"We lost. Doesn't mean it was the wrong battle."

"*Battle*'s the wrong word. I should have said struggle or . . . oh, there aren't words for this. The mistake we made, that we all made, is thinking that we're fighting Antea. That we're fighting Geder."

"All right," Marcus said, pulling the syllables out. "And who is it we're actually fighting, then?"

"The idea of war."

Marcus nodded. The grey at his temples caught the light. His boots scraped against the deck as he shifted, and when he spoke, his voice was calm and careful.

"Grief's a terrible thing, Cithrin, and everyone comes to it differently. You've lost a lot in the last years, and I know how that can affect—"

"I haven't lost my mind. I'm saner now than I have been in weeks. Listen to me. Listen to my voice."

"You sound like Kit now."

"Listen. In Porte Oliva, we thought of it as a normal war. The enemy came, and we prepared for a fight. And we fought. Even though we know that the spiders are there to *make* us fight, we still fought. This has been going on since the beginning of history. Geder wasn't there when it started. This isn't about him or Antea or me. This is Morade wrecking humanity by making us fight."

"I don't know about that. We've got a pretty consistent record of killing each other without any spiders being involved," Marcus said, but she couldn't stop herself to answer his point.

"I thought we would win because we had a better position, better soldiers, better weapons. I thought we'd win it like a battle. Only it's like we were trying to clean something with filthy water. We can't win by fighting, because fighting is what the enemy wants of us. What it goads us into."

Marcus cleared his throat. Cithrin restrained herself from taking his hand. It was all so clear in her mind, but this was the first time she'd tried to say it. She had to find a way to make him understand. Or if not that, at least accept. From the far side of the ship, a rough chorus began a song about a Yemmu tin miner who fell in love with his mule. She could hear Cary's voice in among the others, and Enen's. Something splashed in the water beside the ship. A porpoise or one of the Drowned. Cithrin held her breath.

Marcus sighed. "I don't see that letting them slaughter us is much of a strategy. Dying with the moral high ground isn't as comforting as you might expect."

"I have no intention of dying," Cithrin said. "I think there is another way. But it means making some changes."

"Changes like what?"

"The first is, we're going to the wrong place. The ships need to go to Northcoast, and you and Kit and I need to go ahead of them."

"To see Komme," Marcus said. "Meet with the holding company."

"No," Cithrin said. "You can get me a private audience with King Tracian. You put his mother on the throne. He owes his crown to you. His life, even."

"That doesn't mean he thinks well of me."

"He doesn't need to. We just need to have him in the same room with us."

"And Kit."

"And Kit."

"Because we're going to use the spiders to convince King Tracian of something."

"Yes."

"Something that we don't want to mention to Komme Medean until it's already done."

"That's right."

"I don't know that I like this plan. My history with North-coast includes the corpses of a lot of women I love. I'm not interested in seeing you be one of them. What exactly is your business with Tracian?"

"I want to buy something from him."

"Something?"

"It's complicated."

"Try me."

Cithrin scratched her arm. "You know that the policy of the bank is never to give gold to kings, because they never repay the loan?"

"That may be the only part of your trade that makes sense to me," Marcus said.

"Yes, actually, that's a mistake. It's a bad policy, and I'm going to break it. I'm going to buy a permanent debt of the crown to the bank and an agreement from the king for modified letters of credit to make it circulable. Then when other kingdoms want the bank's holdings, we have a precedent, and the Medean bank is in the center of all those agreements. With royal edicts to back us and existing business partners whom we can run at an advantage, we can build enough transferable letters to let us do...well, almost anything, really."

"I see."

"You do?"

"I see that it's complicated. And you think there's a way to...God, I can't believe I'm saying this. You think there's a way to defeat the *idea of war* with this whatever the hell it is you're talking about?"

"I think this is my natural weapon," Cithrin said. "And it's one the enemy isn't ready for. I know I'm asking for your faith on this."

"And you're sure we don't want to talk with Komme before we start?"

"If it doesn't work, it will be the death of his bank. This isn't something he'd want done."

"Never stopped us before," Marcus said. "Wait here. I'll go find Kit."

Geder

Geder's father wheezed out his laughter, tapping the tabletop with the heel of his palm. His hair was whiter than Geder remembered it, and there were lines at the corners of his mouth and eyes that Geder didn't remember having seen. Perhaps he had, though. Perhaps his father's age was something that struck him anew every time they saw each other, and Geder only forgot.

"And so," Lehrer Palliako said, catching his breath and wiping a tear from his eye, "and so there he was. In the... in the kitchen, with his eyes wide as hands, yes? And saying, *All this is for me?*"

Cyr Emming wheezed along, breathing through his grin. But he kept glancing at Geder, checking to be sure the Lord Regent hadn't taken offense. All around them, the Fraternity of the Great Bear murmured, shutters opened to the soft night air. The breeze smelled of ripe fruits and roasting pork, the preparations for some celebration or feast that Geder would no doubt be obligated to attend.

"And then," Lehrer said, fighting to catch his breath. "And then when the next morning came? The next morning? His nurse came and found me. Told me he was ill."

"No. He hadn't," Emming said and turned to Geder. "You hadn't."

Geder spread his hands in mock sorrow.

"Three and a half pies, he'd eaten," Lehrer said. "Three and a half. Two meat, one blackberry, and half a treacle and walnut. He was on his bed with a hand to his gut and a belly out to here!"

"If someone had told me that they were for everyone at the feast, I wouldn't have done it," Geder said. "That's what he always leaves out of this story. I asked if they were all for me, and nobody said no. I thought they were."

"You were young," Emming said. "Youth always comes with strange ideas."

"He was moaning there in his bed," Lehrer went on. "And he looked green. Honestly green. I was afraid I'd have to call the cunning man."

"It wasn't that bad," Geder said. "I only ate a bit too much."

"A bit too much? A meal too much! Three meals too much! He must have gone faster than his gut could tell him no. I never saw a boy so sick. The feast night came, and he didn't eat a thing. Only sat at the table looking queasy and miserable," Lehrer said, then rubbed his hand on Geder's knee. The old man's eyes were bright and merry and filled with a kind of fond regret. "My poor boy. You tried so hard to do the right thing. My poor, poor boy."

Before Geder's expedition to the Sinir Kushku and his return with Basrahip, the Great Bear had been a place woven from threads of intimidation and desire. The center of masculine life in court, it was the place where Nellin Ostrachallin had composed a series of extemporaneous comic poems so lascivious and specific that Lord Bannien's son had challenged him to a duel on the spot, certain that the verse was mocking his mistress. It was where, as a young man, Lord Ternigan and Lord Caot had entered into a series of debates before King Simeon that had set the framework of the crown's policy toward Sarakal for a decade. To name it was to call into the imagination the smell of leather and tobacco and liquors. It was said that the servant girls there were not beyond quiet favors of a sexual nature. In Geder's early days in the court, it had been a place where being the son of the Viscount of Rivenhalm was much the same as being nobody at all.

Now it was two dozen nicely put-together rooms, some private and some open, where he could sit and visit with his father. The tobacco was still there, but he'd never found a taste for liquor. If the servants would submit to sexual advances, Geder was too petrified by his imaginings of what they would say about him afterward to ever make the experiment. The occasional contest of poetry or rhetoric was amusing enough, but not so profound as his boyhood imaginings of it had been. The expansion of the empire by three new kingdoms had drawn many of the men who would have filled the chairs away to new holdings and cities. Many of the greatest names—Bannien, Kalliam, Maas, Shoat—were dead now. Geder found he almost regretted the change.

Emming's laughter matched Lehrer's, the older men moving from hilarity to chuckling like partners coming to rest at the end of a dance. Emming tapped the tabletop and gestured toward the back of the building. Geder nodded as his advisor and, Geder had to suppose, friend rose from the table and made his way back. Even the loftiest men in the kingdom were servants to their bladders.

"All's well, though?" Lehrer asked, his voice lower now that they were alone.

Geder shrugged. "As well as can be expected, I suppose. There's so much happening, and the distances are so wide. Even using cunning men instead of birds, I feel like I'm working puppets that are working puppets."

"Ah," Lehrer said. "Well. Yes. I'd...I'd give you some words of wisdom, but you have more experience running kingdoms than I do."

"I had word from Elassae. What used to be Elassae. You know the Timzinae in Kiaria got loose?"

"I'd heard," his father said.

"Fallon Broot's gone out to fight them, but they keep fading up into the hills. Won't come down for an honest battle. And the gates at Kiaria are closed, so there are at least a few still in there. I'm afraid..." Geder's throat became unaccountably thick. He coughed to clear it. "I'm afraid we're going to have to burn Suddapal. It's not what I want, but now that Jorey's taken Porte Oliva and we've been welcomed into Newport, it's not as though we won't have any ports on the Inner Sea."

"Ah, that's good. That's good."

"It's just that I'd have kept it. If I could. Suddapal, I mean. And the slaves probably won't take it well."

"War's a terrible thing," Lehrer said, and lapsed into silence for a long moment. One of the servant girls passed by with fresh cups of wine and a silver bowl of fresh bread, butter, and honey. Geder broke off a crust and dipped it into the honey. When his father spoke again, his voice was thin and distant. "I did the best I could by you. I know I wasn't the father you'd have hoped for. But after your mother died, and running Rivenhalm...I did what I could."

"What do you mean?" Geder said. "You were wonderful. Look how it turned out. I'm Lord Regent. I'm running the whole kingdom."

"I suppose that's what I mean," Lehrer said, with a smile. "I'd have spared you that, if I could. Over a certain fairly low level, power's not worth the price of it. Least I've never thought so."

"It's only for a few years more," Geder said. "Aster will make a fine king."

"And may he produce a dozen little princes with whoever he takes as a queen, and save all of us from having to be regent, eh? Truth?"

"True enough, Papa," Geder said.

The evening went on an hour more, then a little longer. When his father rose to leave, Geder went with him, walking out into the wide night air. Lanterns flickered, spilling little pools of light around the doorway where the carriage waited, a little thing with cracked doors and the colors of Rivenhalm. Geder watched his father ride off over the cobbles, disappearing into the darkness. He wished he'd been able to talk about Cithrin with him. He wanted to talk to somebody, but Basrahip was gone and Aster wouldn't have understood. His father was the only man he knew who had loved a woman completely and then lost her. And even then, death wasn't betrayal. It was only as near as Geder knew. And even that...there was no way to begin that subject.

Papa, I was wondering how long I should expect to hurt when I think of her. Does that go on forever? I still think of her body at night. I hate her and I love her both. Is that normal? Is this how things are supposed to be?

How could anyone talk about something like that to their own father? Geder coughed out a small laugh. His own carriage drew up, grand and solid and shining black and gold as if it were a piece of the city itself. He let the footman open the way and help him up. The hooves of his private guard clattered, surrounding him, and the carriage lurched forward, moving into the night. He sat at the window, looking out. They passed the flattened and empty space that had been Lord Bannien's compound before he and Dawson Kalliam and a handful of others had risen up. Not so far away, there was the gate where he and Jorey Kalliam had brought the army into the streets of Camnipol for the first time in memory to fight against the Feldin Maas's mercenary showfighters and save King Simeon and Aster from the plots of Asterilhold. Past that, the hole where he had hidden with Cithrin.

Everyone, he supposed, had some private version of the city, made up of the streets and rooms and windows that they knew best. Violence made the landmarks of his personal city. Perhaps even of his world. The wheels of his carriage rattled against the streets, and then changed their sound as they passed over the Silver Bridge. The Division yawned below him, candles and lanterns on both rims defining the void by their absence. He had a moment of inexplicable fear, certain that the bridge would give way, that he would fall into the vast emptiness at the city's heart. At the far end of the bridge, his carriage turned again and the Kingspire came briefly into sight. The great banner of the goddess flowed from the temple, the darkness turning the red to black. The pale circle at the center caught the moonlight, and the eightfold sigil itself was like a shattered eye looking out over the city, the kingdom, the world.

When the carriage pulled to and Geder let the servants clear the way, he felt at once that something was terribly wrong. The formality of the footman, the way the grooms would not meet his eye, something. It could as well have been a scent on the wind. Without knowing what it was, Geder knew *that* it was.

The master of the household, an old Firstblood man with hair like snow on black water, waited in the great entrance, his throat tight and his chin high. Geder walked to him with a deepening sense of dread.

"Lord Regent," the servant said.

"What's happened?"

"It is nothing...serious, Lord Palliako. Boys suffer worse all the time, but—"

"Boys? What do you mean, boys?" Geder snapped. And then, "Where's *Aster*?"

He was on the triangular dueling grounds at the side of the spire, looking out over the Division. It struck Geder how much the boy had grown and changed in the years since his father had died. The war years. Aster stood nearly as tall as Geder now. His arms and legs were thin, but his jaw was no longer the jaw of a little boy. Not a man's yet, but reaching for it. Geder felt a pang of anxiety at how few years remained before Aster would take the Severed Throne and the empire, and how terribly much there was to be done so that Geder could present him with a world at peace. But that was all for another time. A different night.

He saw Aster's shoulders tighten at the sound of his approaching footsteps. He looked like a religious icon of anger and shame. Geder stopped.

"How bad is it?" he asked.

Aster turned. Even in the moonlight, the swelling of his left eye was obvious, as was the darkness of the flesh surrounding it. Geder groaned and came forward.

"Who was it?"

"Myrin Shoat," Aster said, his voice sharp with anger.

"The tall one you're always sparring with?"

Aster's gaze was fastened on the ground and wouldn't rise. His fists pressed his thighs.

"Was it," Geder said, fumbling for words. "Was it by accident?"

Aster's jaw clenched and released and clenched again. He shook his head once and went still. Geder sighed. He lowered himself down to sit cross-legged on the dry ground.

Aster didn't move. Geder patted the earth beside him, his hand coming away pale with dust.

"Come. Sit. I'll look ridiculous if I'm the only one doing it."

"Dirty," Aster said.

"They'll wash it. It's what they do. Sit with me."

For a moment, he didn't think the boy would. He thought Aster would stand there, towering over him, or walk off. Geder wasn't sure what he'd do if that happened. But four long breaths later, Aster folded his legs and sat down. The lanterns of the servants and guards glimmered from the spire but didn't approach. Aster's gaze didn't rise, but simply fixed on a patch of ground a little closer by.

"You could tell me what happened," Geder said.

Aster shrugged. It was a tight, constrained gesture.

"I could guess," Geder said gently. "I mean, if you'd rather. Ah. Let's see. You were at the Prisoner's Span, and discovered that one of the people in the cages was actually Sanna Daskellin put in by mistake. You were going to have this Shoat person lower you down, but he dropped you and you hit your eye on the corner of the cage."

"Don't make fun of me," Aster said.

"I'm not making fun of you. I'm being ridiculous so that maybe you'll smile."

Aster didn't smile. A tear tracked down from his uninjured eye, silver against his cheek.

"You could tell me," Geder said again. "I won't laugh at you."

Aster was silent for a long moment, motionless as a mouse before a snake. When he spoke, his voice was steady and calm. "He said some things that made me angry, so I hit him. Only I didn't do it very well."

"Things about you?"

Aster shook his head.

"Things about your father?"

Aster shook his head.

"Things about me?"

Aster didn't move, but his gaze shifted up to Geder for a moment before looking down again. Geder shook his head. In another situation, hearing that the boys of the court were mocking him behind his back would have stung and angered him, but Aster's pain was so raw and immediate, Geder didn't have to struggle to put himself aside.

"People will always poke fun at their betters," he said. "It's a rule, like rain goes down from the sky instead of up toward it. Or thunder comes after lightning, not before. It's just people."

"I know," Aster said. "I shouldn't have lost my temper."

"No, you shouldn't have. You're going to be king soon, and when you have to hand down justice and portion out lands and make treaties with other kingdoms, they can't think you're going to fly off and punch someone just because they've said unkind words about you."

"I know," Aster said, a sob in his voice. "I didn't mean to fail you."

"Fail me? You can't fail me. I'm the Lord Regent. You're the prince. I'm the only one who can fail here," Geder said. Aster nodded, but didn't look up. "Did you win the fight?"

"No."

"Ah. Well. You could challenge him to a duel, if you wanted to. Settle it on the field of honor."

"Do I have to?"

"No. But I thought you might want to. It's the sort of thing noblemen do sometimes. Not that I have. Honestly, I don't think I've ever been in a fight that I won." Aster looked up, confused. Geder nodded. "The first time I went into battle, I caught a bolt in the leg, passed out, and missed half the fighting. It's true."

"You faced Feldin Maas."

"Clara Kalliam's guard faced Feldin Maas. I ran for the hills with his letters and hoped no one would catch me. Some men fight, some think, some paint or make poems or win women's hearts. We are what we are. Knowing what our strengths are and what our weaknesses are and making do with them is all any of us have."

"Is that what you do?"

"I try," Geder said, and for an instant, sharp as a blade under his fingernail, he was in the empty banker's compound in Suddapal where Cithrin had once been, and then gone. He closed his eyes against the pain of it and coughed out a rough laugh. "I don't always do very well."

"He's stronger than me," Aster said. "On the dueling yard? He's got better reach. If I challenged him I'd only lose."

"You know, the idea of dueling is that righteousness gives you strength. The combat isn't just who's the strongest. It's who has the truth on his side."

"That's lovely," Aster said, and his voice was almost his usual again, "but I don't think truth outmatches having a better reach."

"Probably not," Geder said.

Far off in the city, a man shouted something, the words blurred by distance. A woman's voice shouted back. Geder looked up at the goddess's banner shifting in the breeze and the clouds and stars beyond it. He lay back, bending his knees.

"You're getting dirt in your hair," Aster said.

"I'll wash it back out," Geder said. "You know...it occurs to me. Not that I'd make the argument myself, but it *occurs* to me that striking the crown prince of Antea could, in some situations, be considered treason."

Aster's good eye went wide.

"I'm not saying it was," Geder said. "Only that some people might take it that way. If they didn't have all the information. Or had very strict ideas. And we do have the royal guard. We could just have them wander over to the street outside Shoat's compound. They wouldn't have to go in or speak to anyone if we didn't want them to. They could just go...*be* there. For a night or two."

It was a relief and a pleasure to see Aster's smile.

Clara

The day of the ambush began with light rains. Her son's army had reached the river the day before, and the trees that grew around the long, slow water seemed to speak in soft voices full of sharp consonants as the raindrops hit the leaves. Clara sat by her tent, smoking her pipe, listening to the noise of the soldiers breaking camp, and watching the faint light of dawn grow stronger. The smell of wet earth and smoke made the air rich and thick as perfume. Her simple breakfast—boiled eggs and coffee—tasted better for being eaten here.

The distance between herself and the soldiers was a social fiction, and like all social fictions terribly important. Traveling in disguise behind the army was a thing of scandal, but it could be explained away as the eccentricity of an older woman who had, after all, been through so much in recent years. It was little reflection on Jorey that his mother was odd. Had she then been incorporated into the army, though, it would have been *his* eccentricity, and a thousand times harder to overlook. So instead, her tent stood a little way off, had its own cookfire and her own servant, because Vincen was still playing that role where there were so many people about to see if he played some other. And so she was not with the army, but rather accompanied by it. She and

Jorey pretended they were in two separate journeys that happened, as if by happy coincidence, to overlap for a time.

And perhaps that was true. Perhaps that was the metaphor for being a mother to a son. It left her feeling soft and calm and only a little melancholy to think so.

"It's raining," Vincen said, appearing from the scrub with a pan of river water.

"It is."

"You're getting damp."

"Not very much so," she said. "And besides, my alternative is to huddle in a tent as if a little water would melt me. I'm too old for that kind of pretense."

"Not too old for the pretense of being old," he said.

"I haven't the faintest idea what you're talking about."

"It seems to me you've given yourself a great deal of freedom in how you live your life," Vincen said, "and you keep claiming it's because you're old. For one thing, you really aren't that old. And for another, there are any number of women in court who die after long lives without ever doing half the things you have."

"It is rude, you know, to dissect a woman's story of herself before lunch."

"The only thing wrong with it is the way it makes you seem less," Vincen said, hanging the pan over her little hissing fire to boil away the impurities. "You aren't yourself because you're old. You're just Clara."

"I don't know who taught you how to flatter, but they did a brilliant job," she said.

"I'm still learning," Vincen said. And a moment later, "You might want to go talk with Jorey today. I heard he had a visitor. A merchant from Sara-sur-Mar's been in the Lord Marshal's tent for the better part of the morning."

"Really?" Clara said. "Is there opinion on what exactly his business is?"

"Nothing I'd rely on," Vincen said.

"Well, then perhaps I should go and find out."

"You probably should," Vincen said, with a false solemnity. "After all, you're very old."

After she'd finished her pipe, Clara made her way down the path toward Jorey's tents. Her own little encampment was well within the circle of the sentries and patrols. No one challenged her. Indeed, many of the thin-faced, hard-eyed men knew her already and seemed to view her with a kind of indulgence. She felt as though she were in danger of becoming something of a mascot to the army.

The state of the men had come as something of a surprise. The campaign had left them hard and slight, like dried-meat versions of themselves. Even Jorey was thinner about the cheeks now, his gaze prone to a fixedness that she couldn't entirely interpret. They moved through the countryside, camp to camp and day to day, with an air of exhaustion balanced against determination, and it left her wanting to send them all home. Many of them had wives and children back in Antea. Farms or trades from which they'd been plucked by the obligations of their lords. She wished that she could tell them all to go back. To sleep in their own beds again. To eat their own food and drink beer and wine and sing along to the performers who stopped at the taprooms and street corners. But of course that was impossible. And even if she had convinced them, Geder's priests would have said the opposite and won.

"I'm sorry, my lady," the guard outside Jorey's great tent of framed leather said as she came near. "The Lord Marshal's in conference."

"Is he?" Clara said, raising her eyebrows. "With whom?"

"Couldn't say, my lady," the man said.

"Couldn't or won't?" Clara said with a smile. "Well, don't you mind. There's nothing I have to say that can't wait a bit. I'll just sit until he comes free."

"It's . . . it's raining, my lady."

"Well, hopefully he'll come free soon."

The guard licked his lips. "Just wait here a moment, my lady," he said and ducked into the tent. The voices that came from within were too muffled to make out words, but she could still recognize the sounds of the individual men. The guard and Jorey. The eerie, unpleasant voice of one of the remaining brown-robed priests. And then another, unfamiliar one. When they emerged, the priest and the guard flanked a wide-shouldered Jasuru man with scales the color of bronze and an embarrassed expression. His gaze flickered to Clara and then rapidly away. She wondered who he was.

"The Lord Marshal's free, ma'am," the guard said, and so she had to go in and see Jorey rather than follow the Jasuru. It was expected of her.

"Mother," Jorey said. "What can I do for you?"

"I'd meant to come ask after that letter you wanted me to carry home, but now I'm curious about that man who just left. He isn't one of ours, is he? Though of course, I mean yours. The only one I really have is Vincen."

"I can get you more servants if you want them," Jorey said. "It wouldn't be a problem."

"That's kind of you, dear, but I wasn't fishing." *At least not for that*, Clara thought as she sat. The Lord Marshal's tent was as large as some shacks. Whole families lived in the poorer quarters of Camnipol in rooms with less space than this. It occurred to her that, since the bulk of the army had come from the siege at Kiaria, the framed leather walls around her had likely been Lord Ternigan's before her plan had set him at odds with Geder. It made the space seem ominous.

"He's a merchant from Sara-sur-mar," Jorey said. "By which I mean a smuggler. He came because he had information to sell."

"Really? That seems presumptuous. Was it something you actually paid for?"

"It was," Jorey said, leaning over his little camp desk. A thin, cheap scroll showed lines of pale ink. A map, perhaps. "Callon Cane's appeared there. Set up a house. Started paying bounties for acts performed against Antea."

"That's a poor choice on his part," Clara said. "If I were in his position, I'd choose someplace to work that wasn't where my enemy was walking toward next."

"Well, you aren't leading a campaign of sabotage and murder designed to bring down the throne," Jorey said. "Our new friend knows of a way past the city walls. A smuggler's tunnel. He sold us the directions to it and the path to Cane's house. I questioned him with one of the priests. The information's good. It isn't a trap, or if it is, it's not one he knew about."

"Not a spy, then," Clara said. "Just a profiteer."

His eyes went empty for a moment, and he sighed. "Father would hate this."

"He would," Clara said. "But which part of it were you thinking of?"

Jorey's laugh was short and bitter. "I was imagining how he'd feel about sending men in like thieves in the night. Crawling through tunnels and assassinating the enemy rather than facing him in the field. But you're right. There are a hundred other aspects of this that he'd have hated as much. Or more."

"Thieves in the night?" Clara said.

"We can't afford another siege. The men are exhausted. I'm exhausted. When Vicarian was here, he'd talk me out of it. Convince me all of this was possible, but without him, now…" Jorey shook his head. "We shouldn't have won at Porte Oliva. It was luck, and Geder sending those weapons. If the dragon comes again, we won't have surprise to help us. Most of these men have been fighting since Sarakal. They've won and won and won, and the only triumph we've given them is another march. Another battle. Another chance to die."

"It's war," Clara said.

"It's not, though. Wars end. This is something else," Jorey said, and dropped his head into his hands. "Maybe I'm looking at it from the wrong end. Maybe this is all the hand of the goddess. The gates opening in Porte Oliva. The tunnel in Sara-sur-Mar. Maybe it's all the spider goddess giving us ways to win the battles when we can barely keep marching anymore, and I'm only being ungrateful."

"Is that what Vicarian would have said?" Clara asked.

"It is," Jorey said. "And when he said it, I'd be convinced. But he's not here, and I'm just not as persuasive."

"So few of us are," Clara said, "but—"

"I am trying, Mother. I am trying as hard as I can to be this man. To be the nobleman and servant of the crown. I am trying to forget that my father died at Geder's hand. I tell myself how much we owe him, and how kind he's been. To me, to you. To Sabiha. And most of the time, I can do it. I can remember how he came to the wedding because I asked him to. How he took care of Sabiha when the baby was coming. Vicarian's let the past go. He doesn't struggle anymore. I want to be like him. I want to believe that all of this is going to come to some perfect and glorious end, and that you and Sabiha and Annalise will all be fine if I can just do what needs doing and not *feel* anything. And some days, I almost manage."

He wasn't weeping. Even the pain in his voice was dry. Her son's soul had become a desert. All the replies she could think of—*It will be all right* and *Trust your instincts* and *Geder is a monstrosity*—would have made the moment worse. She took Jorey's hand and sat with him for a time in silence.

Jorey called the march not long after, and Clara retired to the little cart Jorey had found for her. The grasslands were behind them, the river on their left as they moved north toward Sara-sur-Mar. Vincen drove her team of two old, tired mules with their moth-eaten rumps and long, broad ears. Clara chewed on a knuckle, her mind busy and unquiet.

"We have to get word to him," she said.

"Who, my lady?" Vincen said.

"Callon Cane. Jorey has a path into the city that will reach him. I've seen the map. I think . . . I think I might be able to steal it. Or copy it. We have to move faster than Jorey does."

"Or else we lose another ally," Vincen said.

"Or else we lose Jorey, I think."

Vincen looked over his shoulder, his brow furrowed. "Find the map, then, and I'll go." The meaning of the words was deeper than mere syllables. *Of course I will risk my life to save someone you love.* Clara smiled and Vincen turned back to the mules and reins. She smiled at his back and shook her head. He was an impossibility, she thought. Men like Vincen Coe simply didn't exist. And perhaps neither did women like herself. He'd been right, of course, that it wasn't age that had freed her. It was loss. Her husband had died and she had been stripped of all the roles that had defined her. It should have felt like a vine suddenly missing the trellis it had grown upon, and it had. And it had also been like a cage opening. Jorey was still in that cage, only his was crueler, and the demands it made might be more than he could stand.

She could imagine him, if things went forward as they were now, ten years older, twenty. The misery of pretending to be a man that at heart he was not would tell on him. He would grow bitter, and his wife and daughter would know it. His mother would as well, for that matter. Because, of course, pretending a thing did not make it true.

Vincen stopped the cart, the mules jostling one another and looking back at him. Vincen had no attention to spare them. His head was shifting, like a dog tasting the wind. She tried to follow his gaze, but all she saw were trees by the roadside, scrub beyond them. All she heard were the voices of the soldiers and the distant murmur of the river in its bed.

"What's the matter?" she asked.

"I don't know," he said. "Something. Something isn't right."

"Should I find Jorey?" she asked, and the horns of the advance guard sounded. Vincen cursed and yanked on the reins. The mules hunkered down, their great ears set in defiance. There were more sounds now. Men yelling. Shouting. She looked back down the road, and the sword and bows were struggling into formation, some blades at the ready, some waving uncertainly as a banner in a whirlwind, trying to find the source of their peril.

"Get down, Clara," Vincen said.

"What is it?"

"We have to get you someplace safe."

She moved forward quickly, lowering herself to the road. The dragon's jade felt oddly slick under her feet, like the road itself had become uncertain where it should be. "What's happening?"

"We're being attacked. They'll try to drive us into the water."

"How do we stop them?" Clara asked.

Vincen drew his sword with one hand and a dagger with the other. He pressed the hilt of the dagger into her hand. "I don't know."

The riders burst out from among the trees to their right, proud, tall men in the green and gold of Birancour. She could see four of them, though the screaming seemed to come from everywhere. Up the river and down. The nearest of them looked from her to Vincen and back again, scowling, then spurred his mount in a charge. Vincen dodged behind the cart, pulling Clara with him. The queensman sank his blade into the side of the first mule. The animal screamed and tried to run, the cart lurching and creaking. There were more men boiling out of the brush. Clara tried to keep the moving cart between her and the attackers. The mules ran forward, trying to find a path not already blocked by trees or water, the enemy or the army all around them. She heard Vincen shout before she realized that she'd left him behind.

Something deep happened, and the sounds around her all went quieter. Still there, but also distant. Her head hurt at the back, and she was on her knees now without knowing quite how she got there. A man moved into her view. His tunic was green and gold, and the club he held in his hand was tipped with lead and blood. He lifted it again, preparing to bring it down on her, so she pushed the dagger in her hand out, into the man's crotch. His eyes went wide. It was hard to move her arms. They seemed very distant, but she did it again as he fell. His mouth was round with surprise and distress. She pushed the blade into his neck. It was like cutting an orange. She'd thought killing a man would be harder.

A roar came, like a windstorm or a wave. The thin, black-clad soliders of Antea. The brown-robed priest she'd seen speaking with Jorey earlier strode into her line of sight. He was shouting. *Flee or put your weapons down! You have already lost! The goddess cannot be defeated. Everything you love is already gone! You cannot win! You cannot win! You cannot win!*

And with each phrase, she felt herself folding down. The dying man at her feet looked up at her in wonder and despair. *We cannot win*, she thought. *Everything we love is already lost. Already gone. The spider goddess will take it all and leave us with nothing, and there is nothing to be done. Listen to my voice! Antea cannot be defeated! You cannot win!*

I cannot win.

"Here!" a man's voice called. "To me! To *me*!"

A familiar-looking man pulled her to her feet. There was blood all down the front of her dress. The sounds of the battle were closer now, louder and more real. The pain at the back of her head was sharper, and she felt what must have been a trickle of her own blood running down the back of her neck.

"Lady Kalliam!" the man said. "Are you well? Can you run?"

"I'm fine," she said. "A little tap on the head, but these little fucks will have to do better if they want to kill me."

The man laughed.

"Come with me," he said. "I'll see you to safety."

"Yes," she said. "No. Wait. Where's Vincen?"

The man shook his head. Her heart went cold.

"Where is Vincen Coe?"

Marcus

The Thin Sea that divided Northcoast from Narinisle was calm water, for the most part. The currents were predictable, the winds smelling of land and metal. The small ship with its shallow draft and high masts had been built to travel quickly and maneuver well. The lumbering round-ships with the little flotilla to protect them had fallen away in a matter of hours, slowed by their shapes and their load. Even so, as near as they were to Carse, Marcus didn't expect they'd reach the city more than a day or two before the rest caught up.

Kit and Cithrin stood together at the bow, deep in conversation. Marcus sat at the stern, looking out over the water with a scowl. The white cliffs of Carse were hardly more than a thickening of the horizon. The water they crossed could almost have been anywhere. It was only knowing where they were and where they were headed that made the waves seems familiar.

The last time Marcus had been in Carse, he'd been a younger man, and a hotter one. He'd thrown King Springmere's body off those cliffs first and his head afterward. If he thought about it, he could still conjure up the stickiness of the dead man's blood-drenched hair. The stink of the body. It had been months of work and planning. Schemes and conspiracies. He had cut out all of Springmere's support, undermined the throne that Marcus had given him, until the day came when wearing a crown was no defense.

Springmere hadn't asked him why. Hadn't begged. As soon as the trap closed around him, he'd known why. Alys and Merian. Marcus's wife and daughter. Marcus had imagined any number of things he might say there at the end. He'd practiced whole speeches about justice and falsehood and the kind of cowardice that could bring a man to betray his own allies. *I gave you Northcoast*, Marcus had said a thousand times in the privacy of his mind, *and I will take it back*.

He hadn't actually said any of it when the time came. He'd kicked Springmere down and sawn off his head while the man burbled and screamed. As moments of sublime justice went, it had been ugly, brutish, and unsatisfying. When Springmere's corpse was feeding the crabs and gulls at the base of the cliffs, he had stood for a moment, waiting for the peace that he'd expected retribution to bring. There hadn't been any. His wife and child were still dead because he'd given his loyalty to an untrustworthy man. He hadn't expected vengeance to bring them back, but he had thought that it might ease the pain of missing them. Just a bit.

The cliffs grew from a thick line to a ragged curve. The port at the base was still invisible, but Carse itself would be in view soon. Gulls chased the ship and the sailors cursed at them. Low, pale clouds floated and shifted against the late summer blue. Marcus watched for the city with his shoulders tensed and waited for the blow.

Yardem came up from belowdecks, his nose lifted to the wind and his ears canted forward. He nodded to the ship's mate as he passed, but didn't speak until he came close to Marcus.

"Been some time since we were here last," Yardem said.

"Has. I keep having to remind myself it's not Lady Tracian we'll be speaking with. Her boy wasn't much more than a thumb and an overwhelming sense of entitlement last time I saw him."

"He was a boy," Yardem said.

"Well, he's a king now."

"Is," Yardem said. "Because of you."

"Maybe he'll be grateful."

"Open to a pleasant surprise. Regret that you didn't put the crown on your own head?"

"Are you joking?"

"A bit, yes."

"There was that baker. You remember the one? With the apple tarts shaped like stars? What was her name?"

"Steyen," Yardem said with a wide, canine smile.

"That's right. Steyen. I wonder if she's still about."

"Suppose we'll find out," Yardem said.

"Yep."

They were quiet for a moment.

"They may try to kill us," Yardem said. "Slaughtering the old king can leave the new king nervous."

"That had occurred to me too. But we have Cithrin and Kit. And if he doesn't, though, the apple tarts."

"Yes, sir."

"It's also entirely possible that we're old news. Everything we did was a long way from here, and the world does move on."

"You think they just won't recall us?"

"I can hope."

The docks were crowded with ships of a dozen different designs. Marcus recognized banners and shipping marks from as far as Kort and Suddapal. Carts and dockhands crawled across the wooden piers like ants. The wind was coming in gusts now, complicating their landing. Marcus strapped the blasted sword on his back again. The rash where the scabbard rested against his shoulder hadn't quite healed since he'd stowed the damned thing after fleeing Porte Oliva. The poison that it carried made his joints ache a little. Or maybe he was just getting old.

Kit and Yardem stood with him, trying to stay clear of the sailors. Kit squinted up at the wooden stairs that climbed up the vast cliff face. They'd moved since the last time Marcus had seen them. In his memory, he could still follow the turns and switchbacks and landings of the old stairs, but the cliff face was soft, and nothing that hung from it lasted for long.

"You've been to Carse before?" Yardem asked.

"Yes," Kit said. "Many times. In my experience, sex farces and tragedies of character play well here. Religious subjects and tragedies of politics less so. They seem busier than I recall them being."

"It's the war," Marcus said. "You can usually see a little shifting of the trade ships when there's a good, rolling war on. It isn't usually this much, though."

"I think there isn't usually a war like this one," Kit said. "It seems no place has gone entirely untouched by it. Even those where Antean blades haven't gone have changed."

"That's true," Marcus said. "Wouldn't be surprised if it affected the blue-water trade too. Even Far Syramys will smell the wind off this fire. Truth is the world hasn't seen a war like this one since the last time our new friend was in the skies."

"Same one," Yardem said.

"Sorry?" Marcus said.

"It's not *like* the fall of the Dragon Empire," Yardem said. "It *is* the fall of the Dragon Empire."

"Suppose that's true," Marcus said.

"I don't know that I find that reassuring," Kit said.

Yardem flicked a jingling ear. "Didn't mean it to be."

A guide boat came alongside, a Cinnae man in the bows with a dun-colored speaking trumpet. The ship's mate shouted down to him, and for what seemed the better part of an hour, they negotiated back and forth, until the mate finally shouted a string of curses, tossed away his speaking horn, and called for the sails to be raised again and the course set. The deck lurched and creaked as the low sails caught the breeze and the ship turned for an empty slip. The guide boat moved ahead, shouting and hectoring both the crew and the other boats that threatened to cross their path. They were just starting to tie up at the dock when Cithrin emerged from below. The blue dress draped in Elassean style as if she wanted to remind the king of all the cities and nations that had fallen in the past few seasons. She'd touched her lips and cheeks with red, but only just. She moved across the deck with sure steps. She was beautiful, but not the way a girl searching for a boy might be. It was the beauty of a well-made knife. From the style of her hair to the tilt of her shoulders, everything about her spoke of competence. He tried to see the thin-limbed, frightened, overwhelmed girl he'd met on the last caravan from Vanai. He couldn't find her. She wasn't so many years older than she had been, and also she was. A small sorrow plucked at him that he hadn't been able to make the world an easier place for her.

"Where do we stand?" she asked smartly.

"Customs man should be aboard within the hour," the ship's mate said. "Once he's cleared us, we're sitting tight until the others come."

"Thank you," she said, turning to Marcus and Kit and Yardem. "This should be an interesting day."

"Could put it that way," Marcus said.

"It's going to be fine," she said, her voice solid and certain. Like she was trying to convince herself. "It is all going to be fine."

In fact it was well over an hour before the customs magistrate walked the gangplank over and scowled along the deck. He was a Firstblood man with a bald pate, a ledger in his hand, and an air of grievance that surrounded him like a smell.

"Who's responsible for the fees, then?"

"I'm patron," Cithrin said.

"Mm," the magistrate said. "All right. And what are you carrying?"

"In this ship, or the full company?"

"You've a full company?"

"I do. We're the first ship of twenty."

The magistrate laughed dismissively. "Let's have the tally for both, then. God alone knows where you think to put twenty ships, though. It isn't your private dock, miss. There are rules about these things."

"Of course," she said. "This is ship is carrying only passengers. I am Cithrin bel Sarcour, voice of the Medean bank in Porte Oliva. These are my guards and counselor."

"Names?"

"Kitap rol Keshmet," Kit said. "Sometimes called Master Kit."

"I can manage Keshesti names, thank you," the magistrate said. "You. Tralgu. Spit it out. I have other business to finish today."

"Yardem Hane."

The magistrate snorted. "Nice try. What's your real name."

"Yardem Hane."

"Really," the magistrate said. "And then I suppose you'll try to tell me that this leathery old fuck is supposed to be..."

Marcus lifted his hand in a short wave. The magistrate's face went grey as ash. His ledger fell from numb fingers, the pages splaying out on the deck.

"Think they remember us, sir," Yardem said.

"Seems they might," Marcus said.

The plan had been simple. Send a message ahead to the palace requesting an audience with King Tracian and his master of coin relying on Marcus's name to catch the king's curiosity. It had been a good plan, Marcus thought as the guards marched him and Cithrin side by side up the flights of wooden stairs. The poisoned sword was taken, as were Yardem's blades and the little knives Cithrin and Kit had carried. Four men walked in front, four between Cithrin and Marcus at the front and Kit and Yardem behind, and four brought up the rear. Not precisely an honor guard's formation. They hadn't bound anyone, though, so that was a fine thing.

"Do you remember," he said, "back when you were coming to Carse the first time to ingratiate yourself to Komme Medean and kick Pyk out of your chair?"

"I do," Cithrin said.

"I was going to make myself part of your guard. You wouldn't allow it."

"No, I wouldn't."

"I'm seeing how you drew that conclusion."

"Fame is its own punishment," Cithrin said. Even in the somewhat threatening circumstances, her voice was bright. Somewhere along the way, she had become hard to frighten.

The cliff rose beside them and the water fell away, the masts of the ships pointing up at them like the fingers of curious giants. When they reached the edge of the cliff and the iron stairs that led to the great yard, Marcus's legs ached and his breath was heavy. Cithrin and the others seemed fine, though, so he didn't complain or ask for a moment's halt. The wide, open streets of the city around him were as familiar as a house lived in as a child and seen again as a man full grown. Now that he had seen a dragon, the city made more sense. He could imagine Inys making his way between the buildings, climbing to the ancient perches and looking out over the sea. It was strange, like the memory of a word heard once in some language he hadn't known at the time but explicable now. His own history and the city's both came clear before him.

I have lived my whole life in Inys's ruins, he thought, *and I never understood what I was seeing.*

The king's palace rose up level above level, a massive block of dragon's jade and stone. Walking through the southern gate into the gardens was like seeing an old friend. Or an old enemy. Marcus felt the familiar tension in his back. His lips curled into an unkind version of a smile. Apple trees heavy with fruit made a carefully manicured orchard around a fountain of dragon's jade. His family had died burning to determine who got to sit beside *that* water and eat *those* fruits. If anyone had asked him before now, he'd have said his anger had mellowed. He'd have been wrong. The central fact of his life was still that Alys and Merian were dead, and he would never forgive the world for it.

More guards were waiting for them, though these at least had light and nicely decorated armor. Their blades would kill just as quickly, but it was possible to pretend they were merely ornamental. They led the four of them down a long hall and through a carved archway. The room wasn't made for meeting, though for someone who hadn't spent time studying the architecture of the palace with an eye toward murder, that might not have been obvious. It was, after all, wide and comfortable. The rails and walkways above them on all sides might almost have been intended to open the room and give it the sense of being a covered garden. It was really a place for archers to stand so that, by aiming down, they wouldn't hit the man across the way from them. There were divans of buff-colored silk and tapestries from Far Syramys. A servant poured them water and wine and gave them plates of nuts and fresh grapes, silver bowls of cool water to refresh themselves with. Somewhere above them, as hidden as the archers, musicians were playing softly: mandolin and sand drum and harp. As slaughter pits went, it was hard to improve on.

Cithrin didn't see the room's threat or its potential for violence. She took her seat, relaxing into it like she came here every day. Yardem paced as if simply stretching his legs. Only Kit let himself gawk at the beauty and splendor of the palace, standing in the room's center and turning slowly to take it all in.

"I am impressed," Kit said.

"You're meant to be," Cithrin said. "We're all meant to be."

"That it's intended doesn't take away from the effect," the actor said. "I've played before kings before, one time and another, but I can't say that I've been here. This was what you were hoping for, wasn't it, Cithrin?"

She smiled. "I'd hoped for more respect and less fear, but this will do. As long as we can speak to the king and his master of coin, we'll be fine."

"You're a woman of great faith," Marcus said.

The voice came from the walkway above. "Captain Wester."

King Tracian looked more like his mother, now that he'd

grown to manhood. The fat cheeks had spread to a manly if still-rounded face. The darkness of his hair showed what Lady Tracian's must have been before the grey of age crept in. His personal guard were behind him, but without weapons drawn. The king's robe was a deep red velvet, embroidered with a pattern Marcus couldn't make out.

"Majesty," Marcus said. "Been some time. I heard about your mother's passing. I'd have come for the burial, but I thought people might misinterpret it."

"She'd have understood why you didn't," King Tracian said. "I have to say I'm surprised to see you here. Especially unannounced."

Marcus spread his arms in a gesture of helplessness. "Flying before the storm. If I'd had a reliable way to send a message faster than I could arrive myself... Well, I might have."

Tracian put his hands on the railing. His gaze was fixed on Marcus like he was a puzzle the king was trying to solve. "I've heard some fairly astounding tales about you over the years."

"Most of them are probably exaggerations," Marcus said. "You know how it is when people talk."

"People were saying you woke a dragon and flew across the world on its back."

"You see? Exaggeration. He wouldn't have let any of us on his back."

Tracian laughed, and then stopped and then laughed again. Marcus knew better than to bait the man, but he couldn't seem to help it. The urge to be the man he'd been in these halls, in this palace, was almost too powerful to overcome. He'd killed a king once, and the new king would have been a fool to forget it.

"What brings you?" King Tracian asked, his voice calm and careful.

"Majesty," Cithrin said, bowing deeply. "Captain Wester is with me. He's led my guard since I founded my branch of the bank."

"Yes, Magistra bel Sarcour. I'd heard that too," King Tracian said. "I almost thought the dragon riding more plausible than that General Wester had fallen to guard duty."

"It has its compensations," Marcus said. "But she's telling you true. I wasn't coming here at all. I'd thought we were going to Stollbourne until she told me to change course. What happened before, happened. Right now, the job's less fighting old battles than avoiding fresh ones."

"I've heard about the fall of Porte Oliva," the king said. "You have my sympathy, of course. But I don't know how I can help you."

"I was thinking that I might be able to help you, Your Majesty," Cithrin said.

"And how would you do that?" he asked.

"I was thinking of giving you a great deal of money."

Cithrin

Everything had a cost. Cithrin knew that the way she knew her own body. It was simply the way the world was built. Even an apple given freely had to be carried or eaten or thrown away at the risk of offending the giver. A word kindly given cost the time it took to respond and to think afterward whether it had been truly meant. Having Marcus Wester at her side was a tremendous and likely critical advantage. It had, as she'd hoped, brought her before the king so quickly that Komme Medean and the holding company weren't even aware as yet that she was in the city. That King Tracian's interest and curiosity were built on a bedrock of fear was part of the price of it. It meant having the first part of the conversation in a pit where the king and his guards posed a much greater physical threat to them than they could to him. That was easy enough to ignore. Marcus's cold smile and the way he spoke even the most innocuous words could be a prelude to violence and meant that his part of the work was done, and he needed to be put aside as quickly and gently as she could manage.

She had hoped to spend more time leading up to the proposal. Discussing Antea and the fall of Suddapal and Porte Oliva, perhaps. Something that would leave the king thinking of Geder as the more immediate threat. With Marcus in the room visibly restraining himself from snarling, bringing in the prospect of money at once seemed a better tactic. Gold had the advantage of being distracting.

"I was thinking of giving you a great deal of money," she said.

For the first time, Tracian's attention entirely left Marcus. Cithrin smiled. *Look, there's no animus. We are all allies and friends.* In the corner of her eye, Yardem moved nearer to Marcus. She hoped they would both sit down.

"Well, I can't say I'm averse to the idea," King Tracian said. "But that isn't what I've come to expect. Magister Nison has always been quite adamant that loaning money to the crown was out of the question."

"I am not Magister Nison," she said. "All respect to the man, but his position and mine are somewhat different."

She saw the motion in her peripheral vision as Yardem and Marcus sat, giving the focus of the performance to her. If there was a way, once this was all done, she would have to give the Tralgu a gift as thanks. A plant, perhaps. The king frowned, but there was, she thought, a glint of interest in his eyes. Interest or avarice. One was as good as the next.

"How so? You're both bankers. You answer to Komme."

Cithrin spread her arms the way she imagined Cary would have, playing to the crowd. "I have spent the last year in the teeth of war, and Magister Nison's been here. He is looking for reasons to keep money from you so that his branch can have it. I am looking for ways to give it to you so that we can both be safe. I'm afraid the importance I put on profit may not be as great as it was." She let her voice quiver just slightly. *You see? I'm afraid. Oh so afraid.*

"Don't overplay it," Kit whispered, and Cithrin coughed.

Tracian was at the rail above her now, his hands resting on its edge. She could see directly up his nose, and he, likely, was looking down her dress. It was awkward for both of them, which was fine. The sooner they moved to a drawing room where the walls themselves didn't cast them as enemies, the better it would be.

"A banker who doesn't serve profit's an odd thing," he said.

"These are exceptional times. You've heard of what Magistra Isadau and I did after the fall of Suddapal."

"Komme visits me on occasion, but he doesn't tell me everything he knows."

"But you *have* heard," Cithrin said. *You are king, and you have control.* Truth was the best flattery, when that could be managed. It spoke well of him as a man that his expression shifted toward the solemn when he spoke. It could as easily have moved toward self-congratulation.

"I have," he said. "The ambitions of the Severed Throne have been a subject of a great deal of conversation at court."

"Will you hear my opinion?"

"Well," Tracian said. "As I recall, you are the expert on the private mind of Geder Palliako."

It was meant to embarrass her, so she grimaced as if embarrassed. The king's smile was almost conciliatory, as if sorry to have brought up something so indiscreet. She understood for the first time how deeply King Tracian was out of his depth, and tried not to let the realization show in her voice or manner. "I suppose that's true," she said. "I believe that Antea is on the dragon's path. Its war will not end."

"Even the dragon's war ended," King Tracian said.

Master Kit coughed politely and stepped forward. "With respect, Your Grace, it did not. This *is* the dragon's war."

"It's come back to life like a fire rising from old embers," Cithrin said. "And Palliako is its tool, not its master. It can't be ended in the normal ways. Even if Antea conquered every other throne in the world, the violence would not end. The fighting will come here, and you will need every advantage you can dream of to survive it."

"Antea has no quarrel with me," King Tracian said. "We have few Timzinae here. We have a long history of cordial relations with the Severed Throne. You are the greatest danger I see."

"None of that will save you," Master Kit said. "You may walk as if on eggshells, and it will not keep you safe. You may give Antea everything it asks for, and it will still come to violence. You know that to be true, Majesty. Look in your heart, and you'll find you know our words are fact."

The king's gaze flickered to from Cithrin to Kit and back to Cithrin. "And who exactly is this man?"

"His name is Kitap rol Keshmet, and he's my expert on Palliako's master."

"The spider goddess?" the king asked.

"No, Your Grace. Worse than that. Even gods and goddesses may die. I stand before you as the warning against a particularly bad idea. There is no sword so sharp it draws blood from a mistaken thought."

King Tracian scowled. "I don't understand."

"I will be happy to explain it," Kit said. "It is important that you know. But also, it is important that you have every resource at hand to stand against the coming madness." He nodded toward Cithrin.

"Ah yes," King Tracian said. "The great deal of money?"

"I have the remaining resources of Suddapal and Porte Oliva in my command. I propose to lend them to you for the duration of the war, but I would ask a favor in return."

"Sanctuary?" King Tracian asked.

"No," Cithrin said. "Permission to trade. If I hand you all my capital, I have nothing left to do business with. No way to buy, no way to sell. I would ask that you permit me to write letters of transfer based on the gold I have given you."

"I don't know what that means," the king said.

"Only that the loan I give you, I may transfer to others. After the war, when the world is safe again, you will repay your debt. Of course you will. You're an honest and honorable man. Yes?"

"Of course," Tracian said. She couldn't tell whether he believed it or not, but it hardly mattered.

"Between that time and this," she said, spreading her hands, "I would like the exclusive permission of the throne to issue letters of transfer. Should I wish to purchase a bolt of cloth or supplies for a brewery, I will write a letter transferring part of your debt to me to the seller. So if I were to purchase seven tenthweights of gold worth of barley, I would be able to write a letter transferring seven tenthweights of your debt to that merchant. And when the time came to repay the debt, the merchant would be guaranteed the gold directly from the crown. You would repay him as you would have me."

"In that manner," Master Kit said, "Magistra Cithrin's bank could continue to trade and function, you see."

"It would require that you let it be known that the crown guaranteed the debt," Cithrin said. "You would need to make a proclamation that the letters were to be respected as one would respect the throne itself."

"For the duration of a war," King Tracian said, "that hasn't started."

"Until you repay the loan, Your Majesty," Cithrin said. "Whenever that may be."

Marcus said something under his breath. She couldn't make out the words, but the tone was derisive. Yardem shrugged.

"The danger you are in is real," Kit said. "Placating Antea

will not save you. Listen to my voice. You *must* be ready when this comes."

"How much gold are we talking about?" King Tracian asked. She took a deep breath. When she told him, his eyes went wide.

The master of coin was a thin-faced man younger than Marcus Wester and chosen for the position more by the nobility of his blood than his keen understanding of finance. She sat with the man in a comfortable drawing room that looked out over the sea. Their chairs were leather and wood, and the workmanship so solid they didn't so much as creak. She drank wine and water and ate sugared almonds and salty cheese. He looked over the proclamation she'd drawn up and the terms of her contracts with the crown, scowling and scratching his chin. Kit sat across from her, lending the uncanny power of his voice less often than she had anticipated he would have to. Cithrin kept her hands folded in her lap, waiting for the guards to rush in at any moment, Komme Medean shouting and shrieking at their head.

The two points of critical importance—the exclusivity of her right to issue letters and the consequences of merchants flaunting the crown's guarantee—hung in the back of her mind, the arguments she'd prepared to support them pressing to get out even before objections were raised. When the master of coin did balk, it was at trivia—the price she was charging the crown for silk and tobacco, how to make certain that no false letters were presented to the treasury. Cithrin responded to every query with dignity and grace because Kit and Cary and the players had taught her how to seem one thing while being something else. If her true self had been at the table, she would have been a creature entirely of laughter and contempt.

When she stepped out of the palace, the sun had already fallen into the western sea. A soft wind shifted through the wide streets, rubbing against Cithrin's legs like a cat. A group of children ran across the square, chasing one another with laughter and tears. Seagulls wheeled overhead, their twilight-darkened bodies barely showing against the pearl-grey sky. The agreements were signed, King Tracian's signature and seal already in place. The wealth on the ships still not arrived at Carse had changed as if by a cunning man's trick. At the height of the day, it had been the capital of the Medean bank in Porte Oliva. Now at evening, it was the property of the crown of Northcoast. Not hers any longer. She had traded it all for a parchment and a few hundred words. At her side, Kit lifted his eyebrows and glanced back at the palace behind them. *Have we managed? Did it work?*

Her smile was slow and broad and only a little more certain than her heart.

Marcus and Yardem finished exchanging their own banter with the captain of the palace guard, their voices bluff and masculine and uneasy. The pair made their way toward her, Firstblood and Tralgu. The poisoned sword slung across Marcus's back caught the falling light and seemed to glow green.

"That was it?" Marcus said by way of greeting.

Cithrin lifted her eyebrows. The implicit threat was still in his mouth and the way he held his shoulders. He glanced down the streets around them, not looking directly at her, but watching for dangers she was nearly certain didn't exist. Or at least not here. Or now. She looked to Yardem and made her gaze a question. Without seeming to move at all, the Tralgu looked pained. They were walking the paths of Wester's history, and the tension in him was like seeing someone caught in an unexpectedly harsh current. What had happened here might be dead and gone to everyone else in the world, but he was still within it. For him it had never died, and so perhaps it never would. Or at least not while he lived.

She felt a tug of pity for him. "That was it, and it was enough," Cithrin said.

"I owe Yardem a beer. You owe me a beer. So you buy him one and we're all square?" Marcus said. "That's the magic that's supposed to let you defeat Geder Palliako in the field? Because it seems to me you've just given away a lot of gold."

"I didn't give it away," Cithrin said, walking east. The rising night before her was studded with the first stars. Away to their left, the great carved dragon slept at the Grave of Dragons. Now that she'd seen a living example, she could appreciate how true the sculptors had been to their model. Always before it had seemed like an exaggeration. "I bought something with it."

"Tracian's goodwill isn't worth that much," Marcus said.

"That isn't what I bought," Cithrin said. "I bought the crown's debt."

"That's like owning an empty hole and the air to fill it with, from what I can see."

"That's all he could see too," Cithrin said. "He looked at me and saw a frightened woman with more money than sense. And he thinks he took advantage."

"Well," Marcus said, "he always was a snot-nosed little brat. His mother, at least, was someone to contend with."

"He didn't understand the implications of what he was doing," Cithrin said.

"He's got good company in that," Marcus said, and then sighed. He squinted up at the moon, looking thinner and older and more fragile than her memory of him. She felt the urge to put her arm around him, lean her head against his shoulder as a daughter might to her father. Tentatively, she reached out, touching his elbow. At first he stiffened as if offended, then with a rueful smile he let her tuck her arm through his and walk on into the twilight city. "I suppose it doesn't matter. As long as you understand it."

"I do," she said. "And Komme Medean will too. But he's not going to like it."

She would have liked to spend the evening in the city, moving from one taproom to the next, finding the places where musicians played in the cool and darkness, the gambling rooms where desperate men and women played at dice and tiles. Her time in Carse had been so long ago and with the distortions of memory seemed so brief, she wished she could take a few hours to pretend that the time in between hadn't happened. That Suddapal still stood, that Pyk Usterhall still lived, that Geder Palliako might have found some other lover to occupy his time and attention. The risk was too high. There were too many people there who knew her on sight.

And in truth, what she wanted most was not to have to explain herself to the man whose fortune she'd just committed.

Still, on the way to Magister Nison's branch, she did contrive to stop at a stand where a Dartinae girl sold bricks of cake and little cloth napkins filled with spiced pork and walnuts. She paused for a long moment at the council tower, looking up at its dark windows, ten floors above the cobbled street. Kit told stories of his travels in the city with the troupe and Yardem made laconic, gentle jokes about the people as they passed. She could feel Marcus softening a bit as they walked and the knot in her own belly starting to tighten. It was as if the alarm of his past was transferring into her and becoming an anxiety for the future. Nor was it the far future she feared. Geder and his blades, the spider priests and their creeping madness. They were the terrors of another day.

The moon was high in the sky and the western horizon utterly black when the moment came she could put off no longer. The holding company was built like a keep within the city. She walked to the great iron gate that stood closed against the uncertain traffic of the night. Two Tralgu guards in light scale armor with short, workmanlike blades stood at a rough sort of attention, but their ears shifted forward as she and the others approached.

"I've come to see Komme Medean," Cithrin said before the guards could call her out.

"Household's asleep," the smaller of the two guards said. "You'll have to wait for morning."

Her heart leapt at the idea. It wouldn't be her fault. The guards had turned her away. What could she have done? But, of course, the answer would be obvious. And so she did the obvious.

"Find him or his daughter," Cithrin said. "Tell them Magistra Cithrin bel Sarcour of the Porte Oliva branch has come with news of the war. And that I have a document that they will be very interested in seeing."

Geder

Every day brought more bad news from every corner of the empire. The raids in Inentai were escalating, and the enemy had come to recognize the power of the priests. They'd started to bring huge drums that drowned out even the greatest speaking trumpets the spider goddesses' priests could devise. The second army, as Mecelli had come to call the scraping of loyal Antean sword-and-bows from Nus and Suddapal, were calling the enemy the Children of Thunder. Morale, the reports said, was still high despite the loss of life and the success of the raiders. He could not promise how long that would remain the case.

In Elassae, Fallon Broot had taken the fight to the enemy, defeating the Timzinae in battle after battle, but thus far none had been decisive. He was coming to the conclusion that rather than a genuine campaign, the enemy was trying to draw him farther and farther from Suddapal. He was splitting the small force he had, sending the foot soldiers back to the city where, with the priests to aid them, he hoped they would dig out the roots of insurrection there before the force from Kiaria and the rebellious elements in Suddapal could coordinate. He himself would remain in the field to balance continuing attacks on the Timzinae army with the reestablished siege on the mountain fortress of Kiaria.

Jorey Kalliam and the main army were tracking north

in Birancour, moving toward the apparent new stronghold of Callon Cane in Sara-sur-Mar in hopes that by killing or capturing the man, he could find out where Cithrin, the dragon, and the shadowy leaders of the Timzinae conspiracy had fled after Porte Oliva.

The farms throughout the empire were coming near to harvest, but the work of the newly enslaved Timzinae from Sarakal and Elassae had not been as useful as the same work by experienced and free farmers. It might have been because the slaves were reluctant to work for the kingdom that had broken their homes and had their children hostage in the prisons of Camnipol, or it might have been that they didn't have any experience working farms. Likely, it was something of both. Whatever the causes, the harvest would be thinner than Geder had anticipated. Not starving thin, and so better than the year before, but not as good as he had hoped. Dar Cinlama and the other searchers in the empty places of the world had either found nothing—Korl Essian's forces in the north of Lyoneia and Cinlama himself—or had stopped sending reports—Emmun Siu in Borja and Bulger Shoal in Herez.

More troubling than any of it was the silence from Kaltfel. It had once been the heart of Asterilhold, and the first city to fall under the sway of the empire when that kingdom fell. It was closer to Camnipol than Estinport or Kavinpol, connected directly by dragon's roads. It had practically been an Antean city even when it had been under King Lechan's rule. And of Basrahip and the apostate there, no news at all had come.

"If it were mine to do," Canl Daskellin said, "I'd look at drawing in."

The garden was cool around them. A fountain chuckled and muttered, sheeting water down the bodies of twelve of

the thirteen races worked in dragon's jade. Only the Timzinae were not numbered among them, and Geder assumed
it meant the statues were even older than the false race. Or
that the sculptor had understood that the Timzinae were
not, in fact, human as the other races were. Either way, he
liked the fountain. The trees around them still sported their
summer green, their leaves wide and lush and blocking all
but the smallest dapples of sunlight. It would not be many
more weeks before the green began to retreat and the yellow
and red of autumn took its place.

The seasons were turning again, and the war was not
over. Geder felt the pressure of it like a hand laid at the back
of his neck.

"Drawing in," he said. "And what would that look like?"

"Abandon Inentai, for one," Daskellin said. "It's rubbing
up against Borja and the Keshet. It's already bleeding us
more than it gives back. Split the forces there between Suddapal and Nus, at least for the winter. If it falls to the raiders, we can take it back in the spring."

Cyr Emming snorted and shook his head. "It controls
the dragon's road between Sarakal and Elassae," he said.
"Let Inentai go, and not only do you have a mountain range
keeping your forces in Nus and Suddapal apart, but you've
got a toehold for an enemy to strike north or south at will."

"Well, Porte Oliva, then," Daskellin said. "It's the farthest there is. Cithrin's not there. Her bank's not there. We
have other ports in the south. We don't gain very much by
having it, and even sending messages to it is hard now. Once
the pass at Bellin closes for the winter, it'll be even worse."

"They won't fall," Geder said.

"My lord?" Daskellin said.

"They have temples in them. All of them do. And as long
as they have temples, they won't fall. Basrahip said so, and

he's been right about everything up to now. I say we trust him. Keep to the plans we have. They've gotten us this far. The danger now is that we break faith. As long as we don't do that, everything's going to be fine."

Emming nodded, and a moment later, Daskellin did as well.

"It'll be fine," Geder said.

Basrahip returned in the middle of the night, and without fanfare. Geder woke in the morning and went through his daily rituals of bathing and dressing himself to the point that the body servants wouldn't see him naked, then putting up with their ministrations. He went to break the night's fast at the table in the royal quarters. Aster and Basrahip were both sitting already, slabs of beef and bowls of peppers and honey before them, drinking tea and talking.

The huge priest looked profoundly changed. His dark hair had a dusty look and his cheeks were sunken. Even his hands seemed thinner. His left cheek was marked by a deep bruise that began, almost black, at his cheekbone and flowed down grey and green and yellow almost to his chin. The smile he greeted Geder with was beatific.

"Prince Geder!" Basrahip said, rising to his feet. "I bring glorious news."

"You're back," Geder said, aware as he did how inane the words seemed. Of course Basrahip was back. He knew he was back. But just because it was obvious didn't keep it from seeming the most important thing happening.

"I am," Basrahip said. "Sit, Prince Geder. Eat."

"You didn't send reports," Geder said, doing as the priest said. "I was worried things were going badly. Thing didn't go badly?"

"Reports," Basrahip said, waving a dismissive hand.

"Binding ink onto paper is the death of meaning. It pretends to be words, but it is a stone. A bit of wood. A thing without a soul. The work in Kaltfel is too glorious for such blasphemy."

"I've had reports from other places," Geder said. "All sorts of them. Some days it's felt like I do nothing but read notes and letters from places where things are actually happening."

Basrahip grinned and pointed a thumb at Geder as if he'd just agreed with the priest. "And I have come now with my living voice. There is the difference. In these other places, you have death. Killed words that are neither true nor false. It weakens you. Fills you with despair, yes?"

"Some days," Geder said, trying to make a joke of it.

Basrahip took a plate, spooned peppers and meat onto it, and handed it to Geder. The familiarity and intimacy of it left Geder feeling as if they were just old friends—the kind that made a sort of family—rejoined after too long an absence. That he was the guiding hand of the empire and Basrahip his most trusted advisor fell away, and for a moment he was only Geder and the priest was just the man he knew he could trust.

"You should refuse these letters," Basrahip said. "Bring the voices themselves to you. Hear them as you hear me. In this way all things are made real."

"I'm not sure how well that works," Geder said, taking a bite of the peppers. Their heat had nothing to do with temperature, and he drizzled a line of honey onto them as he spoke. "It's a big empire. Having people bring all the news in person seems like it would slow things down pretty badly."

"You are the man of wisdom in these things," Basrahip said. "I only say that the hard words you have read have weighed you down. The words I bring may still be hard, but they will lift you. I have no greater proof than this."

"Wait," Geder said. "Hard words? Why are they hard? I thought you said they were glorious."

"They are," Basrahip said. "The city of Kaltfel is in chaos, Prince Geder. Through your will, the enemies of the goddess and the servants of lies have been brought forth where they can no longer hide. The apostate claims the city as his own, claims the temple as his own. I came to him myself—a man I have known from childhood—and I begged that he listen to her true voice. And do you know what he said?"

"He called Basrahip an apostate," Aster said, the excitement in his voice bordering on joy. Apparently the prince had some insight into why that would be a good thing that Geder didn't, because it sounded like a bad situation to him.

Basrahip must have seen something in Geder's face, because he chuckled and leaned forward, his massive elbows resting on the table. "From the moment you and I met, back in the temple of the desert, you have known that we brought truth to a world built of lies, Prince Geder. And now the lord of lies has come. We have driven the servants of deceit from the shadows and they take to the streets with their knives and their clubs. They have given up the treachery which was their only strength."

"Knives and clubs?" Geder said. "What the hell is going on in Kaltfel?"

"The last stand of lies," Basrahip said. "The first death throes of the enemy."

"It's because Kaltfel was the first place that we took," Aster said. "It was the first city that had a temple built in it that wasn't Antean to begin with."

"But—" Geder began.

"Listen to me, Prince Geder. Listen to my voice. This is what we have always hoped for. This is the proof that all your work has not been in vain."

Geder tried to chew a bite of honeyed peppers, tried to swallow. It was difficult. His throat seemed tighter than it should have been. When he spoke, his voice was smaller than he expected it to be, more tentative. "We wanted this?"

"The first wave of your power has washed over the world," Basrahip said. "It has brought purity with it, and those to whom purity is a poison have writhed in pain to see it come."

"I suppose that's true," Geder said. "I mean, there has certainly been resistance, even though we didn't start any of it. It was always them attacking us. We never set out to attack anybody. They always hit first."

"Because they feared your power and hers," Basrahip said. "Because in it, they saw their coming death, and they knew that this day—*this* day—would come. The rise of the apostate of Kaltfel is the call to end the age of dragons. He leads the forces of lies, and his defeat will begin the spread of her peace over the world."

"So he isn't defeated?" Geder said. "Kaltfel's in riot, and the apostate is still alive."

"Yes," Basrahip said. "And when his power breaks, her peace will flow from Kaltfel and fill the world."

"And Cithrin and Callon Cane. The Timzinae. And the dragon. How do they fit in with this?"

"There are many servants of the lie. Cut this one down, this one who was in the grace of the goddess and fell from it, and all the rest will come unraveled. This is the battle we have prayed for. That we have worked so long to call forth. And now it is come, and the hour of your victory with it. You are about to win everything."

The hour of my victory, Geder thought, and a tightness he hadn't known he carried released in his back. He felt his shoulders rise like someone had taken a weight off of them. He hadn't realized how much the news of unrest from around the empire had been bothering him until Basrahip came to put it all in its right place. Of course there were troubles. Of course there was fighting and strife. And he had known, because Basrahip had told him, that the enemies of the goddess weren't going to give themselves up easily. It was only in looking at maps and reading the reports of battles lost or only half won that he'd lost his way. Basrahip had told him the truth. No cities with a temple to the goddess had been lost, and now none would be. He took a bite of the beef and closed his eyes, enjoying the taste of the animal's blood and imagining a map with light pouring out from Kaltfel and spreading to the corners of the page. And all of it would be done before Aster took the throne.

It wasn't that there was hope. It was better than hope. It was certainty.

He needed to tell Daskellin about it. Looking back, he could see that the baron had been growing concerned. Probably that was part of why Geder had let himself be worried too. Now that it was clear there was no cause for concern, he had a gift he could share.

"All right," Geder said. "Tell me what we need to do."

"We must destroy the apostate," Basrahip said. "The culling blades we carried made a strong start—very strong. But they carry a terrible weight, even when worn by the righteous. Many of those corrupted by the apostate fell before us, but not the man himself. Of my brothers who rode at my side, only three remain. The time for waiting has passed. We must take your swords and your bows and return to the capital of lies in force. When the corruption is purged, Kaltfel will shine like a beacon, and all who love truth will rise up as one."

"All right," Geder said, and then, "That may be tricky. We've already sent all the soldiers we could spare to Inentai or else Birancour. I could send word to Jorey and have him bring the army, but that would mean going back through the pass at Bellin or else marching through Northcoast. Thanks to Canl, things with Northcoast are fine, but I can't think King Tracian would feel comfortable about having our army march through his lands, even just as guests of the crown."

"We cannot wait," Basrahip said. "Bring what men remain. Pardon your prisoners and arm them and call them forth in her name. Abandon the plows in their fields and the sheep in their pastures. There is no work under the sky more glorious than this."

"Yes, well," Geder said. "I may need some help convincing people of that."

"I am your righteous servant, Prince Geder. As she is the righteous servant of humanity and enemy of all those who would beguile you. This was the work I was brought into the world to complete. I will not fail you now."

Aster, grinning, pounded his palms on the table. His eyes were bright, and Geder felt the joy in the boy's eyes echoed in himself. The end was coming. The last battle that would finally, finally, set the world right and make all the loss and fear and sacrifice have meaning. Then Cithrin would understand what she'd done to him.

Then she would come back.

Outside the unshuttered window, the perfect light of morning shone across the city, brightening the roofs and streets like a fire that never stopped burning. A flock of pigeons wheeled over the Division, falling as Geder watched into the wide canyon to pluck some food from the garbage dropped to its depths. Camnipol, the center of the empire, the center of Firstblood power in the world. And his now to lead and to perfect. In his imagination, Cithrin stood beside him, her sheer, pale dress pressed against her by the breeze, her pale hair and eyes glowing with the light of the flawless, lucid day. Her smile was angelic, her lips soft and wet and pale as snow. He took her hand in his.

I see now, she said.

I knew you would.

Forgive me?

"Always," Geder said.

"Always what?" Aster asked, and Geder was back at the table, a blush rising up his neck.

"Nothing," he said and took another forkful of the meat. "I was just...I got lost in my own mind for a moment. It happens all the time. Everyone does it. Do you want some more peppers?"

"I'm fine," Aster said.

"Basrahip? Peppers?"

"I have no need of them," the priest said. The bruise on his cheek was interesting, now that Geder looked at it. All through it were tiny patches of black, like spent blood.

"All right, then," Geder said. "We'll need to make a plan. I'll call Emming and Daskellin. And...let me see. Palen Esteroth is in the city. He was in the court of Asterilhold for years before the conquest. He'll be useful. I'll have him brought in to consult with on the battle plan. I wish Dawson Kalliam hadn't fallen under the Timzinae's sway. He was the one that took Kaltfel last, after all, but never mind. We'll find a way."

"We will, Prince Geder," Basrahip said though a wide and placid smile.

"And you said that some of your fellow priests, they... ah...they died?"

"Indeed. Gloriously and in her name."

"Does that mean you'll need to initiate new priests?"

"Yes, Prince Geder," Basrahip said. "We shall need more. *Many* more."

Clara

The wide, grassy plains outside Sara-su-Mar, the lush blue of its skies, and the passion of its lovers had made the backdrop of any number of small romances and ballads of youthful love. Clara had never made the journey herself, but the image of it that she held in her mind was perfect and complete. She could not say now whether her imaginings had been romantic fluff, or if violence had greyed it.

The defensive perimeter Jorey had made was clear, the army huddled behind its swords and spears as it took stock and planned. Where his patrols and scouts had gone, she did not know, nor could she ask.

Low clouds pressed down until the sky seemed no higher than the treetops, and the spitting rain soaked the road, her cloak, and the coat of her horse. It thickened the air. All along the roadside, tucked back in the cover of the trees, tents and rough cobbled-together shelters huddled. Men and women watched her pass, their faces bleak and empty. The children who sat at the roadside were too hungry to play. Their faces had taken on the grey of the land around them. They were the small people of the world. Trappers and fishers and hands on the farms so desperate that they could not postpone their business, even though there were armies on the road.

The battle that followed the ambush had lasted hours,

pressing into the countryside before Jorey called their forces to regroup. The stink of churned earth and drowned fires clung to the landscape as if it had always been there, as if the devastation of war had bled back through history and poisoned all that had come before. That was not true, of course. Weeks before, this same low road had likely been cheerful and bright as any of the old songs. That it had always been so corrupted was an illusion. But it was a persuasive one.

Clara kept her cloak tight around her and her head down. She regretted now that she'd taken so fine a horse. The nut-brown gelding stood out among the half-starved nags and exhausted plow mules that shared the road with her. The question hadn't even occurred to her. After all this time, some part of her was still the Baroness of Osterling Fells, whether she wished it or not.

A bend in the road, a grass-covered hillock to her left, and her own preoccupation hid the crossroads from her until it was too late. Five men in cloaks of undyed wool stood in the center of traffic. Their hems and boots were dark with mud, and hoods covered their heads. Their blades were in scabbards, and two held unstrung bows wrapped against the rain. One of them was speaking to a thin young man, bending toward him, interrogating. The young man's head bobbed as he spoke, desperate for approval and rich with fear. An answering fear rose in Clara's throat. The hooded man nodded, waved the young man on, then stepped in front of two girls traveling the same direction Clara was.

Soldiers, then, though in this blighted space she had no way to tell which side's men they were. If they were queens-men, what would they make of an older woman with the accents of Antea in her voice and a fresh, powerful horse beneath her? And if they were Jorey's men, how could they keep from asking what errand took her into enemy territory?

Stopping now, even hesitating, would only draw further attention to herself. She wondered, if she bolted, whether the men would be able to raise an effective alarm. They let the two girls pass, and Clara was certain one of them at least was looking at her with a vague curiosity in his eyes. *Remain calm*, she thought. *Don't give them more reason to notice you.*

She might as well have stood in the stirrups and sung for all the difference it made.

"Hold there," the man in the front said, holding up his hand to her as her horse stepped into the crossroad. "Rein in, grandmother. Rein in."

Clara raised her eyebrows as she might to an impertinent servant, but she brought her little horse to a halt. One of the other men stepped in and put his hand on the reins. He managed to seem polite doing it, which she counted in his favor.

"What's your name and your business on the road?" the lead man asked. His voice had the softer cadences of Birancour, and now that she was near him, Clara could make out the green and gold of his tunic. The wet had darkened both almost to black, but there was no doubt. A queensman.

Well, at least it isn't one of the contemptible little spider priests, she thought, and then smiled. The words might have been in her own mind, but they had been in Dawson's voice.

"Clara Osterling," she said. "I'm looking for my daughter. She was staying near here before the battle, and I haven't found her since. Her name's Elisia. She's a bit younger than you, I'd think. Brown hair? A mark on her left cheek?"

It was ridiculous. Antea was in her blood and her vowels, and there was no way of removing it from either. She could no more pass for Birancouri than she could be mistaken for a chipmunk. The man smiled.

"Can't say I have, grandmother," the queensman said.

"Then you'll excuse me. I have to keep looking."

"Not sure of that. I'm going to have to ask that you come over here with us."

"What for?" Clara asked, feigning confusion.

"Agents of the enemy all around, ma'am. Just have to be sure you're what you say."

Clara made a soft, amused sound in the back of her throat. "Ah," she said. "It's my accent, isn't it? I quite understand."

"Then if you'd just—"

She drew her knife and slashed at the man holding her reins in a single motion. Thankfully, the blade didn't connect, but the boy started back and his grip went loose. She kicked her poor horse's flanks like he'd done something wrong, and together they leapt forward, scattering the queensmen like pins on a bowling green. She kicked again and the poor animal surged forward. Shouts rose behind her, and a woman's startled shriek. Her speed drove raindrops into her bared teeth, into her eyes. Clara bent low over the surging back and held as tightly as she could, waiting for an arrow to pierce her back or a stone to stun her.

For God's sake, she thought, *don't kill me. I'm trying to help you.*

Leaving Vincen behind had been among the most difficult things she had ever done. Even after the wound had been cleaned and the bleeding slowed to a sickening crimson seep, the worst had not come. The cunning men moved on, tending to those among the army's wounded whom their skills could aid to health or else with their passage into darkness, leaving Clara to sit at his cot. His skin had taken on a waxen look that made her think of meat at a butcher's shop. In his fever, he kicked away the thin blankets and then, minutes later, gathered them back to himself.

She sat with him because she could think of nothing else to do. Somewhere in the camp, Jorey and his knights were measuring the cost of the ambush and its effect on their plans. She should have been there, gleaning what she could if not farther afield, acting on what she already knew, and yet it all seemed impossible. Vincen slept in a fever and woke in it, and the two states seemed nearly the same. Near sundown, he raved for the better part of an hour about the need to find a lost dog before the hunt began, and then fell into a sleep so profound that Clara had to watch the rise and fall of his chest to assure herself that it was only sleep.

What would the men think of her attentions to a man who was, after all, merely a servant in her house? What would her boys make of it? She didn't care. She only dampened the cloth again, soothed Vincen's wounded body as best she could, and waited.

Near dawn, the fever seemed to lose its grip. The blankness left his eyes and reason returned. The terrible pressure in Clara's breast and throat eased and she felt the black exhaustion she'd spent the night ignoring.

"My lady," Vincen said, with a weary smile. "I'm afraid I may not manage that errand for you after all."

"I think you may be forgiven this time," Clara said. "You have an excellent excuse."

"Thank you for your indulgence," he said, then sighed and made as if to rise. Clara put a restraining hand on his shoulder, and the weight of it alone pressed him back to the creaking canvas.

"You're not to move," she said. "Not until the fever passes."

"The warning—"

"The warning be damned," Clara said gently. "Callon Cane and his agents have to know they're in danger. There's an army outside their city. It isn't as though we were being subtle."

Vincen Coe frowned. "He doesn't know we have a way in. They'll kill him," he said.

"People die. I can't save all of them," she said, and tears welled in her eyes. She felt no sorrow to match them, they simply came and she suffered their presence as if they were unexpected and unwelcome guests. "This one time, I think we can leave the enemy to their own devices."

Vincen's expression clouded, pale lips pressing together. She felt his disapproval, and her answer was rage.

"No," she said before he could speak. "No, I won't have it. We aren't responsible for the world and everything in it. Not every tragedy is our fault. Not every loss."

"We've come this far so that we—"

"Could do what we can," Clara snapped. "We came so that we could try, but there are constraints. There are limits."

"And have we reached them?" Vincen asked.

If she hadn't been so terribly tired, she would not have sobbed. Truly, staying up all night waiting for a young lover to die before one's eyes was better done at twenty. It took too much energy.

"You cannot go," she said. "And there is no one else that I trust."

"And if they kill him because we didn't warn him?" Vincen said. "If the word spreads that Palliako slaughtered him after all, can you live knowing that there was something else you could have done and didn't? Can your son bear it? Because say you both can, and I'll go back to sleep."

Outside the little tent, a horse snorted. The cool morning breeze stirred the wet oilskin walls, shifting the shadows on Vincen's face as if he were an image on a banner. Could she live knowing there was something she could have done, and that she hadn't?

"What do you want from me?" she asked.

"Take the warning," Vincen said.

"*Me?*" Clara said, and laughed.

"Who else?" Vincen asked.

"What makes you think I could manage that?"

"You're a predator, my lady," Vincen said, and closed his eyes with a sigh. "You can manage anything."

"You're young and romantic," she said, making the words harsh and their harshness an endearment. Vincen smiled.

She could take any horse in the camp. The army wouldn't be moving before tomorrow, she was certain of that, and the city wasn't that far away. Getting access to Jorey's tent would be simple enough, she was his mother, and the tale of gutting the Birancouri soldier had made her more of the army's pet. It could be done. She *could* do it. And so, of course, she had to.

She said something soft and obscene. Vincen smiled.

"Sometimes doing the least necessary is still a heroic work," he said.

"When I said I didn't want to outlive another lover, this isn't what I meant."

"You won't die," he said, the words growing slushy with sleep. "You'll never die."

Everyone dies, she thought. *All of us. And usually, damn you, for things less important than this.*

For a long, anxious hour, Clara combed the stretch of wood, sometimes certain that she'd come to the wrong place, sometimes that the story had been a fabrication from the start, and always consumed by the fear that she would overlook the secret way. That Geder would overcome another of his enemies because she had not prevented it.

When at last she found the entrance, it was with a sense of profound relief. There, in the depths of a grey-green bush, a slightly deeper darkness. Now that she saw to look for it, a uniformity of the forest litter that spoke of being swept to look as if it were undisturbed. The thin rain tapped against the leaves and trickled down the back of her neck as she looked for a place to tie her mount. It seemed cruel to leave the poor animal out in the cold, but it wasn't as if they'd put a stable next to a smuggler's cave. She made do with a dark hollow where the canopy of trees almost stopped the wetness, and looped the reins in a branch.

"I'm sorry," she said, petting the gelding's gentle face. "I'll come back as soon as I can."

She pushed through the brush, twigs cracking against her. The darkness resolved into a sloping passage so narrow that her shoulders brushed both sides. Worn stone steps led down into the earth, and she followed them, her boots slipping a little against the dampness and grime. When the last of the raindrops had stopped, she paused to light a stub of candle. The smuggler's passage made tombs look welcoming. Streaks of slime clung to the stonework, and the walls tilted in against each other, as if on the verge of collapse. Her passage through it seemed to take hours. There was no marker to show when she passed beneath the walls of Sarasur-Mar, when she moved from the wilderness into the city. Her little underworld was circumscribed by a single candle's light, and there might as well have been nothing outside it.

The smell of sewage was the first sure sign that she'd reached the habitation of humans. The stink of it was profound and powerful, and it grew with every passing yard she walked. The passage widened, and the stones became brick—old and weathered and alive with cockroaches. The secret passage opened into the vaulted arch of a great sewer. The rank water shone black in the candlelight, and dead things floated in it.

She followed a stone quay along the side of the wall until it turned away, up toward the light and the streets of the besieged city. She lit her pipe from the last of the candle's wick and threw the last thumb's width of wax to the gutter. If wouldn't have been enough to get her back anyway. She'd need to find a lantern. Assuming the man she was seeking out didn't kill her for her troubles.

She turned the bowl of her pipe down to keep the water from putting out the tobacco and stepped into the street. The house was a thousand times easier to find than the passage had been. The green-painted walls and yellow eaves reminded her of toys that a child might play with. She stood outside for a long moment, then sighed, marched to the bound-oak door, and rapped the iron knocker against its strike plate.

It was almost a full minute before the little viewing window squeaked open and a Timzinae woman's dark eyes appeared.

"Who the fuck are you?" the woman demanded.

"I'm here to see Callon Cane," Clara said.

"You're off your head, then," the woman said. But she didn't laugh. There was no hesitation in her voice. Nor surprise. Any uncertainty that remained in Clara's mind evaporated in that moment and she smiled.

"I've come through danger to see him," she said. "And if you don't let me through, I can swear he'll be dead or taken before the week's out. And likely you will too. Now open the door."

The woman blinked and slammed the window shut. Voices came from the other side. The Timzinae woman's. A man's voice, so deep he was likely one of the eastern races. Clara wished she could hear well enough to make out the words. A cart rattled by behind her, iron wheels against cobblestones. The sound almost covered the scrape of a bar being lifted.

The door opened. The rooms within were gloomy and dim. A huge Tralgu with a bare blade in his hand and half his ear missing stood aside and motioned her in. Clara had the sudden visceral memory of the Tralgu who'd been her own door servant, back in some other lifetime.

"I've come to see Callon Cane," she said again.

"Your thumb."

"They don't take women."

"All the same. Your thumb."

Clara held out her hand, suffered the prick of the blade against it. The Tralgu leaned close to examine her blood, then made a satisfied grunt.

"You'll have to leave the blades," the Tralgu said. "Both of them."

Clara didn't ask how he'd known she wore two, only drew them from their sheaths and handed them over, hilt first. The Tralgu seemed satisfied with that. The woman was gone, and Clara felt sure that she was being watched from places she didn't know.

The bare drawing room looked out over a narrow court-yard, rain running down the window glass like the world weeping. The makings of a fire were laid out in the grate, unlit. The man standing at the window was little more than a silhouette. His greatcoat might have been black or brown. His battered hat sported a wide brim. He was perhaps six inches taller than Clara, perhaps six shorter than the Tralgu guard, who took his place silently behind her. He could have been anyone.

Likely that was the point.

"You don't know me," Clara said. "And for reasons of my own, I won't tell you who I am. I have come to warn you. The forces of Antea know you are here, and they have a way to move soldiers into the city. You must leave at once or else..."

The man turned. His face was bloodless, pale, and aghast. Clara felt the world shift beneath her.

"Mother?" Barriath said, sweeping the wide hat from his head. "What are you *doing* here?"

She stood stunned for a long moment. When the laughter came, it was like a fountain and it would not stop.

Cithrin

Komme Medean sat still, his calm radiating a rage so profound it made the stone of the walls, the wood of his desk, even the air itself seem fragile. His son, Lauro, stood behind him looking distressed and confused but uncertain what he should say, and his daughter, Chana, sat at a side table, her face carefully empty. Cithrin sat across from the soul and name of the holding company in the seat usually afforded to guests. Even Chana's husband, Paerin Clark, was not welcome for this meeting. The blackwood door to the office was barred from the inside, and all the servants had been sent away. If Cithrin started screaming, no one would hear her.

Cithrin felt a pang of anxiety in her belly, but she could bear it. When she smiled to herself, it felt almost like excitement.

When Komme spoke, he shaped each word on its own, giving the syllables a careful and equal weight.

"This is the greatest fraud in history."

"This is a goldmine that will never run dry so long as there is ink," Cithrin said.

Lauro's voice was thin and angry. He was older than Cithrin, and she could see that he knew he was supposed to be outraged without being entirely certain why. "You gave away our money."

"I did not," Cithrin said. "I changed the form of it. From coins and bars to letters that represent them and a royal proclamation that will give those letters the force of law. And exclusive rights to issue those letters in the name of the bank."

"You gave our gold to the king," Lauro said. "We'll never get the gold back."

"Exactly," Cithrin said. "Neither will anyone else."

"But—"

"Lauro," Komme said. "Be quiet. You're out of your depth."

"You gained us nothing," Lauro went on, talking over his father. "So you can write letters against the debt. So what? How does that gain us anything?"

Cithrin smiled. "We can write letters of transfer totaling more than the debt we're owed."

Lauro opened his mouth, then closed it. "No we can't," he said. "The debt's only a certain size. If you write letters for more than that—"

"A debt that will never be repaid can be whatever size we say it is," Cithrin said. "If we choose to put out letters for twice that sum, what difference will it make to the crown? Tracian was never giving up the coin anyway. We all know that. The merchants we're working with probably know that, but there's a royal order to pretend otherwise. If we need to pay someone from outside the kingdom, we can buy more gold at discount. Give the seller letters of transfer worth five tenthweights for every four tenthweights they provide. Who wouldn't take that exchange?"

"And that makes it fraud," Komme said. "Without gold—"

"*Gold*," Cithrin said, waving her hand. "What's gold? A metal too soft to take an edge. There's no power there.

What makes gold important is the story we tell about it. All of humanity has agreed that this particular object has value, and then because we all said so, it does. The metal hasn't changed. It doesn't breathe, it doesn't bleed. It is what it was before. All we're doing is telling that same story about some letters we've written."

"You are advocating that we tell people these letters can be exchanged for actual gold," Komme said. "You are obligating the crown to a greater debt than what we are owed—"

"And it doesn't matter, because that debt will never be called," Cithrin said. "An obligation isn't an obligation if no one truly expects it to be met. And in the meantime, we can create markets that run on letters and do all the same things as markets that run on coin. Only now, instead of minting new currency by toiling in a mine and running ore through a smelter, we write it. If we need more money, we make it."

"But we can only write letters for the amount we are owed," Lauro said, almost plaintively.

"Lauro!" Komme snapped. "Be quiet!"

"Antea can be beaten," Cithrin said. "The war can be brought to a halt. But it requires a great deal of money. More money than we had. Now we can decide now how much money we have. How much money there is to *be* had. We can hire mercenaries of our own. Pay the ones working for Geder to break their contracts. We can offer the farmers in Birancour and the southern reaches of Northcoast better prices for crops like cotton and tobacco, and when Geder's armies come, they'll starve. We can pay bounties. We can hire ships to carry weapons to Borja and the Keshet and arm Antea's enemies there. All it takes is money."

"All it takes is *gold*," Komme said, but there was a tremor in his voice when he said it. Cithrin sat back in her chair.

She'd made her arguments. Going over them again would gain her nothing. Komme Medean was a smart man, and one who understood contracts, wealth, value, and power. Given time, he would see the world through her eyes. Chana pressed a knuckle against her lips, staring at Cithrin as if she were a puzzle the woman could solve by an act of will.

"If this fails," Chana said, and then left the sentence unfinished.

Cithrin nodded. "If this fails, we will fall beneath the blades of Antea or be taken back to Camnipol and slaughtered by Geder's own hand. That hasn't changed. It isn't as though we're at greater risk than we were before."

"And if we defeat Palliako and destroy Northcoast doing it?" Chana asked.

Cithrin shrugged. "The world is burning. Anything that doesn't end in ashes is worth doing. And there's also the possibility that it doesn't fail. Perhaps instead, we shift what people think of when they think of money. Buying and selling with letters of transfer seems new and frightening to them now, but in three, four, five years, it will be commonplace. All of our partners and debtors will have been using them. The throne will have backed them for years. And when that happens, if that happens, we've become the keepers of the king's debt."

"If we're the king's debt," Komme said, "then we're the king."

Cithrin smiled.

"Then we're the king."

They gave Cithrin liberty of the holding company's compound but not of the city. She had expected less. If Komme had had the guards keep her to a room, she would have understood his position. Her record for following the edicts of the holding company could not have been worse. That he gave her leave to sit in the courtyard in the compound's center and drink cool wine in the shade of the trees was a signal of sorts. She was not free to leave, and neither was she precisely a prisoner. She thought of it as being in a sort of personal escrow, kept in place for when she was wanted and until it was clear what she was wanted for.

As such, all she saw of Carse now was glimpsed through the narrow windows along the upper halls. Wide, grey streets and square buildings. High clouds puffed like cotton fresh from the boll. The air of Northcoast was warm enough, but with an undertone that made her think of the first warm days of autumn more than the last cool days of summer. In the courtyard, the vines and ivies rustled in breezes almost too gentle to feel and the fountain muttered and burbled to itself. At night, she didn't sleep, nor did she expect to. At meals, she managed to swallow enough to keep her mind awake and alive, but little more than that. She knew to expect the anxiety, and so it was only an indisposition. The knot in her belly, the shapeless fear and dread, the craving for wine or beer or something stronger. She watched all of it happening to her, almost able to predict when the next wave would wash over her and when it would recede. In the meantime, grapes and cheese, water and wine. Not enough wine to untie her knots, though. She needed her wits more than the peace, and somewhere in her travels she'd learned how to suffer rather than indulge her need for strong drink.

There were a thousand things that might still go wrong. Even if Komme Medean convinced himself to follow her scheme, the ships might be captured or sunk. King Tracian might have a change of heart. Geder's armies might come too quickly, overrunning Carse and Northcoast before her plans had time to take root.

She had loosed her arrow, and she could no more call it back now than pluck the moon from the sky.

The servants and members of the holding company treated her with respect and caution, as if speaking to her were itself a reckless act. She accepted their politeness and reserve as part of the price she was paying for her actions, but they chafed. She could not calm herself with alcohol or with the business of her bank. The only thing left was the thin comfort of news. What little she had of that came through Yardem and Kit and Marcus Wester, and it was not what she had expected.

Yardem's and Marcus's friends among the mercenaries of the north reported that Antea had been taking contracts with whatever companies Geder could find. All through the season, as the main body of the army had chased her in the southern coast of Birancour, the garrisons and keeps along Antea's bloated borders had filled with hired swords, the Antean troops sent elsewhere. Where precisely was less clear. There were stories of fighting in Sarakal against the allies and remnants of the traditional families there, and also of the ongoing siege at Kiaria. There had been a rash of assassinations in Kaltfel as well, which commanded the attention of Northcoast more for its proximity than the scale of the violence. Thus far, at least. In the agonizing, slow hours between midday and twilight, she began sketching out a scheme for outbidding Antea's contracts. So long as they were paying coin for services she could buy with paper, even a loss on her part was a victory of sorts. If she could frighten the Severed Throne into emptying its coffers, the war effort might stumble.

Of the army chasing her, information was considerably more complete, thanks to the reports of Paerin Clark's anonymous ally. Who had been sending the letters remained unclear, but he had managed to make a place for himself first following the army and then, after Porte Oliva, sitting in council with its commanders. The false scent of Callon Cane in Sara-sur-Mar seemed to have distracted the Lord Marshal for the time being, and the season was coming to its close. Jorey Kalliam was as aware as she that winter favored the defenders, and that the men marching in his columns could be made loyal by the priests, but no story of a hidden goddess could feed them. Even a man persuaded that the great powers of the heavens loved him above all else could starve. However powerful a story might be, it had its limits, and the brute material world didn't listen or care what priests and bankers told it.

She was not playing her games against the world, but the priests. The mundane stories of trade against the grandiose epics of slaughter and war. It struck her how deeply deceitful both narratives were. The banks pretended that business was stable, reliable, and a bit dull. The priests pretended that war was glorious. And the kings and regents pretended they were in control of it all.

Looking at it as dispassionately as she could, she gave herself about even odds of evading Geder's reach. Unless some new information came to light, which to judge from history, it would.

For now, all she could do was wait for the ships to arrive. The gold, the pirates, Isadau, and the dragon.

Marcus found her one evening on the northwest corner of the compound's high walls. The nature of the building as a keep within the city was clearer here than anywhere. The setting sun shone through the brick merlons, setting the high walk in stripes of fire and shadow. He wore old leathers, and for once didn't carry the green sword on his back. The years had not been kind to him. She couldn't recall now whether there had been grey in his hair during that last, strange caravan out of Vanai. There was now. It spread from his temples out like frost on a window. Long travel and the poisoned sword had made his face thinner, the lines around his mouth and at the corners of his eyes stark and deep. She remembered his shoulders being broader than they were now and his expression less tired.

She remembered when he'd been her protector. It seemed like a thing from a very long time ago. There was an impulse she couldn't quite fathom to pretend to be helpless around him. To give him that place in her life again, even though she was quite aware it wouldn't fit.

"Captain," she said as he leaned forward, looking down at the street four stories below them. She made her voice sound light, the formal title made an intimacy by also being a joke.

"Magistra," he said, matching his tone to hers. "It's a good building. I was never inside it before this. Didn't really think they'd built it quite so much to withstand a siege. A couple dozen men, and you could hold this place for quite a while."

"The holding company has always been aware that people might grow to dislike it."

"Can't imagine why," Marcus said dryly. "Anyway, I was down at the docks, and the harbormaster's thinking the ships may come tomorrow. Depending on how much our great scaly friend is slowing things down, of course."

"Did he say what the chances were that the pirates have killed everyone and vanished to Lyoneia with the gold?"

"Wasn't something he ventured a guess on," Marcus said. "If they did, though, it's because Inys let them. I don't doubt he'd have been comfortable burning all the ships to the waterline and having the Drowned carry the gold across the ocean floor in carts."

"Might take longer to get here that way," she said.

"Might. Saw your Master Komme coming up here. He still looks like he's swallowed a squirrel."

"He would."

"Really? I thought you and he spoke the same language. Understood each other."

"We do," she said, and nodded at the edge of the wall and the long drop beyond it. "You know how it feels looking down from too great a height? Like the precipice is calling for you? He feels that way all the time right now."

"Does he, now?"

"I assume so. God knows I do."

Marcus leaned his shoulders against the bricks, turning his back to the sun. Cithrin stared out past him to where the great red disk was sinking lower behind the buildings of Carse.

"Kit keeps trying to explain the trick to me," Marcus said. "Part of it, I follow. The other part of it just seems... well, I get lost. I see where getting people to take these bits of scribble instead of actual money lets you afford things you couldn't otherwise. I'm not clear on how that makes the world a place full of justice and equality and all."

Cithrin looked at him. The light of the setting sun had burned into her eyes, and its afterimage obscured him. "Justice and equality?"

"Stopping war's the point, isn't it? Not just this one, but all of them?"

"I don't know about all of them, but this one. And making fewer others. But you've worked for me. Did you think we were making Porte Oliva just and equal?"

"No offense, but that really wasn't the impression I took, no," Marcus said. "That's where the confusion comes in."

"Do you recall Annis Louten?"

Marcus scratched his chin, the stubble making a sandpaper noise against his nails. "He was the spice man, wasn't he? Came to you for a loan."

"He was. And he repaid late, with penalties. The ship he invested in didn't come through, and he hadn't put insurance against it. He had to scrape and save and go without in order to keep us from taking his rooms and his stock. That's trade. Going to his rooms with the full guard and taking the same money from him at knifepoint? That's war. Both leave him just as low, just as poor. He did little to deserve either besides be unlucky. But in one, we take what we want under threat of death. In the other, he gives it because he agreed to.

"If I manage what I hope, people will still starve. Families will still be broken. People who have done nothing wrong will still lose their livelihoods, their health, their homes. You've seen my trade. You don't have any illusions about what I do when a contract is broken."

"Yes, but if someone's given their word, that justifies what comes after."

"How?"

"Justice," Marcus said.

"There are as many definitions of justice as there are people making them. Justice is doing what you said you would do, or being forced to. Or justice is getting back what was taken from your family. Or justice is hurting the man who hurt you. Anyone who wants to make the world just has only to say what justice is first, and then impose it on everyone with a different thought. I don't care about that. I just want to keep people from burning each other's cities quite so often."

From the street, far below them, a man cried out, and a woman shrieked. Cithrin and Marcus looked over the edge together to see the two tiny figures in each other's arms smiling and greeting each other like old friends. The sun slipped behind the buildings and turned the world to rose and grey.

Marcus let a long breath out from between his teeth.

"The way you say it, money does the same thing a blade would," he said.

"It's a tool, the way a blade is," Cithrin said. "But blades aren't my tools, and this is. The violence we do with a contract is the sort I understand."

Marcus

For years, Northcoast had been in the back of Marcus's mind. It had taken on a depth and significance that had nothing to do with the actual stones and skies. Northcoast was the place where the past had happened. Where he had been loved and powerful and betrayed. When he'd left Carse the last time, it had been in a fast boat going south with a king dead behind him and an old enemy on the throne by his hand. It was the kind of romantic gesture young men made because they didn't have any better way to purge their grief. And now he was back, and walking through the city was like the blankness in the eyes of an old lover who didn't recognize him. The taproom across from the great launderer's yard where he and Alys had eaten their meals was still there, but the old man who'd served them sausages and apples and beer wasn't. The empty house where he'd met with his men that last, fatal night before King Springmere earned his place in history as the Mayfly King had been taken over and cleaned. Half a dozen children were playing pebble-tossing games on the same stones where he'd cut Butun Skinkiller's throat. There was a memory. He hadn't thought of old Skinkiller in years.

After Springmere's death, Marcus had run from this city and from everything he'd been when he was here. He'd been a legend. The great general who'd pulled victory from a lost war and then cast it all away in the name of vengeance. Or justice. Or whatever name people wanted to put to it. He'd become a minor mercenary captain and head of a merchant bank's guard. Northcoast hadn't forgotten him, but the Marcus Wester it remembered had been younger, more certain of himself, and hadn't had the rash across his back where the damned sword made his skin itch and peel.

He passed through the city like a ghost. The holding company made room for him and Yardem and Kit, putting them all in a brick-walled storeroom that smelled of wheat flour and old oil. The three men spent their days in the taprooms and at the docks, finding what word they could. They spent their nights at the holding company, sharing information and telling tales and jokes. Cithrin's great scheme still seemed like something a street-corner swindler would do to rook the unwary out of a few bits of silver, but for the moment she was safe from Palliako and his armies. Yardem and Kit made good company when they didn't wander off on religious debates about the nature of truth and doubt and the spiritual roots of wealth. And even when they were talking hairwash like that, having familiar voices while he sharpened his knife or ate rice and meat from the holding company's kitchen or started building plans for what to do when Carse fell under Antea's hammer made the evening pass faster. In the nights, he would lie on his cot, looking out the narrow window at the stars, and try to put off sleep for a few minutes more.

Because the nightmares, of course, were back, fresh and raw and more terrible than they had ever been before.

Kit snored, but not enough to make an annoyance of himself. His blanket was a series of dark brown lumps where he tangled himself. The top of his head poked out at one end, and a single bare foot at the other. Yardem, by contrast, slept on top of his blanket, his eyes slitted but not quite closed, and his sword on the stones beneath him where his hand could find the hilt without requiring him to stand or even roll to reach it. Only his ears drooping to the sides showed the Tralgu was actually asleep.

Marcus scratched his chest. His arms and legs felt like they were sinking down into the earth, limp as overcooked chicken. In his memory, Cithrin looked out over the city and said, *The violence we do with a contract is the sort I understand.* The thought left him caught between pride and melancholy. She spent so much time and effort seeming older, it was easy to forget that she was only just past her girlhood.

She'll be fine, Alys said, walking through the thin spread of trees outside their little house. He couldn't see the details of her face, but he knew it was her with the false certainty that came in dreams. Some part of him was already screaming in anticipation of what was coming. The violence, the smell of burning skin, the feeling of his daughter in his arms, her blackened skin against his own. *She'll be fine.*

He tried to speak, to warn Alys that it wasn't true. Merian was in danger. They were both in danger. All of them. All he could manage was a whisper, and she couldn't hear him. Couldn't tell that he was trying to scream. Behind him, Merian laughed. He tried to turn around, but his body wouldn't move. Something was wrong with him. He felt like he was stuck in thick, invisible mud. Merian's laughter turned to a scream and he tried to run. It wasn't too late. If he could only get there in time. Her scream was constant now, like a storm wind that didn't have to pause for breath. The air stank of smoke and his skin was beginning to peel back from his hands, exposing the meat of his fingers. The bone. The thickened air was ripping him apart rather than letting him through. He gritted his teeth and tried to scream his daughter's name, his heart thudding against his ribs even as the wise, watching part of him turned away, knowing what would come next.

"Sir?" Yardem said.

Alys and Merian were in flames, the child curled in her mother's lap. Their screams reached over the crackle of the flames.

"You should wake up now, sir," Yardem said. "Something's happening."

Marcus opened his eyes and took a deep, gasping breath. The little room was thick with buttery yellow light. Kit knelt on his cot and peeked out the window into the black night. Dream and reality mixed, the screaming and the smell of fire still in his ears and nose as Marcus swung his feet to the floor. He tried to say *What is it?* and managed some part of the syllables.

"Not sure yet," Yardem said. His sword was in his hand.

The death screams of his family moved out from their intimate place in Marcus's ear, out to the window and the dark streets beyond. That wasn't his nightmare, then. People were screaming. He yawned, the force of it cracking his jaw, as he rose.

"Palliako's army?" he asked.

"Could be," Yardem said.

"I can't believe that they could travel so far or so quickly," Kit said. "Do you think it's possible?"

Marcus reached under his own cot, hauling out the vile green sword and scabbard. He slung it across his back. "I know a way to find out. You stay here."

In the night-black city, lanterns flared and people filled the squares. Marcus moved among them, his senses stretched for the peculiar signs of violence. Yardem, at his side, shifted his ears one direction and then the next. The city guard

stood at the corners and choke points where the rush of a
mob could be controlled, but so far as Marcus could make
out, there was no riot, no invasion, no burning buildings or
boiling pitch or flights of killing arrows.

He was in the middle of a wide square, perhaps three hundred men and women in it looking around in confusion that
echoed his own, when the screaming came again, and from
all around him. Yardem tapped his shoulder and pointed up
toward the distant stars.

A deeper darkness moved against the sky, blotting out
stars. The movement gave it shape—wide, tattered wings,
a great tail and serpentine neck. The dragon glided silently
against the night, swooping over the city like a hawk looking for a rabbit. A gout of flame poured forth from the
mouth in a great gold-and-smoke cloud brighter than the
moon. Women shouted, pointed. Men screamed and tried
to push themselves back into the buildings against the flow
of other people coming out. Others stood in openmouthed
wonder. All round the city, lanterns and torches flickered to
life, the citizens of Northcoast flooding the streets or fleeing
them in terror and elation.

Kit was pacing when they came back in, his expression a
mask of distress. He stopped, his gaze shifting from one to
the other in anticipation of the worst.

"Ships are here," Marcus said.

The late morning found the square outside the Grave of
Dragons packed almost too tightly to walk through. Marcus and Yardem had to lead with their shoulders and push
to make any progress at all. For the most part, they got no
worse back than angry looks and some mild profanity. One
man so thick across the shoulders he could have passed for
Yemmu from behind pushed back and lifted his chin, but

Yardem met his gaze and shook his head. The man backed down.

King Tracian's private guard held the entrance, blades drawn. Even they kept looking back over their shoulders to catch a glimpse of Inys as he moved along the long, pale rows. When he reached the soldiers, Marcus looked for the one in charge. A Kurtadam woman in plate armor so bright and gilded, he was fairly sure he could have poked through it with a dinner fork. Not all armor was for fighting, though, and hers did the work of showing who mattered. Yardem at his back, Marcus pushed through to her.

"I'm here to see the dragon," he said.

"You and everyone else," she said, looking past him into the crowd.

"I know him. We travel together," Marcus said. The guard captain ignored him. Yardem flicked an ear. His empty expression wouldn't have read as amusement to anyone else. "I'm Marcus Wester."

"Fuck off," she said.

"No offense, ma'am," Yardem said, his voice deep as thunder. "He is."

For the first time, the Kurtadam woman really looked at Marcus, and her eyes went wide. "Oh shit."

"It's all right," Marcus said. "No one ever believes me right off. But I have come to see the dragon."

"Sorry, I can't do that," the woman said. "King gave orders. No one's to bother the . . . God. The dragon. Marcus Wester and a dragon. What next? Orcus the Demon King?"

"He's back at the compound," Marcus said. "Tracian didn't mean me. You should let me through."

"Not an option. I'm really very sorry."

Marcus shrugged and cupped his hands around his mouth like a speaker's horn. "Inys!"

The dragon's head shifted toward the crowd. The vast, warm eyes found him at once. "Marcus Stormcrow. You have come."

Marcus looked a question at the guard captain. She stood aside. The path down to the graveyard proper was pale and empty. Marcus and Yardem stepped down toward the huge beast. The scars of the battle in Porte Oliva were healed, for the most part. Wide scars striped Inys's flank, roughening the scales and making a range of small shadows when the sun came at a sharp enough angle. The dragon's wings were ripped where the huge Antean spears had pierced the webbing. Inys was still magnificent; there was no question about that. But also ragged and tired. Marcus wondered whether the injuries it had suffered would heal further than they already had, or if this was as whole as the dragon would ever be again.

Inys shifted forward and put a taloned paw into the imprint of some long dead dragon. The expression of grief on the dragon's face was unmistakable. "Arach. This was Arach. She used to sing the most beautiful pieces. I can hear them in my mind if I try to. Her voice was so pure."

"You recognize them from their...paw prints? Or handprints. I don't know what the respectful term is," Marcus said, but Inys took no notice of him.

"She said that all her compositions were inspired by the colors of the stars." Inys shifted, caressing another imprint. Black talons dug into the stone. "Kairade. He was my brother's friend. He knew things had gone too far, but he was loyal. I asked him once to help me stop the war before it went beyond the point that we could mend the damage. His laughter had tears in it. I remember that. No one else remembers it, but I do. I am the only one who knows. And if I'm wrong, if I misremember a name or detail, it becomes true now. I can make the past simply by saying what is so and what is not. Any past that reaches this point, this place, is as good as another."

Marcus looked at Yardem. The Tralgu scratched his arm.

"So," Marcus said. "You're looking better."

Inys shifted his great head, the vast eye focusing on Marcus.

"Well," Marcus said. "Improved, anyway."

"These dead around us," Inys said, sweeping his wings in a gesture that took in everything in the long arcades. "How did they pass? Was it in the war? Was it after? Did Morade turn on his own in the end?"

"Don't know," Marcus said. "I wasn't there, and the records that far back . . . well, could say they're spotty."

"The weapons they brought against me," Inys said. "I have never seen their like before. They were designed to let slaves like you bring down dragons."

"That's what it looked like," Marcus agreed.

"Who made these designs? And why?"

"Again, I can't really say."

Inys settled onto the ground, tucking his huge legs under him like a cat preparing for a nap. His ragged wings folded against his sides. Marcus had the sudden image of a man sitting alone in a room filled with ancient bones. He felt a pang of discomfort, as if he might be intruding on something sacred. He scowled at the feeling and the deference to the dragon that it carried along.

"Magistra Isadau's back at the compound with Cithrin and the others," he said. "Cithrin's plan to end the war seems to have done something, so that's good. I suppose. Unless it just means the Antean army that kicked our asses in Birancour are coming to kick our asses in Northcoast, in which case, that'll be a pity."

"The truth is lost," Inys said. "All truth is lost in the blackness of my sleep and the emptiness of your history. There was a crime. A treason worse than mine. Worse than my brother's. Slaves armed against us. How desperate must we have been to allow it. How terrible that rage."

"We're thinking it might be good to have someone go take a quick look south of the city here. Just in case there's an army on the road. We haven't heard word of Antea crossing into Northcoast, but since there's someone here that can go aloft and check. To see if we're about to be attacked. Which could be important."

"Or perhaps we did not permit it," the dragon said. "Perhaps the slaves rose up themselves. Perhaps these evil designs were born in a slave child's mind, forged in a slave's fire. Perhaps we weakened ourselves with war, and the animals rose up against us, smelling our blood and fear."

"All respect, sir," Yardem said. "There's not a way we can know that. And it doesn't change much if it's truth."

Inys blinked, as if surprised to find them there. Marcus wondered what exactly the plan would be if, between grief and injury, the dragon lost its mind. That seemed a distraction that wouldn't help anyone.

"Would you, Marcus Stormcrow? Would you turn against me?" Inys asked.

No, he thought. *For God's sake, tell the lizard you'll lick his ass if that's what he wants to hear. We don't have time for this.*

"I don't know. Maybe? Depending on what you were doing."

The scales along the dragon's side rippled like grass in a high wind. Acrid smoke leaked out from between Inys's dagger-sharp teeth. "Treason. You would turn your hand to treason!"

"If you don't want the answer, don't ask," Marcus said. "Would I ever say you'd gone too damned far, and no farther? Yes, if you earned it. Would you rather I tell you that I'd follow you to the death of the world and the sky just because you're such a great and powerful you? Because I'm fairly certain I can find you a dozen or so of that sort just by walking back up the path there if you want them."

Inys was silent for a long moment. Long enough that Marcus began to feel little flutters of unease in his belly. Then the dragon chuckled. "You are more like her than you know, Marcus Stormcrow. Not so educated, not so graceful, but carved from the same stone all the same. Drakkis would have laughed with your jokes."

"Honored," Marcus said. "But here's the thing. This war we're fighting is a long way from done, and it's getting more complicated by the day. Back down south, we all thought you were the big damned secret that'd turn things our way. You thought it too. We called it wrong, and so we've pulled back. It's left us weaker and in a less defensible position. If Antea comes here before Cithrin can do whatever it is she's doing, we'll have to pull back again, and we're getting damned thin on places to pull back to. So while I'm sorry your dead friends are dead, I need you to focus on the next few days and weeks. If you're strong enough to help us in the war, that's a great good thing. If having your ass handed to you on a Birancouri platter's put you off your game, that's less good, but I'll manage. What I can't have is everyone making the plan to move forward counting on you if you're too weak. So, all respect, are you going to sit here feeling sad for yourself, or are you going to stand up and do the job?"

"No one speaks to a dragon so," Inys said, his voice deep and resonant as a gong.

"Almost no one. What's it going to be? Do what needs doing? Or mope like a child who didn't get the candy he wanted?"

Yardem flicked his ear, the rings jingling against each other. The Tralgu's expression was pained. *Fair point*, Marcus thought. *May have gone a bit far there.*

The dragon closed his eyes, breathed in deeply, the house-wide ribs expanding, pausing, and falling again. The air filled with a smell like brimstone and hot iron.

"You shame me. Tell me what it is you need, Stormcrow," Inys said. "I am in despair, but not yet in defeat."

"Yes, well. You and me both," Marcus said.

Clara

Of all the things that could have been occupying her mind as she rode back across the dark landscape of Birancour, the one that Clara could not dislodge was the letter she had promised to carry back to Camnipol. She had meant to, of course. She had resigned herself to going back to court, and the one bright moment of it was the thought of carrying Jorey's words back to Sabiha. And Annalise. Little Annalise.

She had letters like it herself, or once had. When Dawson had been away in the field as a young man riding at the order of his dear friend King Simeon, he had been consistent with his love letters home. She must have had fifty of them. More, perhaps. Dawson had had a traditionalist's view of poetry, so each letter included some bit of verse he'd composed for her along with his professings of love and descriptions of desire. She rode now in the darkness, the little horse tramping south through the cool air that spoke of autumn. The soldiers of Birancour were surely patrolling the countryside, as were Jorey's men. The gloom of night gave her only so much cover, and the risk of being caught by either side was great. Barriath rode behind her on a thin mule. He was wrapped in a hooded cloak, and stayed behind her, the way a servant should. Pretending that men she loved were her servants had become something of an expertise of hers, and Barriath had been willing enough to take her direction. He played the role now in case they were seen before they knew it. One played one's role always when it was possible to be seen, or else, more often really, one accepted the risks.

They rode on the turf at the roadside to muffle the sounds of the hooves. They bore neither torch nor lantern, but used the moon and stars to see by. They passed, she hoped, as ghosts across the face of the land, and she could not stop thinking of that letter.

She had taken great pleasure in the letters she'd had in her time. She'd kept them all, except one that Dawson had written when he was in his cups. His appreciation of her beauty had grown more explicit than he was accustomed to putting to paper, and he'd embarrassed himself. She'd had a second letter the next day asking that she destroy what he had written. Not without regrets, she had complied, though she had made him repeat certain parts of the missive upon his return. And she was taking that experience from Sabiha. It felt like theft, though that wasn't true. There would be other couriers than herself, surely. Men sent their wives love letters all the time.

It was only that she'd promised to keep this one safe to Camnipol, and she wasn't going to do that.

"Mother," Barriath whispered.

"My lady," she corrected.

"My lady," he said, a smile in his voice. "Look south."

The light of fires was almost too faint to see, but he was right. They were there. She tried to recall how the camp had sat in relation to the road when she'd left it. She was almost certain that the lights came from Jorey's men. She paused, patted her poor horse on its neck, and turned it south, across the trackless fields. She made no attempt to at stealth now, but talked to her horse in soothing tones loud enough to carry in the black. The sentry's voice was harsh and sudden. Even when he spoke, she didn't see him.

"Who's there!"

"What?" she said. "Lady Kalliam, of course. Why do you ask?"

There was a moment's silence. When the voice came again, it was wary, but less so. "Lady Kalliam? What are you doing here?"

"Well, I went out for a ride after supper to clear my head. The tents can be so terribly stuffy, you know. Only I seem to have gotten a bit turned about, and it took me much longer than I expected. But I have my man here with me for protection and we were quite careful not to go anywhere near enemy territory, so I was entirely safe the whole time."

"You're coming in from the north, ma'am," the sentry said. "That's where the enemy is."

"Really? Are you sure? I thought we were headed east."

"Fair certain you're heading south, ma'am," the sentry said.

"Oh. Well, how embarrassing."

There was a clicking, and a spark, and a thin flame in a little tin lantern. The man holding it was younger than Vincen or Jorey. A boy, almost. His caved-in cheeks and deep-set eyes belonged to a starving man, but he smiled all the same.

"You really shouldn't be leaving camp at all, ma'am. It's not safe."

Clara made an impatient noise in the back of her throat, and then sighed. "I suppose as I'm a doddering old woman who can't tell south from east, I'm in no position to disagree with you. Still, do you suppose we might keep this between us? If I promise very solemnly not to wander out again? I don't like to worry my son."

"I'll have to make a report," the sentry said. "But I'll make as little of it as I can."

"You're entirely too kind," Clara said, then turned to Barriath. "Come along."

The sentry passed the lantern up to Barriath as they went by. The ground became more even. The smell of cookfires and latrines was as familiar as a well-loved song, and Clara angled her horse toward the rough corral she'd taken it from.

"You're entirely too good at that," Barriath said.

"Never discount the power of being underestimated," she said. "And don't talk so impertinently to your betters. You're my servant after all."

"Yes, my lady," he said again, and poorly.

With night folded over it, the camp seemed both smaller and endless. The air was still warm enough that many of the soldiers hadn't bothered to put up tents, but slept in the fields around guttering fires or else in darkness. The flame of Barriath's little lantern ruined her dark-adapted eye, making the blackness outside its little circle deeper. The cunning men's tent called to her like water to thirst. She wanted to go to Vincen, to tell him all that had happened in that dark little house in Sara-sur-Mar. Of Barriath and his comrades and the decision she and her son had made and hoped that Jorey would make as well. She wanted to hold Vincen's hand and make sure his fever hadn't come back and lay her head on his chest to hear him breathe.

It would wait. It would have to.

She had stayed too long in Sara-sur-Mar. Her intention had been to go, deliver her warning, and retreat again at once. Instead, she'd stayed with Barriath, each of them talking too fast, trying to fit all they had to say into a few minutes. Barriath had been building a rough fleet to stand against Palliako, had worked with the Medean bank in

Porte Oliva, had taken Lord Skestinin prisoner and saved a wounded dragon with his ships. Clara had sent reports and letters to the Medean bank in Carse, followed the army in disguise, and engineered the death of Lord Ternigan. Barriath's laughter had been a roar, and the strength of it had lifted her. *And here I thought it was Father I took after.*

Jorey's tent glowed at the seams. Clara's steps felt awkward after the long ride. Or perhaps it was the exhaustion of so long a day. She was not so young as she'd once been, after all. Or the prospect of what she was about to do to herself and to her son and to her kingdom. She wished there had been some way to deliver that letter. To have let Jorey be the man to his wife that Dawson had been to her. There was so very much to regret.

The guard at the door nodded to her, the movement almost a bow, though not quite. There was, she supposed, no set etiquette for how to greet a Lord Marshal's mother in the field.

"Is he awake still?" Clara asked loudly enough that her voice carried.

"I am," Jorey called from within, his voice muffled. The guard nodded again, and Clara passed inside.

He was at his small field desk, as if he had been there for hours. The map before him was marked in red and black. He smiled when she sat across from him, but it was the sort of expression a boy used when he was pretending to his mother that all was well and he had not been crying.

"I don't suppose I can convince you to return to Camnipol before your huntsman's well?" Jorey asked. "I know he's a favorite of yours, but I do have an army full of soldiers that can keep you safe."

"I very much doubt that," Clara said, drawing out her pipe and her little pouch of tobacco. "Jorey, the time has come that we need to have a talk, you and I. A serious one. As adults."

"We don't need to do that, Mother. It's all right."

"It isn't all right. A very great deal of it is wrong. And we're both aware of the fact, yes? Tell me, Jorey. How do you feel about what happened to your father?"

The boy's face paled. He swallowed and looked down at the map before him without seeing it. "He conspired with the Timzinae against Prince Aster," Jorey said.

"That isn't true," she said, and confusion passed through Jorey's eyes. "It isn't, and you know it isn't. Your father was many things, but a servant to foreign powers was never one. What he did was in service to the throne, as he saw it. We are all in service to the crown. As we see it."

"I..." Jorey began and then stopped. For a long moment, silence reigned. When he found his voice again, it was low. "I did what you asked, Mother. I renounced him. I made my peace with Geder, and accepted his forgiveness."

"You did. You made yourself a place in the court. You were not cast out as I was."

"I'm sorry about that."

"Don't be," Clara said. "Don't ever be. We did what needed to be done to survive, and for the most part we have, haven't we? You're Lord Marshal, favored of the crown. I'm...Well, if I had stayed, I'm sure I'd have been welcome at some of the feasts and balls, wouldn't I? Only I didn't. You have a child now, my dear. A baby of your own. There are so many things that you will learn with her. There are risks that you would take yourself without thought that you'd run over glass to keep her from chancing. It's love, and it's right when the baby is small, but then you've all grown up, haven't you? And still to keep you safe...even when the price of the safety is..."

"Mother?" Jorey said carefully. "Are you well?"

Clara dabbed her eyes with her cuff and shook her head. "This war you're leading. How will you end it?"

"I don't know," he said. "I try not to think about that."

"Your father never conspired with Timzinae. Or the bank that this Cithrin creature held. Dawson was raised a certain way, and he did not change. Even when the world did. How would he have ended this war?"

"In my place?" Jorey said. "I don't know. I don't know that he could have. I know that we're chasing shadows, Mother. I can't say it, but I know it's truth. All I can look at is the next step, and then the next, and then the next. Trying to keep my men safe and alive, trying to reach the next goal in hopes that something may happen that I haven't anticipated. It was easier when Vicarian was here. Ever since he took these new vows, he's been sure that everything will end well somehow. When I'm around him, I can convince myself it's...not true even. Possible."

"It isn't," Clara said.

"I know," Jorey said. "But this war is a raft I climbed on to keep my family safe, and the river's going wherever it goes. The best I can go is hold on. For Sabiha's sake. And Annalise's. And yours."

"And your own sake, Jorey? What would your sake look like?"

"There is no my sake. I watched my father slaughtered before my eyes and I renounced him. Instead of bringing my wife respectability, I dirtied her name more. I am leading an army of half-starved men on an endless campaign because..."

Jorey stopped. His hands were in fists.

"Because Geder's priests want you to," Clara whispered. "And everyone knows, but no one dares object."

"Father did."

Clara plucked a bit of leaf from her pouch and pressed it

in the narrow bowl of her pipe. "He was not the only one." She lit the pipe from the lantern flame and sucked the sweet smoke into her lungs. Jorey's eyes were fixed on her. It felt like standing on the edge of a cliff over deep water. She dreaded the leap, but there was no stepping back. She went to the tent's door and sent the guard for her servant. It wouldn't take long. She knelt at Jorey's side, took his hand in her own. "I have been conspiring against Geder Pallaiko and his priests."

"Mother. No."

"Yes. Very much so."

"You have to stop it. You have to stop now, and forever."

"You know that isn't true."

Jorey was weeping now, and his tears called forth her own. A deep regret shook her. Her advice had brought him here. She had been the one who insisted that he make himself a place in court, that he renounce his father, that he compromise and compromise and compromise until he was this. The commander of a campaign he had no faith in, driven by fear and by guilt.

And still, it was better than being dead at Dawson's side. And that had been an alternative.

Barriath stepped into the room behind her, and Jorey snarled without looking up, "Go away. You're not wanted."

"No?" Barriath asked, and Jorey started like the word was a wasp sting.

For an endless moment, they were silent. Two brothers divided by a rift as deep and profound as the one that split Camnipol. Jorey rose to his feet, his fingers trailing from her own hand.

"What are you doing here?" he breathed.

"Anything I can to pull Palliako down," Barriath said. "You?"

"Anything I can to keep him propped up."

"Ah," Barriath said. "And you're doing that why, now?"

"I'm fucked if I know," Jorey said and threw his arms around his brother's chest.

Clara closed her eyes. The blooming, opening sensation in her heart was joyful, but it was not joy. It was relief. It was the feeling of setting down a mask worn too long and finding that the world did not end with the role. When at length her two boys released each other, she motioned for them to sit and to speak quietly. For the second time that day, she and Barriath recounted all that had happened, all that they knew. Or almost all. That she had taken Vincen Coe as a lover seemed a bit more than the situation called for, even now. When Jorey found that she had engineered the fall of Lord Ternigan that had inspired his own promotion, he shook his head at the cruel irony. When Barriath revealed that Lord Skestinin was his own prisoner—alive, well, and still only half convinced that Barriath meant Aster and the throne no harm—his eyes went wide. And Barriath's report of the true origins of the spider priests as the weapon of the insane Dragon Emperor was like a child's bedtime tale come to life, except that it recast everything that had happened in Antea since before the death of King Simeon. The night went on and on, and sleep not even a thought. When she smoked the last of her tobacco, it was the first sign of how long their conversation had run. The birdsong that announced the coming dawn was the second.

Their time together was almost over, and she could see the grief of it in her sons' eyes. Everything had changed for them all, but their situation was the same.

"We cannot allow the priests to know what we've done or what we're doing," Clara said. "The Severed Throne is in terrible danger, and our family—we three—are in the best position to save it."

"Yes," Jorey said, and it was the most beautiful word she had ever heard spoken. She took his hand in her own.

"You are Lord Marshal," she said. "The army is yours. Keep it safe, and stop it from fighting."

"I've already written half my report in my mind while we we've been talking," Jorey said. "I'll tell Geder that the men need to winter over someplace safe where they can rest. Porte Oliva. Bellin. Someplace that doesn't have the local forces harassing us. It's an easy argument to make, because it's true. Come spring, I'll be cautious. Slow. As much time as I can keep us out of the field, I'll take."

"Good," Clara said. "These poor men didn't ask for this. If we can keep them from killing anyone more or being killed themselves, all the better."

"What are we going to use that time for?" Barriath asked.

Clara nodded. "Dawson saw the priests for the danger that they are. We are going to have to do well what he did poorly."

"There are a lot of priests out there, Mother," Barriath said. *And one of them is Vicarian*, he did not quite add. Because he didn't have to.

"I know," Clara said. "I didn't mean to suggest it would be simple."

"How do we start?" Jorey asked.

"With allies," Clara said. "And with the work we've already done. I'm going to have to leave you. Jorey, be careful with yourself while I'm gone, and I will write as often and as fully as I dare. And I'm leaving Vincen Coe with you. See to him. Promise me that."

"Of course," Jorey said. "But where are you going?"

"With your brother," Clara said. "I think it's time I spoke with this bel Sarcour woman, don't you?"

Marcus

The taproom was in the north of the city where the architecture changed, streets narrowing to a merely human size, the great stone towers replaced by wooden structures no more than three stories high. The yard didn't open to the dragon's road itself, but the jade ribbon was less than a minute's walk to the south. Close enough that random travelers in need of a meal might find their way there by chance. The walls were dark and hung with shields of what seemed a hundred different houses. Low benches lined scarred wooden tables and three-legged stools crowded a fire grate longer than two men lying head to foot. The scents of roasting chicken and a spiced bean soup made the air feel warmer than it was. The players liked it for the keep's open invitation to performers and cheap beer. Marcus liked it because he'd never been there before.

A thin Jasuru woman in a flowing gown of braided cotton stood at the center of the room, her hands contorted in claws, her eyes narrow. Her black tongue passed over sharp teeth, and her scales shone the color of brass. With a shout, she lifted her right hand, a sphere of bright air forming around her fist. She gritted her teeth, shouted again, and the globe burst into a bright violet flame. There was a scattering of polite applause.

Cary leaned in against the table, her eyes narrow, as the

cunning woman called forth a second ball of flame, this one orange.

"Maybe you can tell me," she said. "Why is it so many cunning men go in for performance?"

"You'd have to ask them," Marcus said. "Can't see why they wouldn't, though. Impressive to look at, some of it."

At the far end of the table, Hornet said something that made Charlit Soon roll her eyes and Sandr laugh hard enough to slop beer out of his cup. Yardem, sitting beside Hornet, smiled patiently, his ears drooping to the side in a way that made the old soldier look like a patient rabbit. Outside, the night wind had a chill to it that was the first real hint of winter. There would be plenty of warm days still to come. But Carse was almost as far north as Rukkyupal, and if the currents of the ocean warmed Northcoast and chilled Hallskar, it didn't change the fact that it was late to start a long march for anywhere.

No one had said the words yet, but Marcus was fairly sure they'd be wintering in Carse. Long, dark nights in the cold he'd borne once with Alys and Merian. Walking south to Porte Silena was starting to sound like the better option, even if it meant facing the armies of Antea alone and on foot.

"I just would have thought...you know. Calling fire from the air?" Cary said, moving her hands in tight but dramatic gestures. "That has to be good for something more than copperweights at a taproom."

"You mean fighting?" Marcus said.

"For instance," Cary said.

"Not really," Marcus said. "I mean, it's impressive to look at, but if it's not faster than a bow or a blade, it's not a trick you'd be likely to do twice."

The actor bit her thumb, considering, and nodded. "That's a fair point."

"It's the difference between what you do and what I do," Marcus said. "No offense, but what matters to you and Kit and the others is what looks best to an audience. What matters to people like me or Yardem? What kills the other person fastest. The two aren't the same."

"No," Cary said, a distant look coming to her eyes. "I suppose they aren't."

Marcus was silent for a moment. Mikel came in from the darkness. His thin frame made him seem younger than he likely was. He grinned and came to the table, where Halvill made room for him. It was odd the way the players and the guards had become a single group after the flight from Porte Oliva. But sea travel had a reputation for changing people in ways that they did not change back. They sat together now in groups that mixed one with the other and made no distinction. Enen and Hornet and Yardem and Charlit Soon all shoulder to shoulder on the bench. Even Magistra Isadau was there, with her niece Maha. The only ones missing were Master Kit and Cithrin.

No. That wasn't right. They weren't the only ones.

Marcus looked over at Cary. Her hair was pulled back in a thick braid. Her eyes were dark, seeing something that wasn't in the room. Of all the players, he felt he knew least which of her feelings were truly hers and which the artifice of her trade. He'd seen her pretend everything from heartbreak to joy, lust to horror, cold rage to naïve trust. He didn't know that he'd ever seen the actual woman. It was part of why he liked her.

"I'm sorry about Smit," he said.

"I am too," she said, and didn't speak more. Marcus didn't press.

"Captain!" Sandr called from the foot of the table.

"Where's the magistra? She should come with us. Like the old days!"

"Thing about the old days," Marcus said. "They're old."

In truth, Cithrin was still at the holding company's compound, and Marcus wasn't sure anymore whether it was captivity or choice. With the ships in port, the wealth of Porte Oliva had been taken by the king and the proclamation put out that, as an act of loyalty to the sovereign of Northcoast, letters of transfer from the Medean bank were to be treated as the gold they represented. The bank had begun making trades using the papers where real money had been. Marcus had even escorted the first of them at Cithrin's request, walking through the streets of Carse from the branch run by Magister Nison to a fletcher's hall partnered with the bank. The journey had been planned in advance, as clearly a show as anything Cary and the players ever did. Marcus, Yardem, Enen, and half a dozen of Magister Nison's people making a great show of protecting a thin sheaf of papers. It had felt like manning the walls of a fort built from sticks and pillows, but he'd understood the bank's reasons. If they wanted people to think of their bits of scribble as being the same as gold, then they needed to be protected as gold would be protected. That it was ridiculous didn't seem to matter, and so he had scowled at the passersby and kept his hand on the hilt of his sword. Unsurprisingly, no one had leapt to the attack and stolen the papers. Marcus wondered whether anyone ever would.

"We're thinking of putting on The Pardoner's Wife," Cary said.

"Really?" Marcus said, trying to recall which play that was.

"Mikel knows all Smit's lines. It's a short solve, though.

We need more people if we're going to have the full selection to pull from. And there's the problem of not having a cart. Or costumes. Or props."

"Mmm," Marcus agreed, drinking from his cup. The beer was better than he gave it credit for.

"I was wondering if you thought...Cithrin is in a strange position here, isn't she? I mean, she's not precisely locked away and she's not precisely not, if you see what I mean."

"You're wondering if she's in a position to underwrite the company?"

"Wondering, yes. I don't want to presume on the friendship, but there's been a fair amount of work we've done and risk we've taken doing what amounts to her business."

"I can ask."

Cary nodded, swallowed, looked back at the Jasuru woman just as the cunning woman tossed all four of her globes of fire into the air, where they annihilated each other with a series of reports like tiny thunder. The cunning woman spread her arms and grinned. The sweat running down her face and neck made her seem oddly vulnerable. The players shouted and clapped and stamped their feet as she bowed. Enen tossed a bit of silver to her, and half a dozen of the other patrons of the house followed suit. Cary shook her head in disapproval.

"She needs people leading the audience," Cary said.

"You think?"

"Nothing convinces people to throw coins like a bunch of other people throwing coins."

"Or letters of transfer," Marcus said, trying to imagine the Jasuru woman being caught in a storm of crumpled letters.

The door of the taproom slammed open and Kit rushed in. His hair was disheveled and his eyes wide in a way that set Marcus's heart racing before the old actor was halfway across the room. Yardem's ears went straight up, and the Tralgu began to pull himself free of the bench.

"Marcus," Kit said, reaching out, "I think you should come. Now. I believe we have a problem."

"Antea or Inys?" Marcus asked, already walking to the door. Yardem fell in at his left and Cary at his right. He swallowed the impulse to tell her to stay safe in the taproom. She'd traveled with him more than enough to make her own choices about what risks to take.

"Neither," Kit said darkly as they passed into the cool night air. "I suspect this is much, much worse."

In the square outside the palace, a dozen men stood in formal array under a banner of parley. At the center, a thin man in a brown robe held out one arm. In his other was a speaker's horn. A small crowd had begun to form around them and at a little distance, like the audience at a performance.

"Listen to my voice!" the thin man shouted. "I come to deliver the world and the truth! The seat of Antea has fallen to the corruption of a false priesthood, and King Tracian of Carse is now the greatest hope for the true teaching of the goddess! Come out, my king, and we will deliver the world to you!"

"Well," Marcus said. "God smiled."

"I believe I know him," Kit said. "If I am right, his name is Eshau rol Salvet. He came from the same village I did, but went to the temple two years before I was called to it."

"Enemy of the goddess?"

"That I can't speak to," Kit said. "He was devout the last I saw him, but that was decades ago."

"Listen to my voice, great king! I bring you victory and grace!" the priest called, and the square echoed with his voice.

"Where's Inys?" Marcus said, walking quickly forward.

"Flying south last I saw him, sir," Yardem said.

"Find him."

"Yes, sir. Any thought how to do that?"

"Be creative."

"Yes, sir."

"I'll do that," Cary said, and turned back, dashing into the night. Marcus looked after her, then at Yardem. The Tralgu shrugged.

"She'll do that," Yardem said.

"Fair enough. Can you go get the sword?"

"Yes, sir."

"I picked a hell of a night not to carry the damned thing."

"Did, sir," Yardem said and loped away to the east and the holding company. Kit, at his side, opened his fists and closed them. Marcus put his hand on the hilt of his sword. The simple steel was good enough for most work, but the thin priest had men at his side, and five of them had blades of their own. One even wore boiled leather armor. Marcus wondered how many of them carried the spiders in their blood. At the palace, the high iron gates swung open and someone in a bright ceremonial armor of Tracian's guard looked out at the crowd.

This wasn't good.

"Eshau!" Marcus shouted, marching fast toward the group. "Eshau rol Salvet! As I live and breathe. Who ever thought to see you here."

The priest turned toward him, eyes wide with surprise. Kit, trotting at Marcus's side, murmured low, "What are you planning?"

"Planning to distract the bastard while I think of a plan," Marcus said, then grinned and lifted a hand to the dozen grim faces turned toward him. "You must all be Eshau's friends, yes? I'd say it's a pleasure to see you all here, but truth is we weren't expecting anyone."

"Who are you?" the priest asked, his gaze shifting from Marcus to Kit and back again.

"Marcus Wester. General Marcus Wester, once was. Captain now. I've taken up mercenary work these last couple dozen years, but before that I was the one put Lady Tracian on the throne. King's mother. So perhaps you've heard of me?"

"No," the priest said. "We are come from Kaltfel, city at the world's center and true seat of the goddess. We bring the good word that her truth is at last revealed and to call the righteous men of Northcoast to defend her refounded temple against the false priests and vile pretenders who soil her name with their corrupt tongues. A terrible battle is coming, and we alone stand against the forces of lies and falsehood."

To the south, something bright and silent happened, like lightning from a clear sky, but without the thunder. Marcus ignored it. Anything that wasn't raining hell on his shoulders right now could wait.

"Yeah, well that sounds like a powerfully amusing pastime, it's true. But I think you may find the exercise a bit disappointing. You see, we're fairly short of righteous men just at the moment, and—"

"Who is this, at your side?" the thin priest said.

"I think you know me, Eshau," Kit said.

"Kitap rol Keshmet. Apostate."

A murmur passed through the assembled men. The one in armor drew his sword. It was simple blade. Workmanlike. And the man knew how to hold it.

"Apostate. Yes," Kit said. "And it seems not alone in this."

"I am no apostate," the thin man said, lifting his chin

proudly. "I am the one true path to her. I have seen the error the old Basrahip fell into. His pride led him astray, but the goddess is incorruptible."

Marcus raised his hand. "To clarify? She's incorruptible because she's made out of rock. We went and checked, Kit and I. Now, here's the thing. You need to leave. Now."

"I will not be turned aside," the thin priest said. A flash of lavender fire rose up into the air behind him, just the color the Jasuru cunning woman had made. Marcus felt a surge of mad hope.

"All right, listen to *my* damned voice for once," he said. "There is nothing you're going to get out of this city. Not in my lifetime. So you and your little set of religious here just turn around and walk back down the road that brought you."

"What's going on here?" a too-familiar voice asked from behind him. "Who calls for the right of parley?"

Marcus closed his eyes. "This would be a very good time to go back the hell inside, Your Majesty."

"King Tracian," the thin priest said, falling to his knees and spreading his arms. His eyes were glassy and bright. "I come to bring you word of your destiny. You are fated to bring the world to an everlasting peace, and I am your righteous servant."

"What do you mean?" King Tracian said, stepping forward. He was in a long robe of red velvet, his expression confused but also intrigued. A dozen guards stood behind him, their swords at the ready.

"I bring no false parley," the priest said.

"He does," Kit said. "He brings false parley. Everything he says or believes is false. Not even a lie, but a mistake with roots so deep they could pierce the earth to its center."

The thin priest's jaw dropped, his eyes widened. For a

long, terrible moment, the thin priest looked shocked, lost, and alone. It struck Marcus how odd it must be for a zealot to hear himself called a liar with the power of the spiders in his blood to know the enemy was speaking truth. Little wonder these priests were crazed. The thin priest's face went dark with rage.

"You are an abomination! Kitap rol Keshmet, I name you Ensanyana! Black-tongue! Thing of darkness!"

"Thing of darkness?" the king said, taking a step back.

"They knew each other when they were boys," Marcus said as the dozen men drew together, pulling what knives and swords they claimed. "It's a very long conversation and stranger than you'd enjoy. Consider going back in your palace, eh? I'm trying to keep you alive."

"*Apostate!*" the thin priest screamed, and a column of fire fell from the sky. Marcus shied back, the sudden heat an assault. Even closed, his eyes hurt from the brightness, and for a terrible moment he was in his nightmares again, running through the flame to cradle a wife and child already eaten by the flame. He stumbled back, his skin burning. Someone was screaming. He thought for a moment it might be a woman's voice. Alys returned from the dead by some hellish trick of the spider priests. And then the darkness rolled back over him and the cool night breeze.

When he opened his eyes, the night was a thousand times blacker than it had been before. His face and hands were burned, and his eyes ached. The fleeing audience still filled the night with their screams, and King Tracian had fallen unceremoniously on his ass to Marcus's right. The thin priest and his dozen men lay blackened and charred on the stones. Inys bent down as if to smell one, then took the corpse between his vast teeth and chewed it thoughtfully. Marcus heard Kit's voice, soft and reassuring, speaking over

King Tracian's panic-filled gabble. Marcus leaned forward, elbows on his knees, and permitted himself a chuckle.

"The corrupt are everywhere," the dragon said. "So long as they are, chaos will follow them."

"Yeah," Marcus agreed. "Picked up on that."

From behind the dragon, Cary came with the Jasuru cunning woman behind her. A moment later, Yardem Hane loped into the square, the poisoned sword drawn in his massive hand. The Tralgu slowed, the point to the green blade drifting down toward earth.

"Took too long," Yardem said as he reached Marcus's side.

"Appreciate the effort."

"Still."

"Life's full of disappointments," Marcus said. "Might want to put that thing away."

Yardem sheathed the blade as Inys lifted up a second corpse and began eating it as well. A glow of fire lit the dragon's mouth from within like a paper lantern. Marcus stepped across to where the king was only now rising to his feet.

Marcus made a small, ironic salute. "That's two you owe me now, Majesty."

Geder

Sitting in the drawing room of Lord Skestinin's mansion felt strangely eerie. Geder half expected to hear the cunning men still chanting over a death-grey Sabiha, to see Lady Skestinin with her smile stretched tight by her fear. But outside the window, the trees were the deeper, warmer green that came before autumn. The servants in the hall spoke with laughter in their voices. The divan where Geder had slept on those long, terrible nights had been reupholstered in yellow silk to match the new window coverings. Those signs were enough to remind him that the season hadn't been a dream, that it was not summer that was coming in the weeks and months ahead, but short days and bitter cold.

He wore his field gear. Black riding boots, black leather cloak with the hood tucked back behind him. His horse waited outside in bright barding and his personal guard in chain and armed for war.

His decision to lead the force to Kaltfel had been a clear one to Geder and Basrahip. Not all of his other advisors had seen it that way. Canl Daskellin in particular had argued against it.

"You are the Lord Regent," he'd said, pacing the length of the war room, placing his feet carefully among the mountains and swamps of the miniature empire. "Your duties, and with respect, your *responsibilities* to the kingdom go far, far beyond leading a force to put down an uprising. If something happens to you in the field—"

"It will not," Basrahip said, but even his low, rolling voice wasn't enough to take Daskellin from the thread of his thought. Not all at once, at any rate.

"If it were to, the court is scattered across the face of the world. We could not convene a council big enough to name a new regent. Not for weeks. Maybe months. You are more than yourself, my lord. You are the state."

"I won't get hurt," Geder said. "I'll be very, very careful. All right?"

"He's the Lord Regent," Emming said, scowling at Daskellin. "If he can't do what he deems best for the realm, then what's the point of having him?"

Geder nodded his thanks to the older man, and Emming returned the gesture with a bow. Daskellin lifted both his hands, shaking them as he bit his lips.

"I understand why you would want to address this firmly, my lord," he said. "But I beg you to consider the risks you are taking. The kingdom is...in a delicate situation. There are many, many things that require attention, and the potential for crisis is great. I fear...I fear..."

"Say it," Geder said.

"If we lose our Lord Regent," Daskellin said, "I do not think we will be able to keep the kingdom from insurrection."

"I think you overestimate my importance," Geder said, though in truth they were pleasant words to hear.

"With respect, it isn't you as a man, Lord Palliako," Daskellin said. "It's your role. Even after what happened in Suddapal, there are many who think of you as a hero. The man who stopped the Timzinae. Who protected the throne. Now, who defeated the dragon. If you sat in your bath for the next year and did nothing else, your presence here would still give the realm a sense of stability. And we are losing that. There are three armies in the field now. Four, counting this new group. The belief that there is a man on the throne who sees and manages all of it is keeping the realm from flying apart."

"In other times," Basrahip said, his voice rolling out like a distant thunder, "all these things you say might have been true. But this is the age of her return. The answer to the fire years. The end of the fallen epoch. Prince Geder is the chosen of the goddess. He cannot fail."

"I understand that," Daskellin said. "It's only that—"

"He will not fail," Basrahip said, shifting his weight and attention forward. His smile was gentle and wide. "Listen to my voice, friend Canl. He cannot fail. The last battle has begun, and Prince Geder will be there at the birth of the coming world."

Daskellin opened his mouth, closed it, and looked away. He nodded his acceptance and then laughed ruefully. "I suppose it's only that I'm used to normal wars. This really isn't one of those, is it?"

"It is not," the huge priest said. "For at the end of this war, there shall be no others forever."

"Well," Daskellin had said, pressing his toe against the tiny version of Kaltfel, "I suppose that's worth being present for, isn't it?" And that had been the last anyone had said of Geder's staying behind when the soldiers departed for Kaltfel.

A soft knock came at the door, and Lady Skestinin took half a step in. Geder rose and bowed to her, not a full bow. That would have been too much. Just a little angle at the shoulders, enough to honor the lady of the house and the family she was heading now that her husband and son-in-law were gone.

"Lord Regent," she said. "When I heard you'd come, I hoped there might be news. Anything would be welcome."

Anything. Even confirmation of her husband's death. They both knew that she stood there more likely widow than wife. The sorrow and anxiety barely showed. In truth, he couldn't say how he knew. It wasn't in her voice or the expression in her eyes or the way she held her body. It was in her, the whole of her.

"I'm sorry," Geder said. "I'm expecting word from Jorey anytime now, but no. Nothing yet."

"Ah," she said, twisting at her own fingers without seeming aware she was doing it. "I understand. I'd only... Well, yes. Thank you all the same."

"I wanted to see Sabiha before I left. And the girl. Annalise. In case I see Jorey again before I come home."

"Oh," Lady Skestinin said. "I didn't know that was possible."

"Anything's *possible*," Geder said.

He had come to Lord Skestinin's mansion as his last stop before the little army decamped for the westward march. Before that, he had gone with Aster and Basrahip to review the troops, such as they were. The encampment was outside the city walls by the western gate. They were three full cohorts and part of a fourth, but only five bannered knights and no cunning men besides Geder's own. The throne had called for men so many times that those still left to answer this call were weedy youths and old men, the injured of old campaigns who had healed enough to march and slaves of half a dozen races who had been offered their freedom in exchange for fighting on the empire's last battleground. To call them ragged would have been kind, but as Geder and Aster rode past them, they stood as proud as a seasoned army of the purest blood.

They reminded Geder of the boy he'd been the first time

he'd ridden on campaign, fat, bookish, friendless, and despised. And now he was the ruler of the greatest empire since the fall of the dragons. He wanted to give some rousing speech, some assurance that they were there on the work not of dragons or men, but of gods. However raw they looked, however awkwardly they wore their swords, what lay before them was glory. He wanted to, but he didn't. Better to let Basrahip deliver the speeches. He was much more convincing, speaking with the voice of the goddess as he did.

The priest was a structure of smiles and broad gestures all through the review, but Aster's expression was closed. The black eye he'd suffered was gone now, though there was a tiny scar now between the brow and the bridge of his nose where the blow had cut him. A tiny disfigurement that would always remind him, Geder thought, of his enemy. He was willing to bet that Myrin Shoat would live to regret that little scar deeply. The prospect made Geder smile. Aster frowned at him.

"Just thinking," Geder said. "It's nothing."

"I wish I could go," the boy said. "I don't see why it's safe enough for you to go but not for me."

You're still a boy, Geder thought but restrained himself from saying. It was true, but it wasn't what Aster could hear. There was no way to explain war to someone who had never seen it. Never been touched by it. Never heard the voice of the fire in Vanai in his nightmares or seen a woman's silhouette against the flames and thought, *I've done this.*

"Glory's all well and good," Geder said. "But you'll have your chance later. Once you've taken the throne."

"It's all going to be over by then," Aster complained. "The wars will all be ended, and the dragons and the Timzinae will all be dead, and it'll be nothing but peace."

"I know," Geder said. "That won't be a bad thing."

"I just wish I could see it before it ends."

"The triumphs when you come back are the best part," Geder said. "Before that it's mostly a lot of camping and a little bit of shouting."

Aster managed a wan smile. "You're just trying to make it sound bad so I'll feel better."

"Is it working?" Geder asked.

On the way back through the gates, Basrahip rode beside Geder, Aster riding a length or two ahead. The small people of the city bowed their heads as Lord Regent, high priest, and crown prince passed together surrounded by his guard. Three of the most powerful and noblest men in the empire. Geder put out his hand in a gesture of blessing.

"You are well, Prince Geder?" Basrahip asked. "You have lost your doubts?"

"I have," Geder said.

"This is as it should be," Basrahip said. "All of this is very, very well."

"Do I have time to make a stop before we call the march?"

"What you do, you may do," Basrahip said. "You have no need to ask me."

"I'd like to stop by and see Sabiha Kalliam before we leave. And her daughter."

"As you wish," Basrahip said.

Still, Geder had seen Aster back to the Kingspire and made his farewell there. The prince had been brave about the whole thing, and his tutor had been there to whisk him away to lessons. Best to keep the boy's mind occupied. He'd spend less time chewing at himself, worrying for Geder and envying him. Basrahip and half a dozen priests rode back for the army beyond the gates, and Geder had sought out his best friend's wife. She was, after all, as near as he could get to saying goodbye to Jorey himself.

"Yes," Lady Skestinin said. "I suppose anything is possible. I know I never imagined myself living through times like these." For a moment, her reserve cracked and tears touched her pale eyes.

"If there is any way to bring Lord Skestinin back safely, we will do it," Geder said. "And if he's harmed, I will see that a thousand of the enemy are killed in his name."

"Yes," Lady Skestinin said. "Yes, of course. Thank you."

Geder nodded. It hurt him to see her pain and to be unable to do anything to ease it. It hurt him to think of Aster's aching loneliless and anxiety and of the fact that Jorey had already missed the first months of his daughter's life. Lady Skestinin nodded again, much as she had before, and retreated to the hall without taking the risk of further speech. Geder sat again, his hands between his knees, and looked out at the garden. Bees filled the air around the pear trees, drawn, he thought, by the sweetness of the fruit where it had gone overripe and split. A striped grey cat streaked across the ground, fleeing from something or chasing it. Geder closed his eyes, and Cithrin was there, waiting for him. She was neither the cruel one, laughing at him for being too stupid as to believe in her love, nor the repentant one who begged his forgiveness. He couldn't even conjure up her face, not clearly. It was Cithrin because he knew it was Cithrin. It was the Cithrin he'd created in his heart, and who was still there.

I loved you, he thought. *And you laughed at me. Why did you have to laugh at me?*

"Geder?"

His eyes opened, and Sabiha was there. He hadn't heard her come in. Motherhood was agreeing with her. She'd put on weight that widened her face and her hips, brought a warmth to her cheeks. The baby clung to her side, riding

Sabiha's hip like a tiny bear shimmying up a tree. The small, bright eyes found Geder, boggled at him, lost him, and found him again.

"Sabiha," he said. "And how is the perfect girl?"

Annalise made a low *guh* and swung her arms to grab Sabiha's hair. Sabiha winced and gently disentangled her locks from the baby's fingers. "The perfect girl," she said, "is growing like weeds in springtime and doesn't know her own strength."

"She looks wonderful," Geder said.

"She is wonderful," Sabiha replied, sitting down on the chair opposite him. "I hear you're going."

"Yes. After this."

Sabiha shifted the baby to her lap and jounced her gently on her knee. Annalise looked fascinated, and then startled, and then cooed delightedly and waved her tiny hands. Her hair was thin as high clouds on a windy day and the same color as Jorey's. The soft place at the center of her head where the bones hadn't grown closed was visible only because he knew to look for it. Geder imagined he could see something of his friend's face in the pudgy curves of her cheeks. She met Geder's eyes and shrieked with pleasure. Geder smiled.

"I wanted to see my niece again before I left," Geder said, looking directly into the child's eyes. "She's going to be a different girl when I get back, isn't she? Uncle Geder won't even know her."

"Would you like to hold her?" Sabiha asked.

"If I could," Geder said, and Sabiha rose up, scooping the baby to him, to his lap. Annalise was lighter than he'd expected, as if her body were made from fluff and warmth. He held her carefully around the chest, supporting her neck the way Sabiha had shown him the first time, though the baby seemed quite able to hold up her own head now.

"You know my nurse back at Rivenhalm used to tell me that you should whisper all your secrets into the soft place there before it grows closed," he said.

"My mother says that too," Sabiha said. "It's supposed to make the baby grow up wise."

"Is it? I thought it was to give them something while they were still innocent enough to make it clean again. I may have gotten that part wrong. My skull had grown closed when she told me, but I was still fairly young. It's hard to know what really happened back then."

"It is," Sabiha said. "Have you heard from Jorey?"

"Just the usual. Reports from the field. Dry stuff. Nothing personal. You?"

"I had one letter after Porte Oliva fell. He seemed...*happy*'s a strong word. He seemed well. He was glad his mother came."

"They're going to make fun of him for that when he gets back," Geder said.

"If he wins, the jokes will be gentle," Sabiha said, an edge in her voice. "And if he loses, they'll mock him for more than that. It's the joy of court that everything you do is available for the casual judgment of others."

"I suppose I don't see that from where I am," Geder said. "No one but Aster confides in me. Or makes jokes. I'm not complaining, you understand. It's just I wasn't really part of court before Basrahip and the priests came, and after that it was so little time before I was named Lord Regent. I don't know what court life is really like. All my time I've been either below it or above it."

"I've been in the thick," Sabiha said. "It's only people. Cruel and kind, and often both in the same evening."

Annalise blurped in agreement. Geder made a clicking noise with his tongue against his teeth that fascinated her, and she tried to grab for his lips. Sabiha gasped and pushed her hand between them. For a moment, he thought he saw something like fear in her. As if she was afraid that he might get angry with the babe if it tugged at him too hard and dash her to the floor. But perhaps that was only his imagination. Sabiha knew him better than that. Or he hoped she did.

"After this, it should all be over," he said, embarrassed by the words as he said them. *I'm going to save the world. I'd never hurt your baby.* Obvious, thin, and whining.

"That's good," she said. "I'm ready for whatever comes after."

"A world truly at peace," he said. "Not that I think it will all come right at once. There'll still be some work to be done. Ruling. All that."

"I'll take a world that's half on fire if it brings Jorey home," she said. "That's uncharitable, I know, but it's the truth. I just want him back before she starts walking and doesn't want to be held anymore."

"Would it be all right," Geder asked, "if I gave her one of my secrets? Just to keep before I go."

"Of course," Sabiha said.

The baby looked up into Geder's eyes, suddenly and comically solemn. Her thick fingers opened and closed. Geder leaned carefully over her until the thin scruff of hair tickled his lips. He could feel the soft place as a tiny warmth. He closed his eyes.

He whispered, softly enough that not even Sabiha could hear him, "I don't want to do this anymore."

Cithrin

King Tracian's face was red and beginning to peel. Marcus Wester, sitting at Cithrin's right side, looked much the same. It was as if they'd both sat out too long in the summer sun without shade. Komme Medean was at her left, his weathered face solemn as if they were at a funeral. And beyond him, Kit. The four of them together on one side of the table, and the king across from them and sitting in a slightly higher chair. On the pale white tablecloth, a single vivid drop of blood. And from it, dancing crazily, a tiny black body with eight frantic legs.

The point made, Marcus crushed the spider with a stone.

"You're...*one* of them," King Tracian said.

"I am, yes," Kit said. "I believe, though, that my actions and history will speak for my benign intentions."

"It's truth," Marcus said. "Kit's been the driving force behind stopping these bastards since before the rest of us knew they were more than the latest fashion in Antean political cults."

King Tracian put his head in his hands, peeking out between the fingers. The gesture didn't seem intended to be comic, however it looked, and Cithrin didn't laugh.

"The power of having someone like that," he said. "To just say things and have them be true."

"Have them be believed, rather," Kit said. "Please forgive

me, Majesty, but I find these differences are quite important to me. More so, perhaps, than the average person. What we do does not create truth. In my experience, only the world can do that."

"And the dragon..."

"Yes," Marcus said. "It seems that it started that long ago. Inys says he is part of the cause of it. And, we're hoping, part of the solution for it too. But the point here that you should be taking back to your private chambers is that if we hadn't come here, you'd be marching your army off to Kaltfel right now, ready to fly your banner and die to a man. You'd be at war."

Cithrin glanced over at Komme. The old banker's face didn't seem to have moved at all. He might almost have been carved from wood. She kept her own expression smooth and calm, giving away as little as she could.

"So this isn't Antea's Lord Regent," Tracian said. "Geder Palliako isn't the danger we're facing. It's these...these priests that command him."

"No," Cithrin said. "It's Geder. But it isn't only him. The shape that all this has taken, the shape it still takes, began in him. You're right that it won't end with him, though. It will spread the way it almost did here. It may have already."

"You see," Kit said, leaning forward and gesturing with both hands, "as distance grows, the chance for...not even misunderstanding. For differences of opinion, then. They grow. And when all sides are certain—*unshakably* certain—there can be no reconciliation. Only death for one side or the other, inevitably. And I fear that will be true for every division, however small. I believe that, unchecked, men like myself will set the world into an eternal battle of all against all, with no hope of peace. It is, as Inys tells us, what we were made to do."

"So, much like the normal course of history," Marcus said sourly, "but without the restful times between."

Cithrin folded her hands together and kicked him under the table. They could be cynical and despairing afterwards when they were safely back at the holding company and drunk. This was not the time.

Under the red of the burn, King Tracian looked green. "Komme?"

"Majesty," the old banker said.

"What in the name of all that's holy have you brought into my court?" the king demanded, his voice harsh with anger. No, not anger. Fear. Cithrin made a private note of that, even as she dreaded the answer. Komme bowed his head and heaved a sigh.

"I've brought you the only hope you've got," Komme said at last. "We have to stand up to this, old friend. You know I don't like working out in the world where everyone can see it. But being quiet and hoping the storm passes south of us won't work this time. The girl brought you the gold to defend the nation because chances are you're going to need it. Nothing she said to you was false. Cithrin bel Sarcour is more than the voice of my branch in Porte Oliva. I don't say this lightly. She's a genius. There hasn't been a mind like hers for seeing the systems of the world in all my life."

"You trust her, then?" the king asked.

"Absolutely," Komme said with a firm nod, and Kit pressed his lips a degree tighter to cover a smile. It was all right. Cithrin knew it was a lie. All that mattered was that the king didn't.

"All right, then," Tracian said. "You think this war can be won?"

It was the question she'd been waiting for. The one she'd known from the moment the summons came she would answer. She thought of all the words she'd practiced, let her breath out, and pulled up her neck the way the players had taught her to. In truth, there might have been no one in the world better prepared to seem one thing and be another than her.

"No, it can't be won. Not as a war, with soldiers on the field. The more we try that, the more they manage what they were made for. Violence. Dislocation. Chaos. What we *can* do is drive them out of business."

King Tracian frowned, but there was something in his eyes. A glimmer not of hope—it was much too early for that—but of hope's seed. King Tracian was curious.

"How," he said, "would we do that?"

CUT THUMBS! the sheet read in letters half as high as her finger was long. Each one was drawn in red ink with a lining of black to make it easier to see. The writing went on underneath in a less ostentatious script. *The forces of madness are all around us. Protect your mind and your family. Do no business with anyone who will not prove themselves free of the spider's taint! When they say there's no need, that is when the need is greatest! The servants of the spider are everywhere. Never let down your guard!*

In truth, it was not her favorite of the letters. There were five of them now. The first laid out what the spiders were and where they had come from, and the rules by which they functioned. Another listed twenty strategies for defeating the priests in the field of battle, including a rudimentary set of visual signals that could be used with torches or banners to guide troops whose ears had been stopped with wax. But the one that was hardest for her to read was the letter that Magistra Isadau had written to her race, telling the Timzinae what the spiders were and of Inys's creation of their whole people as a measure against them. *We have suffered*, that letter said, *but not without reason. We have suffered because they fear us. And they fear us for good cause.*

Cithrin imagined the copies of the letter coming into the hands of the slaves of Antea. She could barely imagine what it might mean to them. Isadau's words already had the power to move her to tears, and she was sitting safely in the scrivener's house at the south of Carse with the sample copies in her hand and a cup of watered wine sitting on the bench at her side.

"How many can we produce?" she asked.

The master scribe was a dark-skinned woman of middle years. Her forefinger and thumb looked almost deformed by the calluses there. "Done to standard, a full member of the guild could make five copies in a day."

"And how many full guild members are available?" Isadau asked. Through everything, she managed to seem gentle and firm.

"Twenty," the woman said.

"Not enough," Cithrin said. "How many senior apprentices?"

The master scribe scratched her arm. "If we used them, we might have as many as...fifty desks? So that way we could have two hundred and fifty pages a day, but that would be—"

"We will supply paper, pens, and ink," Cithrin said. "And you'll accept payment in letters of transfer."

A shadow passed over the master scribe's face, but at least it passed. "King Tracian has commanded that we will, and so we will."

"I'm glad we understand each other," Cithrin said. She drank off the last of the wine in a gulp and put the cup back on the bench with a sharp click. "It's a pleasure working with you."

"Likewise," the master scribe said.

Cithrin and Isadau rose. The main room of the house was row upon row of desks, and fewer than half of them occupied. That would change. Cithrin could already picture every desk full, the air thick with the scratching of pen on paper. One point in a plan of a hundred, and thankfully not one that had to be paid in coin. Buying paper with paper. There was an elegance in that, she thought. Or it might only have been that she was a little bit giddy.

The plans she'd drawn up in Porte Oliva had been for besting Antea in the field, and not all of them applied to her new framework. But some did, and others she could create with Komme and Chana and Magistra Isadau and Magister Nison.

"Magistra?" the chief scribe said as they reached the wide blue doors that led to the sun-drenched street. Cithrin and Isadau turned back together, each of them answering to the title. The master scribe held up the sample letters. "All of this we're copying. Is it ... true?"

"All of it," Cithrin said.

The master scribe said something obscene.

Walking back toward the holding company, Isadau folded her arm with Cithrin's. Carse was not a beautiful city, but it was handsome. And there were places—the dry fountain of dragon's jade by the magistrate's court, the Grave of Dragons, the glassblowers' street—where it achieved moments of radiance. Still, she missed the close, cramped streets of Porte Oliva and Maestro Asanpur's coffee. For that, she missed Vanai's canals and wooden houses and the gates that had closed off one section of the city from another.

She wasn't certain, even now, that Komme had ever given her freedom of the city. Nothing had been said. But after the last meeting with the king, Isadau had started taking her along. It was almost as it they were back in Suddapal and Cithrin was finishing out the last few months of her apprenticeship. Odd, with all that had happened since, that the thought reassured her. Yes, she'd lost Porte Oliva. Yes, Pyk Usterhall had been lost or killed. She'd spent the gathered fortunes of her branch on a half-mad scheme to remake what the world meant by money, but she was finishing her apprentice work, by God. Perhaps it was just the ritual of it that comforted.

"Do you think we'll manage it?" she said as they turned north into one of the great, dragon-wide main ways.

"That depends on what you mean by *it*," Isadau said.

"I was thinking of defeating the ancient enemy, bringing Antea to heel and the dragon's war to an end. Little things like that."

She's meant it as half a joke, but Isadau's tight smile made her think that perhaps she was on more serious ground than she'd known. "I hope that will be enough."

At the compound, Komme Medean was pacing in the courtyard. His left knee was swollen with gout, and he leaned heavily on a carved oak cane. All through the yard, palm-sized sheets of yellow paper hung from string tied between the walls and trees. The little pages fluttered in the breeze like the banners of a vast miniature army. As Isadau and Cithrin came near, Komme plucked one from its place and held it up to the sun. A line of purple ran along its lower edge, startling against the yellow, and bright flecks caught the light. He looked over at them and lifted his chin in greeting.

"Komme," Isadau said, smiling as she steered Cithrin toward him. "I don't know what these are, but I think they're beautiful. Have you taken to art in your old age?"

Komme's single laugh was harsh, but genuine. He held

out the page in his hand to Cithrin. "I'm doing what you two should have done before you gave all my damned money away. These letters of transfer we're writing? They're too easily forged. Doesn't do us any good having sole right to make these if everyone and their sisters can make copies. We need to find a way to make them distinct, yes?"

The paper felt thick and stiff between Cithrin's fingers, almost more board than paper. Tiny mineral chips glittered on its surface and tiny threads of red and blue spiraled through it. The violet band at the edge was damp. Komme saw her considering the discoloration and smiled sharply. She nodded her question.

"Put it in vinegar and it turns color. Until it dries, anyway. The maker swears that no one else in the world knows the process or could figure it out. My guess is that's lies, but even so, it cuts the number of people stealing our right down from everybody everywhere to a few that are really dedicated to it. The yellow and the flecks? That was my thought. Gives people the idea of gold without the actual coin. Brings them halfway."

"It's a good thought," Isadau said.

Cithrin handed back the page. "I wasn't sure you were going to let the contract stand."

Komme's smile vanished. He pinned the page back in its place on the string. "I didn't have a choice, did I? That's the thing that all your plans and schemes skip. Contracts and letters of transfer and clever arrangements of business? All of it assumes that the agreements can be enforced. Well, his majesty's the one with the crown and the guardsmen, so if he wants the agreement enforced, enforced it's going to be."

"I didn't forget," Cithrin said.

"Give us a moment, Isadau," Komme said, still squinting at the paper and rubbing his thumb along its violet edge. Isadau and Cithrin exchanged a silent glance, and the Timzinae woman uncurled her arm from Cithrin's. Her footsteps faded as she walked into the shade of the house. A sparrow flew past, grey-brown wings fluttering in the air. Somewhere outside the compound, a man shouted. Komme sighed and turned to her.

"You're the worst voice of any bank I've ever seen," he said, and then lifted his palm to her, commanding silence. "I don't want to hear any damned explanations of why you had to do it this way or how the scale of the thing justified cutting me out of my own business. You crossed me. You know it. And you meant to do it."

Cithrin's belly went tight and she nodded. "I did."

Komme's smile had no mirth in it. "Well, at least you've got the balls to admit it. You did this the wrong way, Cithrin. You should have come to me. We should have talked the plan through. You and me and Paerin and Chana. Nison and Isadau. You have a brilliant mind for finance, but you don't have the only goddamned mind there is. You've managed to insult everyone on the company. Did you think about that?"

"I . . . No. Not really."

"You see? That's the problem with you. You've been pretending to be a grown woman long enough you've forgotten you're a girl. Get married, have a couple of children like I did, get some perspective on what risk is, and you'd be ready to run a bank the right way. You were raised badly."

"I was raised by your bank."

"The irony's not lost," Komme said, limping forward to the next yellow sheet. He reached up, running his fingers along its edge like a farmer judging a crop. "This doesn't happen again. Ever. You've made a practice of stepping outside your authority, and you've gotten away with it. It's given you the wrong impression of what authority is and what your role in the bank should be."

"I apologize."

He turned back to her and grunted in pain, leaning on his cane. "You've tied my hands for now. I could throw you on the street. Strip you of your place. It's within my rights. You don't even have a branch any longer. But since the bank's just embarked on this scheme you've created, it would look odd to cut ties now. The bank has to seem more solid than thrones now. Getting back lost confidence is harder than stirring cream out of coffee. Besides which, you're friends with a dragon. There's a certain romance in that, and people like romances when the world's uncertain."

"I'll speak to you first next time," Cithrin said. "I promise."

"Next time," Komme said, shaking his head. "And with you, there may be a next time."

He moved on to the next string, but his gaze was skating over the yellow papers now. Cithrin walked half a step behind him and to his left.

"You've heard the news from Narinisle," he said over his shoulder.

"No."

"Word of your agreement with Tracian's spread. It's precedent. Narinisle's asked for the same arrangement. Herez will too, though I haven't had it formally yet. They're asking why Northcoast is favored over them."

"What are you going to do?"

"Me? Who am I? I just have a holding company. It's the branches who'll make that call."

"Yes, but what are you going to do?"

"Give it to them," Komme said. "Start trading your letters of transfer as widely and commonly as I can. Sell Herez's debt to Northcoast and Narinisle's to both of them until the three are so entwined it's impossible to say who owns what or where someone would go to change these things back to coin. Anything to make the essential lie at the heart of this harder to see."

"Good," Cithrin said. "That's excellent."

"Or it's my ticket to dying in gaol. Either way, I thought you'd want to know you'd drawn even with Palliako."

"How do you count that?"

"He took Asterilhold, Sarakal, and Elassae. You've taken Northcoast, Herez, and Narinisle. I call Birancour a split," Komme said, and spat into the bushes. "Cithrin bel Sarcour, secret queen of the world."

Entr'acte

Captain Karol Dannien

The mountains in the north of Elassae were black crags. The great slabs of stone lay one against the other like some titanic act of violence had been petrified mid-cataclysm. They channeled even the gentlest wind into howling gusts that came from any direction, or all of them. There were just enough wild goats surviving on the low grey scrub to attract a healthy population of mountain lions. The tracks and paths through the sharp valleys were challenging for pack mules, and anything wheeled was worse than useless. The water tasted sharp and mineral.

Karol Dannien had fought in the flatlands of the Keshet and at the Bloody Gate of Lôdi, the swamps south of Kaltfel and the iced-in harbors of Hallskar. In almost thirty years of paid violence, only the Dry Wastes had been a less hospitable stretch of land and worse ground for a battle of any size. But God hadn't asked his opinion, and so there it was.

The aftermath was mostly confined to a pair of slightly less steep inclines. The Anteans, spurred on by the shouting and hectoring of their priests, had charged the high ground, and Karol had had his men roll rocks down at them to break their ranks, following with a charge of his own. It had worked, but it hadn't been anything like pretty. The first clash had come just after dawn, and Karol's men were still hunting down the last of the fleeing Anteans when

dark came on. He wasn't worried about a counterattack.
The mountain lions could pick up the slops for all he cared.
Probably be a nice change from goat meat.

Cep Bailan, his second this godawful endless campaign,
stepped out of his tent and stretched his arms out to the sky
like the Haaverkin was gathering the whole world to his fat,
tattooed belly. Karol hunched deeper into his coat.

"Heat's finally breaking," Cep said. "And past time for it."

"You're too far south. Your kind should stay north of
Sarakal."

"That's only true," Cep said and slapped his massive
chest. "But sometimes you sad little bastards need our help."

Karol sighed. Cep was a brilliant man in a fight and a
good leader before a battle, but the long months in the dark
halls of Kiaria had been too long in close company. Every
night had ended in another volley of insults and crudeness,
and after a half season in the dark hearing the man rain
abuse on Karol's imagined mother, sisters, and lovers, it was
hard not to think some of the joking had teeth.

"Do we have to do the first part again?" Cep asked, plod-
ding after Karol. "I don't know why you do this. It isn't like
they don't know they're hurt. Not like you're going to tell
them anything different."

"They're my men," Karol said.

"If you need to keep saying it, it starts not sounding true,"
Cep said. Karol promised himself for the thousandth time
that he'd never work with a Haaverkin again. "You go on
ahead. I'll meet you with the prisoners. The men don't like it
when I see them injured."

"You laugh at them."

"They're funny."

"Go be sure Chaars has enough men to set up a watch."

Cep scowled, the tattoos on his face warping. He stamped

off down the incline, intentionally making his way across the paths of the black-chitined Timzinae soldiers still carrying the wounded and the dying from the battlefield. Karol sighed. The man truly was a child. But he was good at being sure the other side fell and his own didn't, and that forgave a lot.

The cunning man's tent was overfull, and the soldiers had started lining the wounded on the rough ground outside it. The low chanting and uncomfortable weight of the air that felt like the oppressive hour before a thunderstorm were familiar enough. Someone was on the edge of death, and they were trying to coax him back for another chance at living, at least until the next fight. Karol went down the line of wounded men, smiling at each, telling them they'd done a good job, making light of the wounds they'd suffered and encouraging them to laugh through their pain. And in the back of his mind, a small quiet voice made evaluations. Dead. Crippled. Will recover. Won't recover. Dead. Dead.

Most of them were Timzinae—likely ten out of every dozen—but here and there a Tralgu or a Jasuru lay in the dirt alongside them. Karol himself was one of the only Firstbloods, and he could feel an exception being made for him. Yes, he was like the Anteans, but he was different. He was *their* Firstblood. He was all right.

He paused by a young Timzinae boy he remembered from his calmer days when he'd been running the gymnasium in Suddapal. Another attempt at retirement that hadn't gone well. The leather-bound hilt of a great knife protruded from the boy's belly, and blood soaked his sides. The nictatating membranes covering his eyes were locked closed, but his eyelids were open, giving him the eerie aspect of being both seeing the world and not. It took Karol a moment to place the boy's name.

"Caught a memento there, Salan," the mercenary captain said.

Salan forced a smile. There was blood on his teeth, and his breath came in gasps. "A good knife."

"Looks it," Karol said, kneeling beside the boy and making a show of considering the blood-soaked hilt. "Fine workmanship. Take care of it, and you'll get a lot of years out of a blade like that." *Might recover*, he thought. *Might be dead already.*

"Wish it was someplace else," Salan said. "Like to take it out."

"No, that's not true. You keep that right where it is until the cunning man gets to you."

"Hurts though."

"Knife doesn't hurt," Karol said. "It's the damned hole that hurts. As soon as that steel stopped cutting you, it started holding your blood in. I can't tell you how many men I've seen who would have been fine pluck out a weapon like that and bleed to death instead. Taking it out's a damned sight more dangerous than putting it in."

Salan nodded and put his black hands around the wound, as if promising not to let anyone take the knife out of him. Karol nodded and clapped the boy's knee.

"Did we win?" Salan asked as Karol stood.

"Hell yes, we did," Karol said, glad that he didn't have to lie to say it. "You just stay there and wait your turn. And don't get impatient. We don't rush the cunning men for pin-pricks and scrapes."

"Be all right with me if they rushed a little, sir."

"I'll mention it to them," Karol said with a smile. *Probably live*, he decided. *Probably.*

Before setting up shop in Suddapal, Karol had worked with perhaps half a dozen Timzinae. A couple years of garrison work in Maccia and Nus. A Kesheti prince named Unlil Soyam who'd hired his company to hold the left flank in a massive honor battle. A brief partnership with Sanis Sorianian before she'd retired. That Suddapal was a center of the Timzinae race hadn't been a point for or against it. He'd decided to settle there in the end more for the coffee than the races that made up the fivefold city. The last year hunkering down in the vastness of Kiaria had given him a deeper respect for them. In the deepness and dark of the stronghold, the Timzinae fighters had been thoughtful and professional and no less disciplined than a Firstblood troop.

There were always incidents, but the commander of the siege had treated them with courtesy and respect. All in all, it had left him feeling better about roaches as a people. Not that he'd stopped thinking of them as roaches, but they made jokes about Firstbloods barely being civilized enough to take their pants down when they pissed. That kind of joking was all in fun, after all. And kinder than half the shit that spilled out of Cep Bailan's fat mouth.

All in all, Karol's time with the Timzinae made the part that came next that much more pleasant for him.

Most of the prisoners were disarmed, stripped, and tied neck to neck by a Jasuru Karol had worked with a time or three who had almost certainly been a slaver at some point in her career. The knots were tight enough on them that too much struggle kept the blood from their heads but didn't outright kill them. It was a pretty piece of ropecraft. The great prize was in a little shack they'd put up for the purpose. And the priests—there'd been two of the bastards— were already char and meat on the fire.

Karol entered the shack and nodded to the guards. They each made their salute and left. A small tin lantern hung from the roof, though there was more light leaking through between the boards than the flame provided. The prisoner was on his knees and naked as a babe newborn. His arms were bound behind him, and his ankles as well to keep him from standing. He was shivering, maybe from cold, maybe from shock. Hard to say. Somewhere along the line, someone had thrown an elbow across the man's nose and splashed it over until the tip pointed off to the right somewhere. Blood and spit soaked the ornate mustache, and deep bruises mottled the man's arms and legs. Karol sat on a three-legged stool.

"Well," Karol said. "Here's a turn, eh? Fallon Broot, yeah?"

The prisoner's gaze swam up to him, floated for a moment, and the man nodded. Karol nodded back.

"Yeah, I remember you. You'd not recall me, I wouldn't think. Not sure we ever met to speak to. I was in Camnipol...Lord, years ago. Around the time of that unpleasantness in Anninfort. There was a thing, eh? Believe I saw your manor house. It had the...the little grey tower? Yeah? On the eastern side."

Broot's nod started slowly and then had a hard time stopping.

"Nice place," Karol said. "Not as showy as some of the others, but dignified. I liked it."

"My thanks."

"Come up in the world since then, though, haven't you? Protector of Suddapal. There's a hell of title. Whole city under your protection. Or five, I suppose. Depending how you count it."

"I serve...Severed Throne."

"Course you do, course you do. Thing is, I don't. My plan, just between us, was never to serve anyone in particular again. Train younger men, send them off to fight. That was my angle. It was your people brought the fight to me."

Broot struggled to breathe through his broken nose, coughed, and spat out a huge dark clot of blood. It lay on the dirt, a red so dark it approached blackness, shining wet in the candlelight. The prisoner didn't speak.

"Truth is I came to like Suddapal. And Antea? Well, I didn't used to have much against it, but it's gone out of its way to complicate my daily life. Killed a fair number of my friends, besides. Took their babies to prison back in Camnipol. Put good men and women didn't have anything to do with any conspiracy one way or the other into chains. That just seemed mean, now. Didn't it to you?"

"I…"

"And them priests you've got? They're some kind of Kesheti cunning men, ain't they? Way I heard it, they got poisoned voices or some such. Get in a man's head and just spin it all around."

"Blessed," Broot said, "of the goddess."

"Never much held with that sort of thing myself," Karol said, taking a pipe and a pouch from his belt. "Tobacco? It's stale as dirt, but it's what I have."

Broot didn't say no, so Karol lit the bowl, drew on it until the smoke was as rich as the thin leaves would allow, and then placed the stem of it between Broot's abused lips. The prisoner breathed in and out through his mouth, the smoke curling up around his face. Karol smiled and took the pipe back.

"Now, Lord Protector. Why don't we talk a bit about the city we're both so fond of, eh? Seems like the forces there must be mighty thin to have the man in charge of the place leading the forces in the field. Or was it just that you felt all cocksure and glory-hungry?"

Broot swallowed. Karol took a small, thin knife out and started cleaning the dead tobacco from the bowl.

"All right," Karol said. "Better if I'm specific, then. How many men do you have defending the city, and how are they deployed?"

Broot rolled his jaw, stretched his thick neck. His gaze came up to meet Karol's. The white of his left eye was all bloody red. Karol tamped in a fresh wad of leaf and lit it, knowing before the prisoner spoke the sense of what he would say, if not the precise words.

"I will never betray my men," the prisoner said. "And you will never defeat the Lord Regent."

Karol took a long, slow draw on the pipe, nodding thoughtfully, then took the small cleaning knife and the pipe of burning tobacco, one in each hand, leaned forward, and did something terrible.

It took a few minutes for Broot's breath to slow. The screaming turned to a long, high whine broken only by the ragged gasps when he drew in breath. His cheek and shoulder were pressed against the ground, and bits of dirt stuck to his eyelid. The ropes dug into his neck and his face darkened with blood, but not so much as to kill him or let him pass out.

Karol threw the ruined pipe to the corner and leaned back on his stool. "Truth is, I don't greatly care whether you tell me. Do or don't, I'm still taking that city back, and all the ghost tales you'd care to tell about your great and powerful Lord Regent don't mean piss t'me."

The whine shuddered. Karol sat forward with a sigh and wrenched Broot back up to squatting. He ran a finger along the rope around the prisoner's neck, putting enough slack in it that the blood could flow again.

"You got any brothers or sisters? Children?" Karol asked, his tone conversational. "I got a brother lives in Daun. No children I know of, so I call it none. I'm guessing you've got some family back in Antea. Hell, maybe even a lover on the side. Friends. Favorite dogs. What my father used to tell me, whatever a man loves, that's what you grab him by. Not a kind man, my father, but not a stupid one either."

Broot was weeping now, snot and blood running out his ruined nose. His eyes were pressed closed. There was fresh blood on his belly.

"Here's what you can do for me," Karol said, his voice losing its false gentleness. "You picture them. All of them. And you picture everything you've done to the people under your fucking *protection* happening to them. Because when I am done with you, we will roll back every step you bastards took to get here. All the way back to Camnipol. I will find that little grey tower again, and I will bring every soldier I've got that's lost a son or a mother or any loved thing along with me. And you think right now on how *that* day's going to be."

"Please..." Broot said, and then didn't go on.

"We'll have back for every last thing you broke. Every child you took. Every slaveman's lash. All of it," Karol said between clenched teeth. "And we'll show your Geder Palliako what war looks like when he *isn't* winning."

Dramatis Personae

Persons of interest and import in
The Widow's House

IN THE GREATER WORLD

Inys, the last dragon
Marcus Wester, mercenary captain
Kitap rol Keshmat, former actor and apostate of the
   spider goddess

The Players

Cary
Hornet
Smit
Charlit Soon
Mikel
Sandr

Callon Cane, a convenient fiction

IN BIRANCOUR

The Medean bank in Porte Oliva

Cithrin bel Sarcour, voice of the Medean bank in
   Porte Oliva

Magistra Isadau, formerly voice of the Medean bank
   in Suddapal
Pyk Usterhall, notary to the bank
Yardem Hane, personal guard to Cithrin, also
Enen
Roach (Halvill)
Corisen Mout

Maestro Asanpur, a café owner

Mastién Juoli, master of coin

IN IMPERIAL ANTEA

The Royal Family

Aster, prince and heir to the empire

House Palliako

Geder Palliako, Regent of Antea and Baron of
   Ebbingbaugh
Lehrer Palliako, Viscount of Rivenhalm and his father

House Kalliam

Clara Kalliam, formerly Baroness of Osterling Fells
Barriath
Vicarian, and
Jorey; her sons
also Sabiha, wife to Jorey, and
Pindan, her illegitimate son
Annalise, her daughter

Vincen Coe, huntsman formerly in the service of
House Kalliam
Abatha Coe, his cousin

House Skestinin

Lord Skestinin, master of the Imperial Navy
Lady Skestinin, his wife

House Annerin

Elisia Annerin (formerly Kalliam), daughter of Clara
and Dawson
Gorman Annerin, son and heir of Lord Annerin and
husband of Elisia
Corl, their son

House Daskellin

Canl Daskellin, Baron of Watermarch and
Ambassador to Northcoast
Sanna, his eldest daughter

Also, various lords and members of the court, including

Sir Namen Flor
Sir Noyel Flor
Cyr Emming, Baron of Suderland Fells
Sir Ernst Mecelli
Sodai Carvenallin, his secretary
Sir Curtin Issandrian
Sir Gospey Allintot
Fallon Broot, Baron of Suderling Heights

and also Houses Veren, Essian, Ischian, Bannien,
Estinford, Faskellan, Emming, Tilliakin, Mastellin,
Caot, and Pyrellin among others

Basrahip, minister of the spider doddess and
counselor to Geder Palliako
also some dozen priests

IN ELASSAE

Fallon Broot, protector of the fivefold city
Carol Dannien, a mercenary captain
    Cep Bailan, his officer
    Salan, soldier and cousin of Isadau

IN NORTHCOAST

The Medean bank in Carse

Komme Medean, head of the Medean bank
    Lauro, his son
    Chana, his daughter
Paerin Clark, bank auditor and son-in-law
of Komme
Magister Nison, voice of the Median bank
in Carse

King Tracian

IN HALLSKAR

Magra of Order Murro and
several of his compatriots

THE DEAD

King Simeon, Emperor of Antea, dead from a defect
of the flesh
King Lechan of Asterilhold, executed in war
Feldin Maas, formerly Baron of Ebbingbaugh killed
for treason
Phelia Maas, his wife dead at her husband's
hand

Dawson Kalliam, formerly Baron of Osterling Fells,
executed for treason
Alan Klin, executed for treason
Mirkus Shoat, executed for treason
Estin Cersillian, Earl of Masonhalm, killed in an
insurrection
Lord Ternigan, Lord Marshal to Regent Palliako,
killed for disloyalty

Magister Imaniel, voice of the Medean bank in Vanai
and protector of Cithrin
also Cam, a housekeeper, and
Besel, a man of convenience, burned in the razing of
Vanai

Alys, wife of Marcus Wester
also Merian, their daughter, burned to death as a
tactic of intrigue

Lord Springmere, the Mayfly King, killed in
vengeance

Akad Silas, adventurer, lost with his expedition

Assian Bey, collector of secrets and builder of traps, whose death is not recorded

Morade, the last Dragon Emperor, said to have died from wounds

Asteril, clutch-mate of Morade, maker of the Timzinae, dead of poison

Erex, lover of Inys whose manner of death is not recorded

Drakkis Stormcrow, great human general of the last war of the dragons, dead of age

An Introduction to the Taxonomy of Races

(From a manuscript attributed to Malasin Calvah, Taxonomist to Kleron Nuasti Cau, fifth of his name)

The ordering and arrangements of the thirteen races of humanity by blood, order of precedence, mating combination, or purpose is, by necessity, the study of a lifetime. It should occasion no concern that the finer points of the great and complex creation should seem sometimes confused and obscure. It is the intent of this essay to introduce the layman to the beautiful and fulfilling path which is taxonomy.

I shall begin with a brief guide to which the reader may refer.

Firstblood

The Firstblood are the feral, near-bestial form from which all humanity arose. Had there been no dragons to form the twelve crafted races from this base clay, humanity would have been exclusively of the Firstblood. Even now, they are the most populous of the races, showing the least difficulty in procreation, and spreading throughout the known world as a weed might spread through a rose garden. I intend no offense by the comparison, but truth knows no etiquette.

The Eastern Triad

The oldest of the crafted races form the Eastern Triad: Jasuru, Yemmu, and Tralgu.

The Jasuru are often assumed to be the first of the higher races. They share the rough size and shape of the Firstblood, but with the metallic scales of lesser dragons. Most likely, they were created as a rough warrior caste, overseers to control the Firstblood slaves.

The Yemmu are clearly a later improvement. Their great size and massive tusks could only have been designed to intimidate the lesser races, but as with other examples of crafted races, the increase in size and strength has come at a cost. Of all the races, the Yemmu have the shortest natural lifespan.

The Tralgu are almost certainly the most recent of the Eastern Triad. They are taller than the Firstblood and with the fierce teeth and keen hearing of a natural carnivore, and common wisdom holds that they were bred for hunting more than formal battle. In the ages since the fall of dragons, it is likely only their difficulty in whelping that has kept them from forcible racial conquest.

The Western Triad

As the Eastern Triad marks an age of war in which races were created as weapons of war, the western races delineate an age in which the dragons began to create more subtle tools. Cinnae, Dartinae, and Timzinae each show the marks of creation for specific uses.

The Cinnae, when compared to all other races, are thin and pale as sprouts growing under a bucket. However, they have a marked talent in the mental arts, though the truly deep insights have tended to escape them. As the Jasuru are a first attempt at a warrior caste, so the Cinnae may be considered as a rough outline of the races that follow them.

The Dartinae, while dating their creation from the same time, do not share in the Cinnae's slightly better than rudimentary intelligence. Rather, their race was clearly built as a labor force for mining efforts. Their luminescent eyes show a structure unlike any other race, or indeed any known beast of nature. Their ability to navigate in utterly lightless caves is unique, and they tend to have the lithe frames one can imagine squeezing through cramped caves deep underground. Persistent rumors of a hidden Dartinae fortress deep below the earth no doubt spring from this, as no such structure has ever been found, nor would it be likely to survive in the absence of sustainable farming.

The Timzinae are, in fact, the only race whose place in the order of creation is unequivocally known. The youngest of the races, they date from the final war of the dragons. Their dark, insectile scales provide little of the protection that the Jasuru enjoy, but they are capable of utterly encasing the living flesh, even to the point of sealing all bodily orifices including ears and eyes. Their precise function as a tool remains obscure, though some suggest it might have been beekeeping.

The Master Races

The master races, or High Triad, represent the finest work of the dragons before their inevitable fall into decadence. These are the Kurtadam, Raushadam, and Haunadam.

The Kurtadam, like myself, show the fusion of all the best ideas that came before. The cleverness first hinted at in the Cinnae and the warrior's instinct limned by the Eastern Triad came together in the Kurtadam. Also, alone among the races, the Kurtadam were given the gift of a full pelt of warming hair, and the arts of beading and adornments that clearly represent the highest in etiquette and personal beauty.

The Haunadam exist to the greatest extent in Far Syramys and its territories, and represent the refinement of the warrior impulse that created the Yemmu. While slightly smaller, the tireless Haunadam have a thick mineral layer in their skins which repels violence and a clear and brilliant intellect that has given them utter dominion over the western continent. Their aversion to travel by water restricts their role in the blue-water trade, and has likely prevented military conquest of other nations bounded by the seas.

The Raushadam, like the Haunadam, are primarily to be found in Far Syramys, and function almost as if the two races were designed to act as one with the other. The slightest of frame, Raushadam are the only race gifted by the dragons with flight.

The Decadent Races

After the arts of the dragons reached their height, there was a necessary and inevitable descent into the oversophisticated. The latter efforts of the dragons brought out the florid and bizarre races: Haaverkin, Southling, and Drowned.

The Haaverkin have spent the centuries since the fall of dragons clinging to the frozen ports of the north. Their foul and aggressive temper is not a sign that they were bred for war, but that an animal let loose without its master will revert to its bestial nature. While they are large as the Yemmu, this is due to the rolls of insulating fat that protect them from the cold north. The facial tattooing has been compared to the Kurtadam ritual beads by those who clearly understand neither.

The Southlings, known for their great black night-adapted eyes, are a study in perversion. Littering the reaches south of Lyoneia, they have built up a culture equal parts termite hill and nomadic tribe worship. While capable of sexual reproduction, these wide-eyed half-humans prefer to delegate such activity to a central queen figure, with her subjects acting as drones. Whether they were bred to people the living deserts of the south or migrated there after the fall of dragons because they were unable to compete with the greater races is a fit subject of debate.

The Drowned are the final evidence of the decadence of the dragons. While much like the Firstblood in size and shape, the Drowned live exclusively underwater in all human climes. Interaction with them is slow when it is possible, and their tendency to gather in shallow tidepools marks them as little better than human seaweed. Suggestions that they are tools created toward some great draconic project still in play under the waves is purest romance.

With this as a grounding, we can address the five philosophical practices that determine how an educated mind orders, ranks, and ultimately judges the races...

Acknowledgments

I would like to thank Danny Baror and Shawna McCarthy for hooking me up with the amazing team at Orbit. The book would not exist in its present form without the good work of Will Hinton, Ellen Wright, Alex Lencicki, Anne Clarke, and Tim Holman. And, as always, my thanks to my family for their support during the hard parts.

The failures and infelicities are my own.

About the Author

Daniel Abraham is the author of the critically acclaimed Long Price Quartet. He has been nominated for the Hugo, Nebula, and World Fantasy awards, and won the International Horror Guild award. He also writes as MLN Hanover and (with Ty Franck) James S. A. Corey. He lives in New Mexico. Visit his website at www.danielabraham.com.

Find out more about Daniel Abraham and other Orbit authors by registering for the free monthly newsletter at www.orbitbooks.net.